ODYSSEY OF AN INNOCENT

also by kerry Heubeck

Where Feasts Come Rarely —
A Viet Nam Album

Ancient Customs of Vietnam's Edé People (editor)

Praise for *Where Feasts Come Rarely*

...the photographer and author affectionately portrays the people and the landscape in beautiful black and white compositions, which quietly seduce the reader. Bits of poetry and prose next to the pictures also touch the heart...

Geronimo **review,** June 1999

I have fallen utterly in love with the amazing and radiant book ... so tender, so luminous, so full of care and sympathy...the images were so gentle. And the words only confirm the sense of a sincere heart reaching out to the world.

Pico Iyre, *Video Nights in Katmandu,*
The Lady and the Monk, etc.

...beautiful photos of a beautiful land and people. But somehow both seemed sad—a little wonder, considering what they went through....

Frank Waters, *The Man Who Killed the Deer,*
Book of the Hopi, etc.

...those remarkable pictures... somehow managed to gather up horror and happiness, hunger and hope. Perhaps the greatest threat is the impact of "the alien"; the greatest hope is the still unspoiled naiveté of the children.

John Peters, founder, *World Neighbors*

Kerry Heubeck's book is an exquisite visual experience. His photographs are simple, beautiful, touching, very caring, very compassionate, extraordinarily memorable. From the land of Viet Nam, which has seen so much suffering, Heubeck brings us a powerful message of hope, and a very gentle, yet obviously unrelenting, belief in humanity.... I wish the people of the United States could have seen this book during the years of that war. I am very glad that they are going to see it now.

John Nichols, *The Milagro Beanfield War,*
The Sterile Cuckoo, etc.

ODYSSEY OF AN INNOCENT
stilling the sirens of war

a memoir

Kerry Heubeck

Order this book online at www.trafford.com
or email orders@trafford.com

Most Trafford titles are also available at major online book retailers.

Printed in the United States of America.

ISBN: 978-1-4269-0436-3 (sc)

Trafford rev. 03/09/2011

 www.trafford.com

North America & international
toll-free: 1 888 232 4444 (USA & Canada)
phone: 250 383 6864 ♦ fax: 812 355 4082

for Ami Y-Lai:
Kao khap ko ih.

and to the memory of

Mac Riding

Ya Vincent

CAVEAT LECTOR BENEVOLE

Some say the gods gave us memory so that they might take it away from us in bits and pieces and thus enjoy the ensuing show. I believe events in the ensuing account happened as described; others, on occasion, have disagreed. A few names have been changed, either to protect the guilty or because I just don't remember.

Author's royalties from the sale of this book will be donated to Asia Connection, Inc., supporting health and welfare programs in Viet Nam.

Contents

A NOTE ON LANGUAGE:

Several languages are encountered in this story. The Vietnamese tongue, a language of harmonic and tonal beauty, incorporates a number of diacritical marks in its proper Romanized form. For the sake of simplicity, Vietnamese words in the following text are italicized but omit such marks; their proper forms can be found in the glossary with all diacritical marks and accents. Names and Vietnamese words, however bastardized, but commonly used by us foreigners, are not italicized.

....Tomorrow he shall take his pack,
and set out for the ways beyond,
On the old trail from star to star,
an alien and a vagabond."

Richard Hovey,
More Songs from Vagabondia; Envoy

Prologue

I came by ship, with ship's company,
sailing the wine-dark seas for ports of call
on alien shores...

The words belong to another, surfacing from the past. The middle was the beginning.

Two lithe figures, conical straw hats hiding sun-darkened faces in darker shadows, slide their dugout from the wide sand beach and onto the still sea. Now wading and pushing their slight craft, the two finally step easily over the low gunwales and squat at either end, taking up paddles and dipping them into the placid water. Atmospheric haze shimmers in the mid-day heat and hides horizons in rippling ghostly gray falloff, belying the tropic brightness, blinding from stirred mirrored surfaces.

The one in the bow paddled easily, an almost instinctual movement, and laughed as the other played out the net over the low stern. Carried over the calm waters of the South China Sea, their lyrical language undulated as smoothly as the heat mirages wavered, rose, stretched, compressed, disappeared, and rose again, creating an impressionistic dream of blues and grays and flowing voices softly cascading from the one reality to another. No other life forms joined the illusionary dance, and gradually a track of bobbing cork floats disappeared behind the canoe, closing a wide and ancient circle.

"*Coi di!*"

The one in the bow, naked save for a pair of loose-fitting army green skivvies and his plaited hat, pointed to the south, squinting in the glare, wiping the sweat from his forehead and half smile from his face.

From the nothingness of distant gray haze slid a great warship's ashen bow. Reflections from glass eyes and brass trimming, weaponry, then antennas gradually arose into view. The slight hum of ship's machinery drifted across calm waters.

The shimmering beast gradually separated from the haze of the same non-color and became more distinct as it ever so slowly eased towards the canoe and outstretched net in the distance. Still closer grew the phantom ship, taking form, adding details, growing higher, more menacing, still showing no manlike life aboard. Little wake gave evidence to its passage; still it came on, barely making headway, yet steadily approaching, as a lone and wary gray shark might close upon a trapped prey.

"*Ve di!*"

Agitated, the one in the stern cast off the last of the net, then grabbed a paddle. The tiny craft altered course, heading back towards shore, away from the path of the encroaching man-of-war.

Onboard the American destroyer a metallic voice reached from the bridge into the torrid confines of the gun director. The director, a small turret-like affair crowning the high-rising structures of the ship, swung slowly to the left, the giant binocular lenses, one on either side, rose and fell slightly, then appeared to steady, locking onto their target. The movement of the director, and its dilated eyes, was slower now, more steadfast and determined.

Gilmore's dark forehead was jammed against the eyepieces of the rangefinder. Perspiration had erupted in a hundred places on his young face, clenched now in concentration. The director watch officer, also young, had partially climbed from the cramped interior. He stood half-exposed in the hatch and sounded as though he was arguing with someone standing below. Gilmore finally made out the raspy voice of the XO. He heard the words, "Free Fire Zone..." The watch officer replied something about "common fisherman..." The

XO's voice grew irritated, louder. The watch officer cursed, only half under his breath, then glanced at Gilmore, who had taken his eyes off the optics. "The Gunnery Officer's taking my place." He shinnied out of the hatch.

The two fishermen at first feared the oncoming ship, then decided that once they got out of its way, it ought not pose any threat. They pulled their dugout up onto the beach alongside another already there and stood watching the curious spectacle, something neither had seen before. Then they noticed movement on the forward deck. The two barrels of each of the gun mounts rose, then swung towards the beach, towards their position. Fear returned.

Gilmore was sweating heavily now. His eyes were glued to the optics, hands tightly clenched to the focusing handles. He continued calling out range and bearing to the target. The guns were now locked into the motion of the director, jerking occasionally as Gilmore swung more to the left. "Mounts one and two locked and tracking." More mechanical commands. One barrel blazed and recoiled, the noise deafening.

The fishermen saw the flare from the gun just before hearing the explosion, still uncomprehending for a moment; then fear struck hard and they began running. They did not know enough to separate. The second round was on target.

The middle was death, whether by my hand or another's. But, as so often, that dark angel also carried with it a weak but viable birth. In adrenalin and egos one of Huxley's great doors of perception began to open. All was not as it seemed. I was not led in, but the portal opened. Eiseley knew of those moments: "Every now and then, however, there comes an experience so troubling that the kaleidoscope never quite shifts back to where it was. One must then simply deny the episode or adjust one's vision. Most follow the first prescription; the others never talk."

An element of brass, tarnished after more than a score of years, sits before me now, cut and molded into a receptacle for man's ashes. It once bore the markings of death, a cylinder of simple gunpowder and Armageddon. "H.E." for High Explosive. Numbers: 5" 38. War became mechanized when brass was born, and at that point personal responsibility for killing began fading from consciousness; mechanized and depersonalized. It's easier to kill now.

Better than any jeweler's polish, the mind brings back the reflections now hidden by time's tarnish: a shell casing ejected onto the blistering deck those many years ago, designed by man's hands solely for the purpose of death. A projectile that "wasted" the lives of those two fishermen. It was also responsible for leading me on an odyssey of more than a few years and the proverbial thousand *li* about this small globe.

The remainder of that sultry afternoon the phantom ship poured tens of rounds onto that solitary shore, aiming at two small dugout canoes; so that, finally, the day's report could read: "Two KIAs; supplies; and two enemy craft destroyed." The irony being that a technicality of regulations prevented the KIAs from being confirmed. So even by prevailing standards the taking of two lives proved worthless, though I suppose the "enemy craft," dugouts though they were, counted for something on the Admiral's scoreboard of the day. There is no fine line between reality and lunacy.

Fate and Monkey

"There was a rock that since creation of the world had been worked upon by the pure essences of Heaven and the fine savours of Earth, the vigor of sunshine and the grace of moonlight, till at last it became magically pregnant and one day split open, giving birth to a stone egg, about as big as a playing ball. Fructified by the wind it developed into a stone monkey, complete with every organ and limb. At once this monkey learned to climb and run; but its first act was to make a bow towards each of the four quarters. As it did so, a steely light darted from this monkey's eyes and flashed as far as the Palace of the Pole Star. This shaft of light astonished the Jade Emperor as he sat in the Cloud Palace of the Golden Mists, surrounded by his fairy Ministers."

from *Monkey*, by Wu Ch'en-en (1505-1580 A.D.)
translated from the Chinese by Arthur Waley[1]

Sing in me, Muse, and through me tell the story...

Fate, I believe, is something of a comical goddess. I'm not sure she doesn't cavort about some nights with that Oriental trickster, Monkey. Together they make an awe-inspiring pair.

---

[1]   New York: Grove Press (1958, ©1943)

I was finishing college in the mid-sixties, just about the time that non-war in the East was coming to popular and unpopular attention. Though, at the time, I was too naive to have any particularly strong political feelings one way or the other, I had what seemed good sense enough not to want to go. Graduate school seemed a logical and honorable alternative and so I headed towards a master's degree. But then my time in the sun was up, as was my number, for the military draft.

Insufficiently motivated in academics to pursue further studies, with the draft board in close pursuit, I decided that if I had to go into the service I'd choose the one least involved in that far-away affair; besides, I liked the sea. So into the office of the Navy recruiter I marched. And so began my education into the workings of bureaucracies, and the games of Fate and Monkey.

After close to a year enlisted, an acceptance to Officer Candidate School came through, which I grabbed, having had enough of mopping floors or swabbing decks. Then I had a choice: Did I want a ship on the west coast or east? Easy. Ships on the west coast sometimes deployed to WESTPAC, or in common English, the western Pacific, i.e. the shores of war. Ships on the east coast made show-the-flag tours to the sunny Mediterranean. East coast it was. A month more of irrelevant training, and I reported aboard.

Two weeks later Fate smiled wryly, Monkey chuckled. The ship received orders to join one of the very few destroyer divisions from the east coast to be deployed to WESTPAC, and the coast of Viet Nam and that war that had never been declared by our government.

Even before that fateful cruise the mischievous and divine duo had begun their games with that good ship, a gray boat, as old as I. I was told that it had been built for an expected life span of eight years. Two 5" gun mounts were positioned forward. At one time there was a mount aft also, but then the Navy modernized and added ASROC (Anti-Submarine ROCket), a nuke. But the engineer's math was a little off, and after they slid her off the ways she floated so far down in the stern they had to do something—so they just took off the after gun mount. She floated better.

An empty hangar bay sat behind the stacks, used now for storage and occasional bull sessions. It had once housed DASH (Drone Anti-Submarine Helicopter). DASH was an exciting remote-control toy, until, on another ship, it headed for the California coast one practice day with a torpedo attached under its belly, thumbed its nose at the controller and kept right on going, in spite of all radio signals to the contrary. Now the empty hangar was all that remained.

ASROC too became something of an embarrassment. Once a year the officials designated a ship for a trial of the system, just to prove, in that especially obscured mentality of the military, that nukes are safe. Fate pointed her finger: we were chosen and soon headed to sea.

We had not yet entered the target area when a loud "WOOSH!" sent a shudder through the ship, and the nuclear-capable rocket streaked away prematurely; 180 degrees away, to be exact, from the target. In pretesting the system, the only graduate of Annapolis on board had pushed the wrong button.

But I digress.

> *Now they made all secure in the fast black ship,*
> *and, setting out the winebowls all a-brim,*
> *they made libation to the gods,*
> *the undying, the ever-new,*
> *most of all to the grey-eyed daughter of Zeus.*
> *And the prow sheared through the night into the dawn.*

The year was 1969. After a number of training exercises we were pronounced "ready for sea" and so began our passage to the East, by heading west of course, through the Panama Canal and up the coast of Mexico to San Diego. It all began pleasantly enough. On the long haul from the California coast to Hawaii, with some time to ourselves, I began reading *The Day of Infamy*, Walter Lord's consummate history of the Japanese attack on Pearl Harbor.

> *The sun rose on the flawless brimming sea*
> *into a sky all brazen...*

We were scheduled to enter that port just after sunrise. The calm sea was a mirror reflecting the blue sky. As First Lieutenant (a job in the Navy, not a rank), I was stationed on the forecastle, a splendid vantage point from which to identify all the landmarks about which I had just read. Goddess Fate and Monkey winked at each other.

The ship was just easing into the narrow channel. A minor glitch: the bridge could not raise Harbor Control on the prescribed radio net. Never mind: it was an early Sunday morning, probably following a late Saturday night. Finally picking out the saddle in the mountains through which that tremendous enemy airborne invasion had passed, I began describing the happenings of that famous day, another sleepy Sunday, some twenty-seven years earlier, and indicating the relevant geography to the seaman accompanying me there on the fo'c'sle.

I was recounting how the Japanese planes had flown a tight formation through the gap in the green mountains, then dropped down and headed for their individual targets. I was becoming involved in the story, but someone interrupted and pointed back to that mountainous breach and at dozens of tiny specks passing through it. Then we began to hear: a pulsating drone that could only be produced by scores of airborne engines all approaching at the same speed. The growing formation fanned out, dropping lower.

Talk over the sound-powered phones became less official, more agitated. The bridge still couldn't raise Harbor Control.

The specks were growing larger, the sound, louder. The multitude was composed of small single-engine planes. *Old* small single-engine planes. They looked like specters out of history books. *They looked like Japanese Zeros.*

Then, with the newly risen sun glinting off their sides, we saw those other rising suns painted under their wings. The Captain, Executive Officer, Officer of the Deck, and Radio were frantically working every radio net they could find, to no avail. Such a cacophony of voices passed among lookouts on the sound-powered phones no one could get anything straight. We were passing Hickam Field, and parked on the ramps were ghosts of World War II planes.

The Zeros began diving. Explosions! We could see mirages of men running excitedly, falling about the flaming wrecks. We passed a marker in the channel mandating a five-knot harbor entrance speed, and were passed ourselves by the Ward, a destroyer that didn't exist anymore on the roll of U.S. warships, heading out to sea at flank speed. She had been one of the few to escape from that harbor's devastation during the Japanese attack. Monkey laughed.

The channel was too narrow for a turn. New dimensions of reality shook us all.

Finally, as if nothing extraordinary was taking place, a voice came up on the radio and simply gave us a berth number and directions to tie-up. Not until alongside did we learn of the making of a future film, about the attack on Pearl Harbor, to be called *Tora! Tora! Tora!* Sunday had been chosen for the attack scene so that Navy pilots could use their day off-duty to fly the planes.

The Trickster had played his game and introduced to us, in a few brief moments, an element of war we had tried to ignore until now: fear. Only, in his inimitable way, he added another, more important realm, which not until much later, caused me to ponder: that sudden and ineffable break with reality.

***

We continued westward, using much of the transit time for readiness exercises and the studying of innumerable new codebooks and regulations for operations in a combat zone. The "Maddox Incident" in which a destroyer had been supposedly attacked by a high-speed North Vietnamese patrol boat in August of 1965, had made us all just a little edgy (this was before the fraudulent aspect of this incident had come to light).

Each of us harbored his own anxieties on crossing that invisible line through the water, the boundaries delineating "the combat zone"—a line that gave us an added bonus in pay as well as a few added personal insecurities. Little time passed before we were inaugurated into the complexities of warfare communications within that zone.

CIC (Combat Information Center)—that dark compartment behind the bridge with all the radar scopes and whatnot) first picked up an unidentified contact on surface radar some twenty-five or thirty miles away, traveling fast for a surface vessel, some fifty knots or so (not out of line for an enemy high-speed patrol boat—one of which had supposedly attacked the Maddox). Then the magic words, "constant bearing, decreasing range," meaning it was running at a course calculated to intercept us on our present heading. The officers on the bridge were thrown into a bit of a fluster, attempting to raise the contact on radio (to no avail) and changing speed and course (the contact changed direction in order to continue to intercept us). I can't recall if General Quarters were called or not, but I do remember that tension had noticeably increased.

Then, finally, a voice came up on a radio net reserved for local air traffic asking "Hopechest," our call sign, to respond. More confusion as the codebooks were broken out, the proper codes for the date looked up; a challenge code was issued to the inquiring voice. The response was silence.

Anxiety reached an apex. The challenge code was issued again, louder and more frantic. Nothing.

Finally, "Angel 3" came up on the radio, told us in no uncertain terms what we could do with our code books and suggested that if we wanted our muthafuggin mail we could come around to a heading off the wind and drop our speed to fifteen knots. About this time a lookout reported what happened to be a low-flying U.S. helicopter.

The Trickster was not done with us.

After some general off-shore fire support, and then plane guarding — chasing a carrier around Yankee Station for a while, we were given what we were told was an important mission to provide fire support to a night attack on a VC position clinging to the side of "Monkey Mountain," overlooking Danang Harbor. The significance of the mountain's name escaped me at the time.

We were to enter the harbor at dusk, anchor, set up radio contact with the spotters, and provide support when and where called for. We were to be close. There seemed a good chance we might get shot at.

We eased into the harbor to the precise location given; dropped the hook. This scared more than just the captain, for even with our boilers up and a sailor standing by with a sledge to break a quick-release link in the anchor chain, we were about as close as one could be to the state of a very large sitting duck.

The anchor drug; we were drifting toward the shore. My imagination placed not only 122 mm mortars but also heavy artillery in the hands of our enemy nestled into the flank of the mountain, just waiting. The sun had long disappeared over the blue-hazed mountains.

We moved; dropped anchor again.

Anchor dragging again.

Moved; dropped the hook again.

"Bearings constant, Captain. We're holding."

We waited. The hardest part. The attack wasn't to begin until 2300 hours. We waited. The captain grew nervous. He stationed roving lookouts on deck, tossing grenades over the side every five minutes to discourage any would-be sappers.

We waited. The repetitious "THUD" of concussion grenade explosions underwater heightened the tension. Monkey, with a slant to his eyes, smiled.

We waited. Nature did not.

2230 hours: The tide begins coming in. The ship begins swinging on her chain.

2245 hours: We're swinging good.

2257 hours: Our gunless stern is facing Monkey Mountain. In modernizing our sleek man-of-war, the U.S. Navy opted for nuclear capability over one of the most basic tenets of either ancient or modern warfare; cover your ass.

There was little we could do with a nuclear anti-submarine rocket/torpedo at the moment. We really wanted a gun mount back on our fantail. As it was, we called Mission Control and explained our dilemma: We couldn't shoot. I could swear one of those Army bastards chuckled in the background...but then, perhaps it was our primate friend of the gods again. Trickster was becoming quite attached to the good ship with the call sign "Hopechest," And fate was drawing me closer to the land of the Lotos-Eaters.

***

And so it was that we came to the middle,

> *Think of a catch that fisherman haul to a halfmoon bay*
> *in a fine-meshed net from the white-caps of the sea;*
> *how all are poured out on the sand, in throes for the salt sea,*
> *twitching their cold lives in Helios' fiery air:*

That episode marking an otherwise quiet Sunday when the deaths of two simple fishermen gave birth to an unknowing quest. It was perhaps the most awakening experience on that voyage, but certainly not the last of consequence. Fate and her cohort had one more surprise they had saved for our homeward journey.

If our ship's entry into this war was marked by an introduction to the beginning of a war past, it should not come as a surprise that, before leaving the arena, I was to be indoctrinated into the climactic end of that great world battle, an end of shadow and fire carrying with it a dark and explosive prophesy to the world itself.

We were leaving the zone of combat, and had suffered nothing worse than a minor collision at sea. The ship had received orders for an extra liberty port in Japan on the way home. It was a port that had not been visited by an American Man-of-War since that great war to end all wars, and the Navy Department wanted a report on the possibility of future visits by its ships.

Kure, an industrial area located some twenty-five kilometers from Hiroshima and known for the construction of some of the largest super-tankers in the world, was itself a town of little western influence. It promised a rare look at the more traditional life of that complex country. We, as did the Navy, failed to recognize the significance of the date of our arrival.

On August 5, 1970, we slowly maneuvered to the municipal pier, a structure obviously designed for smaller craft than ours. We noticed a gathering of people, fronted by several apparent dignitaries and pretty young girls in kimonos. That our liberty call promised an enrichment to the community's coffers was not to be doubted.

Not until tying-up did we realize that the gathering was actually composed of two groups, one welcoming the American sailors with the key to the city and open arms; the other, vehemently protesting the imperialists' arrival on the eve of the twenty-fifth anniversary of the most devastating man-made event in the history of this small planet and its inhabitants.

Just a quarter of a century ago the same government's military that was now tying to its shore had dropped the atomic bomb on Hiroshima, only a short distance from where we now gazed upon our welcoming committee. Our mingled and mangled past was not to be forgotten so easily.

That dark moment of history came to searing life for me as I later walked the landscaped path towards Ground Zero, now a peace park and reminder to the world of man's capabilities to destroy all that he has been given. Parents played with young children on the manicured grass, and other children's burned and disfigured faces flashed before me.

East Wind and North Wind, then South Wind and West,
coursing each in turn to the brutal harry.

The fragrance of the blooming gardens mingled in my mind with the stench of burning earth and flesh; the busy sounds of the streets nearby turned into the screams of air-raid sirens, shrieking winds of flame, and the death-cries of man, woman and child. And that was only the beginning, for with that one detonation we had unleashed a new power that would forevermore hold our world in fear of its unbridled strength. Once let loose, these particularly ghostly dogs of war could never be recaptured. That was the difference.

The sights and sounds and smells of that horrible scene returned again and again to me. I actually became dizzy, my legs weakened, and I had to sit upon the earth, that scarred and sacred earth.

the grey-eyed goddess came to him, in figure
of a small girl child,

A run-away ball rolled toward me, followed by a beautiful and shy young child. I rolled it back. I could not hide the tears streaking my face.

"Arigato gozaimas, Ojisama."

She had bowed, and actually thanked me, then hurried back to her parents.

***

There was one further incident, which comes to mind now, that occurred before I left that ship. We had returned to homeport from our wartime experiences, thinking it was all over. Then a message clacked its way over the Teletype: We had been chosen to conduct a burial at sea. The body was that of a Navy pilot who had been killed in that same zone of conflict. We knew nothing more of his story. Fortunately, as it turned out, his family chose not to attend the burial.

We had steamed a number of miles out of port, and were just making way in a calm sea. The honor guard stood at an uncomfortable attention flanking the casket, rifles at their sides. The ship slowed, and finally stilled on the quiet ocean. The chaplain spoke a brief service, commending the body to its marine grave. The honor guard raised its weapons for a loud salute, then the coffin was lifted and slid over the side, plunging into the green depths. I heard a superstitious sigh of relief behind me.

The palpable feeling of unease among the crew began dissipating. We started to return to our duties, when someone hollered "Wait!"

The bier had popped back to the surface, now bobbing in the gentle swell. We watched silently; gulls wheeled overhead. The ship's company remained quiet, staring at the reluctant casket. The hush became discomforting. Agitated conversations arose, particularly among the officers, about what should be done. The captain elected to wait a while longer. The body's box, though specially weighted and built to allow the sea's entry, continued to float defiantly in view, with no apparent desire to descend to a deeper abode.

At long last the captain called over the master-at-arms, and with other officers joining in the discussion, finally decided on a course of action. Each of the honor guard was issued additional clips of live ammunition, and on command, began peppering the floating chest and its contents with dozens of holes. After many long minutes the corpse and its container grudgingly slid from view, a less than noble retreat from life.

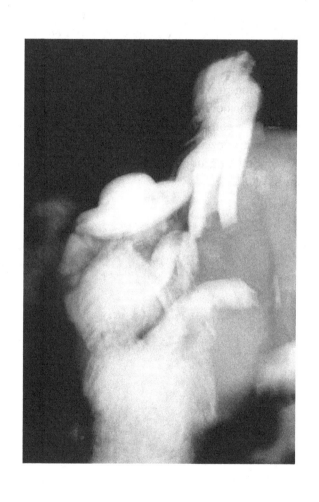

The Seeress

"It's almost as though you were given a second chance." Those exact words were to mean little until they were tossed at me, again, some four years into the future, half a world away. But, never mind, that's another story.

She was a seeress. I know that now. Yet on that warm winter day her appearance fooled me. There was no red-painted hand palm or neon obscenity in the front yard of her home. A friend had simply suggested that I might like to talk to this woman.

I was embarrassed as I paused at her front door, and perhaps a little frightened. Or maybe that had come later. I hesitantly knocked, ready to flee after five seconds if no one answered. But it seemed the door was immediately, though quietly, opened and a kind and gentle face peered through the screen door. "Yes?"

"I believe I...ah...believe I had an appointment."

Even through the mesh of the rusted screen I could feel her eyes. It was not a feeling of intrusion, simply one of friendly knowledge.

"Ah...,but it wasn't in your own name, was it?" There was no accusation, just a question.

Mistress: please: are you divine, or mortal?

I was surprised. I had neither given her my name nor the name in which the appointment had been made.

19

"Won't you please come in?"

Now with the screen door opened I saw more clearly the small frail body, the friendly and open face. She proceeded to speak intimately of my life in the present even before we sat.

> *But the grey-eyed goddess said:*
> *"Reason and heart will give you words, Telemakhos;*
> *and a spirit will counsel others. I should say*
> *the gods were never indifferent to your life."*

Then she took my hand. Her's was wrinkled, warm and dry, still soft and light. I felt an apprehension, but not a dangerous one; simply a feeling that I was suddenly vulnerable. Open. Nothing could be hidden. She was telling me things I knew...but things that only I knew. And she knew. My repertoire of experience had not prepared me for this. I *was* frightened.

And then she slowly slid into my past; first, the most recent, then further and further back until she was speaking of three generations of family history. I sat, spell-bound. Just as easily she traveled with me in tow into the future. She spoke of events that seemed quite improbable. I know better now. She spoke of this writing; she spoke of friendly spirits; she spoke of darkness; and, she spoke of Death. Then she whispered, "It's almost as though you were given a second chance." She would not elaborate.

And just when I realized I had been holding my breath for what seemed like minutes, she said, "and in three days you will encounter one with the initials M.W.C. Very soon after your meeting you will ..."

I protested. I would not do the things of which she spoke.

> *I would not trust a message, if one came,*
> *nor any forecaster my mother invites*
> *to tell by divination of time to come.*

"You need not worry." Her tone, even more than her words, were calming. "If you take care, all will come out well, and you both will be richer for the experience."

Though part of me had come to this meeting wanting to find answers to unaskable questions, I basically had come as a non-believer; and I still could not fathom all that she has told me. This last was her answer to my disbelief; her proof to me, if I would accept it.

She asked for nothing, and spoke a kind farewell.

It was a week later when suddenly her last words returned. Without remembering, I had become involved in the relationship that she had predicted. Ah! But the first name of the other person did not match the initials. Part of me felt, at least, a weak victory.

I spoke to the other, and told her of the meeting with the old woman and of her prophesy concerning our adventures; and finally, with a victorious smile, I mentioned how the woman had been wrong, at least, with her first initial, though the others matched.

She looked at me quite seriously, then laughed; "The name by which you know me is really a nickname; my birth name is M_____!" I must have blanched, for inwardly I cringed with a sudden realization: up until this moment I somehow had deluded myself into thinking I had been dealing with an improbable, but possible, string of coincidences and vague generalities. The Seeress had given me her proof.

Pigs and Chickens

The Navy had maintained a policy, up until that time, of counting a ship's cruise in WESTPAC as a personal tour in Viet Nam, meaning of course that one would not unwillingly be sent back to war again if he had so served. So when the old woman had told me I would be returning to that country at least twice, once as a guest of our government, I knew she had to be wrong. I had no desire to be a part of the continuing maniacal destruction.

But Monkey intervened. The Navy needed warriors and so changed its policy, retroactively. My tour aboard the ship was coming to an end. I called the Detailer's desk in Washington where that Goddess Fate sat pointing her finger so indiscriminately, or so I thought. Yes, I was due for rotation; yes, I was single; yes, I was coming from sea duty; and yes, I was going "in-country," to Viet Nam.

At this point my mind was torn, almost schizophrenic. I wanted no part of the war; but, I was intrigued, curious; there was a certain dark attraction...So, in the end I swore to the detailer that he would have to come look for me in Canada first, should he come up with orders for a combatant position; but, if he could find a non-combative job, I'd go.

Looking back, I realize now that my threat meant little to that anonymous man in Washington. He could have cared less. It took the Goddess to find a solution. Soon I was packing my sea bag for twelve weeks of intensive Vietnamese language training in San Diego, having been assigned to "Operation Helping Hand," Headquarters: Saigon.

The flight into Tan Son Nhut, Saigon's international airport, is probably one every man and woman who ever went that route at that time will not easily forget. The long hours aboard gave too much time to reflect, ponder, wonder. This was the real thing, not just some boat ride off the coast. Some of those young faces would not come back. Some would only return in those ubiquitous body bags. Those who would return alive would probably do so bearing one type of scar or another. Some made noise of false bravado; most were quiet.

Darkness had settled by the time we braked on the tarmac that spring evening in 1970. The stewardess opened the door: sultry, humid air quickly replaced the artificially conditioned atmosphere of the plane. An Army sergeant with an M-16 slung casually over his shoulder was yelling directions. Descending the steps: sounds of choppers somewhere on the darkened distance. I wiped the quickly forming sweat from my brow and felt sick to my stomach. We could hear popping and see tracers on the horizon. The stewardess at the door quickly wiped her eyes.

"Operation Helping Hand" was a slick public relations move at a time the military was drawing fire from critics of the war. The idea was to provide social assistance to families of the Vietnamese Navy during that phase of the war known as Vietnamization. "The training and materiel were sufficient that the U.S. Navy could concentrate on turning over their part of the war effort to the Vietnamese." Our job as "Food and Shelter" advisors was to demonstrably improve living conditions of Vietnamese Navy dependents so that a sailor would not have to worry about the security of his family and thus could concentrate on the job at hand...presumably winning the war. Projects included housing, school building, fishing, and animal husbandry.

In the infinite wisdom of the military bureaucracy I had been selected to assist a small group of animal husbandry advisors comprising a part of "Operation Helping Hand." This small band of farm boys, sailors, brigands, and thieves became affectionately, and at times not so affectionately, known as "Pigs and Chickens."

Setting up small projects of swine and poultry production at some fifty Vietnamese Navy bases along the thousands of miles of coastline, islands, rivers and throughout the Mekong Delta, the group needed a veterinarian, a position held by the Army and Air Force, but not the Navy. Seeing an M.S. degree in veterinary science on my college record, the detailer had looked no further. To him that meant veterinarian. In fact, my degree was far removed from that of a veterinarian, but the powers didn't seem concerned with details. Though I had some experience with large animals, there were two classes of livestock I had particularly avoided: of pigs and chickens I was completely ignorant.

I know of no group of men less homogeneous than Pigs and Chickens. It was a loosely bound herd of individuals ranging in ages from eighteen to sixty-some; administered by a young Lt.(j.g.) cowboy from Oklahoma who practiced his lassoing from behind his desk whenever he felt the need, and chewed Redman, but never perfected his spitting aim; and headed up by an ancient and grisly first class petty officer, known only as Moses, and who had been in Viet Nam so long his eyes were beginning to slant.

The first premise of the group was that you couldn't work effectively with animals within the confines of a military structure. Consequently, military structure was thrown to the monsoon winds. In a war and a country being run by the military this premise was to cause a few problems.

Offices for Pigs and Chickens were ostensibly a part of Psychological Warfare Operations (PSYOPS), itself housed in the headquarters of Naval Forces, Viet Nam (NAVFORV), an immense fortress-like edifice in Saigon on the corner of Phan Dinh Phung and Doan Thi Diem. Keeping to its founding principles, actual administration of Pigs and Chickens was conducted across the street in the back room of Hoa's, one of those typical Vietnamese shops selling everything imaginable, legal or otherwise.

Hoa, a small young lady of perhaps twenty years or so with immense business acumen, supported her parents and extended family from the small shop that was actually the front room of their home. Somehow, she always managed to have space and cold Beer "33" for her Pigs and Chickens boys. Hoa's aging father, known to all as Papasan, considered himself the honorary board chairman of our group and took part, albeit usually silently, in all proceedings and libations. His stool backed up to the wall, alongside which a worn and deflated bicycle inner tube hung from a piece of clothesline. Its purpose eluded me until I first witnessed him taking his place, then resting his right elbow within the inner tube (placed at just the right height) so that his drink was never far from his mouth and minimum energy was needed to get it there. A worn collection of scratched Hank Williams, Johnny Cash, and Merle Haggard albums took turns circling about Hoa's ancient Victrola.

Jim, the young j.g. from Oklahoma, introduced me to all this. We were, on paper, co-managers of the operation. Being a part of PSYOPS had its advantages, as no one really seemed to know just exactly what PSYOPS actually did. Its official offices were recognized by the sign above the door:

LET ME WIN YOU HEART AND MIND,
OR I'LL BURN DOWN YOUR GODDAMN
HOOTCH.

There was an indistinct aura of secrecy about its functions, and also a rather direct link with the admiral, which caused more than a few to think twice before entering its portal on mundane business.

Such links gave us individual, high priority, blanket travel orders, for we sometimes carried highly perishable vaccine. It was not uncommon for a lowly seaman from Pigs and Chickens to bump a Major off a flight to the Delta. We were not always liked, but generally tolerated.

Jim handled the bureaucracy, logistics, and paperwork well, though I don't think he enjoyed it any more than I. My function was to lend some sort of management to the field operations as well as contend with aspects of animal health and illness. Jim, by far, had the toughest job; I was given the opportunity to travel the length and breadth of that mysterious country, monitoring ongoing programs and assisting new projects.

In retrospect, there were probably two items that lent an undefined respect to Pigs and Chickens. The open-ended, high priority travel orders were a rarity and allowed us to go and be anywhere we wanted at any time; the PSYOPS ID card intrinsically said, "Don't ask questions."

Most of that small group had little respect for uniforms, or for that matter, the rank they sometimes represented. Almost routinely Jim was receiving complaints of his men's appearance in the field, and god-help-us-all, in Saigon Headquarters on their occasional return. As to rank, we were organized, loosely, as it were, not by rank at all but by experience. It was not unusual for a seaman, born and raised on a farm, to be telling a lieutenant what to do. This sanctioned disregard for rank on the job unfortunately often led to similar blatant disregard off the job, raising some hackles on unindoctrinated individuals along the way.

I did not appreciate the full value of our license until one humid evening in the Delta. Johnson, a farm boy from Iowa who never saw fit to climb the ladder from the lowly rate of seaman, and I had been visiting several projects in the delta near Vinh Long. We had made acquaintance with an Army Intelligence Officer who liked what we were doing and had assisted us not only in catching rides on some Hueys going our way, but also by diverting one or two of the choppers to our destinations, thus saving us considerable time. I had no idea how he obtained such priorities; I only knew we were treated with what we silently felt to be an undue respect by the dispatchers and pilots.

Tom, the intelligence officer, greeted us as we climbed out of the last ride of the day, scurrying beneath the still-spinning rotors, trying to shield our eyes from the blowing dust. He had a place for us to spend the night, and an Army jeep at our disposal, and was determined to show us the sights.

We cleaned off a couple layers of grit, sampled Army chow, then headed to one of the local bars. By mid-evening I realized other American soldiers had disappeared and that was when Tom explained there was a curfew in the area but, not to worry, as an intelligence officer he had a certain autonomy. Next he was going to take us to the Pink Gate, perhaps one of the most notorious whorehouses in the Delta, to have another beer.

Through back alleys and side streets we passed the soup carts, hawkers and other night activities of the Vietnamese, until, coming out of town, we turned down a dirt road and pulled through a metal gate, caught in the jeep's headlights, colored a shocking pink. I remember thinking that the electricity was out; the interior was lit by the soft glow of kerosene lanterns. It was a small house and only several girls were about. Probably, they had not been expecting any business during the curfew.

We bought black market American beer, and Cokes for the girls; sat listening to Peter, Paul and Mary, and to Tom explain how this was one of the safest places to be as it was often patronized by some of the higher-ranking officers in the area and hence was seldom bothered by the military police.

We had had a hectic day, having gotten caught on the fringes of a firefight and become involved in a subsequent medivac. We were tired from the excitement and thankful for a quiet place to sit and drink and talk. The girls weren't pushy, and as soon as they learned that we were only looking for the environment and not the services they seemed relieved. They joined in the banter when the conversation demanded, were friendly, but certainly not obtrusive.

Then the alarm went off! A petite young girl came running into the front room: *"Dai Uy, Dai Uy*...MPs come, MPs come! They see jeep in front."

Tom was quick. He told the girls to hide us and he would explain his presence with his "intelligence" identification. Johnson and I were hurried into a large closet filled with cleaning equipment, and the door locked with a key. There was little room to be comfortable, but we could hear the goings-on through the slatted door.

"Excuse me, Captain, but may I see your ID?...You realize, of course, there is a curfew in effect, and also this place is out of bounds? Are you the only one here?"

Tom apparently showed his identification and curfew pass, then asked to speak privately to the MP in charge. I could just make out the low tones of discussion, but not the words.

"Well, we still need to see if anyone else is here." Through the slats we could hear heavy boots pacing into other rooms, and doors being opened and closed.

"What's in here?" The closet door was unsuccessfully tried. Several girls' voices rattled off excitedly in Vietnamese. One spoke broken English, "Sir, only small room for clean; Mamasan have key. She no here." The door was shaken by the knob again. We were both holding our breaths. The glare of a flashlight shot up through the angled slats. We each automatically stepped back from the light; Johnson, unfortunately, into a metal mop pail!

"Hey Sarge!...Think we got something here."

"Alright, we know you're in there. Come out with your hands up." It was something out of a poor movie script. I was hoping for a word from Tom. Nothing.

Not knowing what to do, I realized we couldn't come out if we had wanted to; we had been locked in. Silence, I heard the bolt open and close on someone's firearm.

Then Tom's voice, first in Vietnamese, instructing one of the girls to get the key; then in English, "Sergeant, I'll take responsibility for this, but first I need to explain a few things."

The door opened. "Alright, hands behind your heads." We were frisked for weapons, which neither or us carried.

Standing before the MPs, Johnson was explaining that he must have left his ID card in the Army barracks; but, yes, he was Navy. I realized then that his worn and unorthodox uniform had not one insignia of service, rate, or name. Of course he had no dog tags. I showed my PSYOPS ID and orders, vague but important looking. Tom stepped in.

"Sergeant, the Lieutenant and I..."

"Captain, the Lieutenant, as you call him, is wearing Captain's bars."

It was no use explaining that the Navy had different names for the same ranks.

"Sergeant, I know I can trust you. I apologize for not telling you sooner, but this involves a highly confidential matter; in fact, it' s classified 'Top Secret'. Are you familiar with this man's organization?"

"You mean...what's it say here...'PSYOPS'?"

"That's right."

"Well...ah..." He was groping.

"Go ahead, Lieu...Captain, tell him what outfit."

"I'm not sure..."

"We can trust the Sergeant." Tom glanced over both shoulders, moved closer, and whispered, "Sergeant, have you ever heard of 'Pigs and Chickens'?"

"PIGS AND CHIC..."

"Not quite so loud, Sergeant!"

"Pigs and Chickens..." Less of a question.

"That's right, Sergeant. I knew you had heard of them. Top Secret Navy Intelligence outfit. Believe me, there's a good reason this man doesn't have any insignia or ID. Now please keep this strictly to yourself, Sergeant. We can't have the word getting out in the wrong places, can we?"

I thought Tom was pushing our collective luck a little far, but I deferred to him in silence.

"Ah, no Sir."

"Good. We're very close to uncovering a very large dope ring and contraband operation, and we have strong proof it's operating from this house." Tom glanced over his shoulder again towards the girls huddled in the other room, then continued whispering, "The operation's big enough that the Army and Navy are working together, and the Navy pulled in its top in-country team..."

"Pigs and Chickens?"

"That's right, Sergeant. You're welcome to call in my credentials right now, but I must ask you to remain silent about these men, otherwise you'll blow certain infiltrations that have taken us months to achieve. I'll take full responsibility."

"Pigs and Chickens..."

"That's right, Sergeant; you're looking at two of their finest."

He was repeating to himself, "Pigs and Chickens."

As he and his men were walking out the door I could hear him still mumbling, "Well, I'll just be goddamned...Pigs and Chickens!"

***

My fatigues were still a dark glossy green; their insignia still an unfaded black. I was yet a greenhorn, an "f.n.g." in local parlance (fuckin' new guy). A week spent in the office trying to learn what I could of this strange operation had infected me with a growing itch to get out to the projects, and most of all out of the Saigon atmosphere.

I planned a visit to one of the closer projects on the coast near Vung Tau. I was to travel with another PSYOPS officer who had business at a fairly sizable River Patrol Boat Base. Many of the Navy bases were largely Vietnamese now, but with American advisors still occupying key positions. It turned out that this was one of the unfriendliest American groups I was to meet. There were contributing factors to this lack of hospitality, of which, at the time, I was unaware.

Nevertheless, Ivan and I finished off the business of a rather unpleasant day, then went for a meal in the small American mess. We ate in relative silence, stared at, but not spoken to.

Dusk was turning to night as we left the mess hall and Ivan suggested we take a walk down by the docks on the river to enjoy the first cool breezes of the evening. As we walked towards the PBRs and Swift Boats tied to the embankment Ivan took out of his pocket what looked like a pack of Vietnamese cigarettes and offered one.

Not until that first long draw did I realize that I was not smoking tobacco. I glanced at Ivan. He smiled and took a deep drag.

Now I had had some experience with "Mary Jane" before in the States. But each time it had been a real hocus-pocus affair with everyone sitting in candle-lit circles on the floor passing a joint from hand to hand. Whether by insufficient quality or quantity I'm not sure, but it had never affected me much, and I had become a little turned off by all the "oohs" and "aahs" and "Oh Wow, Man!" of the ceremony. So I wasn't much concerned now.

We were sitting on the concrete sea wall to which the boats were tied. The night was quiet; we hadn't spoken. I slowly realized that for the first time in my life I was stoned out of my mind! How long had we been there? I'll never know; I had become engrossed, spellbound, in listening to the silence. It was the most complete and awe-inspiring hush I had ever known in my life, and it was exquisite. I was just at that point of intoxication where I didn't want to try to get up, because I wasn't sure that I could. But as long as I remained still I was perfectly, perfectly, comfortable. Time had become a flexible dimension, and other dimensions I had never before encountered came swimming into view. And the silence of the night was the most beautiful...

A thundering and stunning explosion ripped through my senses! I was blinded by the sudden flash, the blast tearing at my eardrums!

I did not know what had happened. I did know that I would be dead in but a moment...in fact I casually wondered why I was able to be thinking at all, even now. Somehow I was able to break down that moment's event into very small elements of time, and stretch those elements into whole, much larger, conceptual spaces, filling each with long ponderous thoughts. I was dead, but that was alright. It had been painless, and all together rather honorable. I was resigned to my fate; I'm sure catatonic in appearance.

I suppose minutes passed, perhaps just seconds, maybe hours. There was simply no context for time. Slowly, I realized I could move my head. I could see my surroundings. The ethereal fog was disappearing. I was whole. I probably wasn't dead; not even wounded;

I certainly had no feelings of pain. The boats came into focus, sitting as before, calmly, tied to the wall of the river embankment. Circles of ripples peacefully lapped their sides.

Someone laughed in the darkness—a foreign high-pitched laugh. Two dark Vietnamese faces emerged from the watery shadows behind the stern of a PBR. Joking to each other, almost chin deep in the black river, they went about the task of picking up the stunned and bloated fish now floating to the surface. Then I saw the string of grenades looped around the neck of one of the sailors.

An instrument of war had been turned into a tool of harvest, and in that instant, the kaleidoscope of my mind's vision shifted a notch again, and did not shift back.

***

For me, at least, and I surmise for more than a few others who escaped physically from that non-war of our generation, one sound continually reverberates in the subconscious, in that dark corner of the mind. It emanates deep from the soul seeking its reflection in reality. And once found it bursts the time capsules of the senses, releasing multitudes of strange monsters from the past—the kind of images from which nightmares are made.

It's not the sound of 'in-coming'—for some no doubt that scream will also forever linger—but that's not a sound easily called back or triggered in normal life.

This sound pulses as the heart does; but, there's a difference: it comes from a great distance and its intensity increases as it approaches; and when it gets to where you think *it can't get any closer, it can't get any louder, it can't get any more piercing,* that screaming throb keeps coming...louder, louder!

It enters the third eye and pierces the mind and shoots to the base of the spine so that nothing else exists: *only the continuous beating of the rotors.*

The throb of the rotors: rotors of the gun ships; rotors of the medivacs; rotors of the Jolly Green Giants; of the Loaches; of the Cobras. Accompanying the pulsing throb is the searing blood-brown dust kicking up in your face, and the screaming of the wounded, and the moaning of the worse-than-wounded...and the silence of the others; the silence still somehow a part of that throbbing, beating nightmare. I was to see enough.

A mission of dozens throbbing across the top of the canopied jungle or over bombed and defoliated lunar landscape; a pick-up, an insert.

When we hear that sound now, no matter where we are, no matter how long it has been, we're intoxicated, frightened, and returned. Reality loses its easy parameters. Time-painted memories burst the gates, and we're back, our hearts beating with the rotors. We taste the dust and squint the eyes, and cover our ears if we can. But the throbbing, beating rotors keep coming, now from our very souls. And the sweat glistens on our brows, a sweat not of heat but a sweat with the pungent stench of fear, but more than fear.

What is excitement but the adrenal intoxication stemming from a momentary escape from fear; and the ultimate excitement of that war, to be remembered, if you win. The ultimate addiction: worse than that of any of the opiates of nature or chemicals of man. And it is prescribed freely to the youth of each generation, the most susceptible of all; the minds still empty of references, of bases of wisdom—the only antidote.

Without the constant injection of this new addictive, other passions fade and become annulled...as with any other drug. Viet Nam veteran R. L. Barth, in his poem *INSERT,* well describes those afflicted as, "Junkies of terror, impatient to shoot up..." That's why we went back; why we couldn't love, why it wasn't worth talking.

Now Zeus who views the wide world sent a sign to him,
launching a pair of eagles from a mountain crest
in gliding flight down the soft blowing wind,
wing-tip to wing-tip quivering taut, companions,
till high above the assembly of many voices
they wheeled, their dense wings beating, and in havoc
dropped on the heads of the crowd—a deathly omen—

34

Climbing out of the webbed seating of the C-127, trying to blink back the blinding white tropic glare of Phu Quoc's sun and letting my ears adjust to the quiet of the sudden dying of the loud engines, expecting a relative silence of this normally peaceful South China Sea island; something was disturbing. My ears were still ringing, but then I heard; no, I felt, the throbbing.

Like mosquitoes on the horizon, two Cobras were coming out of the west, heading towards this small military landing strip wedged between the calm sea and the silent mountain. The Cobras swung in low, hovered, then perched. Still the throbbing. Now the engines cut...dying. For one who has not seen a Cobra head on, loaded with armament, I can only say it is evil. Its appearance is death, the modern Fifth Horseman of the Apocalypse. I know of no other weapon of war so macabre in appearance.

The Cobras on Phu Quoc were a new sight and an enigma to me, for I had been here several times before and had always enjoyed its serenity: a small fishing village, where *nuoc mam,* the best fish sauce in the world, is made. To be assigned here by the Navy was seen by many as a vacation. There wasn't a war going on here. Why then, the Cobras?

A footnote of this island's history tells of an aging clan of believers in the old Messiah of Eastern communism; believers in deciding their own fate, believers in their own nation. A largely uneducated group of farmers and fisherman, these Viet Minh had played their minor role in keeping the land for themselves, irritating the Japanese and French invaders alike. And now they were old; most of their youth had left for better things...they now simply wanted to work their own land and waters in peace.

So, an unofficial truce slowly grew on the island, even during the American escalation of fighting elsewhere. Those sympathetic to what was now the other side drifted to the largely unoccupied northwestern end of the island and reestablished their lives. Until the coming of the Cobras, this had been sufficient.

But then a colonel came to Phu Quoc apparently with advancement on his mind. He decided that the communists posed a threat and thus needed to be eliminated. His tools: the deadly Cobras.

And so they came. I happened to arrive the same afternoon as their first mission. Their presence bothered me somewhat, though at the time I probably could not have put my finger on the irritation. Not until that evening did what was happening come into focus.

The Phu Quoc Officer's Club was something of an ambitious name—a Quonset hut with some cots in the back for transients like myself, a few chairs, a refrigerator that worked when the generators were running, and a somewhat ancient bar from god-knows-where, capable of supporting about four pairs of elbows at best.

Most evenings we preferred to wander into the village of Anthoi and sit on the low stools of the one shop selling *Ba Muoi Ba*, the warm local beer, and talk about what it was going to be like getting back to the world. But tonight I decided to patronize the Officer's Club.

Two new faces graced the territory. The older, perhaps 25, spoke with bravado and beer. The younger seemed more interested in the libations. He seemed so young to me that the thought occurred that were he back home he probably would not have been served. The Army warrant officers were being treated with Navy honor, and probably never had to buy a drink; and then there was the curiosity of the old hands as to just what these flyboys were up to. For the first hour or so of drinking the conversations were fairly general. My first notice of anything unusual was when someone turned down the music, and the noise level quieted. By this time the Army pilot and gunner were obviously beginning to feel the effects of Navy hospitality, and the younger was speaking, using his hands as flyers are so apt to do when describing their flights.

"We came up over the hills and there they were...the 'slopes' and water buffalo...working the rice paddies. On our first pass some of the women actually waved. We circled, swung in low, and I started in with the mini-guns. There wasn't much cover...they ran ever' which direction. Kind'a like shooting my grandpa's chickens in the yard when they didn't have no place to go...And this bird's so maneuverable we'd just take one after the other...come down behind them and just walk the rounds right up their asses...Bam!—another

36

gook greased...then go after another. When we got done with all them Charlies we just started on the buffalo...but this time we got some practice in with the rockets. Just like some high-tech African safari, man, 'cept there wasn't much left of the targets. 'Cept for the gooks' bodies, that place was pretty desolate when we left. Never seen nothin' like it...What a day!"

***

I had been in that chaotic country perhaps half a year. I no longer felt myself the greenhorn; my fatigues had become worn and faded. I was beginning to count down the days until I could return to the world; yet I still wasn't a short-timer. My days remaining in-country were still measured in three digits.

Somehow I had lost the enthusiasm with which I had begun this adventure. I was beginning to see the insane aspects of even our positive contributions. We were such a spit in the bucket. Originally thinking that we were working within the system to add a positive element to the American involvement, I soon came to feel a puppet, adding only righteousness to a very foul deed. I was depressed and lonely. The constant traveling had shown me much of the war, and that was depressing too. It had also kept me from forming any close relationships.

Though always paranoid of the dope scene, I had begun to find solace in the escape of the herbal nectar. Nothing serious; I had seen too much of the effects of the hard drugs on acquaintances. Nevertheless, Cambodian Red provided an easy evening's escape from the insanity around me. I could occasionally get a full night's sleep. It was also partly responsible for the introduction to a sanity-saving friendship developed from the dust of war.

It happened during that mid-term of depression, abetted by a return to Saigon, the capital of war, where generals dined on steak and champagne, where you could feast atop the Brink's, serenaded by a Philippine band and scantily clad dancing girls, while watching tracers bounce over the horizon, or Puff the Magic Dragon illuminate the outskirts; where you could walk down Tu Do and find any vice you so desired; where you could sit on the veranda of the Continental, eating fine French pastries, sipping rich dark coffee from the highlands, and watch the many scarred and limbless beggars reaching out somehow for pennies or piasters; or the young American soldiers, returned from the field for a few days respite, swagger their new-found manhood from bar to bar; or a sleek *ao dai* blowing in the soft tropic breeze, or the petite young girls forced into prostitution by the war's economy; or worse still, its terrors, luring the wealthy round-eyes into dark alleyways, in miniskirts and caked mascara, forsaking the ways of tradition, scorned by even those they supported.

> *Note all things strange*
> *seen here, to tell your lady in after days*

Like no other place in the world, a city in war presents the contrasts of life in its most insane proportions: where admirals' aides gave daily briefings on KIAs and body counts and reduced the insanity to simplistically colored maps and charts; where brilliant men spoke of ludicrous objectives, and self-seekers wrote up commendations and medals for themselves, while the babes of war were being killed.

With reason, the Saigon Warriors were spoken of disparagingly in the jungles and waterways and hills of battle. What did they know of dirt and grit and the scream of 'in-coming' and cold C-rats and foot rot, and blood and fear and tears and loneliness and pain and cold and heat and body bags and leaches and malaria and sweat and despair and death. All this the Saigon Warriors simply reduced to body counts and objectives—neatly. When faced with such unreality the generalities come too easily; and I had the advantage of these city dwellers, for I could return to their steaks and steam baths at will.

Into Mammon's city I had returned, seeking solace and finding only more despair, when a new acquaintance suggested a good meal and a new place he had found. He called it simply "The Compound."

Several miles from the more infamous bars of Tu Do and the center of Saigon; down a refuse-strewn street in a fairly typical low-rent neighborhood; a place where refugees who could afford a house came. Narrow two-and-three storied buildings jammed wall to wall fronting a narrow sidewalk. No yards. Plants and washing occupied the roofs. It got its name from a walled-in compound across the street where Vietnamese Army officers received training in English, so they could better understand the eccentricities of their American advisors. Because of the army's presence, the street was blocked off to traffic with the ubiquitous concertina wire and a sleepy-eyed Vietnamese military guard. The combination of its military neighbor, the concertina and guard, and a few greenbacks shoved into the right pockets protected the Compound from the usual invasions of MPs and the otherwise mandated closure at curfew.

There was no sign. You had to go with someone who knew where it was if you didn't know. Thus it didn't get the riffraff and drunks wandering in off the streets. It was also one of the few places I knew where the clientele was mixed, both Vietnamese and American men. I never witnessed any altercations. It was marked like every other place on the street with a lone light bulb over the door.

Some of the girls were young and uneducated from the countryside, but most had either grown up in Saigon or been there a number of years, and many were college-educated. Unlike the bars downtown I don't think I ever saw a miniskirt being worn, always the traditional *ao dai*. Another aspect of the place that seemed unique was the loyalty the girls had for Ly, the matron. Never, to my knowledge, was there a hint or desire to cheat Ly of time or money. I certainly could not foresee that this refuge was to become my temporary home several years later.

Put bluntly, the Compound was a whorehouse, but it didn't fit the usual criteria. True, the interior was fairly dark, but the music was soft, most often Vietnamese anti-war songs. The girls didn't push you to buy them Saigon Tea. I noticed that conversations were as often in Vietnamese as English. There seemed an honest friendliness. There was little make-up in evidence. A woman, appearing to be in her late thirties, a little overweight now, still maintaining that fragile oriental beauty, amicably greeted us. It would have been sinful to address her with the bastardized "Mamasan" so popular with GIs to indicate a madam.

This was a different world from the Tu Do bars, or Cach Mang steam baths, or House 411 with its swimming pool, rowdiness and exhibitions. This was a refuge to the senses, a hiding place from insanity, a respite from war.

A slender girl detached herself from a group of giggling friends and approached my companion; and, even though we were wearing civilian clothes, she addressed him in Vietnamese by his rank, as is the custom; for in that lyrical language and culture only in the closest relationships were names used in address. Obviously, they were friends, and were happy to see each other again. The three of us sat at the far end of the room talking quietly of friends and families. I was feeling a relaxation I had not known for more than a half a year. Chris offered a pack of *cansa* around. Mai laughed, and said no thank you, she was crazy enough. I took one, and on lighting it, inhaled deeply the warm sweetness. I drifted slowly into a dream-world of softness. The light half-sad music worked its magic on my ears; the soft-flowing *ao dais* moving across my vision gave rhythm to a gentle undulation of delicate pastels that I allowed to slowly fade from focus into a fragile swirl of color. I was awake, but completely relaxed, soothed to that indescribable state of oneness with my immediate surroundings.

> *The opiate of Zeus's daughter bore*
> *this canny power.*

Chris had earlier told me of his unique friendship with Mai, deep though surprisingly platonic. I envied them their closeness, but appreciated being allowed to be a part, and seeing for once something of genuine value.

Perhaps there was a soft rustling, or a feathery lilting laugh; I don't really know what caused me to turn about in my chair and look up the stairway leading to the floors above and behind me.

Now it occurred to the grey-eyed goddess Athena
to make a figure of dream in a woman's form...

I know only a beautiful form appeared there. And even in my current condition I knew that the beauty reached far beyond the surface. Gossamer robes lifted ever so slightly and rhythmically to an unseen wisp of a breeze. She was standing, floating, above the quiet scene around me, silently taking in all that was occurring. Once again, I knew not what was real, what was drugged intoxication. A pang came to my chest for there was a sadness about such beauty. I was not to learn the nature of that sadness until much later.

Mai spoke to her, she replied quietly, descended almost spiritually, and came and sat with us.

So might Artemis
or golden Aphrodite have descended;

Her name was Lan, and her voice held the delicacy of a golden whisper. I do not remember much of that first conversation. We talked for perhaps an hour, and then she politely excused herself, saying it was time that she must return home.

With this Athena left him
as a bird rustles upward, off and gone.

I began fighting the possibility that I had seen only an apparition, enfolded in the drugged haze of my mind.

At the doorway Mai and Chris reached for each other's hands and said a quiet goodbye. The guard pulled back the concertina to allow us passage and we walked silently through the quiet of a city in curfew. My mind dwelt on how such beauty could incorporate such sadness; the tragedy, inferred but not spoken. A new and mysterious element had been thrown into my life, and with it came a surge of forces temporarily dispelling the black despair I had known such a short time before.

and she will cower and yield her bed—
a pleasure you must not decline.

In the deranged world of a country at war, Lan's friendship brought occasional and temporary sanity. It was a reprieve from the lunacy around me, and without it I should probably not have emotionally survived those times. But in the end, it was just that, a reprieve, and I eventually left that land questioning not only reality, but quite often my own sanity.

Days of a Wanderer

*In life
there is nothing worse than wandering.*

The days of a wanderer can bring knowledge; but, it is the night that harbors painful wisdom. Not without agony come the omens of the dead, the cries of the subconscious, or the meanings of prophecies past.

The release of commitments seems at first a gain of liberty, freedom; but the rootlessness, especially to one so inured to a family and land, soon turns to a bitter cold loneliness that can never be shaken. And the questions in the night; that abysmal sense of worthlessness, having no direction, anchors itself to the soul and begins eating away at man's sanity; always in the night.

*"Go on, go on;
wander the high seas this way, take your blows,
before you join that race the gods have nurtured..."*

From a distant realm of war, in the spring of 1971, a child, a boy-soldier, returned to his native land. He was returning to sanity. He was leaving behind death and strange beauty and the smells of incense and cordite, the sound of choppers, the fatigue of boredom, and the fright of incoming; he was leaving behind the dust and heat,

45

and another child's smile, gone now; and he was leaving behind a subtle new power over life that was available to him nowhere else in the world; and some of these he only thought he was leaving behind. He was confused, but he was returning.

The child returned with the markings of a man, not realizing they were only markings. But one quite close to the child saw those markings quite differently. That one saw those markings as a sign of rebellion against all of life's worthy values. Each in his own way was right.

And so it passed that the one admired so by the child dismissed that child.

No one asked, really asked, what that boy-soldier had left behind; nor with what extra burdens he had returned, for it had been falsely assumed that the boy-soldier had sense enough to know what to leave behind and what to carry.

He was returning to his world; but there was not the joy he was expecting; in its place was an apathy he could not relate to the macabre lunacy he had just left. If this was the real world, he had lost touch with truth.

The kaleidoscope had shifted again, as quickly as before, and he could not adapt to the shift; and so he remained silent, and moved on.

> *"Dear child, whatever put this in your head?*
> *Why do you want to go so far in the world—*
> *and you our only darling?"*

The other was one who, without words, understood the chaos of my mind, and accepted my inconsistencies. I think he knew I needed a guide who would not appear a guide. He has always been a brother to me.

Reentry to the American world without war had in fact come as a great shock to me; but I had become too programmed to admit that fact to myself. The others had been affected by that great tragedy of our generation, but not I, I told myself.

Yet I needed an escape, and a friend. The escape appeared in the form of an ancient VW bus, precisely valued at $400. Materially, I'm not sure it was worth that; psychologically, it was worth every penny, and more, which eventually it wound up costing. The friend was Jeff. We had studied, conspired, worked, played, and gotten drunk together since college days.

We filled the rusted van with all manner of non-necessities and headed for any open road, generally following the sun. Though not knowing it at the time, a year would pass before a circle was completed; and for myself at least, that would only mark the beginning of a much larger circle, both in distance and time. That circles were beginning to form, even in my ignorance, was a healthy sign. We were drifting. And there was time.

We had reached the Dakotas and were passing into that region known as the Badlands. The desolation touched me morosely, yet I was intrigued by the eons exposed in the windblown cuts and washes and exposed fossils; thousands of years lying there before us. What had those bones and grains of sand witnessed during time spans inconceivable to me? I was suddenly quite small, very young and extremely naive.

Besides the evidence of the elements' effects, so apparent throughout the Badlands, the elements themselves were not to be ignored. Our tent, pitched not so far from the road, seemed in the middle of nowhere. A waning moon holding her stance against the wind rose hesitantly above a distant silhouetted butte, finally behind a dark sweeping quilt of clouds. The winds were gathering, as omens do.

Embers from our fire swirled, then flew into a darkness of barrenness and years past. It was the same wind that had been blowing for millennia, and we felt very much alone. The omens forbade unnecessary talk, and we tried to sleep, but the probing and howling of the tempest prohibited even that solace; and finally, in a gust, the tent was swept from its moorings.

And it was the following day, not far from Wounded Knee, that we buried our first engine. It had died a weeping and traumatic (but certainly not noble) death. As one might imagine, with the events of the day following a sleepless night, our mood was not joyful. Miles and miles we were eventually towed through the bleak wastes, and early in the evening we entered the summer-heated metropolis of Rapid City.

Depressed and deprived of transportation, we opted to splurge that night. We found a small and rather down and out motel, and had our first showers in days. Hot water bathing brought some relief to the spirits. The prospect of real beds added to the growing feeling that we might as well make the best of a bad situation. We still had not decided what to do about the decrepit vehicle, standing now as a broken-down war horse, tethered outside the door, for our budget had not counted on replacing a motor that was to cost more than the whole vehicle.

"What the hell, let's go get a drink."

The Elk Horn Bar and Grill was smoky. A large population of pseudo-Stetson hats and high-heeled boots were in attendance and the blue and red flashing neon of the juke box gave a pallid appearance to the various Levied couples on the dance floor. We took the two remaining stools at the bar.

Just sitting down, we had not noticed the two dark-haired women to our left.

"Boy, you two look like you just buried your best friend."

"Worse."

And a conversation began. As simple as that. They took pity on us and our story. Before the evening was over we had been invited to move, the next day, into the home of a Sioux family living not far from the Oglala Pine Ridge Reservation, while we searched for the cheapest means of replacing our extinct engine.

A few days lengthened to a couple of weeks, and we came to know, ever so slightly, a culture as different from ours as any I had seen half a world away. Kay and Thelma were kind to us and did not laugh at our foolish questions or Anglo ways. There were small children and there was a grandmother who told of the old ways, in her own ancient language, for she spoke no English.

What to me had been simply history from the pages of a book became the recent living past, and there was still anger stirring. Wounded Knee was not forgotten; relatives had been massacred, and that was only the beginning of a retinue of grievances against the white man; not the least of which was the societal emasculation of their own men, for prejudice seemed doubly biased against that gender. So few had been able to find meaningful or significant means of supporting their families near the reservation that many left the area to seek jobs elsewhere. Others, less fortunate, succumbed to drink or drugs, or other activities that led to jail. Whether by tradition or not, the culture had become predominantly matriarchal.

Upon hearing story after story of deceit and rape I began to wonder on the nature of prejudice; for how could these people have witnessed such atrocities at the hands of my race and still treat me so kindly? It was a trait I was not to learn from my homeland, but one I was to see again in a land far distant that I was trying to forget. These friends could make distinctions between an individual and his government, between an individual and the masses, between an individual and his ancestors. And I was coming from a South where prejudice was still dying a very slow and extremely painful death. Slowly, I was learning.

I was to learn other truths from Thelma and Kay. They were, each, strong individuals; one was to play an important role at the second round held at Wounded Knee, the militant round that was to make front pages in the not too distant future of 1973. I was seeing frustrations turn a desire to work within the system to build a better world turn to the activism that resorted to rifles and live ammunition. The formation of hatred was not a pretty sight to behold; the shame was that a reason existed for its birth.

We finally gathered and placed the pieces that would enable our war-horse to proceed, and it was difficult to find more excuses to linger, in spite of the kind hospitality offered and the fondness that had grown among us. The unknown road ahead beckoned.

On the morning of our departure Kay had planned a surprise picnic. The four of us lay back on the cool grass beneath the cottonwoods, each contemplating the unique blend of friendships that had developed so quickly; and how, by turning a key, they would be left for fate, even more quickly; more fossils for that forlorn landscape of the mind.

A beautifully beaded Sioux medallion now hangs in a place of honor within our home. It has ridden many miles hanging from a rear-view mirror of a dilapidated van, and it has travelled many more miles in the pockets of several backpacks, through this country and a number of others. A piece of fossilized tortoise shell, some millions of years old rests in the dust of a seldom opened desk drawer. Few know the significance of either. I cannot say I do not believe in sacred amulets.

Jeff and I journeyed into higher country; snow-crowned peaks became common sights. Nights were cooler, glittering with hints of jewel-like frost. We camped beneath towering firs and ponderosas, alongside meandering and rushing streams. Small and large campfires stole our minds for many hours of many nights.

Sometimes deer or elk would come close to our campsites; on rare occasions, a bear. There seemed always present the birds and small mammals: squirrel, chipmunk; opossum, and raccoon. One cold night a skunk joined us by the fire in those cold Rockies. He spent the night, seeming to enjoy the warmth and companionship, not departing until he had shared breakfast the following morning. Wilderness became the soothing therapy I would learn to return to again and again in times of need.

We kept ourselves mostly to the mountains, enthralled by the majestic peaks and abundant wild life. Many times we crisscrossed the Continental Divide of this great land, weaving through high passes and lush valley meadows. Fall was bringing a chill to the air and playing drunken painter with her autumnal palette.

Camped in a high valley, we made plans to climb one of the easier of the major peaks of the Rockies, hoping to glimpse a herd of wild sheep known to be in the area. The trail started out easily enough, but soon we were resting every several minutes. I seemed particularly affected by the altitude and incline, and began lagging behind as the footpath became more vertical and less obvious.

About halfway up the slope, and feeling especially winded, I noticed a lone hiker approaching from below us. Actually whistling as he walked, a solitary Japanese jauntily passed us as if on a Sunday stroll, said his hellos and strode onward and upward. In only minutes he once again passed us, this time on his way down after reaching the peak. We stood amazed by his unapparent strength and brief time he must have spent looking over what must be one of the most splendid views the region had to offer. We nicknamed him "the Kamikaze," and labored on up the trail. In my fatigue I had failed to recognize him as a messenger of the Seeress.

The view from the summit was indeed spectacular. For my efforts I was awarded my first taste of the true mountain climber's euphoria, that feeling of being above the world, by one's own efforts. Though clouds were forming over the next range, the atmosphere was clear, and miles and miles reached out to us.

But then, the clouds approached faster, swirling overhead; the sun was quickly covered and nearby flashes of lightening interrupted the increasing roar of the wind—all as we witnessed the changing spectacle.

Atmospheric electricity stood our hair on end, and then the hail began. The scene both above and below us had changed within minutes, and it was obviously time to descend. Pelted by hail, and now a driving mixture of sleet and rain, we hurried down, slipping on loose stone and mud. The rain and wind continued, and by the time we reached camp it was already dark. Both of us were shivering form the wet cold and exhaustion. Then we realized we had not been farsighted enough to place some firewood in the tent to keep dry. That night began as one of the longest and coldest I can remember... and I remember it well, for it was the night I traveled thousands of miles and backwards in time to meet a lost kin, and to warm myself from the chilling rain and sooth my aching muscles; it was the night of the beginning of another circle fulfilling the prophesies of the Seeress.

To remove my mind from the constant shivering I had begun thinking of warming experiences of the past; for some reason the nationality of the lone hiker of the afternoon came to mind. A haze drew over my eyes, a haze of soft yielding steam rising from the enfolding heat of a Japanese bath in the suburbs of Sasebo.

I had come in from the freezing rain, shed my shoes at the door, and been greeted by a kind and middle-aged lady wrapped in a housecoat, and bowing. She spoke no English; Harumi translated. No, it was not too late, "please take this wrap and come sit with my husband while I prepare a humble late-night meal."

The husband was a small man of glittering eyes and a peaceful smile of welcome. He was an uncle to Harumi, and again she translated, this time, my answer to his question. "Yes, I was in the Navy...on a destroyer."

Ah, he had great respect for the American destroyer crews, for he had been in the submarine service of his county during that Great War and they had to constantly be wary of the American destroyers. Obasan entered with a tray of steaming soup and rice delicacies wrapped in kelp, and a pot of rich steeping tea.

"But those for whom I have the greatest respect were those in my sister service, even though, at the time, we were enemies. I understood their loneliness. To be below the surface of the sea, yet dependent upon the air above, without much communication, and so far from their homes, wives, and children.

"There was one American submarine I remember in particular. She alone had caused the greatest damage to our fleet. She was like a ghost...we were all searching for her, then she would surface suddenly in our midst, do her damage and disappear even before we could take bearings. Her men were daring...I know."

"We were patrolling the Straits of Formosa, and the waters were dangerous, but she eluded us each time. I do not know the truth of the matter, but it is said that she died from her own fish...her own torpedo, her last. You know it is the custom of all submariners to save the last torpedo for the trip home. But this boat, she used her last, and it returned to her, not wanting to be away; and I heard that only the several men in the conning tower escaped alive. This brave boat: she was named for a fish in our sea; you say, I think, *Tang*."

Even before he had mentioned the name, my stomach had been knotting and, in spite of the heated room in which we now sat, my skin prickled with goose bumps. I had heard the story before, from the elders of my family; and I was to hear it again on my return from an old woman who was telling me of my past, and of the past of others related to me. My uncle had been Engineering Officer aboard the *Tang* on that fateful voyage. He had not been lucky enough to escape. He was my godfather, and his life and death had just been brought back closer to me by this aging Nipponese, closer than any of the words of my family—for he had been in those cold seas.

We sat up many more hours, though I cannot remember the other subjects of conversation. I do recall that an intimacy of rare proportions grew among us four that damp and cold evening. Though of different cultures and even times, we shared a warmth of blood ties and family tragedies.

Outside, the frigid rain continued. Obasan yawned and pardoned herself. It was truly late. Harumi led me to the sleeping room. She quietly took my clothes, disrobed herself, and silently motioned me to step into the now steaming room of the *furo*. We lathered, rinsed, then stepped into the soothing heat of the deep bath. The aches and chills swirled away with the steam and fiery water. I was relaxed and my mind at ease. The eventual transition to the quilted *futon* took place as in a dream.

I awoke to the warming sun, breaking into the room...breaking into the tent...and I knew that sooner or later I would be returning yet again to the lure of the Orient, as the Seeress had foretold.

***

With icy fingers and chilling breath, Winter chased us from her lofty abode. We were soon heading south with the flocking waterfowl. We entered Mexico, and on the first night there we were introduced to the camaraderie of a small cantina and the headiness and dangers of the devil's own brew: a lick of salt, a tad of tequila, and a bite of fresh lime.

The morning barely found the three of us: Jeff, me and a tired old van, which by this time had acquired the name Down-Hill Racer; awakening with dry swollen tongues and carburetors, unconquerable pains of heads and guts, about nine million swarming flies, and an unimaginable stench about us.

On painfully rising through the clutter within the bus to the open window, I discovered that our overnight parking space was not on the breezy Pacific shore to which we had drunkenly aimed that previous rainy night; but instead, the very epicenter of the town's dump. We left our own offerings to the gods of inebriation and refuse, and limped grievously southward.

The two humans were ultimately to recover; not so the luckless van. We were some seventy kilometers north of Mazatlan when an explosion to our immediate rear brought the mighty Down-Hill Racer to a coasting and sputtering stop alongside the desolate mountain road.

Inspection showed a shrapnel-scarred engine compartment and pieces of a dead motor, still smoldering. We kicked a few rocks and watched the dust our feet dejectedly stirred in circles. We didn't say much; we didn't have to. Part of our dreams had been killed with that cantankerous engine, the second now to succumb to the demons of the highway.

For hours we sat behind our crippled monster, staring at the silent and lifeless road. No hint of human activity showed itself, though we could see for miles. We waited...and waited. The sun passed its zenith, and we waited still.

Our savior was to take the form of a speeding home on wheels, one of the large recreational vehicles becoming popular with the more affluent travelers back then. It passed in a spray of dust and gravel, but slowed and pulled to the side of the road; then sped backwards to our wounded vehicle. A peace symbol was scrawled in the dust of the back window.

Seeming too old to be of the hippie generation, still sporting a beard, longish hair, and love beads, a man in his fifties stepped from the luxurious motor home and asked if he could be of assistance. He introduced his son; then told how his son's draft number had been selected, and since he did not believe in the Viet Nam war, he was taking his son out of the country. As to our problems, we were not to worry, he had a tow strap and would be happy to pull us into Mazatlan, where we might find some remedy.

Upon swinging out onto the highway, our relative joy at having been rescued altered to abject fear by the time we had traveled a mere hundred meters. Tied some six feet from the rear of this gigantic joy wagon, we were speedily swaying around mountain curves and approaching velocities the Down-Hill Racer had never experienced in its protracted life span. With its worse-than-fading brakes and loose steering wheel, that life span seemed about to come to an abrupt end, more than likely drastically shortening ours as well.

The harrowing drive finally halted in front of the VW dealership of Mazatlan. We thanked the driver profusely, in reality for turning us loose, and entered the vaulted doors, already knowing what we would find out. Rebuilt engines were available, and one would cost more than twice what we paid for the vehicle. We had reached our first south-of-the-border Catch 22; for such an amount would use up the rest of our funds.

Morosely walking out, we were approached by a miniature Pancho Villa, wearing grease-covered overalls. Between his broken English and our abortive Spanish we finally came to understand that he was an excellent mechanic, but not appreciated by the management; and if we would meet him after work he could possibly help us with our problem.

The early evening meeting, at which we provided the *cerveza*, proved less than conclusive, but nevertheless promising. He thought he could get us a cheap and good running engine, and he would install it himself. He would check back with us the following night.

One night led to two, then three and four, and we were about to forget Pancho, when he showed up breathless, explaining that tonight was the night he would install our new engine. He would take care of everything. We thought little of the fact that he seemed anxious to make sure we were leaving town as soon as our van was fixed and paid for.

True to his word, Pancho showed up before dawn, driving the Down-Hill Racer proudly up to the curb. He took great pride in showing off his good work, and after inspecting the purring motor we paid him the agreed sum. Happy to be on the road again, we packed our belongings and headed out of town in our newly renovated warrior.

Proceeding through the outskirts of town, we passed another apparently broken-down VW on the side of the road, jacked up with its engine compartment open. We chuckled something to the effect that we knew how the poor bastard felt...then, at the same moment turned gaping at each other with the sudden realization that the other vehicle's problem was simply that it did not have an engine. We hurried our departure from Mazatlan.

We kept mostly to the coast and countryside, camping on warm tropical beaches and sometimes in fields of brown-furrowed maize stubble. Our time was leisurely and restful. We passed Christmas in Oaxaca, taking part in the festive gaiety of the plaza and stately midnight mass in the cathedral. But our interests lay towards Yucatan and we slowly drifted in an easterly direction. A dot on the map indicated a village on the Gulf Coast that seemed an appropriate locale to bring in the New Year.

Pavement soon gave way to gravel, then rutted dirt tracks, and finally to nothing more than seldom used cow paths. We continued, determined to follow the map to its logical end. After hours of first-and-second-gear bumping we could go no further. The Gulf of Mexico lazily lapped a somewhat dirty beach before us. A few scattered, deserted and ramshackle huts lay behind the palms and brush. We had found our village and coastal retreat, but after frustrating hours of uncertainty and vexation it was hardly what we had in mind. We didn't even have any beer, much less a New Year's Eve dinner we had planned to buy at the local market. It was too late to return the way we had come, for we would surely lose our way in the approaching darkness. In the year we would eventually travel together, this day came the closest to trying our friendship, for we both had arrived in silent and foul moods.

Not bothering to move the van from the middle of the track where we had come to a stop, we finally decided we ought to search for something to eat. Rummaging through the trash that had accumulated within the vehicle, Jeff finally surfaced with a dented can of El Paso brand tamales that we had managed to avoid since its purchase in the states.

A fire was not worth the trouble, it was hot and humid already. We couldn't find the can opener and so jabbed open the can with a jackknife. Though the village was deserted of people, we soon had company: two scrawny pigs, three nearly featherless turkeys and five similarly dressed chickens, all eyeing the canned tamales. We weren't hungry anyway, what we really wanted was a drink. Our heads rested in our hands as we watched the animals sniff and peck at the rations we had thrown on the ground in front of them. Eventually, they too agreed it wasn't worth eating, and meandered away.

We must have sat for an hour, hardly speaking, wiping the sweat and swatting mosquitoes that had emerged in the darkening heat. We began to speak on varying subjects, lonely, on what should have been a festive eve, trying to find some humor in the situation. We were speaking of various friends, one couple in particular who had seen us off...Our memories clicked at the same instant: they had given us a gift upon our departure, some eight months earlier. We had hidden it from ourselves, saying we would know the right time for its unveiling. Clothes and sleeping bags and tools cascaded from the open doors and windows as we searched. Once again Jeff arose victorious form under the accumulated clutter. His right hand held up a quart bottle of expensive bourbon. The eve of the new year had been saved.

We wandered the by-roads of Yucatan, exploring the ancient Mayan ruins: Labna, Chichen Itza, and Tulum, as well as lesser known and unexcavated piles of rock. They were all interesting, but until creeping into the jungle and finding Palenque, still partly overgrown with the lush vegetation of the region, I had not been moved by the majestic sights before me. Palenque was different. It was alive; the spirits still lingered.

We had approached the mossy ruin late in the afternoon. The dirt road was still damp from an earlier rain, and moist perspiration dripped from the greenery. I remember no other tourists about. We walked into the plaza silently; each, I think, feeling the sacredness of the place. We roamed the trails and passageways separately, experiencing the uniqueness surrounding us.

I rubbed my hands over walls of stone carvings worn smooth by a millennium of winds and rains and I could see the carver, stepping back to take pride in his work. I sat on timeworn steps, and music of the life of that day came to my ears. Priests descended from the altars atop the great pyramid; the tart odor of burning copal incense reached my nostrils; smoke hovered in the humid atmosphere, caught below the tiered jungle roof.

In this world exist sacred places, and we had been fortunate to come upon one in our wanderings. Such sanctity may indeed be temporal, for I'm not sure the same places that struck me with such awe would impart similar emotions today, surrounded by throngs of camera-toting tourists. It nevertheless exists.

Exploring the ancient ruins, especially in the tropical heat, can be exhausting work; so we headed to the islands off the coast of Yucatan. Cozumel was beginning to get a little crowded; they were even talking about putting in an airstrip. Isla Mujeres proved more to our liking, and we lingered. Camped on white sand just above the shoreline and below the coconut palms, we soon fell into a routine of pure unadulterated laziness and, aside from occasional snorkeling, a walk or a swim, we did little but take our ease. Yet even this idyllic existence would not long curtail the eventual call of the road.

We were becoming experienced now in the wiles and antics of the Down-Hill Racer and began noticing familiar symptoms. Knowing we could not afford any more shrapnel in the engine compartment we decided to part ways with the less than faithful companion. An obliging Mexican entrepreneur, less mechanic than macho, made an offer. Upon acceptance of the illegal deal, we once again departed town quickly. From Chetumal onward we traveled whatever local transportation was available, including Shank's mare.

I was beginning to learn a few of the simpler truths of Buddhist philosophy through experience. Through the Indian villages of Chiappas, the southern highlands of Mexico, we trekked, our burdens actually lightened now that we had left our own transport behind. We had decided to aim towards Peru and see for ourselves the high Andes and remnants of that ancient Incan realm. Slowing our pace as we passed through the colorful Indian villages and towns of Guatemala — Chichicastenango, Huehuetenango, Panajachel — we each were attracted to the indigenous cultures, in spite of their poverty.

In fact, an aspect of that poverty drew me into further introspection; not the destitution itself, for I had seen plenty of the misery, sickness and death that was the result of impoverishment. But I was also finding an honesty of emotions, a noble contentment with life that was rare in the rich society from which we had come.

Also we were learning what we had been missing while driving our own vehicle. True, we had been able to set our own timetables, and there were a few out-of-the-way places we had been able to visit at will, but now the life aboard the local public transportation introduced us to a romance of the road we had not known before.

Granted, the seats were most often cramped and crowded. Quite likely a seat mate may have drunk too much on market day and ended up vomiting at your feet; or your neighbor asks you to hold a basket of chickens while she nurses her child; but these slight annoyances can be forgiven as you listen to the music of the attendant, "Guate..., Guate..., Guateeee..." singing out the route's destination; or the songs of the happily inebriated in the back of the bus; or the many sounds of the livestock on board; or watch an Indian babe knead a full breast just before going to sleep; or an old woman quietly saying her rosary; or listen to the wrinkled man explain to you of life in a language you can't possibly follow and still you understand even more than he's telling you; or share a warm tamale wrapped in a corn husk with a young child; or perhaps a little *aguardiente* with the fellow across the aisle.

Not that I would choose to travel this way the rest of my life, and I'm fortunate to have the option; but the value of the experience far outweighs its cost, and has left me with many pleasant memories, and not a few life-long friendships.

As I write, the name Panajachel brings back memories of scores of small frozen chocolate-covered bananas devoured with an appetite that could only have been generated by the shared tokes of the evil weed smuggled through customs by a fellow traveler in the hollow poles of his tent; the pleasant boat ride across the lake and meanderings through Indian villages nestled beneath the volcanoes; the fantastic meals that could be had for less than fifty cents...

But much of that is gone now. I've since had the opportunity to revisit that lakeside town, now almost thirty years hence, and it has been found. High-rise hotels, and crowds, and street-side hawkers have taken over. It's a paradox of progress, of which I was a part; but there must be some way that the dignity of a locale and people can be maintained in the harsh face of growth.

Chichicastenango, the name itself sings; with men burning copal on the great reaching steps of the colonial church, and women selling baskets and pottery. To enter the church is to step into the life of a religion itself, as native tradition mixes with imported orthodoxy, the smell of incense and the glittering of hundreds of candles glow across the floor amid small offerings; the only place I know where the effigy of St. Tomas is put out in the rain if prayers to him are not answered favorably and promptly. Just as many prayers are offered to a stone god on a nearby hill.

An impatient nature goaded us onward and we traveled rather rapidly through the remainder of Central America. The impassable terrain of the Darien Gap blocked our journey through the tail of the isthmus, and so we island-hopped into Colombia, finally threading our way up the Magdalena Valley to Bogotá. We visited friends for several days and made plans for our further descent into the southern continent of the Americas.

Our first stop was Cali, where we overnighted in a local bordello, not realizing that fact until our departure the next morning. By car and narrow gauge rail, bus and truck and cattle boat, we passed through southern Colombia and Ecuador. Often slowed by irregular transport and schedules, or no schedules at all, landslides and the sights of pretty women, Indian markets and Montezuma's Revenge, we nevertheless plodded more or less southward, eventually reaching the unexpected great northern desert of Peru. Surprised by the vastness of this wasteland in a country where we expected to be immediately confronted by the giant Andes, we slowly gained respect for what appeared insignificant spaces on our tiny traveler's maps.

Lima was another large city, and neither of us was a city person. We visited museums and cathedrals but were anxious to get into the mountains.

The train for Huancayo was scheduled to depart at eight in the morning. It was a ride we had been looking forward to, for the scenery was said to be spectacular, and the rails themselves climbed from near sea level to over 15,000 feet.

While waiting for the delayed departure we noticed a young woman of unique and striking features; we couldn't decide if she was Indian or Oriental. Our curiosity ultimately overcame our reticence and we approached her with our barbaric Spanish. She laughed and replied in excellent English, introducing herself as Isabel. We soon fell into a relaxed camaraderie and agreed to travel together that day on the rail passage rising east into the Andes.

The three of us were to spend some several weeks journeying together through some of the most spectacular country and interesting peoples and history this earth has to offer. Isabel's mother was Quechua Indian; her father, a Chinese immigrant. She spoke Quechua and Aymara, as well as Spanish and English. She was traveling to various villages and towns to purchase artisan wares and crafts to export to the States.

Jeff and I may have been slow, but we were quick enough to recognize the opportunity before us. Had she tried, I don't think Isabel could have escaped our clutches. Her knowledge and appreciation of the cultures and geography of her home country became evident even before boarding the train. She appeared happy to share not only her knowledge, but also her wisdom.

What others may have made of our strange trio was of no concern to us. We were a sister and brothers exploring a land and meeting its peoples. We shared cold and rain for several days and nights in the backs of open trucks crossing snow-capped ranges; we shared hot Indian meals and gut-warming pisco, and chicha, the fermented beer made by a circle of women chewing corn and spitting the distillate and the day's gossip into the pot around which they sat; we shared history and music and small peasant rooms; and laughter and poetry and hours on the only corner in Ayacucho waiting for a ride; we shared serapes and ponchos and the voices of spirits drifting from chambers of centuries-old ruins; mountains of unparalleled splendor, and quiet guitars and singing *charangos* and haunting flutes and pan pipes; we shared the laughter of Indian children, and also their tears; and we shared the gifts of each other.

We trekked ancient paths of the Incas and slept in mist-enshrined ruins of that extinct empire, awe-struck by our mystical surroundings. We gazed upon the majesty of Machu Pichu from the Inca trail high above in the golden light of the magic hour, and we saw a civilization below us working stones and terraced fields, cooking and weaving, nursing infants and proud mothers, and artisans, laborers and warrior priests. And we could hear their songs in the wind of the Sierras.

> *Summering Dawn*
> *has dancing grounds there, and the sun his rising;*

A condor soared over our heads, dipped in unseen airs and disappeared. A lone Quechua flute echoed in the distance a mournfulness of lost ages. The times were idyllic, and we basked in those times, leisurely drifting where the spirits directed. The past often spoke to us in the breezes and stanzas of old Quechua poetry and worn rocks of ruins warmed by the mid-day *altiplano* sun. And we listened.

> *...El sol y la luna*
> *el dia y la noche,*
> *la primavera y el invierno,*
> *no en vano ordenaste.*

!Oh, Uira-cocha!
Todos ellos recorren
el camino que les senalaste;
todos ellos llegan
a la meta que les destinaste,
adondequiera que quisiste...

from *Himno A Uira-Cocha,*
Mil Anos de Poesia Peruana

...the sun and the moon
the day and the night,
the spring and the winter,
not in vain did you order.
Oh, Uira-cocha!
All of them journey
the road that you showed them;
all of them arrive
at the goal to which you intended them,
wherever you wanted...

We sailed on rafts of reed upon the highest navigable lake in the world, and sat with weavers, laughing with them at stories they spun with their llama hair and sheep wool and wooden looms.

Divine Kalypso,
the mistress of the isle, was now at home.
Upon her hearthstone a great fire blazing
scented the farthest shores with the cedar smoke
and smoke of thyme, and singing high and low
in her sweet voice, before her loom a-weaving,
she passed her golden shuttle to and fro.

We gossiped with old women, drank with old men and walked home at day's end with child-shepherds and their flocks in the late glowing light of the high plains. Small and large circles were

63

beginning to close, as other ones, greater though less perceptible, were opening. We were slowly working our way back to the north and the coast. Isabel had to return to Lima. Our funds were running low; Jeff and I had been traveling for close to a year.

Peru is a great country, as diverse geographically as any country I know; the great northern desert; thousands of miles of wandering coastline; the highest mountain ranges in the southern hemisphere; and the last ecological frontier above the surface of the sea, the headwaters of the might Amazon. To this latter fascinating region we decided to direct our attention on the homeward journey.

We found ourselves walking the short dusty street of Pulcalpa, a slight scar of a clearing stolen from the jungle. The town's one boarding house and bar seemed a leftover from a cheap movie set, complete with kerosene lanterns and torn mosquito nets, scarred wooden tables and warm beer. A barefoot child approached with the skin of a freshly killed boa constrictor he'd be happy to sell to the gringos as a souvenir of the jungle.

We plodded to the crippled docks on the Ucayali, sweating from this slight exertion in the oppressing heat and humidity. The river was narrow here, still flowing strongly. From this point upstream only the smallest of riverboats and launches plied their trade. Tropical apathy was apparent everywhere; a subliminal realization that man's efforts were just as susceptible to the hurried decay of time as the once-green vegetation that falls to the moist ground of the jungle.

"Yes, there might be a boat heading down river in a day or so. Why don't you check back tomorrow?"

The object of our wait was a well-worn and experienced riverboat, carrying a cargo of beer and bananas. The beer was destined for the less accessible river villages along the way; the bananas apparently were headed further downstream. On top of the pile were a few odds and ends of machinery parts and special orders that had probably been ordered a year ago. A couple of screened sleepers for better paying passengers were supposed to keep the mosquitoes at bay. After several days of unexplained delays we finally boarded, and cast off, heading downstream and north.

This was another world from the high sierras. Fresh-water dolphin crossed our bows and strange animal voices called out to us from the jungle-entangled shore. Rice, freshly caught fish and fried plantains served our diet for three meals a day. We saw the piranha and heard stories of their deadly mass attacks. The crew delighted in frightening the gringo travelers with their tales of Amazon atrocities. Once or twice a day we would pull into small forest-entombed villages whose only access to the world was this mighty river. We'd walk the paths worn by bare feet and sit in the shade as transactions took place at the water's edge. The river was high and some of the lower hamlets were flooded so that dugouts appeared the only method of getting about. Dark eyes watched us from roof beams, peering through loosely thatched roofs. We soon became accustomed to the beating rhythm of the ancient diesel engine, and it played bass drum to the night melodies of the jungle. The lonesome guitar of a fellow traveler accompanied the symphony, and once again time assumed variable dimensions.

A week on the river, and the river itself was growing wider and swifter. We began meeting other boats, and soon tied up at the docks of Iquitos. We were back in a town with vehicles and electricity and beds and baths. Though we were ready for these luxuries a sadness joined our debarkation. We were on the road home. Closing circles were already becoming constrictive. I thought back on a poem by Antonio Machado that Isabel had shared with us:

> *Caminante, no hay camino;*
> *El camino lo haces tu al andar*
> *Y nunca mas lo volveras a pisar.*
>
> *Traveler, there is no road;*
> *You make the road you walk*
> *And never more will you return to tread on it.*

We moved on to Leticia, in the rain forests of Colombia, and hitched a ride on an old army plane into the metropolis of Bogotá. Reaching Miami International Airport without enough change left to make a long-distance phone call, we were fortunate enough to have friends who would accept the charges and give us a lift.

Second Circle

It had all been an escape. But I was not ready for the reentry. I became something of a hermit, seeing only those friends who allowed me my solitary ways. Those few seemed to understand.

I spent much time in the darkroom, developing images of timeless faces we had met along our recent wanderings...their meanings obscure even to me. Invisible tendons connected these faces with the ancient Quechua poetry Isabel had introduced us to; and, with much help from those more fluent in the Spanish into which they had been translated, the words slowly evolved into my own language. I was being drawn into the words of men and women whose spirits had passed from this earth more than five hundred years ago, and by the faces of their descendants still seeing life much as their earlier relatives had.

I went back to creased Mayan faces and discovered the words of the sacred *Popuh Vuh*. Sentiments flowed from those indigenous to the Central American Highlands.

And finally, from files of negatives, I pulled images of those from that war-torn country I had escaped over a year before, and their voices sang to me from venerable Oriental poetry I had been reading.

I didn't know quite what was happening, but I allowed it to slowly evolve. There were gaps and silences and missing faces. The puzzle was incomplete, but it existed.

I ventured to a great metropolis to get advice from an old teacher concerning the photography I had been doing. After his review he gave me two names; one was well known among students of that medium. He ran one of the first photographic galleries in that city. I don't think he understood any more than I what I was doing, but he was intrigued, and kind, and offered me a showing of my photos to be held that following summer.

I was not an avid fan of the monster city in which I now stood, looking for a second address. Jostled by crowds and deafened by the noise, I was about to give up when I caught sight of the browning card on the mailbox in the darkened hallway. I pushed a button, the door unlatched, and "Whoizit?" was hollered down the dimly lit wooden stairwell.

I was about to meet Nancy and Jack, a pair who would take me under their collective wings. They ran one of the first photo agencies in the big city. They suggested how I might begin capitalizing somewhat on my penchant for the road and use of the camera, and provide not a few excuses for future travels. They also gave me an interesting introduction thousands of miles and half a year away. But all this would come to pass in its own time.

I returned to my southern homeland, listless, doing odd jobs, not enjoying what I did. An opportunity arose for a free trip to Colombia if I would help a friend in shipping a horse to Bogotá. I accepted, and, in late 1972, was soon back to exploring parts of that country I had not visited before. I contacted another friend I had met on the plane flying in from the Amazon earlier that year. She was living in Ibague and invited me to visit. That visit was to be an introduction to two very different aspects of this lovely country.

The bus passed rolling hills and high-mountain coffee country. Small *fincas*, farms, dotted the flowing landscape. Alicia and her friend Daisy met me as I stepped off the crowded vehicle. Names sounding the contrary, Alicia was from the States though her Spanish was fluent. Daisy, a Colombian, was living with Alicia and Pablo in a small two-room house located in one of the poorer barrios. The dirt-floored house had no running water or electricity.

That evening my eyes were to be opened to a large part of the world that, up until now, I had only witnessed from the fringes. Pablo was a young communist, extremely active in the underground activities of that party. I had known of Alicia's political leanings, but I was not aware of the degree to which they had progressed. Both were exceedingly dedicated individuals, believing strongly in their convictions and actions. The plight of the poor...the oppression by the wealthy: the roles played by their country's government, and more devastatingly, that of my own. Likewise, the influence of the multi-national corporations soon became more obvious. Imperialism and neo-colonialism took on shades of a closer reality. I came to see how even some of the best-intentioned individuals often played into the hands of the New Colonizers. And I learned about the word "revolution."

Though I did not agree with all that was being said, I began seeing as they were seeing; and for me, that was an even more important lesson. For it seemed that only when such insight is utilized can true communication exist.

My mind drifted back to two Indian girls of the Lakota Sioux, and how they had begun trying to work within the system, but were soon turned to more violent actions, forced by the system itself to resort to less noble means. Here again I was faced with another story of repression. It could have been this century or a hundred past, this land or a hundred like it. I'm not sure we ever learn.

The next morning we rose early and walked into the crisp predawn darkness towards the center of town. The milk truck, a vehicle of dubious parentage and questionable age, was waiting. We climbed to a wooden seat above the open back and huddled together for warmth, watching our breath drift into the darkness; a few words from the driver and we were off to a spot I will remember the rest of my life.

Soon we were bouncing along deeply grooved ruts, erratically climbing a rising and narrowing valley. The sun hesitantly rose over the mountains to our right, casting a clearing light upon the valley's mist and life itself into the meadows. Smoke drifted aloft from scattered chimneys; sheep and cattle and horses dotted the dark-green pastures, and wiry dogs came out to the road to announce our passing. The truck occasionally stopped and picked up a filled milk can, steaming from its fresh warm contents in the cool morning air. The driver would leave an empty can in its place alongside the road. The walls of the valley were becoming more steep and closing in on the worsening tracks until, finally, the truck stopped at what appeared to be the end of the road.

A boy in ragged pants and sweater was sitting across a burro and waiting. He slid from his mount and unslung two milk cans from another donkey beside him and lifted them into the back of the truck, took the two cans offered by the driver and tied them back onto the pack saddle. Then, as if just remembering something, went back to the cab of the truck. The driver handed him the day's newspaper, and he tucked that behind one of the cans. Not one word had been spoken.

The child mounted his sleeping steed, kicked it twice in the ribs, and started back up the trail from which he had come. We scrambled down the side of the truck, said our goodbyes to the driver and hurried after the disappearing trio. The trail was becoming steeper and more beautiful, winding through pine and hardwood, chasing the source of a swiftly flowing mountain stream tumbling from the head of the valley, itself becoming more of a canyon. We climbed for some forty minutes. The trail took a switchback, made another, and suddenly the canyon walls disappeared and before us lay the most exquisitely lush hidden valley I had ever encountered. The grass was deep in length and color. In the distance, three waterfalls cascaded down steep cliffs from a land of perpetual snow. Fat Holsteins grazed in the foreground.

Surrounded by this storybook scenery sat a rather stunted mountain cabin, situated close to one of the cliff faces down which fell one of the rainbowed cataracts. A tiny wooden sign hanging above the porch simply announced, "El Rancho."

Pablo explained to me that the owner, who was away at the time, was a friend. A lawyer who had apparently done well in the capital city, he had simply wearied of the urban lifestyle and traded in his practice and home for a few cows and this lush parcel of land. Occasionally he would venture down to town for a day or so to visit and purchase supplies, as apparently he had yesterday. I had yet to see the final lure of this Colombian paradise.

The three led me to the other side of the modest home. Steam rose from a series of interconnected natural hot pools. The smell of sulfur hung in the air. Daisy pointed out the miniature canal flowing from the pool at the base of the frigid waterfall into this system of basins. Each pool contained a different blend of scalding hot spring water mixed with the chilling mountain stream. We disrobed and slid into one of the hotter baths.

> *Ice cold*
> *in runnels from a high rock ran the spring,*
> *and over it there stood an altar stone*
> *to the cool nymphs, where all men going by laid*
> *offerings.*

It was a refuge, which each of us needs at times. I have since learned to return to such havens as this quite easily in my mind; and "El Rancho" has always been there for me, never changing. There are a few places of peace in this world. I was glad to have found one.

From Colombia I returned to the states with little in the way of plans for the future. I was drifting, but getting nowhere. Pressure was beginning to accumulate, from both outside and within. What was I going to do with myself?

A phone call from the big city developed into an opportunity to photograph wildlife in East Africa, possibly for a profit. I grabbed the chance, and before long was making plans for a journey to the Dark Continent. Its mystery had always intrigued me. I had always harbored a desire to see the last of the great herds free on their own ground, the mighty cats, and the rest.

I remember a sad departure. My mother had brought me to the airport, and I could see in her eyes hints of tears, and reflections of my own listlessness. I think she must have known, more than I, that this trip, ostensibly for several months, would hold the potential for a much longer separation from the family. We were not able to talk about it, but we both knew.

and now my son, my dear one, gone...
a child, untrained in hardship or in council.

Now the dim phantom spoke to her once more:
"Lift up thy heart, and fear not overmuch.
For by his side one goes whom all men else
invoke as their defender, one so powerful—
Pallas Athena; in thy tears she pitied thee
and now hath sent me that I so assure thee."

The flight was long and tiring, and it gave much time for unwanted reflection. I was escaping again, not even knowing from what or towards what. Did any of it make any difference? Here I was, traveling somewhere I had wanted to go all my remembered life, and I was depressed as hell. And I was alone. I felt that loneliness; it would not leave me. I was making the final jump; ties I had somehow held onto in the past were being irrevocably cut. I did not know why. A new circle was forming; but of its construction, all I knew was the pain.

I'm not sure what preconceptions I held of my destination, other than those of darkness and mystery. They certainly didn't include Colonel Sander's Fried Chicken and the Golden Arches we passed, driving into Nairobi from the airport. I was entering another big city...and each one was becoming more like the last. I wasn't aware at the time that I was soon to meet a sister to the Seeress in this metropolis, and even encounter my old antagonist and teacher, Monkey.

I had been invited to stay at the home of friends I had known in Asia, and on arriving, they mentioned that they were taking off for several days to relax at a rented cottage on the beach north of Mombasa. I was invited to come along. It would be a chance to see some of the country before taking off on my own. Still unsure of my own directions, it seemed a reasonable suggestion; I was still tired from the long flight.

We crossed the dust of Tsavo, and in several hours passed through the traffic of Mombasa, then headed northward along the coast, finally pulling up at a small white cottage. The Indian Ocean lapped at the pristine sand. The sun was still a couple of hours from setting, and after helping to unpack, I decided to take a walk up the beach, hoping to unravel muscles and mind.

I must have been walking for over an hour. The tide was coming in and the sun was approaching the horizon of dunes. The sand felt good beneath my bare feet. The sea breeze was beginning to blow irrational cares and fears to the dying sun. The sea was fairly shallow for several hundred meters out and massive boulders and rocks lay scattered about in the water. They were being covered now by the incoming tide.

I thought I noticed movement far out on one of the rocks, but it was hard to make out with the waves now breaking over them. I walked out into the sea. There it was again. The tide was reaching higher now, and the waves were growing with the evening wind. I could make out some type of animal, nervously jumping from rock to rock. Then I saw. The tide had captured a small monkey unaware on the furthest rocks, and he appeared afraid and trapped.

I approached him cautiously, for I had dealt with frightened animals before and, no different from the other two-legged beast, they were unpredictable. I thought if I stood close to him for a short spell he might become used to my presence, and be more accepting of my help. He cared little for what I thought, springing suddenly at my chest. He grabbed hold for dear life, chattering something beyond my understanding, and climbed onto my shoulders, shaking the water from his feet.

I thought he would scurry away as soon as we reached the shore, but he stayed sitting on my shoulder, a hand loosely holding onto my head. It was a wild stretch of beach and there were no signs of other humans about. The green-brown brush came down to the dunes, and in the twilight the epoch of man had disappeared. I sat with Monkey upon the beach. He voiced more words of his language and then began grooming my head, searching for nits, or whatever prize he might find. After several minutes he swung down and looked into my face. I began mimicking his actions, letting my fingers wander through his fur. He sat, content with my quiet movements.

Time disappeared, as did the separation of species. We were simply two beings, comforting each other on the shores of a sometimes inimical and fragile world.

Though perhaps we used not all the same symbols, I think Monkey and I communicated quite well. He did me two great favors, for which I will be forever in his debt. The first was simply his welcome, by which he informed me that I was indeed on the right road. My doubts and depression disappeared. I was simply happy to be where I was, happy that this road was part of my karma, and I should be content to follow wherever it led.

His second message would perhaps have even a greater and more far-reaching effect upon my life, for, in all my dealings with animals, it was Monkey who introduced me to my brotherhood with all the other creatures on this planet. We *were* one, and our destinies *were* shared. Each of us needed the other. It was a simple message, one I had listened to before, but not heard.

Indeed, we sat and conversed for a considerable length of time. The sun had long since passed below the dunes; the moon was now shining brightly, and millions of stars cast down glittering reflections, bouncing lightly off the swelling ocean. We were in and of our own world, unmarked by man's signs. The diverse pathways, upon which Fate and Monkey had led, brought me to this place and this meeting; and I understood now that it was okay not to understand; simply to accept.

I rose to loosen my cramped legs; Monkey climbed back onto my shoulder. We walked back down the beach, he sometimes riding and talking, at other times scampering along, ahead or beside me. At last we could see the lights of human habitation, and Monkey stopped. We both knew that I was to return to that other world. Our farewell was brief, and he trotted into the underbrush.

I'm not sure, but at times since, when I have felt particularly lost, I sometimes catch a glimpse of a small child-like creature scurrying before my eyes for a piece of a second. At those times a wave of peace will come over me, and I know I can safely continue down the untried road.

With Monkey's introduction, the wildlife of East Africa proved a delight to the senses. For three months I traveled the numerous game preserves of the several countries. I seemed extremely fortunate in encountering many species to whom this land belonged, and I would sit for hours upon hours, often within reaching distance of the great and small beasts of this firmament.

Whether true or not, I felt accepted, simply as another being sharing in the day, the sun, the water, the shade and the breeze, and even the night. Though I persisted in the photography, it was not now my primary concern, and oftentimes I would lose possible opportunities for the lens, merely because it seemed an intrusion into the lives of others, whether four-legged or two.

An Acacia or Baobab always seemed available under which to pitch the tent; and many times herds of wildebeests, gazelle, or giraffe would come out onto the plains close by to graze in the evening air. As the sky turned its many hues at the end of the day, and darkness eventually draped the land, the night songs would begin, and different tongues, far older than mine, would sing and echo in the vast wilderness; a lion's yawn or a zebra's laugh.

> *Dawn came up from the couch of her reclining,*
> *leaving her lord Titonos' brilliant side*
> *with fresh light in her arms for gods and men.*

I awoke beneath majestic Kilimanjaro, the old man. Soft clouds haloed the snow-capped peak in an air so clear I could have touched the summit had it not been irreverent. It seemed as though every species on this continent had gathered on the plain before me, paying no mind to the human's tent. The gathering reached as far as I could see.

Monkey's cousins were noisily playing morning games in the trees behind me; and when I turned my back on them to gaze at the legions of living beings on the savannah, I heard a closer chattering and scampering. I swung around in time to see my breakfast disappearing into the high foliage. Anger was impossible; there was no reason not to share, as they had all shared with me.

My morning offering was to return great dividends two years hence, when I had need to return to this place of peace and time of tranquility, though thousands of miles away. Only later would I understand.

Masai-Mara and Tsavo, the great Serengeti and Amboseli, Marsabit, Maru, and Ngorongoro were each to welcome me in their own special way. While at the latter I realized my proximity to Olduvai Gorge, and so came about traipsing that sun-struck desolation filled with the genetic memories of eons of man's evolution. From these very sands came fragmentary proof of our own antiquity, and grasping and seeking through the ages. And to me it was right that this birth place should be found here, so close to the other animals that had found their niche, and who seemed certainly more content than ourselves with that finding.

The rainy season was approaching, already blocking my intended overland journey into Ethiopia, and so I found myself back on the northern coast of Kenya, camped near Monkey's beach. I was editing film, the best of which was due to be sent back to the market of the big city. I was also trying to find a dhow sailing north, on which I might continue my journey.

I had heard of an island, Lamu, further north along the coast, where dhows often stopped to trade on their routes through the Indian Ocean. I had to wait several days, for the tracks north along the coast had recently been made impassable by the rains. The delay was fortuitous.

Several times we had to get out and push the makeshift bus through the calf-deep mud, but finally arrived at the landing from which launches left for the island. We disembarked from the small boat amid hundreds of others; for unbeknownst to me this was the eve of Malidi, one of the most sacred days of the Muslim calendar. Lamu was the center of Islam for all of East Africa. The small town boasted some twenty-two mosques.

Just as the weather had prevented us from arriving sooner, so had it retarded the entry of a number of large and ancient wooden sailing craft, now appearing in the small remote port, all bearing pilgrims voyaging here for Malidi. This tiny island town was now playing host to tens of thousands of devout Moslems, arriving from places as distant as South Africa and Saudi Arabia.

The village was old beyond memory, famous in olden days for its harem schools; its streets were narrow walkways and paths, flanked by high mud-plastered walls. With its lack of vehicles, the Lamu I was seeing could have been a thousand years back in time.

Following strict Islamic tradition, the women of the island wore *bui-buis*, black coverings extending from head to foot. But I was to notice later the African improvisations as the sea breezes lifted those somber clothes into the air and I would briefly witness the modern street dresses worn beneath, always flagrantly bright in color. I was learning that what we as wayfarers often saw of a culture was often a mask hiding deeper and often contradictory characteristics.

Prayers echoed madly from minaret to minaret, often amplified by loud speakers. But towards dusk the town quieted and people began moving silently towards its center. I had met some other travelers who had come for this occasion, and we decided to find out more of what was going on. We were slightly apprehensive, for we had all heard stories of the Muslim lack of tolerance for infidels.

Night shadows darkened the aged buildings; we walked quietly down one of the innumerable paths towards the town's core. The pathways themselves were already packed with the reverently mute lining the walls; we expected to be stopped at any minute and prevented from going further.

A man, wearing a white *kaftan*, approached. He said nothing, but as if he were expecting us, took me by the hand and led us further into the dark maze until we entered a large open area with a high crude stage erected at its apex. The sight was stunning.

In the several buildingless acres before us quietly sat two seas, one of darkness and the other of light: men, all in white *kaftans* sat on the ground to our left; women, in black *bui-buis*, to our right. The massive space was filled with thousands and thousands of souls...all upon the ground in complete silence. A giant Taoist symbol of yin-yang had inadvertently been formed by the sinuous border between the two sides.

Our guide directed the two women to the right, the other male to the end of a line of white, then led me further forward. We came close to the dais, and then wove among rows of men, finally coming to a space held open between two elders. He motioned me down, and departed. The two flanking men glanced at me, nodded, and returned to their silent prayers.

In that silence of the multitude an energy was produced that was both vibrantly real and ecstatic. I had never experienced anything remotely similar before. I was shaking. It was another experience wherein time disappeared, or at least became so erratic it was impossible to conceptualize. My senses were lost to the power about me.

At some point during the night several muezzin mounted the platform above me. The words of their Arabic prayers were lost to me, but the significance of what was taking place went deeply into my being. It was not the specific religion, but the gathering, on such a large and basic scale, of individuals to share a faith, an energy, a hope.

So you may hear those...thrilling voices;

Chanting began, first by one side, then answered by the other. Bodies swayed and sounds unified; the tension increased as if an electric current flowed from body to body. Then suddenly:

Silence.

Men descended from the pillared stage. They walked the rows of hushed observers, and stopped in front of each. A white-bearded sage stood before me. He hesitated...then lifted his scarred hand over my head and sprinkled something dry and light, as some pollen might be. He turned to a follower and took a small urn, and raised that over my head. I felt the drops, warm and penetrating. He motioned to hold out my hands, and he poured more of the scented fluid over them. He stared into my eyes, softly smiled, and passed on. I shivered uncontrollably, though the African night was warm.

I was kneeling, and it seemed not long, when the chants began again. A new vigor was evident in the pulsing rhythm; the seas swelled and rolled with a tide of human emotion, into which I was being taken. Drowning.

Hours must have passed, for when the ceremony concluded and we four had regrouped, the night sky was already making way for the first light of daybreak. None of us spoke. Another and I walked soundlessly to the eastern shore of the island and sat before the august breaking sea.

***

I had been unable to locate a boat sailing from Lamu to the coast of Ethiopia, and so returned to my camping site near Monkey's beach. Louise, who had accompanied me to the beach that morning following the magic eve of Malidi, visited for a few days before returning to her teaching job in Nairobi. Although I was going to try to find a dhow out of Mombasa, she left me her address, in case I should have to pass Nairobi again. For more than one reason it was good that she did.

I had no luck in Mombasa, and returning to the same camping site, I decided to take a late afternoon swim to relieve my heated frustrations. The ocean was refreshing and I lingered in its coolness. The sun was descending and the light was warm and intimate. I walked the soft sand beach to the spot where Monkey and I had made acquaintance, and I thought of his messages. The sky was growing dark by the time I returned to the tent. I reached inside to get my towel...There was no towel. The back of the tent had been knifed open. There was no pack, there was no camera bag, no wallet or passport. A torn sleeping bag was all that had been left me.

> "Stranger, there is no quirk or evil in you
> that I can see. You know Zeus metes out fortune
> to good and bad men as it pleases him.
> Hardship he sent you, and you must bear it."

My thoughts went immediately to the film. Besides the boxed and processed transparencies were three rolls of exposed film I had not yet had time to develop. I had used them on an encounter with a pride of six cheetah on a kill at sunset. A giant black-maned lion had interrupted their feeding, and stolen the gazelle's carcass. The light had been golden, and I had been close. The interactions and expressions of the animals had been engrossing. None of them had paid the slightest bit of attention to me. The brood of cheetahs climbed a nearby acacia, fought and played, and sat staring into the dying sun. It had been my best shoot, and the film was, with the cameras, gone.

With the help of others, I later recovered most of my clothes and the pack that had been discarded hastily in the nearby bush. Surprisingly, the traveler's checks had been lifted, but cash, wallet, and passport had been cast aside with the clothes not far from the tent. The cameras and most of the film had been taken.

Whether from despondency or a local bug, I soon became ill. I was to lose close to twenty pounds in less than two weeks. After several days I managed to catch a tourist bus from Mombasa to Nairobi, and called Louise from the first hotel at which the bus stopped. She picked me up, took me to the house she shared with an older woman, and put me to bed. I was miserable, but I was now in caring hands. To be in a home with a real toilet aided my plight considerably. And circles were being completed, as I soon discovered.

Louise's housemate, Mavis, was of English descent, but had lived in East Africa all of her life. She had seen immense changes take place and history made in that once British colony, having lived through the Mau-Mau rebellion. She was a great storyteller, and she was much more.

One evening, after I had begun feeling better, the conversation evolved to the subconscious, the supernatural, reincarnation, and other related subjects. Mavis, who claimed to have experienced some unique happenings in these fields, mentioned that she often consulted the Ouija Board. The word stirred my memory; four years earlier the

Seeress had suggested that a benevolent spirit stayed close to me and if I ever met someone who had experience on the Ouija Board I should perhaps see if it were possible to communicate with this ethereal entity. Regardless of my skepticism, I mentioned this to Mavis.

Heavy shadows swayed in the darkened room as the candle flickered on the small table. An old and fragile Bible, a family heirloom, rested on a shelf below the board. We sat in silence, as minds cleared. I found it suddenly quite easy to reach into a quiet pool of infinity, and my mind was at ease. Mavis took my hand and placed it on the marker below hers. The marker shook, then started turning. I looked at Mavis. Her eyes were on a piece of paper, over which she held a pencil. She asked me to voice any letters or symbols on which the marker stopped. The board did not seem within her field of vision.

Words began forming...then phrases. Mavis was kept busy writing as I spoke the letters, one after the other. She introduced the speaker as her usual contact, a famous personage of English literature, about whom she was to tell me much more at a later time. She started speaking...the board answered. The marker was spinning so rapidly I could hardly keep pace with it.

A pause...the marker took on a new rhythm, incomplete sentences interspersed with good old American cussing. Mavis laughed; she knew the speaker well. They had visited often this last year on the board.

The tone, the style of phrase, seemed somehow familiar. I was laughing at the light obscenities. Mavis asked the speaker to introduce himself to me. He said, "He knows who I am...," and spelled out the name of a very well known American writer, whom I had always revered and whose works I had almost completely read. He had died a couple years earlier. Mavis interrupted and said I needed only think of my questions or statements. There was no need to voice my thoughts as long as they were concise. We spoke on many subjects, some of which I don't believe Mavis could have known. Then he asked me to give a message to his family, and spelled out an address in California.

Mavis spoke again of someone close to me and asked the speaker for assistance. The modulation changed abruptly. The marker spun, but neither Mavis nor I could make anything of the combination of letters. There were spaces, as if between words, but of no language with which we were familiar. The confusion lasted some minutes, and there seemed frustration beyond my own.

The marker stood still. We sat for a long minute. Each of us let out a sigh, mine of exhaustion. We both were disappointed with this last demonstration; yet I was astonished at what I had just witnessed. I could find no explanation within my experience. I doubted that Mavis either would or could have disillusioned me so thoroughly. She carefully extinguished the candle after putting away the board and Bible. We moved to another room and sat quietly. She asked to look at my hand... "No, the left."

She, like another I had met, began telling me of my life, mostly of times past. I felt strange...some kind of opening taking place. And then she said:

"It's almost as though you were given a second chance."

***

Prevented by the rains and trade winds from overland or sea travel to Ethiopia, I eventually caught a flight to Addis Ababa. I was still weak from whatever germ warfare that Kenya had visited upon my intestines, but I was recovering. The departure was saddened by the fondness that had grown between Louise and myself, but I could not escape the magnetic pull of continual movement.

I arrived in Addis on the eve of the annual meeting of the OAU, the Organization of African Unity, and it seemed as though every bed in the city was filled. I finally located a small hotel with a cot to offer. I was back in a lonely mode. I had vague ideas of visiting several historical sites in Ethiopia, and gradually working my way north towards Egypt, but answers to the broader question, of where I was really headed, eluded me and added to my despondency. Separated by years and thousands of miles, the words of two women—still the exact same words—haunted me.

Use your eyes:
these things are even now being brought to pass.

I inquired as to a cheap place to eat and was directed to the local version of the YMCA nearby. Depressed and lonely, I entered the huge dining hall, filled to capacity with hundreds of dark faces, now all staring at me, the only white among them. I suddenly knew what it was to be of a minority. The atmosphere was different here, where, unlike Kenya and Tanzania, English was rarely spoken, even in this capital city. I found an empty seat and ate silently, with little appetite.

The tempo of conversation around me changed momentarily, and I looked up to see an older white man, walking with a cane into the cafeteria. He found a place on the other side of the room and disappeared from view. I wondered to myself how he was handling the apparent cultural and linguistic barriers, then let my mind amble on to other inconsequential matters.

In my crowded solitude I walked out to the balcony, and stood with a cigarette and growing doubts, overlooking the street scene below in the dwindling light. I was sadly envisioning a quiet smile of a good friend I had left that morning, when an American voice behind me offered a polite greeting.

The elderly man with the cane leaned upon the railing at my side. His face was kind, and he did not rush into conversation, as if he felt my mood. We watched the movement below fade into the twilight. He introduced himself and asked some general question. I soon found myself sharing many words with this gentle man beside me. We had bypassed the superficial talk of casual acquaintance. I turned the conversation to him, for I was curious; he posed an enigma to my generalized sense of travelers that might patronize the cheaper haunts such as the one we had just left.

He began with a story of his participation in another of the great wars, like the one that had been brought back to me time and again in other stories and incidents. Part of my self-indulgence lifted from my shoulders then, as I realized that each generation has its war, and many had witnessed far worse than I.

John spoke of a dying buddy's head in his lap, and his own doubts and questions arising from the blood left staining his hands. Then he mentioned, "a second chance."

I was enthralled by this simple man's honesty and sincerity of expression; and in our hours together that evening this gracious person gave me something I had been seeking these last several years...a focus, a direction and a reason for being. He showed me that simply caring was not enough; one must act upon one's convictions.

He had acted upon his, and in so doing had founded a movement, which by this time had spread its influence into hundreds of small and poor villages about the globe. He was a modest person, and I later learned from others, as well as from firsthand experience, just how great his contributions to his fellow man had become. The organization, which he had founded and was directing, helped support small, self-help community development projects in some of the most poverty-stricken areas of the world. He had instilled in the workers a very strong sense of self-determination and a vital philosophy governing the movement's principles and peace-making activities. And a true peace and tranquility I had rarely seen, shone within him.

It was then, in this great man's humble room, to which he had kindly invited me, that I realized that circles had indeed been forming in my life. For the first time I was able to see them, and at least partly understand their complexity and contrasting simplicity. I did not know the means by which I would complete the circles, but I did know they meant returning to something from which I had been running. I only had a glance at the influence these few hours with this noble person would eventually have on the wanderings of my life, but even then I knew he had affected me greatly.[2]

***

After remaining several days in Addis I struck north towards the Simian Mountains. The simple problems of food, transportation, and lodging in Ethiopia were to prove some of the most difficult of

---

[2]   John Peters, founder of World Neighbors

all my traveling experience, for the Amharic language and script was indecipherable to me, and my own language was virtually useless. In the wake of a few days being lost, but generally heading north, I found myself standing beside a dirt track, two mud huts and a scrawny mange-infested dog at my back, gazing at an extremely sleep visage of mountains in the foreground.

I stood there in the sun, debating the advisability of tackling such colossal inclines by myself, without maps or much in the way of dwindling food supplies. Odds were hitting about fifty-fifty, and swinging towards the down side when a battered truck stopped briefly nearby and a sun-burned, but otherwise white figure, dismounted from the tail gate into the settling dust. The dog barked once, halfheartedly.

Grahame, an English barrister I was later to learn, was slowly pursuing his way back home from Australia. His timely appearance was the impetus I needed.

We traded for a few eggs and some *injera* and *wat* with an ancient inhabitant of one of the huts, and arranged to leave all but the major necessities of our belongings in her care. Bolstering each other's courage, we crossed the dirt ruts and aimed up one of the eroded trails towards the high Simians.

For me at least, the trek was difficult and tiring, but certainly not lacking in beauty. Grahame was an insufferable comic, and often I wasn't sure if my shortness of breath was due to altitude, exhaustion, or continual laughing fits. In itself, our sighting of the rare Walia Ibex gave sufficient value to the climb, and the scenery became more spectacular the higher we went. Finally, nearing dusk, we saw an escarpment, and on breathlessly reaching the edge, we were awarded a view unequalled on that continent, for below us stretched the rest of Africa.

That night we sat in simple celebration, and exchanged tales of wandering, as embers glowed and breathed with the fresh mountain breezes. It was another night just a little closer to the stars, and the journey itself regained importance.

The next day we chose different trails, and so went our own ways. As I descended worn switchbacks I contemplated the gifts of the wandering spirit: for how else could one experience such spectacular and diverse environments of this globe, and begin to glimpse how they all fragilely fit together; the different cultures, so dissimilar and yet all exemplifying the oneness of humanity. The road had become my school.

I eventually returned to that same mud hut, thanked the guardian of my belongings and turned back to the dusty road to await some form of transportation. If the road is the school, then, surely, waiting is its tuition. Several dry broiling hours passed before the first vehicle came into view. As it approached closer I could see that the small Beetle contained two occupants and a backseat filled to the ceiling with provisions. I didn't even bother sticking out my thumb...but the dusty yellow VW stopped and a young couple got out to stretch.

"Care for a ride?" Good English, with a heavy German accent.

I must have looked dumbfounded, for they laughed, and with a bit of magical rearrangement my knapsack and I were folded into the backseat. They too were going to Axum, and I was welcome to join them as far as I wished. Despite the cramped quarters, no more confining than the few local busses, the ride and conversations were enjoyable. Arne was a writer for a German magazine and had been in Addis covering the OAU meeting. He told of Idi Amin stealing the show with his daylong ranting on the subject of fizzy-water. In an Africa fraught with problems, this commentary seemed indicative of government response in more than one case.

Late that afternoon on a desolate hilltop we were stopped by men claiming to be police. One crumpled military style cap was all that was visible of any uniforms. They informed us that we could go no further that day for there were *shifta*, brigands, in the valley below who would surely relieve us of all our valuables, if not our lives. We were uncertain just how long we were to be stranded, or why the police did not seem interested in doing anything about the bandits. Our insistent questions were met with shrugged shoulders and eventually the demand that we unpack the car so that the pistol-toting chief could check for contraband items.

Communication was poor at best, and tempers on both sides occasionally rose in the heat, until guns were pointed. It soon became clear that the canned food as well as a few assorted personal items had momentarily been declared contraband, and consequently confiscated. We had fallen into an old highwayman's trap. Thieves' honor protected us the rest of that night, though I can't say we slept any too well.

We were allowed to continue on the following morning, and nevermore did we hear stories of bandits. We visited Gondar and Axum, ancient sites of the oldest of the Christian religions. Slowly, over bad roads, we wound our way north. After days of dusty passage through obvious famine we reached the northern city of Asmara, where our first stop was an Italian ice cream parlor.

Arne and his girlfriend Dany were flying out to Munich, so I began exploring the best route into the Sudan. I had heard many stories of the kindness of the Sudanese, but until actually entering that country I had discounted such comments as simple exaggerations.

Throughout the Sudan I carried the extra baggage of an immense and unquenchable thirst. It was the driest and hottest country I had been in yet. The proprietor of a rooming house in Khartoum suggested moving my cot into the front yard of sand, as other Sudanese would do; but that first night in the capital I was still a little gun shy from our experience in Ethiopia. Thus I baked the night out while others enjoyed the cooler evening air. The second night I joined the line of cots and rusty bed springs fronting the dirt street.

I had previously read Alan Morehead's *The Blue Nile,* and just completed *The White Nile,* and enjoyed wandering this town at the junction of those mighty rivers, the site of so much history. Large earthenware water jars were placed in front of many shops, and I soon learned to carry my battered tin cup wherever I went, and direct my path past each of the water sources, dipping into each in turn. The atmosphere was so dry that perspiration would quickly evaporate; and twice a day I had to force myself to urinate.

It seemed that wherever I went someone would offer some kindness or help. I was invited into poor homes to share meals with people with whom I couldn't speak...but not for long, for a small child would run out and return in minutes with a student who was happy to practice his English and translate. I had guides wherever I went. The seemingly innate graciousness of these people appeared limitless. For once I was not simply stared at as *"Hawaya," "Mazoongu,"* or *"Farange."*

> *Our guest and new friend — nameless to me still —*
> *comes to my house after long wandering*
> *in Dawn lands, or among Sunset races.*

One of my new local friends, Suliman, accompanied me to the train and helped me get into one of the old wooden cars, already packed with passengers. The wooden benches were filled beyond reasonable capacity. It would be close to twenty hours before there would be a place to sit, and thirty-six hours before reaching our destination at Wadi Halfa. Temperatures would hover between 120 and 130 degrees Fahrenheit during the day, and didn't seem to slack much in the night. At each stop the clay water urn at the far end of the car would be filled—and emptied in minutes. The car was so crowded that it was impossible to move, and so cans and cups and any utensils available would be passed over the heads of the passengers. Those without any containers would ask politely to share one passing overhead, and so it might be several passes before one's cup was returned with the precious water. In such conditions I expected tempers to be volatile, but on the contrary, everyone went out of his or her way to accommodate others. The windows were opened by necessity, and the blowing sand of the Nubian Desert left a fine grit covering everyone and everything. In spite of the kindness of all on board, our arrival at Wadi Halfa did not come too soon.

Below us was the mighty Nile, flowing calmly below the surface of Lake Nasser, and a rust-streaked paddle-wheeler with the words "Nile Navigation Company" barely legible through the grime and rust along the side. A barge tied to the starboard side was already filling with people and belongings. Years later I was to read of this same boat catching fire and capsizing losing many passengers to the waters of the dammed river.

The voyage down the Nile and through Lake Nasser to the Aswan Dam brought a humid relief to the after taste of the dusty crossing of the Nubian Desert. Though still hot, the slow passage would sometimes stir breezes from the water's surface.

I encountered one English speaker on board, a lawyer from Khartoum. He claimed to have once been the "advocate" of the president. Apparently his opinions differed from those in power and he had just spent sixty days in prison. He spoke of the political unrest and growing dissension among many of the Sudanese. His words came back to me years later as I listened to news of the revolutionary activities taking place in that country.

From Aswan I traveled north to Luxor intending to visit the famed Valley of the Kings. There I met with two other travelers, and together we roamed the ruins and riverside town.

At twilight we were standing near the river staring at an old house that had obviously seen earlier days of splendor, but was currently falling into disrepair. An aged figure in worn raiment of faded mourning-black stepped down from the portico and greeted us in perfect English. We were invited in for tea.

The house had belonged to Gamila Teufik Andraos, the one-time Pasha of Luxor, and in its time had played host to some fifteen kings. It had once been the seat of power reigning over forty-five towns along the Nile; but, after the revolution, the lands and part of the house and its antiquities had been confiscated. Half of the home was now occupied by the Arab Socialist Union. Over tea and Egyptian delicacies we listened to stories of earlier times; the speaker, an aging daughter of that once powerful family, shared her memories of glory and honor. After some hours the narrative came to a whispered end in the darkened house. We sat for several quiet minutes, then the old woman rose and went about the task of lighting several kerosene lanterns. She had already returned to her loneliness and solitude.

The next day a young boy offered to show me some of the lesser known ruins for a few coins. Following our trek about dunes of sand and rock he suggested we visit his family for tea and fresh bread. The mud-plastered front of their house was built against a low cliff, and on entering the cool and dark interior I discovered that the remainder of the house consisted of a series of caves carved from the cliff side. How many generations of this family had lived here the father could not remember; hundreds and hundreds, if not thousands of years these caves had been home to a flowing line of fathers and sons, mothers and daughters. The contrast with the previous evening's environment stuck to my mind, and I wondered how many revolutions this land and family had seen, still living in conditions not unlike their ancestors of the pharaoh's time. Cycles of history repeated themselves, and victors vanished into the fog.

> *"Stranger,*
> *you must come from the other end of nowhere,*
> *else you are a great moron, having to ask*
> *what place this is. It is no nameless country...*
> *Why, everyone has heard of it, the nations*
> *over the dawn side, toward the sun,*
> *and westerners in cloudy lands of evening."*

***

Circles were again closing, and my wanderings sought new directions. Moneys were becoming low, and I had reached the end of plans I had made, but I knew that I would not be returning just yet to my homeland. Drifting had eaten into my blood as a parasite, craving more, and a listlessness inhabited my soul. Thoughts of the East stirred my dreams.

> *"We are not here on Ithacan business, though,*
> *but on my own..."*

Fellow travelers had spoken well of Greece, a short and cheap hop from Alexandria, and so it was there that I arrived with little in my pocket but ideas of further travel. Mid-summer had appeared and tourists had invaded this land of sunny isles and cobalt seas, and, although illegal for a *farange,* jobs were not so difficult to come by. One position availed itself: working for a local animal protection league, which sounded interesting until I discovered it entailed the gassing of itinerant felines captured from the streets of the capital.

Thus my next couple of months were occupied as dishwasher and eventual short-order cook for a small restaurant near Athens' Syntagma Square. The time was restful, and the routine of steady work and income and good fresh food was appreciated. I met other travelers and learned of overland routes through the Mid-East, and plans began forming.

My time in the land of Odysseus proved a catharsis to the spirit. I wandered ancient ruins at dusk and sat in a centuries-old amphitheatre in the spectral moonlight of the Peloponnesus, watching actors living out the immortal words of Sophocles. I drank retsina with Cretan farmers and listened to war stories of another era, and I walked the birthplace of Apollo, listening to winds of thousands of years spin music of mythic yarns. I was finding it more difficult to separate the real from the myth, but I was not troubled by that difficulty: myth and the words of spirits were becoming a greater part of my reality; all part of the road's education.

I was fortunate in that time to encounter other wanderers, each questing in his or her way; and from these others I would learn of roads I had passed up, or not yet taken. We would often journey together for short spells, sharing food of the spirit as well as of the earth. I was beginning to realize that the passage might well be more important than the destination.

Autumn had arrived, and though the skies were still clear, the crowds were disappearing. I left the port of Piraeus with a little more in my pocket, and a more clear direction in my head. I knew now that I would eventually return to that land still wracked with war, that land form which I had launched these meanderings. It was a decision these several months in Greece had worked up from my subconscious, and I felt good about finally knowing where I was headed. If the listless spirit of the wanderer had been cast upon me by demons of a strange land, I would return to that land and at least confront those demons face to face.

The route back was to take me through further circles of time and realms of sights alien to my eyes.

East by East

Mykonos, Delos, Santorini, Crete: island hopping across the Aegean in company with an American artist of Latvian descent, we lounged on fine sand beaches and wandered cobblestone pathways through mountain and coastal villages. From her I learned yet another horror story of this planet's past wars: a Latvian family escaping their oppressed homeland, having only enough money to buy food for the children; food that had been poisoned by the oppressors.

Our paths separated at the Island of Crete, and I continued on the local ferry to Rhodes, from where I hoped to find an easy and inexpensive route into Turkey. Rumors floated through Rhodes as ashes upon the wind: first, it was Hoof and Mouth Disease, then a Cholera scare in Turkey, and no ships were departing for Turkish ports. On later investigation it seemed the real problem was simply a political statement being made by Greece over the Cyprus situation, attempting to use the tourist trade as throwing stones.

For the right amount of drachmas the captain of the "Myhaven," a small boat rocking alongside the pier, could take care of the departure and visa formalities and requirements that had been impossible to obtain from the officials. I had met several others who were looking for passage across that short expanse of water, and so we pooled our resources and embarked well after the shroud of night darkened the quayside. The slight fishing vessel was a pleasant change from the much larger passenger ferries, and an aura of intrigue accompanied our voyage over dark tossing waves to the gateway of the East.

Our boat landed at the small port of Marmaris, where we heard nothing of the reported health scares. Several of us found a bus heading north to Izmir, where one more took us on to the Golden Horn and Istanbul.

> *You are a tramp, I think, like me. Patience:*
> *a windfall from the gods will come.*

On the boat from Rhodes I had met another wayfarer who was to become a companion, and more than a guide, for the next several thousands of miles. Drew was quiet, and had the ability to fold into whatever environment she encountered...to become a part without missing a step. Oriental charm radiated from her almond eyes, and only very superficially hid a deeper wisdom of the East. She was a good traveler, a good teacher, and an excellent friend.

We knew of a train departing weekly from Istanbul for Tehran, and after several days of sightseeing and visa-applying we climbed aboard. I was surprised by the number of western kids traveling this route, and after talking to several, discovered that to these few, at least, the lure of this part of the world lay in the cheap and readily available dope.

> *They fell in, soon enough, with Lotos Eaters,*
> *who showed no will to do us harm, only*
> *offering the sweet Lotos to our friends—*
> *but those who ate this honeyed plant, the Lotos,*
> *never cared to report, nor to return:*
> *they longed to stay forever, browsing on*
> *that native bloom, forgetful of their homeland.*

It seemed a sad commentary on our society that many of these young travelers would see little of the many strange and beautiful sights and cultures through which they were passing, burying themselves in the euphoria of drugged bliss. On the excuse of expanding minds, I saw many being shrunken. Of course, three days on a Turkish train had the potential for driving one to most any diversion.

Throughout my travels I was finding that I was drawn by certain place names, even though I knew little of their historical significance: Addis Ababa, Chichicastenango, Wadi Halfa and others. We were approaching another about which I knew little; yet one which stirred an uncommon interest. Meshad was one of the holiest cities of Islam that could be visited by an infidel. The fasting month of Ramadan had just begun, and the holy city was crowded.

After the usual hours needed to obtain visas for future travel into Afghanistan, we walked the streets, passing busy markets and ornate mosques. Turkey had truly been the gateway to the East with its blend of civilizations; we were now in the cultural center of Persia, another world. We mistakenly walked too close to one of the mosques, and a group of men and boys began shouting at us and some of the younger ones picked up stones. We were learning the sovereign place of religion in this society.

We drank the hot sweet tea of rug merchants, surrounded by thousands, perhaps millions, of dollars worth of Persian carpets, piled to the ceilings, and listened as they explained the means of evaluating their elegant merchandise. And we met students voicing a growing unrest with the government of the Shah. Hints of underground rebellion were whispered. It would be several years before such revolution was to take over the country, with dramatic headlines and consequences for our own government.

Through Turkey and Iran we had moved fairly quickly, but we were soon to come to a country in which I wanted to slow my pace. In fact, one of the reasons I had delayed my stay in Greece as long as I had was that the king of Afghanistan had recently been overthrown, and the borders to that land had been closed to outsiders. Though I knew little of that nation, a foreign term had been with me for years, and that word was intricately tied to Afghanistan. The frontier had recently reopened, and I was hoping to learn more of that magic word: *Buzkashi.*

Buzkashi is, without a doubt, the roughest equestrian sport known to man. Traditionally, it is played with the headless carcass of a calf or goat, filled with sand. In the past a game might last for days, and stretch across miles of the barren steppes. Only in recent years had knives been outlawed from the game; and it was still not uncommon for spectators and players alike to be killed in the all-out frenzy of the sport—if it might be called that.

Buzkashi's attraction to me lay not so much in the unbridled fever of the contest, though I cannot deny that part of its allure, but rather the superb training of the horses and what has to be the best horsemanship on this earth. I had grown up with horses, they were in my blood. I had had the opportunity to play polo in college, a game directly descended from *Buzkashi*. I was about to enter the land that fathered these great horses and riders, and I was anxious to see all that I could of its mysterious attractions and peoples.

The border crossing into Afghanistan was worse than even the usually chaotic scenes we had come to expect of such entries, mostly due to the demanding Iranian officials. By bus and truck, a dilapidated van and tired feet, we eventually crossed the delineated no-man's land, and arrived in Herat late in the dark of night. But already we were feeling a fresh breath of openness and an indescribable sense of cultural freedom we had felt missing in the heavier atmosphere of Iran. We encountered more smiles.

Waking early, we stepped into a dusty bazaar of another century. Camels and fighting cocks, hawkers and gypsies, bakers and barbers, donkeys and dogs, kids and vegetable venders...the marketplace was alive as if life had just been discovered with the rising sun this very morning. I had a feeling of less refinement than what we had left the day before, a greater coarseness that came closer to the basics of life; life itself that was more real. The hearty laugh of the man sharpening knives reminded me I had not heard such an ovation of life in the last thousand miles. Just then I realized I had been tense for weeks, and that tenseness was now escaping, and a gladness for life was entering my spirit. Welcome to Afghanistan.

We proceeded down to Kandahar, and then up and across the desert towards Kabul. The journey was hot and cold, long and dusty...and beautiful.

Minutes before the sun was to grow to immense and fiery proportions, just before disappearing below distant dunes, the driver stopped where no landmarks could be seen and the crowded passengers disembarked quietly from the rickety bus into the all-surrounding sands. Hands and feet were washed with the small amount of water carried on board. Men and women separated, carrying prayer rugs out onto the waves of dunes; and because we were east of Mecca, they knelt to the west, bowing heads to the ground, then raising hands to the sky, all the while facing the giant globe of fire momentarily resting upon the fragile rim of the earth. In that moment I saw the beginning of man's religion.

> *O my dear friends, where Dawn lies, and the West,*
> *and where the great Sun, light of men, may go*
> *under the earth by night, and where he rises—*
> *of these things we know nothing.*

Suddenly I was transported to the dawn of mankind's realization of himself, alone in the enormous entity of the universe, recognizing that which was greater than himself; questioning and praying to that greater unknown. Religions' evolutions since that time have been mere bangles and beads added to the act. I had been allowed a sight into the most distant realm of man's mind; and I was stunned at the beauty and simplicity of that revelation.

We silently boarded the aging bus and sat, hushed, upon the wooden benches crammed inside. The driver started the engine and we eased into the twilight and growing darkness settling over the vast expanse of desert. In cold starlight we could sometimes pick out the fires of nomads and the dark mounds of their tents scattered about the lonely sand, and the silhouettes of distant camels.

Arrival in Kabul was late at night, and a small boy led us to a home that, for a few pennies, offered a room and a warm bath, something that was becoming more and more a luxury. Soon gone were the desert chills of the night.

Kabul was a rest stop, and a welcomed one. I caught up with two months of mail, and the words of distant friends reminded me that there were many different journeys upon this earth; I had chosen but one.

Several days were required to obtain the visas that would be needed to enter Pakistan and India. In the meantime I learned that, because of the dethroning of the king, the Royal *Buzkashi* game, which was normally held this time of year, had been outlawed, as with everything else remotely associated with the late royalty.

That was the official line. From locals we found out that this, the biggest game of the year, would simply be moved a great distance from the eyes of the capitol and its new rulers. It was to be held in a matter of days, ironically only a few kilometers from the Russian border, far to the north. We needed to find transportation to Kunduz—and I couldn't even find it on the map.

By busses and trucks Drew and I eventually found our way to that town, high on the steppes of the Hindu Kush. We passed through wild and apparently barren country, and as we bounced along the dusty road into town we could see caravans of hundreds of camels and horses trekking toward a gathering spot east of the ancient grit-blown village. Twilight was enveloping the dirt paths and mud-dabbed walls of shops as we sorely stepped down from the only mechanized vehicle on the street and stretched our legs. The daylight hours of fasting were about to end, and people began coming into the previously deserted dirt streets. We asked directions for a place to stay, and were pointed to one of the two "hotels" in town.

After dropping our packs in the naked room we set out to find a place to eat, for no food had been available during the day because of Ramadan. We followed the generally masculine crowd towards a building set at the town's crossroads, and were soon being directed up worn wooden steps into a large open room filled with entreating aromas and men sitting about Afghani rugs and boisterously breaking the day's fast.

We headed for an empty corner, with all the men's eyes directed at the unveiled woman at my side. I began feeling slight apprehensions, though Drew seemed to be handling the situation well enough. A loud handclap drew our attention to one of the larger parties feasting in the center of the room. The head of the rug was motioning us to his group. We attempted a polite decline, but the master would hear nothing of the sort. Soon we were sitting to his right as guests of honor.

> *"Welcome; and fall to; in time;*
> *when you have supped, we hope to hear your names,*
> *forebears and families—in your case, it seems,*
> *no anonymities, but lordly men.*
> *Lads like yourselves are not base born."*

We had no common language, nor interpreter; but in moments were laughing, gesturing, and communicating with each of the party sitting about the large carpet overflowing with dishes of exotic fare. We feasted on unknown delicacies, as well as the more common curries, shish kabobs, and pilafs. Stories were told with much signing of the hands and stuffed mouths, and soon we were embarked on language lessons of the better obscenities in each tongue, to the delight of the party as well as others who had gathered about to join in the gaiety.

Finally with little food remaining, the men around us began wiping their hands, unable to stuff more down laughing gullets. The laughter died slowly, and then the man to the left of the host let out a loud and prolonged belch. The guest to his left immediately followed suit. The eruptions continued half way around the carpet before I realized what was happening. I clenched, for I'd never learned to belch on command. The noisy train continued to Drew who performed admirably and quickly.

A pause. Silence. Seconds passed like hours in the forced quiet. A minute passed. Finally, an undignified squeak of a burp shot from my mouth. I looked up. Silence.

The host burst into a guffaw and applauded my miserly effort! Laughter and hurrahs broke from the others. In this harsh land where it is said a man did not draw his knife without drawing blood, even if it meant his own, I had been saved a severe embarrassment, if nothing else, by a simple courtesy of my host; international relations could be left to the proper reign of the diplomats.

The next morning was bright and crisp. As we walked the main thoroughfare of this small town, listening to the tinsmith hammering out an ancient melody and watching the uneven tracking of the horse-drawn carts belie the stability of ages, it seemed to me that the year of the Islamic calendar, 1393, was more appropriate to the scenes about us. Little reminded us of our presence in the twentieth century.

Friends from the previous night's entertainment waved and motioned us on the gathering crowds of men, camels and horses on the outskirts of town. We watched as caravans of loaded camels walked with the timeless grace of the desert towards a large assemblage of dark circular tents, about which milled hundreds of other animals and people. On drawing nearer we could see the horsemen readying their mounts, and crowds of spectators were beginning to accumulate along the boundaries of a large rectangular field. Native dress differentiated various tribes. Horses ranged from fine Arabians to Mongol ponies, and many appeared to be crosses of the two, all in excellent condition.

Kastor, tamer of horses...

From the rising excitement of the crowd we could tell that the *Buzkashi* would begin soon. The riders, *Chapandaz,* were tightening girths, mounting, and warming up their steeds. A shrill whistle blew, and the *chapandaz* convened on the field in two lines stretching completely across the playing area. Teams from various regions were grouped together. To my untrained eye this was the last time any organization on the field would be apparent.

Another signal, and the riders advanced to a circle marked in the ground near our end of the field. I could see the calf carcass lying within the white circle. And then, on some cue that I had missed, pandemonium struck!

Horses were rearing and striking out with their front legs, riders were yelling and using their long wooden handled quirts on other *chapandaz,* fighting to get to the carcass. Dust rose from the melee, often obscuring the assaulting hooves and gnashing teeth as the rearing horses slashed out at each other and at opposing riders. Then, one horseman broke free, clinging to the side of his mount, holding on with only a heel and a handful of mane, his free hand dragging the already mutilated corpse beneath the horse. The mob was instantly at a full run. The lead rider swung up onto his pony as he threw the calf's body across the pommel of his saddle. Others were closing as they raced toward a distant marker.

The game did not relent for the rest of the day. The sand-filled corpse would change hands often and dramatically. At times the play would leave the rough boundaries of the field, horses and riders scattering groups of spectators that had been lining the playing area. Whips and their long wooden handles were used more often on other players than on the horses. The horses themselves took as active roles as their riders, and when, on the rare occasion a horseman fell, his horse would continue charging whomever was carrying the carcass. Feats of equestrian skill such as I had never seen were crossing my eyes every minute. I was witnessing communication between mounts and masters unparalleled in the world of horse and man.

As the sun reddened and grew closer to the horizon, one *chapandaz,* charging ahead of the others, galloped across the beginning circle, throwing the torn and ragged carcass into it as he passed. The crowd cheered. I had seen the *Buzkashi.*

***

It took us almost a week to negotiate our way from Kunduz to our next destination, most often traveling in the back of trucks, sometimes in makeshift busses of Russian origin, and once atop such a contrivance along with men, children, chickens and goats. We were headed towards the Bamyan Valley and its famed caves, and one of the world's oldest, and certainly largest, Buddha, unexpected in this Islamic land.

We most often overnighted in *chi khanas,* small and friendly teahouses, scattered at about half-day intervals along the trade routes. Such shelters usually consisted of a single large room centered upon a large samovar and simmering pots of hot sweet tea. Simple meals would generally be available with no charge for sleeping overnight. Journeys lasting more than a day usually meant coming to know traveling companions fairly well. Even though there would rarely be a mutual language, basic communication hardly ever seemed a major problem.

Rambling the hills and caves of the Bamyan Valley, we became caught up in the pastoral atmosphere. We climbed alongside the giant Buddha, defaced these many years by the hands of Genghis Khan and his invaders centuries past. We met up with three Germans traveling in an old van reminiscent of Down-Hill Racer, only theirs was called "a yellow monster named Gilb." We hitched a ride across barely discernible tracks, higher yet into the Hindu Kush, to the cold and frighteningly beautiful Bandiamir.

Lakes of various sizes and shapes were scattered among peaks and barren high plains, each at different altitudes, having naturally dammed themselves with the deposits of various minerals at their spillways. Each was a dissimilar color ranging from emerald green to royal blue, some taking a reddish hue, others the powder blue of the sky overhead. The lunar landscape dictated a reverent approach, and we roamed the fantastic scenery quietly.

We supped and eventually slept that night in a tiny one-room hut, and were entertained by our hosts with the soft music of a diminutive drum and a hand-made stringed instrument. The wailing of a chilling wind outside joined the music, and the harmony of the two was not unpleasant.

> *These autumn nights are long,*
> *ample for story-telling and for sleep.*

No other buildings had been in sight across the vastness surrounding us when we stooped to enter the small structure. I felt to be among the last of my race as we listened to the songs of the high steppes. That night I squirmed more deeply than usual into a worn and warm sleeping bag.

The next day, a cold one, we caught a ride in the back of an open truck returning towards Bamyan. The truck was constantly breaking down, and every time we started up an incline the driver's son would run along behind, ready to chock the back wheels should we fail to make the climb, brakes apparently being a rare luxury.

Just after starting out we passed a bearded and turbaned old man on a tired old horse, slowly negotiating the rocky trail. A few of the younger Afghanis jeered at his decrepit pace. He paid no mind, and continued on his way. Several hours later, as we sat by the side of the road waiting for the driver to jury rig the carburetor, the old man and old horse stumbled by. The boys were understandably quiet, pretending not to see the lone rider. He approached closer, surveyed the truck, snickered rather loudly, and the horse and man ambled on down the dirt tracks leaving us and our modern transportation behind and slightly more humble.

It would take us over eight hours in the high cold wind to traverse the seventy-five kilometers down to Bamyan. A short part of that time was occupied in the middle of the trail, not fixing broken machinery, but watching an impromptu cock fight.

Several days passed before we were able to locate a vehicle headed out of the valley towards Kabul. During that time we walked by the river and up into the hills and cliffs overlooking the tilled fields, adobe buildings and compounds, and the graveyards with their bright red streamers rippling and ripping to the winds. And we watched as man passed through the patterns below us in his own small way.

A single camel trekked across the stark hills to the north, outlined on the horizon against the high peaks behind him, and I beheld for many minutes his lonely venture. I felt somehow akin.

The chilly excursion back to Kabul passed quickly in the back of a truck of singing and laughing Afghanis. Beautifully clear voices lifted melodies to the winds and mountains, along with the dust of our retreating vehicle careening down from the foothills.

The poetic symphonies stayed with us on the night of our arrival in the capital when we were taken by friends to a small candlelit restaurant to relieve the chills and hunger of the road. Sitting on well-worn Afghani rugs, with steaming dishes and the ever-present tea, we listened to three men playing soft music with finger cymbals, a mellifluent drum, and a soothing stringed instrument similar to a sitar. One of the players lit a chillum and passed it among the few, and already mellow, listeners. The peaceful evening toyed with our senses, as sounds and smells and memories brought us a little closer to the soul of Afghanistan.

The autumnal season was ebbing rapidly, and as much as we would have liked to see more of this fascinating country, the road again beckoned. A bus, as always crowded to the gills, transported us over the Khyber Pass and into Pakistan and the storied crowds of the Indian subcontinent.

In Peshawar we caught a horse cart to the train station, arriving in time to board the midnight special to Lahore. The train became so congested that Drew had to exit through the window when we arrived. There were several places in India we wanted to visit, but our main objective at this point was to get into the western part of Nepal before the winter snows closed off the mountain passes leading in from the south. So we continued our pace through Pakistan, eventually climbing onto the Amritsar boarder train to Delhi. Third class rail fare had its advantages, but space was not one of them. The train was late and slow, and crowded was too nice a word.

Delhi, another massive city, held few attractions for us, and we hastened to leave as soon as possible. In Agra we walked the grounds and ramparts of the imposing Red Fort, then followed the road to the Taj Mahal.

The grounds were crowded, and sulfurous smoke from the fuming factory stacks on the opposite side of the river drifted over the landscaped gardens and magnificent structure. We each had a feeling that this was not how we wanted to see this jewel of history, built more than three hundred years before. We departed sadly and quickly and roamed the marketplaces of the town. Nearing dusk, we decided to return...perhaps the crowds and fumes had thinned. We were unprepared for the majesty that awaited us.

A light mist was rolling in over the river, and as the sky darkened from the burgundy sunset a full and glorious moon rose from the east. Very few people remained on the grounds, and we walked alone and barefoot, sandals in our hands, over the cool and smooth marble terrace of the elegant mausoleum. The artful filigree decorating the walls actually glowed with the golden radiance of the giant moon rising over our shoulders. After many minutes of standing in respectful awe of the beauty encompassing us, we walked out onto the grass alongside the reflecting pools and sat, arms wrapped about our knees, staring at the radiant edifice. Neither of us spoke, recognizing that we were in a sacred and transcendental space that had not existed earlier that afternoon.

There *was* someone else on the grounds, for the light strains of a lonely flute drifted in with the mist, barely perceptible at first. The mist settled about the terraced base and the slender minarets and graceful domes rose from the cloud, blushing from the moonlight and the lonesome refrain of the Indian flute.

We stayed, mesmerized, as the dew settled over us and lightly dampened the grass, and scattered diamonds about the moon-and-star-lit monument. We stayed, silent in this splendor of nature and man, until the early hours of the morning when we were due to board the train to Kanpur. Even then we hesitated to leave, and I pondered the magical flute that seemed to appear at so many of the mystical places I had visited. My fortune was indeed grand.

Travel through India, as so many before me had discovered, forces one to come to terms with his or her own attitude towards humanity. The masses of poverty continually affront the senses, and one must either go mad with frustration, retreat into the Hindu words, "This is a world of suffering, and one must take himself away from it—the suffering is a part of their karma," or become a Mother Teresa. The sanest approach for the traveler seemed to be to offer what one could and continue forward...it was a compromise that, ultimately, only served to soothe the superficial conscience—it did little else.

***

The pastels of early dawn were subtly dispelling the darkness entombing Benares as we stretched the cramped train ride from our muscles and looked about. The banana vendor was asleep in her basket, wound into a womb of wicker. A lone old man sat piling and re-piling scraps of paper among three worn out sandals, pointing at old pictures torn from a ragged newspaper, issuing a poetry of sounds, speaking first to hawkers, then to no one in particular. A cow lay in the lobby of the enquiry office, and we gingerly stepped around her. Monkeys scurried about the roof tossing back missiles thrown at them, along with their own excrement. Having earlier disposed of my small moneys, I refused *baksheesh* to a one-armed and scarred boy, and immediately felt like the shit the monkeys were tossing at passers-by.

Another frail and anemic boy slept, with no clothes or covering at all except the fading shadows tying him to the base of the urine-soaked wall. The Sanskrit symbol of *OM*, coarsely painted on the wall, guarded over his fetal body.

The sun had still not risen as we wended our way towards the sacred Ganges. Streets were filled with the to-and-fro movement of thousands of bodies. Mist, rising from the river's ever-flowing waters, climbed to mingle with the dust of the crowds and growing amber light; and in spite of the small noises, a sacred atmosphere quieted our voices.

Down the long steps to the great river, past lines of beggars on either side: every malady, mutation, and amputation assaulted our eyes. A funeral procession wound toward the burning *ghat*s, already aflame with several corpses.

Hundreds of bathers, pilgrims to these sacred waters, were immersing themselves in the ritual of the Ganges, oblivious to the several small boats of tourists already passing along the shoreline. We hired a small craft, and soon were floating with thousands of yellow flowers into the current, as an intruding amber globe of a sun struck through the fog to silhouette the masted boats lined on the sand banks of the far shore. High above us more monkeys climbed the roofs of the temples and palaces of the maharajas. Ashes from the burning *ghats* settled on our shoulders and the flowing water. Only the bodies of holy men, children under eight years of age, and smallpox victims would not require this fiery purification.

I had been fortunate to have traveled upon the waters of many of the world's great rivers: the Mississippi; the Rhine; the Nile; the Amazon; the Mekong. But never had I known one so revered, and so intricately tied to the lives of its supplicants, from birth to death.

We later walked the streets and pathways of this town, visiting temples dedicated to Shiva and Krishna, and other deities of the Hindu faith. We were passed by colorful processions leading us on to smaller temples.

I paused in the middle of crossing a crowded thoroughfare—a bearded man was approaching from the other side, his white robe glistening in contrast to the dirt around him. An aura glowed about his head; in fact, his whole body radiated with what can only be described as a beatific energy. He likewise stopped several paces from me as he noticed my stunned stare. His eyes closed for a moment, and an ever-so-slight smile of exquisite peace touched his face. His eyes opened, he nodded, and passed on.

I now believe in holy men.

India is predominantly Hindu, and yet it is also the birthplace of another of the world's great religions; one that, at a later time, was to give me great solace and refuge thousands of miles from its source, and my homeland.

Drew instructed me in the four stages of the Buddha's life as they are represented in this country by four sacred locations: Lumbini, where he was born; Bodh, where it is said he obtained his enlightenment; Sarnath, the place he gave his first sermon, known as *DharmaChakraPravartara;* and Kushinagar, his death-place.

It was to Sarnath we traveled, to sit among the Stupas and peace of the sanctified ground. Drew read aloud words of the great man, translated through centuries, and we contemplated journeys of all kinds. It seemed a fitting farewell to this land of contrasting peace and turmoil upon which we had briefly touched.

The one road through the hamlet of Sonali was dark; we could only make out a few small hovels along the side of the empty thoroughfare of this border crossing. A knock on a door and sign language seeking a place to spend the night out of the cold wind brought a smile to the matron of the house as she invited us in. It was late, and even though we tried to make her understand that we had sleeping bags and floor space would be fine, she unceremoniously kicked the old man off the mat-webbed bed and the dog from under it. Then with much fanfare presented us with the pride of the household. Our protests went unanswered.

We had entered Nepal, home to the Yeti, the Third Eye, and the rooftop of the world, the majestic Himalayas. There was still a ten-hour crowded bus ride ahead, but we were looking forward to the trip. Coming up from the crowded and hot flat table-lands of northern India, the scenery before us was a breath of fresh cool mountain air, as each bend in the road granted new sights of lush greens and bounding streams, sky-reaching cliffs and approaching mammoths of mountains.

Each relay of transportation has its resident philosopher, and this day's savant boarded with us at Sonali. Soon into the trip she decided my lap was the only suitable place to ride out the journey, her aged weight that of a sparrow. Entreating persuasion by her son to return to her seat brought only screams at him, so I settled in to learn some of the ways of the East.

She soon removed the top of her clothing, and began fondling her withered breasts; all the time talking to herself and any others who would listen. She climbed over the seat, quite agile for her apparent years, then sat upon the floor for a while. She made to climb out the window, crawling over others in the way; and when prohibited from this, returned to my lap. She began telling me of her persecution in a language only my heart could translate.

"Can mortal man be sure of you on sight,
even a sage, O mistress of disguises?"

"The days have grown too old and wrinkled; the sun's glare burns my fading eyes. I wish for a tear to quench my soul's thirst, yet tears too have passed the ages with the wind, and a vacuum is left within my mind—dry...the sand is blowing, scorching what's left of my life's fluid. Blood has turned black, and black has turned to demons, and demons to my corpse, gnawing so ever consistently at my bones. These breasts that have nurtured the sons of the earth in their time, now suckle only the vermin of darkness and decay. Defy time's mocking rush...ha!...I've died before. I want now to touch, to feel...he moves away from my grasp. He ...they, you, laugh at the ageless, laugh at the truth and wish not, in your laughing, to be touched by the dirt, the filth, the earth. Nor will you touch the sky.

"So deep...the sky is my womb, and sparrows, and ravens, and vultures fly into the sun; the furrows of my substance bear only carnage and rot and stink...and are picked at by my own offspring from before; themselves sired by the vulgar jackals that laugh in fear and chew their own tails in mocking sanity. Let them laugh."

"She's crazy, of course...a little old."

"Watch the dog's eyes—Ah! Now they turn away. Fear rides the steed of deceit. That young bitch pretends to avert its stare—No! Look at me. Look! Ah...you flinch. It hurts a little to look. For in looking you're feeling, and in feeling, you're me. And in me, you'll die, just a little. Here, take these clothes, touch this ravished tit of time. Yes, you open your eyes wide in disgust; open your eyes to see, but don't, you're blind. Your eyes have been eaten away so gladly by the same rats of plague which have torn out my guts. Let their watery mouths chuckle and titter, their laughter is but defecation; so much shit to be balled up and rolled away by the gluttonous beetles of this earth, themselves destined to fall to their backs, waving their legs at eternity, unable to right even their own bulbous bodies.

"There: I vomit on your purity, your innocence, your white sacred cloth, your Christ, your virginity. Turn away; yes, it is better, for you want to puke too...at least you now feel ...without my touch."

"Yet I still can remember. Here, let me but touch that child... only he laughs with me. So much this child of life could teach, but you with your mute and deaf religion would pay no heed. Yes, take him away from my bosom for he might learn of life and come to harm. A sorceress she is. Yes, the darkness is mine...I remember...

"A mist, distilled by the night's breath, nourishing life's growth in its sleep, silently ascends to kiss the rising, glaring globe of that life's source. Tranquility descends the glowing slides of light piercing the leaves of the sky; illuminating the floor of the forest in tiny glittering gems of fire, lighting the valleys with the voices of the birds and the gods, and lighting the ever-awake stream with sparkles of clarity.

"Quietly, I can rest in such space of the past, Leave me be, for I am not of your world. Let the bus go on..."

Her gray eyes peered into mine, and the tenseness left her body. Tears finally coursed her wrinkled face, and she remained quiet the rest of the trip.

***

The streets of Pokhara were silent, cold, disorientingly dark. A child led us by the hands up an incline, and finally into a lightless room. He ignited the wick of a rusted lantern, and we followed him up wooden steps to a cavernous chamber, with two slender cots emphasizing the vast space around them. The shutters were closed to the night's frigid air.

I awoke to the soft creeping light of predawn, lifted myself upon an elbow, shivered from the crisp chill outside the quilts, and pushed open the wooden shutter.

When primal Dawn spread on the eastern sky
her fingers of pink light...

Crystalline brilliance floated into the room; a vision of pure enchantment greeted my eyes. The snow-crowned Annapurna Range of the Himalayas rose before me, some 26,000 feet into an air so clear I might reach out and touch the great summits, glowing with oranges and pinks of a rising sun that could only be seen from the heights of those peaks. I felt a new vitality, a lightness, a tonic of Nature's regal blood.

That morning we allowed ourselves a splurge and moved into a ten-rupee (one dollar) room closer to the quiet lake on the outskirts of town, with even more sweeping and grandiose views of the great mountains rising from our feet. We found a dugout we might take upon the water, and paddled to the center of the lake, resting there in the peaceful reflections of glistening peaks and royal blue sky. It was a day each of us would remember as one of the finest either had known, surrounded by such amazing natural beauty and our own contentment.

> *Even a god who found this place*
> *would gaze, and feel his heart beat with delight ...*

Our days were golden, as we walked the countryside and trekked mountain trails and ridges of sunset colors. They reminded me of another high range of peaks, and I thought upon the magic of this earth's highlands.

We sometimes paused to speak, in our limited fashion, with families threshing the last of the year's dry-land grain crops, maturing to the color of the sun onto the mountainsides. We sat with one family, high on the trail winding down from Nautanda in the warm late afternoon, trading words of different languages, when the young mother excused herself and disappeared into their tiny one-room house there on the high slope. She returned to the door some minutes later and proudly offered me a small cup of fresh warm milk. It was sweet to the taste, and I thanked her in my stumbling new words of that land, wondering to myself of its origin—for I had only seen one bullock that helped in the threshing. My thoughts must have been obvious, for she smiled, undid her halter and cupped a full breast in her hands, proud of her gift.

They were days in which a part of myself said, "Linger," but my destination was creeping closer in space and time, and another voice demanded that I continue on the road eastward.

Drew and I boarded the bus for Katmandu, and sat quietly through the journey, for our own circle was coming to a close, and we had become more than good friends. I had been fortunate in the blending of our paths, for I had learned much from her. She had shared her immense knowledge of Eastern religions and cultures with me, and she showed me the beauty of living within a philosophy of simplicity and love. I often felt remiss in not being able to return all that was given, but this she accepted with a knowing and quiet smile. She had introduced me to the wisdom of the *I Ching,* and she had given me of her own wisdom, rich beyond her years.

Katmandu, though sizable and having modern aspects, still struck us with a certain Eastern medieval quality, pleasant in which to roam. Its remoteness and primitive atmosphere contrasted distinctly with the different sets of international tourists and freaks (among whom we were usually included), whether tripping on scenery, cultures, dope, or the amazingly diversified food scene. It was a meeting place of differences; we hoped it would not be conquered by the intruding influences.

We followed more chanting religious processions to quaint and old temples. We ambled through the old city and across the suspension bridge traversing the Vishnunati River and up to the Swayambhu Temple, overlooking the city and out upon the mighty range of the Himalayan summits behind it. Only later did I learn this was also known as the Monkey Temple.

I should have realized that my old friend of the gods, and past guide, would have his say in the rites of passage from one journey to another. I had almost forgotten his presence, and I was returning to his home territory.

We sat upon the ground, leaning against an ancient stone wall, within view of the giant stupa and its all-seeing eye. My mind was torn, for since the Burmese border was closed, I would be making a rapid jump from this city into the far-East, returning to that land from which I was running. It was a giant step into uncertainty, and I was having second thoughts. It would be so easy to continue on with Drew, find a job far from war and hatred, and prolong this pleasant subsistence in strange and beautiful lands.

I had been lost in my thoughts, when I heard a chattering above me. I looked up and there he was, sitting upon the temple wall, staring at me. In that instant, Monkey's message burned into my mind, and I knew that my pilgrimage must continue alone. Drew turned and looked at me; she took my hand, for she knew the decision had suddenly finalized.

> *...they kept on to their journey's end. Behind them*
> *the sun went down and all the roads grew dark.*

With a fake student ID card left over from sunny days in Greece, I obtained an exceptionally cheap airline ticket from Katmandu to Saigon, by way of Bangkok. Drew and I lingered in the chaotic lobby of the airport until the final call. It was a farewell I had not looked forward to. As the agent was hurrying me to board I remembered a small golden Buddha that had hung from my neck since those days in that ravished country to which I was returning. As I lifted it over my head I suddenly understood, in a Zen-like flash, why I had placed it there. It now belonged to Drew. I couldn't speak, nor could I hide my tears from the stewardess welcoming me aboard.

Lines of a song echoed again and again in my mind:
"I'm leaving on a jet plane,
Don't know when I'll be back again.
Oh, Babe...I hate to go..."

The physical act of getting on a plane and in a matter of hours being thousands of miles distant was an alien and discomforting sensation after almost a year of traveling only by land or water. I was entering a time and space warp; and drastic changes were about to take place, without even the benefit of the gradual acculturation afforded by overland travel.

The plane rose up through the clouds of fantasy and broke into the clear atmosphere of the high world. There was Everest, reigning over the rest of the earth...a giant attended to and fronted by ridge upon ridge of snow-capped pawns. I was lonely and frightened.

Land of the Dragon

I was completing a circle about this earth that I had begun several years before, and a different kind of fear flew with me that day into Tan Son Nhut. It was not the fear of war or injury or death; it was something strangely distinct. Perhaps I had arrived at that root of all fears—the unknown. I was stepping into a new realm of journey with no maps, little resources, and a lot of doubts.

(It was December of 1973. On January 28 of that year a "Cease-fire" declared earlier at the Paris peace talks took effect, a dubious declaration that supposedly allowed the Americans to leave with honor. The South Vietnamese saw it as abandonment. The last American troops were pulled out on the 29th of March, ending almost ten years of US military presence. However, the Americans were not done with this country, nor was the war over. Though I didn't know it at the time, some 8500 US "civilians" remained in-country.)

I caught a ride into Saigon, and began walking familiar streets. The American soldiers had gone, though more round-eyes than I had expected were still evident. The bars were still in business, but traffic had obviously slowed. The market off Nguyen Hue was just as I had left it, and there was the crippled girl selling flowers on the corner, and the friendly old man and his hand-made musical instruments, the sandal maker, and my favorite soup cart.

I found myself on Doan Thi Diem, and there was Hoa's; and a rush of memories. "Papa-San" sat on the same worn stool, puffing on the same cracked pipe. The only change seemed a new pair of aviator's sunglasses he kept pushing back up the bridge of his nose. "Ah...*Dai Uy* Pigs and Chickens!"

I was remembered, and felt pleased. Papa-San called for a toast, "*Chin, Chin.*" In five minutes I had all the news and gossip; then life returned to normal. Too many had come and gone, and I was but another. Papa-San went back to his reveries. Hoa went back to figuring the previous day's receipts. I returned to worrying about what I was going to do.

Ideas were gradually formulating. I had heard much about the hill tribes. Montagnards, as the French had called them, and their cultures interested me. They were the indigenous peoples of this country, and the more that I learned, the more their story paralleled that of the treachery visited upon the American Indian.

The majority of the twenty-two tribes lived in the Central Highlands, a high plateau and mountainous country roughly coinciding with the borders of Viet Nam, Cambodia and Laos. They were, by our standards, primitive peoples, subsisting predominantly on slash-and-burn agriculture; although the war had been responsible for a large percentage being forced to move into deplorable refugee camps. Their numbers were being decimated by both sides of the political struggle, with accompanying poverty, malnutrition and disease. Historically, a certain amount of animosity, prejudice and mistrust existed between them and the ethnic Vietnamese.

I had decided to search out the many volunteer organizations for possible jobs. Because my funds were at an all-time low I would take whatever availed itself for the short term, as long as it was peaceful and constructive, but would keep looking for an opportunity to get into the highlands where I might learn more of these people. Although I had had the chance of getting to know something of the rest of the areas of South Viet Nam during my time with "Pigs and Chickens," the Central Highlands was one region I had only visited for short spells. I wanted to see more of the mountainous terrain and its inhabitants.

First, I needed a place to stay, and price was certainly going to be a deciding factor. I was walking through one of the parks that still afforded the relief of greenery and space from the fumes of oil-burning two-cycle cyclos and diesel army trucks crowding the swollen thoroughfares of this once lovely city. I realized I was only a couple of blocks from that haven I had discovered mid-way through my in-country tour, at 19 Nguyen Van Trang: the Compound. I'd go by and see if there was anyone I still knew, or even if the place was still open. It was an area that might offer some cheap accommodations, in a relatively quiet neighborhood.

The sun had just passed its zenith, and I really didn't expect to find anyone there, even if it was still operating.

I stepped around the bicycle leaning against the doorjamb, and knocked hesitantly. The door opened, and Mai stood staring at me in sincere disbelief. She broke into a laugh and took my hand, leading me inside. Mai had been the first person I had met here some two and a half years before. She was a friend of Chris, who had introduced me to the quiet bar and house of whores and good friends.

We spent some time reminiscing: she had received several letters from Chris, but they had come farther and farther apart, and now it had been almost five months since she had last heard from him; Lan had moved on—stories were conflicting, whether she had married, or perhaps gone big-time, moving to Tu-Do...Mai couldn't say. Business had obviously fallen off drastically since the American troops had pulled out. A few thousand contractors had a difficult time filling the boots and beds of 50,000 troops. But, somehow, Chi Ly, the madam of this illicit establishment, had managed to keep her steady girls clothed and fed and provided them with some money to send back to their families in the provinces. How she did this Mai and the others didn't know, for receipts hardly paid the rent. Chi Ly took care of her own.

Noc, another friend from before, brought three bowls of *pho* to the table, and the three of us sat and ate the steaming noodle soup amid laughter and fond memories of friends come and gone. The war had a way of enriching camaraderie, even that of short duration, to an intensity hardly known without its influence.

Just as I was mentioning my search for a place to stay Chi Ly came through the door with a filled market basket in each hand. Her singing voice had preceded her, complaining about the most recent price increases at the Saigon market; if her girls were going to continue eating so much, they would all turn into fat water buffalo, and then she would have to change her honorable profession.

After greetings of laughter, and jokes about how the *Dai Uy* was so love sick he had to travel half way around the world to come back to see her girls, Chi Ly listened to my plight, sitting on a barstool in thoughtful silence. She smiled, "I wondered when you might return. I've been saving a room with a view for you."

She had, in fact, at the top of the building, with its own shower, an immaculately clean room that had gone unused since the troop pullout. She'd loan me a hot plate, but I'd be welcome to eat with the "family." I walked up the steps remembering a drugged vision of a lithesome beauty floating above these stairs. I shook myself from the reverie, and threw my tattered pack into the corner.

I looked out the open window over the brown smog that had settled onto the streets of the city below. At this height the air was relatively clear and a fresh breeze blew the curtains into the room. I turned and sat upon the cot, leaning back against the wall. An extraordinary sense of being home after two years of being on the road encompassed me. I smiled to myself, thinking of some bachelors' dreams of living over a house of ill repute.

***

I found the office of the Council of Voluntary Agencies and spoke with the director, Ong Long. Surely, with over eighty registered agencies I'd be able to find some type of rehabilitative work. I left a resume that he promised to bring before the next meeting. I took the list of agencies, many of which I had never heard, and started pounding the streets and knocking on doors. I spoke with people dealing with everything from orphanages to eyeglasses, bicycles to bibles. I found no jobs.

After several days of talking with directors and sub-directors, and friends of friends and possible leads, I sat back on my cot, blisters on my feet, exhausted. To top things off I was having a good bout with Uncle Ho's Revenge, and Uncle Ho was winning. I nodded off, and awoke in the early morning hours to the sound of artillery not too far away. Someone had laid a cover over me.

An overdue and hasty trip to the toilet, and I lay back down. The shooting continued...and then a heavy and earth-moving explosion. I sat up and leaned on the windowsill. The southern sky was ablaze with a huge fiery cloud. I couldn't go back to sleep. I was depressed and sick. Which one followed from the other, I'm not sure.

The dark hours stretched into eternities of doubt and self-indulgence. What a fool I had been to return to a war I had come to abhor. How was I to get myself out of this quagmire? I was virtually broke. And I'd probably end up catching the clap from the sheets, without even the satisfaction of having obtained it first-hand.

The daylight brought news that the VC had accurately lobbed a dozen or so rockets into the fuel dump at Nha Be, only a few kilometers from downtown Saigon. Rumors floated everywhere in this capitol of idle hearsay. My depression was not allayed, and the only reason the diarrhea had subsided was that there was nothing left to be emitted.

I was knocking on doors again, handing out resumes, thinking I could still be trekking the high Himalayas, if only I had not acted so foolishly. I was half-heartedly listening to the Deputy Director of CARE when I caught the word "Montagnards." He was explaining a project near Kontum, up in the highlands, that CARE was assisting. He was interested in the possibility of starting a livestock project at the small hospital there, a program that might eventually lead into village projects in the area. Would I be interested in putting together such a program?

It would take a month or so to get the paperwork written up and approved by the New York office; he'd keep me posted. I walked out of the white building into the traffic on Cong Ly with a bit more sprite to my blistered step. At least there was a possibility, not only to do something constructive, but also in the geographic area I had wanted to get into. There was one more agency on my list for the day; I'd make that one stop, then treat myself to a cold beer with Hoa and her father.

I walked through the gates of an imposing and starkly clean compound. I should have realized the nature of its mission by the symbol on the gatepost, a cross presiding over a globe of the earth. Somehow I missed the hint. I stepped into the director's office after he had had time to peruse my *curriculum vitae.* He spoke well and quickly. Said his prayers had been answered (I took that as a figure of speech), he'd been looking for someone with just my qualifications. He wanted photo documentation of the various activities of his organization, the largest non-government agency working in this country, and he wanted to set up a photo lab as soon as possible. Also he wanted me to fly to Laos, a neighboring country in which he was also directing operations, to meet with a nutrition team that had been making a survey of villages in the north of that land and had encountered a number of animal deaths recently...I might be able to make some suggestions. Could I start tomorrow? He'd make arrangements for me to fly into Vientiane on the eighteenth of the month when I could meet with the nutrition team there.

This man made quick decisions; I was awestruck. For over a week I had found nothing, and suddenly everything was happening. I murmured something in the affirmative, thanked him for his confidence in me, turned and promptly tripped over a large BUFE ("Big Ugly Fucking Elephant"—a ceramic specialty of this country, aptly described by its acronym) on my way out the door. Could a person who buys BUFEs really be trusted?

I started work the next day, after first letting the director know about the possible future arrangement with CARE, which would definitely not start for a couple of months. If he didn't mind a short-timer, I could sure use the job. No problem.

We began immediately with the photography of this huge operation. Refugee and child feeding programs, housing for street boys, a baby home for pre-mature, mal- and under-nourished infants—now some seventy babies; a lot of apparently good things were taking place, but something I couldn't put my finger on began bothering me after just a few days.

Sometimes things seemed just a little too American; one or two of the people seemed just a little too good. Some became good friends, particularly the Vietnamese, but others were just slightly too holy to be able to joke with. I was beginning to encounter the "Tom Dooley Complex," that characteristic of assumed omniscience of many western do-gooders at the time.

After a week of working with the group I began to see how fanatically evangelical some of its members were, and I was beginning to feel a little out of place. I had a talk with the director, explaining that perhaps I was not of the same ilk as the majority of his workers, and I just wanted him to know so that there were no false pretences or illusions.

I concluded by stating that I thought he should know that I was living on the top floor of a whorehouse. He thought for a moment.

"Well...just don't park the car in front." From that time on we understood each other fairly well.

Not many days passed before I was winging across the country with a visa and one-way ticket into Laos. (I wondered about that ticket—but the man assured me that for accounting purposes it was better for the Vientiane office to buy the return fare.) I was to meet the head of the nutrition team at a local hotel. He would be in the capital only this day. Then I was to travel into some of the areas in which they had been working and where they had identified the possible livestock problems.

I missed him by twenty minutes. He had left the country. Had he left any notes for me? Nope. Humm...

I walked the dirt streets of this capital trying to find the organization's office. I had no background in the Lao language and just getting directions proved difficult, but the people I met were friendly enough, and soon I was staring at the logo on a front door. Before long I was making plans for getting out into the countryside. Though the office personnel knew as little as I about the evasive nutrition team and its survey.

At the end of a long day's journey from Vientiane I entered a land of ancient oriental wall hangings: the sun was dropping quickly behind a distant blue-green ridge upon which spirals of smoke rose hesitantly from thatched huts nestled among whispers of clearings in the giant bamboo forests. Abrupt limestone cliffs and monoliths towered over a haze-layered stream coursing through the valley; mist already mingling with the fading light. Sounds of cocks crowing and children laughing occasionally penetrated the silence.

We were far to the north of the Laotian capitol, close to the Plain of Jars, and not so far from the Chinese border. At the moment there were no sounds of warfare, neither guns nor aircraft. A primitive peace enveloped the terrain, and I could have been viewing a scene from thousands of years before. I stood gawking at the apparently unspoiled beauty, until a hand gently touched me on the arm and motioned me to follow down the jungle path.

Within part of an hour we entered a cleanly swept clearing. Half-dozen thatched houses stood about its rough perimeter on bamboo stilts. Nondescript dogs, golden-brown children and beautiful tamed jungle fowl shared the spaces beneath the huts, each making use of the end of the day in its own way. An elderly man clasped his hands in front of him and bowed a greeting, the led me to one of the houses.

> *Savages, are they, strangers to courtesy?*
> *Or gentle folk, who know and fear the gods?*

These friendly people were the Muong, or Meo, as called by the Lao. I was told that the word "Meo" actually held a connotation of "savage" or "heathen" in the Lao language...and yet nothing could have been further from the truth. Perhaps there was another side, but I was seeing a gentle people whose lives centered upon their families and the giggling children, too polite to point at the strange foreigner in the midst.

For the next several days I was guided along mountain paths from village to village. Communication was, by necessity, basic, but sufficient for what I needed to learn at the time. Most of these people were refugees themselves, having been forced from their ancestral lands by either one or both sides of a war that wasn't even supposed to be here.

I rarely heard the fire of guns during these days of hiking through the forests of bamboo. And yet the evidence of war was never quite far enough away. There was little in the way of food: rice; perhaps some wild greens; and on occasion of celebration, a chicken would go into a broth that might feed twenty people or more. And yet it was always lavishly shared, and I never went hungry.

I could understand the reason for sending in a nutrition team, yet the answers seemed simple enough. As to the livestock: evidence of disease was apparent, and sometimes easily diagnosed. But after sitting with the elders of the hamlets I came to realize that the major loss of livestock, whether buffalo, elephants, swine, or poultry was always simply the war. Once again I'm hearing stories of helicopters practicing with their weaponry on the larger beasts, seemingly only in macabre joy; cadres of the Lao government coming through the villages in the day, catching or shooting whatever they could for food; and their counterparts of the Pathet Lao passing through at night, silently catching up what remained. The people, the animals, and the land itself sometimes seemed to have little chance.

On the last day of walking these beautiful mountain trails I entered a charred clearing. Even the wild birds were silent in the vicinity. I felt a strange presence surrounding me. The two Muong men with me were quiet, but apprehensive. I could tell they wanted to continue quickly down the path. The ringing in my ears grew noticeable and played eerie rhythms to my mind, and bones, and soul. I was a little scared, but not by anything of this world; not the war or its weapons.

Spirits sang mournful dirges in this green-canopied cathedral, and though I wanted to leave, I was frozen in burned and dusty tracks, listening to growing cries and wailing.

That carbonized clearing was still respectfully called by its one-time name: the Village of the Little Elephant. The Little Elephant and its village home had become victims to the cruel war, and none of the beings of that village had survived...nor had their spirits been properly laid to rest.

This I learned after the men had physically propelled me from my catatonic stance and hurried me from the unquiet silence of the jungle's scar. I had to catch my breath. We walked down the mountain, each in his own solitude, and arrived in Bon Xon just as dusk was settling into the valley.

I needed several days back in Vientiane to meet with government officials concerning livestock vaccination programs for some of the more basic diseases endemic to the area, and so returned to the capital. Christmas was approaching, and I faced spending that holiday alone in a bleak hotel, when one of the office volunteers asked me to accompany a small group going to visit several village projects a half-day's ride southeast of town. I gladly agreed and was soon wandering more jungle trails, this time along the Mekong.

We were walking between hamlets when one of the villagers led us into the dense undergrowth not too far from the main trail. We stopped before a tangle of vines rising before us, and several seconds passed before I noticed the rusting metal, twisted beneath the green sepulcher.

The remains of an American warplane were rapidly being consumed by the thick vegetation. According to our guide it had only lain here for the past year or so. It had come down from the sky during a period of heavy bombing in the area, not too distant from the Ho Chi Minh Trail. The plane had fallen long before the U.S. government had admitted to carrying the war across the borders of the neighboring countries.

The wreckage was just barely recognizable. Should any men have gone down with the plane, their bodies most assuredly would have been consumed by explosion and fire. A forensic expert would be needed to identify any human remains, should any be found.

After several days of meeting with officials and attempting to piece together in my own mind the diverse programs of animal disease control sponsored by the government and various contributing agencies, I returned to Saigon to present several possibilities to my employer.

In spite of my recommendations to try to work within the existing framework of ongoing programs—I had already seen too much "reinventing of the wheel," a malady particularly common to government and voluntary organizations working in third world countries—the alternative of beginning our own program was seized upon by the somewhat impetuous director. I later came to see that this outcome was inevitable.

I also had suggested waiting until the end of the monsoon season when the effectiveness of such a program could be increased, and access to the areas would be easier, thus unfortunately writing myself out of such employment, even though it was a project that greatly interested me; but I was assuming eventual approval of the CARE project, and that was my first priority. This suggestion was likewise disapproved; we would start right away. At least I was guaranteed an interesting job until I found out about the other.

The logistics of organizing a regional control program for livestock diseases proved challenging. Three premises seemed basic: focus should be directed towards the primary killers (besides the war) for which effective vaccines existed; if we were going to work outside the existing system, the method of organizing had to be simple, easily perpetuated by the people themselves, and economically feasible. In a primitive area, such as where we would be working, the educational aspects of such a program would, in the long run, perhaps prove the most important, and thus would have to be thoroughly considered.

In studying the existing programs, and trying to learn from them, some interesting facts came to light. The Laotian government, heavily supported by the U.S. government, relied by necessity on the United States Agency for International Development (USAID) for the construction of such projects.

It seemed, as I had witnessed elsewhere, that the American "experts" had simply taken over, and input from the Laotians themselves was minimal, if it existed at all. This was in spite of the fact that some very talented and well-educated Laotians were available. I was seeing another example of "We know better." There seemed an indelible, though unwritten condition: "If you want our millions of dollars, you do it our way." The recipients had little to say in these follies.

The less obvious paradox of these lessons in ongoing history was that if these friendly people were to learn anything from us, it would be in rejecting our imposing doctrines. These people would choose to become masters of their own fate. Such activism would eventually disregard and even expel their American teachers. Few Americans seemed ready to learn the lessons taught by the results of our French predecessors' activities here in Indochina.

And yet, here I was, ready to invent another wheel. It was a paradox of my own activities that would constantly return to pester my conscience: to be a part and not be a part. The philosophy of the Tao was seeping into my mind, yet I was insufficiently enlightened to apply its lessons completely to what I was doing. Thus onward into the maelstrom I continued.

Vaccines for the more prevalent animal diseases were available in Laos. The problem was that they were being imported by USAID from U.S.-based companies in Taiwan, some at a cost exceeding $2.50 per dose. Such an expense would be minimal to an American farmer at risk of losing his prize cow; however, to a Muong refugee, it would simply be impossible. Our organization had agreed to support such a cost for the project. However, for the possible continuance of such a program after our passing, it hardly seemed feasible, economically or logistically.

Right next door, politically and geographically speaking, Viet Nam, with aid from the French and Americans, had developed the production of vaccines geared to the endemic strains of animal diseases prevalent in Southeast Asia. Over the years the vaccines had proved effective, and costs had been reduced to an average of a couple of cents per dose. USAID had been actively involved in this program, yet the word seemed to have never quite gotten across the border, in spite of periodic regional conferences and constant traveling back and forth of officials from all the countries concerned. The strains of vaccine would more likely be appropriate, the cost was certainly more reasonable, and the logistics surely easier, or so I thought.

Lao officials were intrigued with the idea of making the money go more than a hundred times further, with a more appropriate, closer, and less expensive product, but since it wasn't their money they'd have to check with USAID. I should have known. No, USAID was too tied to its already approved multi-year program. I suspected that a "Big Business/Big Government Complex" was somehow involved.

And so it came to pass that with the aid of some concerned Laotian government officials we began smuggling vaccines into their own country. I felt proud to be on the side of the "inscrutable" Asian in this game of foreign aid and advice.

The next step was to select and train the cadre for the initial vaccination teams, themselves to become trainers if the program was to prove successful. With job opportunities virtually nonexistent in the refugee areas this proved mostly a problem of selection from the myriad applicants. Rather than experience or educational backgrounds, we looked for qualities in individuals that seemed to promote a more far-reaching view of what we were attempting to do; people who looked at the activities as more than just a job. In the end, selection relied more on gut reaction to personalities than any other factor. I remained as far in the background as possible; easy enough to do with my lack of language. I had the advantage of a team leader who understood our goals, and whose desire to succeed more than made up for any lack of technical abilities, something I could help with as time went on.

I was back in the land of the towering limestone cliffs, green mountains, and giant-bamboo jungles. I was intrigued by the unending uses to which these ingenious people had put the ever-present bamboo, surrounding us in its hundreds of varieties. The entire house in which I was now sitting was constructed from bamboo: without nail, wire, or string. Our bowls and chopsticks, drinking cups, and other utensils were all of bamboo. We ate the young shoots of the plant, and our baskets were fashioned from it.

It could be burned for fuel. We cooked, ate, and drank from and of it. We slept on mats woven from strips of bamboo, and the roof that kept the chilling monsoon rains from me was of this same beautiful material. We listened to haunting cords of its music from a dozen different instruments of this lovely and unique grass. I began to appreciate the sacredness of this plant.

Though I had experienced some fairly primitive living conditions in my travels, these in which I now existed were approaching the basics, without which survival would indeed be precarious, if not impossible. After a few days of becoming acclimated to the unvarying diet, bathing in the river downstream from where we took our drinking water, and open-air toilet habits, I began reconsidering the necessities of life with which we in our modern world had surrounded ourselves. To view them now as luxuries gave me a new appreciation, not only for those luxuries, but also for the lives of these people, who for thousands of years had subsisted on such basics; and whether by desire or necessity, took their pleasure from simple human relationships and the beauty of nature. I had become too ingrained in the ways of my culture to give up these ways easily; but there were lessons to be learned here if I would but open my eyes. To make do with what one had, and find pleasure and peace in so doing, gave one a strength of contentment uncommon to other societies.

We had decided to implant several conditions into the program on which we were about to embark. Before any vaccinations were to begin, the teams would speak with the village chief of each locality and explain the project as thoroughly as possible and try to answer any questions. It would then be up to him as to whether we vaccinate or not. If he chose to accept the team's services it would have to be for all the animals in the village; an all-or-none proposition. Also, the village would have to provide at least one individual to accompany the team to learn the techniques involved. Thus each village would have someone knowledgeable in the process and who could conceivably continue the program if they desired or should ours fail for any reason.

Lastly, we required that, with the rarest of exceptions, minimum payment be made for the services. Such payments could be made in-kind if funds were not available, preferably in food. These in-kind payments could be used to pay the cadre doing the vaccinations, or revert into the refugee feeding programs of the parent organization, thus releasing other funds for vaccine purchase and transportation costs. This established an economic base for the program, and, I think, also injected some dignity into the process, adding a certain psychological value to the service.

With these simple terms we seemed to have at least a possibility for continuity of the program. The weakest link in the process was the continual supply of vaccine. We'd have to take our chances on that.

Again walking the mountain trails from hamlet to hamlet, I began seeing more evidence of the war's presence. Literally thousands of pockmarks of craters from bombs and heavy artillery dotted the forests and mountainsides, as pox scars might profane the face of a beautiful maiden. We had to be careful to stay on the trodden paths, for land mines and unexploded ordnance were not that uncommon. I had witnessed the injured being carried to the road at Bon Xon for transportation to the nearest medical facility, a day's ride away. That such a handsome land and people had been so insanely and horribly affected by a war of politicians was turning me even more against our government's involvement in the conflicts of this and neighboring countries.

In societies such as these, education was more traditional than that of my upbringing, or even of the Lao schooling system. Disease was often explained in terms of wronged or bad spirits, and sometimes we had to account for our actions in similar terms. I became accustomed to such explanations, and even, I suppose, came to take something of a different outlook on my own world. As I came to see that every animal and object had its own spirit, little different from my own, I gradually gained more respect, and stood in greater awe, of the natural world around me. It was an extension of one of

Monkey's last lessons, and certainly one of the philosophical roots of most Eastern religions.

Some of the village chiefs, usually after a thoroughly democratic meeting with everyone in the village, would choose not to avail themselves of our services. We thanked them for their time and would head on to the next hamlet.

One particular village was actually divided into two hamlets, physically separated by the incline of a large hill. The lower hamlet decided not to vaccinate; the upper one wished to do so. We decided there was sufficient separation between the hamlets to go ahead and vaccinate in the upper collection of thatched huts.

Two weeks later we had a visit from a representative of the chief of the lower hamlet. All of their pigs had died; those of the upper community were fine. Please, would we return to bring the good spirits in the needle to the new animals they had just acquired. We complied, and the bamboo telegraph went to work.

From that day on, other villages were sending requests for the services of the teams; never more were refusals to vaccinate encountered. I felt as though we had just passed our first test, whether the vaccinations had been responsible or not.

It was a good omen on which to leave, for I had just received a message from Saigon: "Pig project approved." On my last night at Bon Xon the elders dug up a jar of particularly strong *lao hai,* the local version of homemade rice wine. Amidst the laughter and conversation I reflected on my short stay in this beautiful land and what we had accomplished. There were now five teams walking the trails between villages. Acceptance was greater that I had hoped, and I was impressed with the speed with which the vaccinators had learned their skills. The last several days I had simply been sightseeing; I really wasn't needed, and that was good.

An elder of the village approached, sat before me, and lifted my wrist. He then tied a slender thread around it, as did others who followed him. The amulets were to ward off any evil spirits I would encounter on my future travels, while away from their protection. I choked up, for I had come to know these people as my family.

The next day I caught a ride in an Air America chopper heading into Vientiane. Within minutes we flew across the lands I had been hiking for the last several days. We passed over the small village clearings scattered across the verdant slopes; more obvious were the barren defoliated areas and the patches of naked bomb craters defiling the green carpet below. We soon were skimming across the Plain of Vientiane, and then I was back in the Lao version of civilization.

From cold-river bathing to hot water and indoor plumbing, had simply by climbing onto a magic carpet. The changes always seemed more magical and unexpected on the return—a quick trip through cultural evolution.

I ended up with an extra day in Vientiane before I could catch a flight out. Even though the small hotel in which I was staying was close to the town's center the only noises of the night were incessant barkings and howlings of the local dogs, and an occasional out of sync rooster. The change to a soft bed and time to kill left me restless, and I rose before the sun and ambled the quiet streets in the soft orange light.

I pass lines of Buddhist monks and their students, barefoot and bareheaded, robed in varying shades of yellow, themselves passing by women and children waiting in doorways with offerings of rice for the out-held bowls. The sun rises behind a temple and the sudden harsh light divides the scenes into contrasting diagonals of shadows and brilliance, and the monks proceed through these zones of darkness as life passes through stages of Yin and Yang.

The outdoor market scenes are universal and timeless as the sellers gain energy and warmth from the morning sun. Still the market seems as much a social gathering as a commercial one: children playing under tables of vegetables; featherless chicken carcasses hanging by the neck; vendors chatting over steaming bowls of noodle soup, all in the apricot blush of morning's radiance.

There was a good chance I might not have the opportunity to again visit this enigma of wartime capitals. In most places it hardly seemed a city at all, but a conglomerate of rural villages, replete with noisy cocks, barking dogs, and bare-bottomed children playing in the pot-holed streets of dirt.

But then a gunship would buzz the rooftops, a deuce-and-a-half would hurriedly and noisily scatter dogs and kids from the blanketing dust and diesel fumes, hauling off the young boy-soldiers to fields of brown, blue, green and crimson red. And shaven-headed bonzes in tones of saffron's time walked barefooted past stupas and whorehouses. A gray USAID Bronco sped past an ambling pedicab, its driver covering his nose and mouth from the grime and soot with his black and white checkered scarf. How must it be to see the twentieth century world from under the conical straw hat?

The sun was high and heat had long since dissipated the delicate matinal wash, leaving a harsh white brilliance and sweating humidity in its wake. Shadows were rare. The crude sign with the English words, "The White Rose," and a paint-pealing picture of that bloom hung above me. A twangy country-western voice and sound of accompanying guitar sifted through the open doorway; the melody and its parent tape slightly stretched from overuse. The cooling darkness inside was inviting, and I decided it was not too early for a beer. My feet were tired and hot, and the mostly sleepless night was taking its fee. My appreciation of the morning's beauty had dissolved with the mist, and I was again falling into a depression of boredom while questioning my existence in this foreign world. The all-American music tempted a desire to return to more familiar surroundings, away from the bittersweet strangeness around me, to possibly speak with someone whose mother tongue was my own. Two round-eyes sat at the bar. Their size, and particularly excessive paunches lapping over belted midriffs contrasted with the slight hill-tribesmen I had left in the mountains, and the Laotians on the streets outside. I immediately felt a certain regret at having entered the legendary white man's bar; and yet another, more basic, craving continued to draw me inside.

A pair of young dark-skinned girls sat with the middle-aged men, laughing in a stilted and broken GI English. A third girl who could not have been past her teens materialized and took the seat beside me, placing her hand on my thigh as she introduced herself and asked if I would buy her a coke. The fact that the beer and coke money was coming from a salary paid by one of the largest evangelical organizations in the world did not escape me; pangs of conscience and situational humor played back and forth with my mind.

The men inflicted me into their conversation, such as it was; one was a contractor with a large American construction firm, the other, a pilot with Air America. War stories were soon superseded by talk of women, oriental prostitutes in particular. They could have been talking about Christmas toys or late model cars that soon lost their individual attraction and were traded for brighter and younger models. That the two girls sat by their sides as they discussed relative anatomical differences seemed not to bother the Americans in the least.

> *One of them found her washing near the mooring*
> *and lay with her, making such love to her*
> *as women in their frailty are confused by,*
> *even the best of them.*

I left with the mixed emotions of a hypocrite, critical of others despoiling the same flowers that I turned to in my loneliness.

***

Here I sit, atop one of many pig crates in the middle of Tan Son Nhut Airfield, watching the vapors of heat rising from the tarmac, turning camouflaged planes of war into shimmering mirages, listening to some forty-odd swine succumbing to heat exhaustion, and wondering what in the hell I'm doing. Just getting here had been a full day's work. The animals are panting heavily from the heat and probably are going to die. They're sunburned already, and there's no cover to get them into the shade. I've been splashing them with water that I've hauled across the field, bucket by bucket...insufficient and temporary relief at best. I'm alone except for the screaming pigs. I try to find someone in charge, but the Vietnamese I encounter act kerry Heubeck

as though I'm speaking Swahili. I know my Vietnamese is bad, but I've usually been able to get my point across before.

The trucks that deposited us here over six hours earlier have long since deserted...and I'm feeling very much by myself. The flight has been canceled three times already, but the Colonel assured us he'd have the plane this morning. So much for friends of friends. It's beginning to appear that no one wants a planeload of pig shit on his hands, and no one wants to fly into the Kontum airfield, a place with a deservedly poor reputation for air traffic. Calling in the favor with the Vietnamese Air Force Colonel may not have been the best idea after all.

By late afternoon the heat reflecting off the concrete is even getting to me, but finally some cargo handlers are helping get the heavy crates into the belly of a C-123. The Vietnamese pilot is telling me he's running out of time and he's not about to have his plane sitting on the ground in Kontum, with NVA guns looking down on it from the closely encircling mountains...We'll be "combat unloading" and he's getting his ass out ASAP...did I know the fighting had moved closer to Kontum last night? "What would anyone want to take pigs into Kontum for now anyway? Plan on selling pork to the NVA? Load up."

We descended rapidly in a tightly spiraling circle. I could see the small town below me, the old Catholic church and bishop's compound, as well as the bombed out ruins surrounding the deserted airfield. We bumped twice.

The huge tailgate of a back door is already lowering; engines have slammed into reverse; the loadmaster is unhooking tie-down straps. Jesus...They're starting to shove the crates down the rollered floor and we're still hauling up the runway! The pilot was serious... crates begin dropping from the still moving aircraft—if the pigs don't die from the heat of this afternoon I'll have to shoot them for all the broken legs!

And suddenly there I was standing with the last crate, watching the lumbering plane climb into the sky. At the end of the runway lay the rusted and twisted carcass of another C-123, caught in an earlier affair, the likes of which this pilot had obviously not wished to encounter. The sun had just hidden itself behind the rounded mountains to the west and cumulus and cirrus clouds were turning a dozen different hues of mauve. I felt the sudden and tangible peacefulness of the twilight.

> *I moved here to the mountain with my swine,*
> *Never, now, do I go down to town*
> *unless I am sent for...*

Bill had already arrived on his bike; John and Harry, a few moments later, one in the old van-turned-ambulance, the other in something resembling parts of various trucks pieced together to form one noisily moving vehicle. We began loading as darkness closed in. Occasional flares, drifting over the nearby hills on the other side of the airport, lighted our progress.

One could hardly be faulted for not recognizing Minh Quy as a hospital. Its piecemeal structure sat off the dirt road heading into "Indian Country," a couple of miles north of town. Montagnard families, mostly of the Bahnar Tribe, camped on the grounds surrounding the hospital buildings, waiting for various family members to be discharged. Cooking fires dotted the dirt yards, and dark-skinned kids played with a variety of evolutionary misfit dogs. Old men, dressed in loin-cloths or tattered hand-me-downs from missionary boxes, leaned against spindly trees smoking black tobacco in hand-made pipes while women, many wearing only long black skirts, tended sooted pots over low fires, or sat talking as they wove intricate designs onto blankets unfolding from their hip-looms, nursing young children in the process.

On entering the wards, the unaccustomed eye saw only chaos. Swarms of native people passed in every direction; a rare white face appeared every now and then; rusted army bed frames, jammed together, lined the stained and peeling walls; only woven-fiber mats covered the oxidized springs of the beds. Two, and sometimes three, small brown patients occupied each cot. IV bottles dripped as bowls of rice were passed about. Moaning could be heard from one quarter; laughter and crying from others. Difficulty arose in mentally trying to separate ambulatory patients, families, friends, and staff. A few of the dark women wore simple gray and white habits of the local religious order. There was a strange and unique bonding that could be felt among everyone present, built up from the hospital's fourteen-year history of serving this ethnic minority.

Minh Quy Hospital was founded by an American, Dr. Pat Smith, in 1960. Ya Ti ("Big Mother"), as she came to be called, was a legend in her own time. She restricted the hospital to service for the Montagnard tribes-people in the area. It was a kind of reverse discrimination in which we all participated, the ethnic Vietnamese being served at the province hospital in town.

The hospital catered to some 200 in-patients and approximately 150 outpatients daily. The staff fluctuated as people came and went. The current handful of foreign doctors, medics, nurses, administrator, and a handyman came from diverse places in the Americas, New Zealand, Australia, India, the Philippines and Viet Nam. Local nurses were trained on the premises.

The present compound, donated by the village of Kon Monay Xolam, had been overrun by the Viet Cong in 1968, following the Tet offensive. The hospital was moved to temporary quarters in an abandoned schoolhouse in the town of Kontum. Because of the continued uncertainty of the military situation, the temporary quarters served as the hospital for four years. In April and May of 1972 there was considerable fighting in and around Kontum. The hospital was again badly damaged when it was occupied by government troops. Mine fields had been laid about its perimeter by three different armies. Shortly after the "Ceasefire" in January of 1973 Pat decided to move the hospital back to its original buildings. Repair and renovation were proceeding, but I could see the vast extent of the unfinished job remaining.

The pig project at Minh Quy had several objectives. The hospital had been relying heavily on donations and grants from outside agencies for its day-to-day expenses, much of which went to feed staff and patients (some basic medications came from the Ministry of Health). Supply of adequate protein had always been a problem since the onslaught of the war. We hoped that the swine program, if successful, would begin leading the hospital towards self-sufficiency. Likewise, we hoped to eventually reach out into the surrounding villages, increasing and upgrading the existing porcine population, a traditional livestock of the Montagnards. The process would take time. We hoped the continued hostilities, in spite of the "Ceasefire," would allow us that valuable element.

I had been hesitant to bring in purebred stock, recognizing their increased susceptibility to local diseases and parasites, yet their breeding offered certain advantages in rapid reproduction. For this reason only a small portion of our herd consisted of bred pureblooded stock. The larger part was made up of younger crossbreeds. Though originally of pureblooded imported ancestors, all of the animals had acclimated to this country's stressful environment over at least several generations. We would experiment with various methods of introducing the cross-breds as breeding animals in the villages, mating them with the smaller and hardier native stock. It was going to be interesting.

The animals were temporarily housed in an old abandoned pigsty in the Kontum Bishop's compound that he had kindly allowed us to use for a short while. In the meantime we began construction of our own barn on land belonging to the hospital. In spite of the fact that we built to basic local standards of such structures, such pride went into its construction by all the Montagnard workers it soon took on a beauty uncommon to pig barns. Because of the proximity of enemy forces and their constant threat to take over the town, not a few jokes were made regarding the structure. One morning I arrived at the nearly completed building to find a small sign hanging over its entryway: "North Vietnamese Officers' Quarters."

Before construction had even begun, we were faced with a major problem. The only land available for its site was on the back perimeter of the hospital grounds, a land long unused because of the minefields laid there during the fighting in years past. Several monsoon seasons had come and gone, and chest-high brush had grown up in the area. I was almost ready to scrub the project, or at least try to seek funds to purchase more suitable land—a delay we didn't need right now.

Here at the onset I grew really despondent, for the last thing I wanted was to risk the lives of the men working on the site, most emphatically including myself; and yet I knew not where or how we could obtain other land. Then Harry and Bok Tuan, the leader of the Montagnard workers at the hospital, paid a visit.

The men had gotten together and decided that since it was their pig barn, they wanted it on the grounds of their hospital, and they would hand-clear the area of the minefield in which we were to build. It was their decision, they said, not mine to make. Bok Tuan concluded by saying that they had had some experience with unexploded ordnance on their own rice fields; they could handle it.

I was skeptical, and still felt the responsibility of such a decision; yet the enthusiasm with which Bok Tuan presented his case, in the end, swayed me. We proceeded slowly and carefully.

The Bahnar have a saying: "Carry a baby as you would a fragile egg." The grounds were cleared with no less concern. In the end, six bushel-baskets were collected, over-brimming with anti-tank mines, anti-personnel mines, grenades and M-79 rounds, "three-whisker" mines and "Bouncing Betties," and an assortment of hand-made, jury-rigged explosives. The collection was formidable. Even more amazing was the fact that no one had been injured in its gathering. There were a half dozen patients in the hospital now with injuries caused by accidents with such monstrosities as lay before me, and yet Bok Tuan and his men had survived. I was thankful, and simply hoped we had them all.

Another aspect of the program, which caused me not a little apprehension, was the problem of pig feed. Especially with the purebred stock, we needed a ration superior to the shaved banana stalks and rice hulls commonly fed to village swine. However, even if I had the funds, how could I justify feeding animals a diet superior to that enjoyed by the majority of the human population around me? It was a dilemma that often kept me awake at night. I sincerely felt that eventually we could cross breed and upgrade the existing village stock, producing more and better livestock that could not only survive, but also thrive, on the local fare. But were the means justified? I still don't know.

Our compromise and salvation lay in the millions of tons of surplus commodities that our country had shipped to the war zone for "humanitarian purposes" under Public Law 480. So much PL 480 surplus had been poured into this country that tons and tons lay rotting in warehouses, and eventually had to be declared "unfit for human consumption" and usually destroyed; all while people starved or children died of under- and mal-nutrition. This was but one of the many examples of gross wastes which accompanied the war. I began seeking inroads into acquiring some of these condemned commodities.

The task would have been easier in previous years when Americans, USAID to be exact, had control of these foods; however, with the exception of the commodities controlled by the Voluntary Agencies, the majority of PL 480 goods was now in the hands of the Vietnamese government. If our bureaucracy and red tape were bad, theirs was a nightmare.

With the help of some "informers" we discovered that a large supply of "Food for Peace" commodities had lain for three years in the government warehouses in Ban Me Thuot, a provincial capital in the highlands to the south of us. These foods had recently been inspected and declared damaged and unfit for consumption. Because of the existing black-market value of such goods we were still to have difficulties in obtaining them.

We finally found the warehouses and achieved entry. I stood below mountains of water-damaged and rodent-infested bags of bulgar wheat, corn-soy-powdered milk mixture called CSM, granola, and other blends and concoctions devised by state-side nutritionists in search of answers to the world hunger problems. I silently wondered on the nutritional value of rat manure.

For the fifth time in two days we returned to the Province Chief's office. The Colonel was unhappy. He wanted to know why he should sign off now for something he was told two years ago he didn't have.

I glanced at the newspaper lying on his desk. The headlines read, "NVA attacking Kontum." As if we didn't have enough problems. Fifty-six signatures later I was the proud possessor of a number of truckloads of damaged commodities. Trucking fares to Kontum had just doubled following the recent news, but I wasn't about to let the bird in the hand revert to the bush of the black-market.

Before leaving Ban Me Thout I had lunch with a gracious family of the Rhadé tribe, friends of the Montagnard with whom I was traveling. Little did I know I was dining with my future in-laws.

We later visited other friends of my Montagnard companion, and as we sat about the traditional earthenware jug of *pi-e,* sipping the rice wine through a straw of cane, I became a little uncomfortable with the secretive nature of our meeting. I was having a difficult time following the conversation, as it had begun in Rhadé. Gradually, as they became more comfortable in my presence, the men shifted to Vietnamese for my benefit. It had always been easier for me to understand the Vietnamese language spoken by the Montagnards than by the Vietnamese themselves, for it was a second language to each of us, and thus generally spoken more slowly and in a more basic nature.

This meeting was to be my introduction to FULRO, the underground Montagnard group that sought local autonomy for their people, and ended up fighting both sides of the more publicized war surrounding them. I progressively became aware that these good-natured men had just been involved in a scrape with several government soldiers caught pillaging one of the Montagnard villages.

I was straining so hard to understand, I missed what was just said. I asked the speaker to repeat himself . Yes, they had just killed three soldiers. They were now seeking a safe-haven from recrimination.

> *Must you have battle in your heart forever?*
> *The bloody toil of combat? Old contender,*
> *will you not yield to the immortal gods?*
> *That nightmare cannot die, being eternal*
> *evil itself—horror, and pain, and chaos;*
> *there is no fighting her, no power can fight her,*
> *all that avails is flight.*

I gazed upon the several men sitting around me on the dirt floor of the small hut...boys, really; each younger than myself. I thought back to other meetings in Iran, Colombia, Sudan, and Rapid City...other individuals ready to fight the oppression weighing on their people. Before me was one of the results of that fighting: Death and scared kids looking for a place to hide. Was there no end, no better way?

Following a restless night, I left Ban Me Thuot the next morning. Though a relatively short distance to Kontum, the trip took the full day and rides on a bus, a plane, another bus, a motorcycle, a truck, and finally a walk of several kilometers before reaching the hospital. It seemed a minimum of a day was required to get anywhere in this country. I spent the travel time in contemplation of the world I had brought myself to, and in wonder about the future.

The next day I walked back to the water source of the hospital with John and Harry. John was an ex-Sea-Bee, who returned to Viet Nam after he got out of the Navy to marry the fiancé he had left here. He was doing a tremendous job of supervising the reconstruction of the hospital. He possessed a truly self-less nature, and took his work at Minh Quy with a solemnity that belied his friendliness. He would later become administrator of the hospital, taking over when Bill left.

Harry was a Tennessee farm boy, born of German immigrant parents. A jack-of-all-trades, he had indebted himself to the hospital with his ability to fix or jury-rig anything placed in front of him, from the dilapidated van *cum* ambulance, to the sophisticated x-ray machine. His jovial personality transcended all language barriers. He presently was supervising the construction of the pig barn, working closely with Bok Tuan and his gang. Harry had likewise returned from the Army to marry his wartime sweetheart. He had showed up at the hospital one day and simply asked if he might be of assistance. He and Bill were our *cumshaw* experts, able to procure anything, legal or otherwise, on extremely short notice.

The three of us crossed a fallen log over the meandering stream, gingerly stepping around an ingenious Montagnard snare trap set to catch small mammals or amphibians. The trap was intricately fashioned—all to catch a mouse for dinner.

The field into which we navigated seemed barren; bomb and artillery craters perforated the landscape. And then I noticed the metal objects projecting from the sand. I looked around. Thousands of rounds of ammunition lay about us; everything from 175 mm projectiles to M-16 rounds. Hundreds of grenades. The shiny colors of M-79 rounds. I spied several white canisters to my right and walked carefully over to see what they were. Just as I saw the initials W.P. stenciled on their sides I remembered the particular care with which we had handled similar containers in the Navy. "Willy Peter"—White Phosphorus...The deadly fire that wouldn't go out.

All this had been jettisoned here by a retreating ARVN battalion during some of the more recent heavy fighting. One child now lay in the hospital with no legs, a tribute to the lethal power of a small brightly colored M-79 round he had picked up here for a plaything.

I lagged behind as the others began walking on. I stood alone and imagined the drone of B-52s approaching...the fear in the nearby villages as the uniquely terrifying sound drew nearer... crying children afraid of the unknown world invading theirs...the solid thump-thump-thump of distant bomb loads dropping upon ancestral lands...and the closer, thundering explosions of the 500 pounders, shaking the very earth with blinding flashes, and leveling destruction...and more crying, this time in the knowledge of death and loss. I could hear the cries and moans, whether of the now dead, or the once living, I know not; I was simply experiencing a barren piece of land...and more hapless spirits. I shuddered, caught my breath, and trotted to catch up with the others.

We later crossed the infamous Kontum Tank Trap, a ditch and its offspring of a mound, half circling the town to the north. Miles of deep trench dug by hand, each hamlet of each village responsible for so many meters of strenuous digging. All the stupidity of the war was dug into that "Trap"—within thirty minutes the North Vietnamese could create a crossing every NVA tank in Viet Nam could roar over at flank speed.

We returned to the house loaned to the expatriate hospital staff by the Bishop of Kontum. A Belgian doctor, a woman, had just arrived with a twelve-year-old Bahnar child. The boy looked to be six or seven. The boy's parents had been killed when their village was bombed two years before. The child was an epileptic, and mentally impaired, whether from previous injuries or some congenital defect I did not know. He was crazy like a fox. He spoke Bahnar, Jarai, Vietnamese, and GI English. He knew exactly what was going on. He easily talked me out of my one flannel shirt.

The doctor was bringing the boy back to his home area, after having been away these two years, hoping to find relatives or friends who could give him a family. Traditionally there were no homeless in the Montagnard societies; the war was changing that, but I had little doubt that the woman and child would be successful.

I excused myself, and in the growing darkness, withdrew down the outside corridor to my bare room and cot. The day had stirred my mind, and I wanted to be alone.

I tossed back the dark mosquito net and lay upon the faded and scratchy army blanket, my hands behind my head. Why were any of us here? Were we really alleviating pain, or simply giving an excuse for others to cause more? What *was* Karma?

And then I realized, I cannot be here for them. Too much ego is wrapped up in altruism. I must admit to being here for myself. In spite of our great rhetoric, the overall effect may very well be nil, or even worse, to these people. I will do what I can, perhaps I will earn another chance for myself.

Those were the words in my head...I hardly could know their meaning. But those words took me back to an old woman, a seeress, speaking of my life..."It's almost as though you were given a second chance..."

I got up from the cot and went outside to sit in the small courtyard of the building. As my eyes adjusted to the semi-darkness, a familiar chattering attracted my attention.

I had been told of the gibbon that Marcelle, the French/Bahnar cook, had befriended, and who had his own house in the center of the courtyard, but I had forgotten his existence with the many happenings of the last several days. There on the roof of his house, idly trailing a secretly acquired spoon back and forth across the corrugations of the metal roof of his house, sat my old friend Monkey. Looking up at the bright starry night, he then turned towards me, with what I had to think was a smile.

It had been a while since our last meeting, and I was elated to now be living in the same home with him. I felt a rising lightness coming into my head. My cares would be worked out as long as I gave myself up to the Yin-Yang working of the Universe. Monkey spoke and I heard the words of Lao Tzu, echoing over two thousand years of man's folly:

"Acting without design, occupying oneself without making a business of it, finding the great in what is small and the many in the few, repaying injury with kindness, effecting difficult things while they are easy, and managing great things in their beginnings: this is the way of the Tao."

***

Minh Quy quickly became home to me. The staff was an interesting and good group of people. We each had our quirks, but the close living and working conditions produced few and only relatively minor squabbles, much less than might be expected from such a group and situation.

I made a particularly close friendship with Bill, the lanky crew-cut redhead who took care of the administrative duties of the hospital. This entailed everything from managing finances to buying the just-baked morning bread before sun-up, obtaining black-market gas to keep the hospital generators going when no fuel was supposed to be available, straightening out personnel hassles, talking the Ministry of Health into increasing their monthly allotment of antibiotics, transporting patients to specialty clinics in Saigon, and a thousand other items that no one else wanted or had time to do.

Bill took the innumerable interruptions to his already hectic schedule in stride and rarely became flustered. I admired his linguistic abilities: his command of the difficult and tonal Vietnamese language seemed flawless; he rattled it off as quickly as he did with English, French, or Spanish.

The secret to Bill's unflagging energy appeared to dwell in a never-empty glass of "Dago-Red," a particularly addictive concoction consisting of an exceptionally cheap local red wine, half a bottle of Biere Larue, and a healthy squeeze of fresh lime. The glass was rarely far from hand. I've never seen Bill in the least bit intoxicated; it was simply a tonic that helped the day go by a little more smoothly.

I soon got into the habit, at day's end, of stopping by Bill's room and office for a brief discussion of world philosophy or the day's happenings over a cooling duplicate of his energizer. He rarely commented on the accompanying perfume of swine excrement that I brought with me.

By now I had lived in Kontum for close to a month, and the small-town atmosphere, with all its rumors and gossip and friendly neighbors, aided the feeling of quickly becoming a part of the local life—the women in the open-air market politely covered their mouths and laughed with their sparkling eyes as I amateurly bargained for a pair of local underwear; one of the two Indian merchants, with a not-so-innocent smile, stepped from his stall offering tea and a long spiel on why I should purchase at least fifty meters of his finest silk, knowing all along that yesterday and the day before we had already discussed my lack of appreciation for the finer things in life; the small cafe where several of us might stop at the end of the day to enjoy their fresh yogurt over shaved ice and the conversation of the local philosopher; the owner of the nearby sawmill who daily complained of the war-generated shrapnel embedded in the local hardwood logs that continually tore up his saw blades; the elderly couple who carried heavily laden water pails on bouncing shoulder poles to their immaculate green garden on the deserted land of the airport perimeter, surrounded by the ghosts of bombed-out homes, who seemed to enjoy the respite of stopping for a few minutes to chat on the weather and latest rumors of VC attacks; little Yanh, the gate-keeper's son who accompanied me everywhere, continually pulling up his falling shorts, rarely speaking, but never-the-less silently offering his approval or disapproval on any subject at hand;

the silent Buddhist graveyard across from the old French Catholic Church; the bicycle rides along the glistening fields of new rice and the Bahnar villages with their stilted houses, followed by running children shouting, "*Ong My, Ong My...*"; all this was having its effect, and I found myself slowing down...to listen, watch, converse.

I sat at the little desk in my room, the shutters open to the cooling night air, penning a few lines into my journal under the soft yellow light of a slowly dripping candle. Not far from the window a Boy Scout jamboree sent sounds of gaiety, laughter, and song into the room with the breezes. The consistent sounds of whistling and thumping artillery barrages into the nearby mountains lent a sound of unreality and insanity to song and night.

I thought on the words of the diplomats in Paris who had signed the documents declaring the Ceasefire. During my last stay in Saigon I had run into Moses, who had worked with me in the Navy Pigs and Chickens program. He now was a "civilian" working with the Vietnamese Navy, retrieving ammo from American ships off Yankee Station, all apparently in defiance of the new peace accords. Even Moses was becoming fed up with the corruption in the high command.

The military situation seemed to be closing in. Dak Pek, not too far to the north, had been overrun; Dak To, just up the road, was almost continuously under rocket attack.

The previous night the Catholics of Kontum had organized a procession of candles and the Virgin, her image carried upon a small raft floating above their shoulders, circling the hospital in flickering light, singing and praying for the security of the hospital, Kontum, and their families.

Some Bahnar men had recently been abducted from their village, and the rumor had it that they would be used for the upcoming prisoner exchange mandated recently in Paris. It mattered little which side did the abducting.

I remembered the Montagnard fable of the Barking Deer, a small defenseless animal caught between the talons of the eagle and the claws of the tiger, each trying to save it. The echoing whistles and thuds of out-going continued to rattle the windowpanes throughout the night.

***

The headlines of the Saigon paper had read, "30 CHILDREN KILLED AS VIET CONG ROCKETS TEAR INTO DELTA SCHOOLHOUSE." I pedaled on down the potholed road towards the hospital, thinking how fortunate we were that the artillery sounds that had become so constant were always out-going. And then I saw the new gun emplacements that had been effected earlier that morning.

Three monster 175 mm self-propelled cannons had been placed directly alongside the hospital. They were now firing round after round over the buildings and into the verdant mountainsides overlooking the tin roofs painted with faded and peeling red crosses.

Again, the distant flashes, puffs of smoke, and moments later the not-so-far-away thumping sounds. How much artillery could a group of soldiers take before they started firing back at the big guns behind the hospital that were responsible for such deadly harassment? And then what would the headlines read?

I leaned the bike against a tree and headed towards an obviously upset crowd gathered on Minh Quy's open portico. Wondering about the commotion, I worked my way into the center of milling villagers.

A corpse lay at my feet. Covered to his shoulders with a sheet, I readily recognized the still face of the young Montagnard nurse. He had been one of few words and quiet smiles. Suicide, a new malady to this ancient race; and no one seemed to know why.

Women, some holding infants to their breasts, knelt about the body, crying. Others rocked back and forth on their knees, chanting laments as tears drifted unencumbered down streaked brown cheeks. Echoes of the powerful eruptions of the nearby guns irreverently bounced off the hospital's walls, as projectiles whined overhead.

I looked closer at the face below me. Something appeared as a bead of sweat on the almost smiling upper lip. I really wasn't sure he was dead...but I knew he was.

> *Of mortal creatures, all that breathe and move,*
> *earth bears none frailer than mankind.*

Another sound took over from the beating of the guns, a new staccato upon the tin roof. The gray massed harbingers of the monsoons had been accumulating these last several days over the same mountains now being shelled. I wondered if I was the only one seeing such obvious signs of the spirits' displeasure.

The oppressive humidity had given way with a sudden breeze to the cooling drops that now began disappearing into the dust. Tiny rivulets began coursing down and off the corrugated tin overhead.

Children ran out from under cover of the eves, nakedly splashing in the new puddles, already forgetting the death behind them. Supple adolescent girls stood with raised faces below gushing rainspouts, washing their hair with shampoos of tamarind and mirth. Water dripped from blinking eyelashes and raised chins, streaking slim necks, coursing between young uplifted breasts, soaking dark skirts clinging to youthful thighs. Innocence laughed with sparkling eyes and pattering rain. New life had followed death, and the wetness soaked into the parched earth.

***

As I wedged into the cramped seat of the bus, diesel fumes rose from its mufflerless undercarriage, directly into crowded coughing faces of even more would-be passengers. Everyone finally squeezed aboard, replete with accompanying baggage of boxes, bags, baskets, bundles of vegetables, chickens, and one screaming pig.

I conversed with the polite and curious elderly couple sharing the seat, their luggage spread over our knees; and then lapsed into a reverie for the remainder of the several-hour ride from the high plateau to the coastal city of Qui Nhon. We began the drop over An Khe Pass, going by several twisted bodies of armored personnel carriers lying up-ended or on their sides; the new rust already blending with the camouflaged green of their ruptured metal hides.

Friends had notified me of more damaged PL 480 commodities that were supposed to be destroyed soon in this seaside town. The local authorities were pleasant and understanding, but told me it would still take at least another day to complete the paperwork and signatures. I decided to walk the beach, but access to this attractive coastline was hampered by the hundreds of refugee shanties lining the shore. The rather primitive tidal sewage system of these quickly raised huts left odiferous reminders to the squalid conditions above the low-tide flats. I changed my mind and climbed the eroded embankment to find an inexpensive restaurant where the smells might be more appetizing.

The Hoa Lan Restaurant occupied the street corner. The few round and scratched Formica tables within its shadowed interior looked out through its open front onto the varied street-side activities. A pleasant and robust young woman with the hands and accent of the countryside came to the table and described the limited menu. Fresh fish seemed enticing after the limited diet at the hospital.

As I sat on the low stool, sipping the warm sudsy beer, a middle-aged woman approached. Her language resonated with the bastardized GI English of an era gone these last couple of years. She appeared on hard times, and I too quickly labeled her as a has-been "Mamasan." She offered her deal quickly, with a half-hearted manner that knew defeat before she had begun. Well, she had a sister and a girlfriend. She was walking away as the words trailed in the litter of the street. The encounter was depressing, and I finished the Beer "33" with one long swallow.

An older man, lanky to the point of emaciation, walked up to the table with a sprightly gait and a lively smile of brown teeth. He carried a battered suitcase with a sign attached. His easily understood hand language rapidly told of his deaf and mute condition. He turned the side of the suitcase towards me, the word "Masseur" was crudely painted on the sign. He offered a sample of his services, but I tried to politely decline. I felt ungiving, and to sooth my conscience,

149

held out a cigarette. He accepted, and in his way asked if he might sit down. Not until then did I notice the following of street kids who were edging closer. They giggled behind cupped and dirty hands. I looked at the old man as he smiled at the children. They came closer and sat around his feet looking up into his wise and kind face with the expectancy of youth. Other youngsters joined the growing circle. The man shrugged, and with a knowing smile, raised both hands as if a signal.

> *The crier came, leading that man of song*
> *whom the Muse cherished; by her gift he knew*
> *the foods of life, and evil...*
> *the gods deal out gifts, this one or any—*
> *birth, brains, or speech—to every man alike.*

The silence was immediate. Open mouths and staring eyes centered upon the aging Othello on his impromptu stage. His soundless story began as he raised himself from the stool, his hands twirling in the air. His face became a thousand masks; and I, as the other children around us, sat transfixed, awed by the master mime before me.

His story was a hilarious parody of a fat nine-foot American descending in his helicopter to settle upon the land of Viet Nam for the first time. For the next half-hour I had difficulty breathing for laughing so hard.

All too soon his parable was concluded. As I wiped the tears of merriment from my face, he turned and bowed to me, and then to the children...and he was gone.

Van, the waitress and cook, had been standing behind us, quietly enjoying the show. She now placed my cooling meal before me, and asked if I might wish anything else...perhaps another beer.

> *"You're a wanderer too.*
> *You must eat something, drink some wine, and tell me*
> *where you are from and the hard times you've seen."*

I noticed that I was still the only customer in the Hoa Lan. I asked her if she would have a cold drink and join me while I ate, as long as no other diners showed up. She seemed genuinely pleased at the invitation and quickly returned with the drinks, sitting across the table from me. She laughed about the mime, and it seemed a rare laugh, as if she had not had occasion for such an emotion in a long while.

She turned quiet, and the conversation, such as it was, drifted into silence a number of times. She was patient with my struggling Vietnamese; she occasionally interjected Americanisms into her few sentences. Though she was polite and smiled, it was a sad smile, and I couldn't rid myself of the feeling that a great hurt lay beneath her kind exterior.

Darkness had emptied the street before us, and when I glanced at the clock on the wall I realized the hour of curfew had long passed. No other customers had entered. I asked Van if she knew a cheap place in the vicinity where I might overnight. Her answer took me by surprise. She had a small place, and I would be welcomed there. In fact I would do her an honor if I would come, for there was something she wished to show me.

I was as much puzzled as surprised by Van's invitation. She had neither the appearance nor demeanor of a prostitute, and yet such a proposal would hardly be viewed as proper conduct in a traditional Oriental culture. At any rate, there seemed little in the way of alternatives—and besides, I was curious.

We pulled the large metal accordion doors across the face of the darkened restaurant, and Van latched the giant antique lock in place. We walked the empty streets in silence and soon turned into an obscure alley; through doors, and ultimately into a diminutive cubicle with a small double bed, cupboard, and dresser. Several photographs stood framed atop the chest of drawers; otherwise the room was bare.

Her voice asked me to sit. There was only the bed. She had been facing away from me, and when she turned her eyes were red, and moisture teared her cheeks. She handed me the photos from the dresser.

A military funeral was taking place somewhere in Middle America. It must have been cold, for collars of overcoats were drawn up over necks and mouths, and hats were pulled low. Scarves were sometimes evident, and heavy clothing was blowing. Trees were bare of leaves. A grayness, more than from just clouds, had enfolded the scene. A flag-draped casket centered the picture. I could just make out part of a mound of dirt beneath the yellow striped canopy. An Army honor guard stood at attention on either side of the coffin...

A boy-man with closely cropped hair and closely cropped smile stared at the camera, trying not to show too much pride in the new dress uniform, the solitary National Service Ribbon, the Marksmanship Medal pinned to his chest. Colors of the American flag stood to the left rear, slightly out of focus. The dark blue background clashed with the uniform's color. His eyes were young and bright, highlights reflecting from the double strobes...

Two children, probably about three- and four-years-old, stood in mid-distance holding hands. Their Amerasian features distinguished them from the other children playing in the background at the Saigon Zoo. Their Western clothing was new and brightly colored, red and blue plaids, more yellow stripes. Their smiles were being dictated by the proud parent, obviously standing to the right of the photographer...

I looked up. A face of quiet pain stared at the last photograph I held in my hand. Van had been quiet during the long minutes I had spent looking at the pictures. She wiped her eyes and spoke.

During the last month an American nun had finally convinced her to give up her children for adoption. They would go to the States, the land of the free, and have a much better life than that which she could provide here. After all, their father was dead.

The children had been picked up the day before. The last words she had heard: "Mommy, aren't you coming to Saigon with us?"

***

Saigon was its usual caldron of heat, humidity, and grime, blaring horns and mufflerless Hondas. Nevertheless, after a month or so in the Highlands, I usually looked forward to a few days of change, splurging on good meals, enjoying hot showers, sometimes a few too many drinks, and visits with friends. Ostensibly, the trip was for picking up funds and supplies for the project and running errands for the hospital.

I was particularly looking forward to this trip, for my old traveling buddy Jeff was arriving for a visit. His original plan had been to take the summer vacation from his teaching position and travel parts of Asia. He was hesitant about visiting Viet Nam, but we were close and hadn't seen each other in over a year and a half. I convinced him that tourists came into the country every day—there were thousands of soldiers, though little publicized, who had spent their year of war without ever hearing a shot fired. Perfectly safe, not to worry, I said. Jeff shared my interest in different and "primitive" cultures; and in the end it was not so difficult to prevail upon him to come the extra mile.

The government flight on which we had hitched a ride from Saigon was late arriving in Pleiku, and by the time the jitney had dropped us on the quiet street of Kontum, darkness had already settled into the valley. The thumping of the howitzers was far enough away that I had ignored them; to Jeff's unaccustomed ears they were obtrusive. I reassured him.

We talked into the night, catching up over a bottle of black market bourbon. Phyllis, one of the nurses, told us of a few rockets that had hit the village of Paradi, close by, and others that had actually landed in the outskirts of Kontum the day before. She seemed to think they were simply isolated incidents, geared to perturb that day's local elections.

We walked across the grounds of the hospital the following morning. Camping Montagnard families circled pots of rice, others of wild greens, boiling over open fires. Friends called out greetings and waved.

Three particularly cheerful members of Bok Tuan's crew were repairing a water line between the two main wards, and I took Jeff over to introduce him. The air was crisp and clean, the sky clear, and the morning promised a beautiful break in the monsoon weather. We talked with the workers and joked over the nearly completed pig barn, and then Jeff and I headed in its direction.

I doubt that sixty seconds had elapsed since we had turned from the three men digging the trench. The explosion ripped at our eardrums and the concussion forcefully hit our backs. A moment passed when I had no idea what had happened. We turned in unison to the sight behind us.

Black smoke was still rising from the chaos between the two damaged buildings. One wall of the eastward had been blown in, and we could hear patients screaming in the smoke. Shattered timbers and broken block and twisted metal braces dangled from hidden, swaying threads. A smoldering hole now obliterated the once neatly dug ditch. Three bodies lay buckled and bloodied nearby; heart-rending moans seeped from the mouth of one, the others were silent.

Hysteria passed through the compound as a nightmare tornado. Just as I reached one of the bodies I heard the whistling of the next rocket. The second explosion heightened the screaming of women and crying children.

I thought of the big guns on the other side of the hospital fence line, the obvious target of the in-coming projectiles. Several days before, a few of the staff had tried to talk the soldiers into moving the artillery, but there was always a higher command, and in the end they gave up. Here around us lay evidence of the arrogant stupidity of war. At no other time had I ever so fervently hoped, one might even say prayed, for improved accuracy of enemy artillery.

A third round exploded near the hospital but did no damage. Other rounds continued their satanic whistling overhead. The doctors decided to evacuate the hospital. Ambulatory patients and families quickly gathered their few possessions and hurriedly began the long walk up the dirt road towards town.

Emergency surgery still occupied the operating room. Other doctors, nurses and aides were treating the wounded. The 175 mm cannons began answering the rockets, and the increased sounds of war were not easy to bear.

I think all of us were frightened, but fear rode unpronounced the rest of that day, with the exception of the small children who had not previously known this face of war. We were kept busy lifting patients, moving necessary equipment, speeding from Minh Quy to the Provincial Hospital and back. The in-coming continued, sometimes hitting close to the road.

Compresses to stop the spurting blood, probes to find the damaging shrapnel, IVs to replace vital fluids, stitches to sew rips in blackened flesh, splints to hold shattered bones—slipping on the blood in the corridor, holding dripping bottles of serum, lactose, saline, holding a patient down while a doctor probed a deep and painful wound, holding a head up to a glass of water.

Two bodies lay on the cool tiles of the outside corridor; enshrouding green sheets slowly spotting with growing circles of dark crimson. Women knelt in moaning bereavement. Another rocket whined overhead. Dogs barked, several howled. Ya Vincent, friend of children and all animals, refused to leave until everyone else, including the dogs, were safely away. Several other nuns remained with her, some stoic, some hysterical, all senselessly brave.

After the last of the patients had been moved Jeff and I helped in minor ways with the makeshift operation on the one survivor of the three workmen. Prognosis wasn't good. His wife stood crying just outside the door, holding a child's leaning head to her side. Hours passed quickly, and as the sun dropped to the mountains the rockets ceased, the guns slowed, as in respect to a descending god. Bill, Jeff and I stood near the torn earth of the first explosion. The skies were quiet. A kind of low-level alpine glow turned the smoothly rounded mountainsides a warm vermillion. Smoke rising from cooking fires in nearby Montagnard villages spoke of twilight's peace and a twilight's lament.

By that evening we all agreed that the VC had probably sharpened their aim sufficiently that Minh Quy was safer than our present location, and, exhausted as everyone was, the evacuation reversed itself, in a much more orderly fashion. By midnight patients and staff were back to their accustomed environment, tarps hanging over the rent walls.

One of the Montagnard girls who had helped throughout the day approached us, and silently placed a slim brass bracelet over Jeff's wrist—appreciation for a stranger's help. The bracelet, a part of the hill-people's tradition, had most likely been forged from a spent artillery shell. Jeff turned to me with something of a sardonic smile, "Not to worry, huh?"

***

I sat in the courtyard of our stark living-quarters, my back resting against a wooden pillar, drawing circles in the dirt with my bare toes. Monkey sat nearby, obsessed with the colors of a child's comic book, tearing page by page from its spine after perusing its contents. In spite of several hours of operating, the third casualty of the rocketing had succumbed two days ago. Three simple graves lay behind the hospital, fresh dirt mounded over the shallow interments.

My mind played back the scenes of those harrowing hours. I had gained respect for all these people. Minor squabbles paled as I realized the dedication and selflessness each exhibited during that trying time. The word "hero" became redefined for me as I realized it was not so much how one handled the heights when one was in full control, such as with a great athlete, but what one did when control was lost. Masks and facades were shed, or rather torn from egos, and true people emerged with all their foibles and strengths, naked to the world's sight.

That day had also torn from me one of my secret dreams. For years I had aspired to the great photo-journalistic tradition demonstrated by people like W. Eugene Smith. That great photographs had the power to move, beyond words, often answered the controversy over the necessary intrusion of the photographer in times of pain.

I realized now that I was unable to invade the sacred privacy of individuals in torment. I had carried a camera with me on that morning of horrible surprise. I had dropped it at the time of the first explosion, and had not thought to pick it up until the next morning. I was coming to understand, indeed to *feel,* the sentiments of those cultures and individuals who saw the camera as an invasion of their spirits, a thief of the most sacred possession of a person.

The responsibility inherent in the use of that tool was too seldom appreciated. There is a certain dignity of people that should not be infringed upon, unless invited. And if pain can be alleviated, or even soothed, that seemed a higher priority.

I'm glad there are others who feel differently than I, for the world needs them as a reminder to the collective conscience. Unfortunately, there are few photographers who have the compassion, the ultimately painful compassion, to lay witness to such pain and horror, without either entering into the scene, or adding to the pain with their own insensitivity.

***

Not long after the rocket attack, the mood at Minh Quy shifted perceptively. Pat, the founder of the hospital, had returned from over a year in the States with her two adopted Montagnard boys. The pig barn had been completed and was ready for occupancy. These happenings were sufficient cause for celebration and a blessing by the spirits.

Tribesmen and their families, some having walked several days to attend the upcoming festivities, began arriving at the hospital, carrying large terra cotta jars. A tangible feeling of gaiety and new life brought quicker smiles to faces, giggles from children and adults alike.

Greenery festooned the corridors and entranceway to Minh Quy. Rice wine jars had been lined up between trees. A pig had been sacrificed to the spirits of the land upon which we had built, and the remaining carcass was democratically butchered to provide for the several hundred participants expected. Tables and mats placed in front of the buildings were rapidly becoming inundated with bananas, grapefruit, breadfruit, star fruit, dragon fruit, and a dozen other varieties whose names I did not know.

On the morning of the ceremonies I was presented with an intricately woven loincloth and shirt of Bahnar design. I hesitated in laying my white buttocks bare, but the spirit of the occasion mandated the change. Not a few guffaws ensued, from both foreign staff and Montagnards alike; the latter being a bit more polite in their comments.

It was a day of festivities, speeches, native dances, quantities of food and too much homemade rice wine. The war and its misery were forgotten for the while.

> *But now it entered Helen's mind*
> *to drop into the wine that they were drinking*
> *an anodyne, mild magic of forgetfulness.*
> *Whoever drank this mixture in the wine bowl*
> *would be incapable of tears that day—*

The pleasures were real, and I remembered the words of Aldous Huxley: "If ever I want to make merry in public I go where merrymaking is occasional and the merriment, therefore, of genuine quality; I go where feasts come rarely." I think he would have enjoyed this day.

We finished the last hours of the night in the hospital kitchen, the domain of Ya Vincent, the jolly Montagnard nun who had taken a western name and this western greenhorn under her wing...along with every other child who stepped foot on the place, and every bird and animal she could find. Ya Vincent had become my special friend; I always could find solace, or answers, or a quick laugh and ever-present smile on this happy woman perspiring over the fires and kettles of Minh Quy.

The girls were making risqué jokes aimed at Jeff and myself, and Ya Vincent could hardly contain her laughter long enough to translate the more difficult lines. We sipped rice wine from scavenged IV bottles, laughing about having the only pig barn with its own minefield. On another day that laughter would come back to haunt me.

***

Jeff had left for other parts, with his own stories to tell. John (the ex-Sea Bee who had helped so much with reconstruction of the hospital) and I managed to move all of the pigs the several miles to their new home, making use of the ambulance/van and pickup—the two would never smell the same again. Rain of the season had hampered the move and it was dark, wet and cold when we shoved the last shrieking animals into the overloaded van for the final run. We were bushed, and thinking of a warm meal, cold beer, and dry clothes, when John made the comment that he sure as glad we hadn't had a flat tire all day. We were about a half-mile from the barn; the cold rain was coming down particularly hard in the darkness and I couldn't see well enough to negotiate around the flooded potholes. We hit one deep crater especially hard when the blowout occurred. We were rarely guilty of such hubris after that.

***

The military situation around Kontum had hardly abated. Mam Buk was reportedly taking over a thousand rounds a day and seemed certain to fall. Dak Pek had been overrun. Dak To was taking rockets daily. The out-going from the huge guns still close to the hospital increased noticeably, and their targets were sufficiently close that we could watch the explosions on the hillsides. Aerial bombing began some six kilometers from the hospital. Silence was becoming an unknown entity. The local Province Representative of the American Consulate stated that there were from 75,000 to 100,000 NVA or VC troops in the province. He added that there were probably three regiments in the hills right outside town. Evidence seemed to dictate that when the big push came, Kontum was the obvious first target.

The hospital was going through a certain period of instability itself. Pradhan, the idealistic doctor from India, was returning to his homeland. Bob, an ex-medic, was returning to the States for his final year of medical school. Harry and his wife were gone. We gained, to the chagrin of many, a resident anthropologist who seemed at times as out of touch with reality as the recently arrived young doctor who could sometimes be seen chasing the geese around the buildings with his stethoscope swinging wildly about his neck. Bill had departed with his Vietnamese family, and the administrative duties of the hospital fell upon the shoulders of John, who carried a full load already.

The thirteenth of July saw more rockets falling in the vicinity of Minh Quy. Fortunately, ARVN had moved their cannons across the road, removing at least a small amount of danger from the hospital. I straddled my bike on the crest of the hill, watching twenty-some rounds explode harmlessly along the side of the road ahead of me, or in the adjacent rice fields, only meters from the Bahnar village of Kon Monay Xolam; itself alongside Minh Quy. This was a luckier day.

I was later approached by a young Montagnard girl, crying, "My family has nothing to eat, please give me just a little corn." How many times could I say, "It doesn't belong to me." I can't say, "If I gave it to you I'd have to hand it out to everyone." I thought of the young conscientious worker I had fired for selling feed on the black market. I was sitting on thirty-five tons of CSM. She saw the refusal in my eyes, and turned away. I had never felt so wrong in all my life.

All I would have had to do, to maintain the dignity of us both, would have been to offer payment in kind for one of the many small and trivial jobs left undone. I resolved myself to this solution in the future, but cried inside for the travesty I had just committed. No wonder these people could not understand the strange foreigners; the indigenous communal ways were so much more humane. What great temptations and barriers we placed before them.

*All beggars come from Zeus, What we can give
is slight but well meant—all we dare.*

I found myself dropping into a long spell of depression. The world seemed to be closing in; I began questioning the very values that had placed all of us here. Were we accomplishing good, or merely creating dependencies that would cause greater pain once we were gone? And there seemed no doubt that sooner or later we would be gone.

The time came to return to the Saigon office to take care of accounting matters, and to pick up some medical supplies for the hospital. On arrival, the staff there seemed as depressed as I. News had just arrived that Dat, the young driver and messenger for CARE was dead. He had once confided in me how he had abhorred the idea of going into the army. His father had died years before, and so his mother had helped him get forged legal papers saying he was the only support she and his siblings had. It wasn't far from the truth.

Several days before I arrived he had been arrested. This morning, before any trial could take place, his mother received a message from a prison official that Dat, an exceptionally healthy young man, had died from an unknown illness. The family was unable to reclaim the body. No one knew what, if anything, could be done.

I took care of business as soon as I could. Saigon had little to offer in alleviating my gloom.

The seaside restaurant in Nha Trang was a little more opulent than what I was used to, but the CARE director had recommended the food and, since I was in this city on an errand for him before returning to Minh Quy, I thought I might as well give it a try. I hadn't eaten all day on the trip from Saigon and supposed myself hungry. Perhaps a good meal would pick up my spirits; the depression of the last week or so had really gotten me down. The waiter brought the bountifully served plate; I looked at it, and felt nauseous. I paid my bill and went back to the hotel room, wishing for the morrow's trip to be over.

161

On return to the hospital I mentioned my depression and continued loss of appetite to one of the doctors. He looked at my eyes, then asked if I had noticed the color of my urine lately. It had been quite dark the last day or so. A quick blood test diagnosed Hepatitis "A," The young doctor mentioned that depression was a characteristic symptom of the disease. It was nice to know I wasn't going crazy, but the fact alone did not alleviate the gloom. I thought of the grime on the walls of the Hoa Lan Restaurant in Qui Nhon several weeks past, the smell of sewage along the beach.

That I had an excuse to lie all day under the faded army blanket, and do absolutely nothing, day in and day out, was the one bright spot of the affair, for I had little desire to do anything. I tired quickly, even of the many and various paperbacks in the staff library. I could sometimes hear Monkey outside the window, rattling pans, berating someone advancing into his territory uninvited, or simply chattering to himself. Occasionally I would notice the heavy sounds of the big guns, but I paid them little attention. Though I wanted to do nothing, I began feeling guilty of simply lying there while the others were busy.

A Montagnard and his wife had been helping me with the animals, and I felt content that they could handle the daily chores, but several sows were close to farrowing and I felt the need to be present as that time approached. It was to be the first production of our herd, and I didn't want any mistakes.

The message was brief: eight piglets had been born, but died soon after delivery. I wondered what else could go wrong. I had the feeling that, had I been there, I could have averted the deaths. This, our first litter, was to be a symbol; maybe it was.

I dropped my feet to the floor and sat up. I stayed there until the dizziness disappeared, resting my head in my hands. Finally I was able to get into the cut-offs that had been hanging on the back of the chair, and slipped into a pair of sandals. Because of my lassitude we had lost the first born of the project.

However slow my movement, the activity was rejuvenating. Fresh air and sunshine, and even the smell of pig manure, got the juices flowing again. Friendly faces forced me to smile; smiling forced away the depression. As the days drew on, we had several more litters in fairly quick succession, all robust and healthy. The world was again a happy place in which to be.

It was a Sunday morning in the first days of September. Most of us were lingering over a second or third cup of rich highland coffee, unhurried in taking on our abbreviated chores of the day. An explosion, differing from the sounds of outgoing, came from the direction of the hospital and barn.

A group of the Bahnar staff had gathered at the entrance to the barn, and I hurried to the gathering. In the center of the small crowd stood a Vietnamese boy in his teens. Blood covered his face, white tee-shirt, and army pants. His speech was at first incoherent, as he gesticulated wildly. Slowly we pieced together his story.

A heavy battle was being fought for the last several days near Dak To, just to the north of us. ARVN was apparently taking a substantial beating. Three young soldiers decided they had had enough and headed south through the hills, removing the tops of their uniforms, hoping to avoid quick recognition should they be seen.

They had stayed away from the road, avoiding other troops. Seeing the barn and hospital ahead they hurried through the brush, thinking they might find a hot meal and perhaps a safe haven from which they could contact their families. Unfortunately, they had rushed directly through the remnants of the old minefield laid by their own army several years before. Only fifty meters from the barn the leading youth tripped over a slight and rusty wire hidden in the underbrush. The boy standing before us remembered nothing after that until stumbling up to the barn. He was crying, "Help him...he was my best friend."

Geam, the barn worker, volunteered to go with me to see if the other two might still be alive. He knew the area and the main paths well, and if we stayed on them we shouldn't have any trouble. The others standing about remained quiet. Several took the bloodied soldier to the hospital to cleanse his wounds.

The area of the blast was evident enough. In undergrowth, mostly chest high, an almost perfect circle, perhaps twenty meters in diameter, had been wiped virtually clean by the explosive. I expected to see two bodies.

Geam pointed. The soles of two army boots protruded from under a bush at the circumference of the scythed area. I stepped closer. I could see the fatigues neatly tucked into the top of the boots. I parted the brush. Legs extended from the boots.

The body simply ceased to exist at the waist. Bone and entrails protruded from the belted pants; the marks of the notorious "Bouncing Betty," a deviously designed anti-personnel mine that sprang into the air about chest high before exploding. To blow a foot off wasn't sufficient any more. Made in the U.S. of A.

The execution of the other youth had not been so clean. Obviously our help had been superfluous from the onset. We carried what remained of the bodies to the hospital.

We only told the ARVN commander about the two bodies. To convince him that the remains should be picked up by the army took considerable time, and not a small amount of patience. It had been an imposition on his Sunday's rest. We left biting our tongues.

By the next day, rumors had circulated throughout Kontum: the hospital had mined the area around the pig barn. We were never to have any problems with theft, or even many local visitors.

***

With its close to a decade and a half of history, Minh Quy had acquired a certain apolitical reputation within Kontum Province and surrounding areas, particularly among the hill tribes of the region. Whether real or imagined, at least a part of the staff felt a certain immunity to the activities of the war; it was not uncommon for several of us to take a Sunday afternoon walk along village trails stretching into the mountains or along the swiftly flowing Dak Bla. We stayed away from areas of fighting, but otherwise felt fairly safe in our wanderings into country ethnic Vietnamese and other westerners refused to enter.

One exceptionally clear Sunday morning, several of us decided to venture across the Dak Bla and follow the trails meandering along its far shore. The river had been rising with the advent of the monsoon season, and a boatman gave us a ride across in his dugout. With a toothless smile, he told us of a short cut where we might avoid some of the lower and wetter spots. The trails had been worn by thousands of bare feet over hundreds of years, and I took pleasure in removing my sandals and walking that much closer to the smooth earth.

With the exception of avian songs and the murmuring streams descending to the river, we mostly walked in silence. The trail would sometimes lead along the river, rising upon twenty-foot cliffs, or pass along stepping-stones strategically placed at the water's edge. It would cut into the jungle, canopied thrice over, green, cool and moist. Wild fruit trees grew along the paths, which always seemed to take the most natural routes, crossing streams over fallen logs, around boulders and giant virgin teak trees. Man's trails had obviously originated from those of other animals; and he had accepted their guidance.

I remembered other times in an earlier year, walking such trails in fatigues and heavy boots, frightened beyond description, seeing the same foliage only as camouflage to possible ambush. Beauty had not been part of the vocabulary then.

We entered a small clearing; some half-dozen bamboo and thatch houses stood upon stilts waist high. We were quickly seen by children playing under the closest house. Some came running up to greet us, others ran to tell their parents. It happened that Dr. Christian, a particularly good pediatrician, was accompanying us. It was his first excursion so far from the hospital on foot, and probably the first time he had taken off in several months; needing convincing to relinquish a day from the hospital.

The doctor recognized one of the children at about the same time that child's parents saw him. They were overjoyed at his appearance; he had saved their son's life only a short time before. They ushered us up and into the one-room structure of their home. We stooped below fringes of thatch, and sat upon the bamboo-slatted floor, as we were bid.

The boy's father appeared within minutes, carrying an earthenware jar about two feet tall, which he placed in our cross-legged circle. He took a three-foot length of plastic intravenous tube down from the rafters, its origins obvious. He then filled the jar with water and worked one end of the tubing down through the rice hulls floating on top and the fermented rice at the bottom of the jar. A small stick, broken into the shape of a "T," was placed across the top of the vessel. He sucked from the make-shift straw, spitting the first brown mouthful through the slats of the floor, took a swallow, smiled widely, filled the jar to the brim again, and passed the tube to the doctor.

Though normally a non-drinker, the doctor recognized his responsibility in all of this, thanked the host, and proceeded to drink from the tubing until the level inside the jar broke away from the marker across the jar's rim. The host refilled the jar with water and passed the tubing to the next person. Water in, wine out.

While we had been so occupied, the wife and children were busy tending a small pot over the fire, and slicing the tender parts of a banana trunk into wafer-thin wedges. The rice wine was just making its second round when three wooden communal bowls were placed among us. the fare was simple: rice; *rau muong,* a leafy spinach-like vegetable; the thin slices of the banana plant cooked with a field mouse, simmered in hot peppers. The parents were proud that they could offer us meat, a rarity to their diet; and we ate with appreciation.

Politely breaking away from a rice wine jar is a difficult proposition, for the utmost courtesy possible of a Bahnar guest is to become intoxicated in the house of the host, demonstrating a true friendship built on trust. We explained our plans to reach Kon Mohar in time to make the return trip to the hospital before darkness fell. Reluctantly, but kindly, the host allowed us our way.

The trail passed a small waterfall, crossed the stream again, and rambled through more lush greenery. A group of young Montagnards and one Vietnamese approached in a single file towards us. They wore pieces of uniforms of a shade of faded green we knew to be typical of the North Vietnamese. They all carried arms: mostly Chinese AK-47s; an M-79 grenade launcher; and one M-16. They were obviously FULRO, and the side to which they paid allegiance seemed apparent. We stopped.

The Vietnamese, resting one hand upon the handle of his sidearm, and slightly raising the pith helmet over his eyebrows with the other, appeared agitated. He asked the darker-skinned Montagnard leading the group, "Who are the foreigners?" His accent reminded me of the teacher from the North we had had in Navy language school.

The Bahnar leader momentarily ignored his question, smiled, and greeted us by name. He then turned to the Vietnamese and, speaking in that language, said, "It's alright; they're from Minh Quy...the hospital."

We spoke for a few minutes. The North Vietnamese seemed somewhat taken aback at this openness to Americans, but remained quiet. We asked no questions and said our goodbyes; the group stepped off the trail, allowing us to pass. I thought of the sign hanging over the entrance to the pig barn, jokingly proclaiming it NVA officers' quarters.

We arrived at Kon Mohar in the early afternoon, and by then the heat had penetrated even to the shadowed mountain trails. An elder of the village greeted us with several *cai bi dao,* melons resembling giant succulent cucumbers. Their juices soothed our thirst. We visited with some friends, and then climbed down a switch-backed path to the river below. Children were playing and laughing in the swift current of the shallows. The adult foreigners joining them raised the level of gaiety several decibels.

The splashing water was irresistible. The day's heat and fatigue washed downstream with the current. This was the Dak Bla, the same river flowing past the hospital. John and I decided to take advantage of the cooling waters, and float back to Minh Quy. The others chose to return by the way we had come.

The meandering of a river's path is rarely noticed unless one is fortunate enough to have an aerial view of that water's course...

an advantage I wouldn't have for another month. The current was strong, augmented by monsoon runoffs; nevertheless, our aquatic folly would take some five hours, half way through which we admitted to each other our chills and possibly impetuous choice of return route. By that time we had passed those places where we might have easily stepped ashore and joined the path returning to the hospital. High bluffs now rose on either side of our passage.

We were passing Ap "C," a resettlement village situated back from the edge of the southerly precipice, when several rifle shots echoed between the river's walls. A distant guard was yelling something back over his shoulder, pumping his carbine in the air. We waved our hands, and he raised his rifle again, this time aiming towards us. The pinging splashes caught our attention before we heard the reports from the gun. We ducked beneath the muddy water and swam for the near bend in the river that would take us out of the rifleman's sight. Finally surfacing with gasping breaths, we glanced at each other, and began a more determined swim to our destination.

About a mile before the current reached Minh Quy the high bluffs descended to gentle slopes along the river's edge. The first place where we would have the opportunity of climbing upon dry land was at the village of Kon Satieu. The sun was approaching the western hills, and we were chilled to our very bones.

Unfortunately, the landing was occupied by the women of the village, all in various stages of undress, as this was the time and place for their daily bathing. Strong tradition decreed that no man witness these baths; equally strong physical need demanded that we get our hypothermic bodies out of the chilling waters as fast as we could. Tradition forsaken, we shouted our apologies as we raced through the shallows and naked bodies to the accompaniment of astonished shrieks, giggling, and good-natured admonishment. In spite of our weariness, we jogged the remaining distance to the hospital in an attempt to regain some warmth.

***

In the past couple of months I had come to know members of the New Zealand Red Cross Team stationed in Pleiku, a little over an hour's ride to the south of us. They were an interesting foursome, engaged in various community health and development projects in that neighboring province. They would sometimes bring patients to the hospital for specialized needs. The majority of their work likewise involved the Montagnard tribes-people.

I had become particularly friendly with the team leader, Mac Riding. His grizzled appearance, crow-tracks at the corners of his smiling eyes, and sometimes-shaggy beard, belied an age similar to my own.

> *...he seemed no man at all of those*
> *who eat good wheaten bread; but he seemed rather*
> *a shaggy mountain reared in solitude.*

I suspect that the eight years he had spent as a solitary lighthouse keeper off the coast of New Zealand added to the wisdom and sharp humor of his words. I doubt that I have ever known a man who knew himself so well, and consequently was quick to know others.

Mac and the rest of the team were interested in our program, and particularly the placing of improved breeding stock into resettlement villages. They were working in several hamlets where they felt such projects might be beneficial. Thus we often spent time together, visiting selected sites, talking with village elders, discussing possibilities.

The companionship of the Red Cross Team served as an escape from the closed circle of Minh Quy relationships that had begun to feel confining. As good a group as it was, the twenty-four hour daily working and living association eventually became not dissimilar to the psychotic burdens upon a crowded crew of a small ship out to sea for months on end.

As enjoyable as relations proved with both Montagnard and Vietnamese in the area, linguistic and cultural differences made most associations a work of labor; and sooner or later, a friendship among one's own people granted a relaxation that could not be found elsewhere.

Mac and Leoni, the New Zealand nurse with whom he was especially close, became the kind of friends I had been seeking for what seemed a long time. I had never been one for crowds; one or two close relationships always seemed more satisfying than gaggles of superficial associations. The three of us became close, and enjoyed an uncommon bond.

The Red Cross Team had come to visit one weekend, and we decided to visit the Dakia Leprosarium on the outskirts of Kontum. The French priest in charge had proudly asked us to visit his pig farm on the grounds.

On entering the vast and immaculately landscaped holdings of the Catholic diocese we each felt the special quality of peace emanating from the quiet surroundings. The leprosarium of Graham Greene's writings came to mind, and I understood why he had chosen it as an escape from the rigors and reality of life.

We walked the silent and immaculately tended paths with an effervescent nun, her face glowed with kindness; was she always so cheery? Small groups of Montagnard lepers worked quietly at gardening chores; children played on the closely cropped grass, but there was no yelling or screaming; a covey of whispering nuns passed and smiled.

The path to the barns led through a field that had been allowed to lie fallow. Two giggling Bahnar women looked up with toothless grins from their kneeling position on either side of a giant anthill. They motioned for us to approach and held out stumps of hands covered with the crawling delicacies for which they had been digging: hundreds of large scurrying red ants carrying burdens of white globular egg casings. The women wiped more ants into their mouths, laughed, and a few escapees scampered from the corners of their smiles. We were invited to join the feast. A crawling acidic sourness rewarded our tastes, and we passed on down the footpath.

At the end of our visit we sat back against giant Royal Palms, planted decades previously. We lazily conversed and let our minds

wander in the serenity of the environment. There was no war here...
that was restricted to outside the gates. Peace so close to its antithesis
seemed hard to fathom, but here it was. Yet a closing circle towards
death was also present; the absence of the very boisterousness of life
I missed, and in the end we moved on.

***

As November approaches dark skies herald the earnest onslaught
of the monsoons. Days pass without sight of the sun; penetrating rains
pound the earth and swirling winds whip ponchos and rain gear to
eventual shreds. Once chilled in the wet gusts, a body soon longs for
the tropic heat so often characterizing these equatorial lands.

Montagnard villages lie quiet during such dark and wet days.
Motionless bodies huddle in dark blankets around smoldering
hearth fires; rarely are voices heard. A ceaseless rain falls upon
an already soaked land. New rivers course through stepped forest
paths, and the Dak Bla continues to rise. Men have chained
dugouts to higher ground and more sturdy anchorage. A few
women are dangerously trying to rake firewood from the growing
torrent.

The river is taking on a somber and malevolent guise. Undermined
banks crash to the rushing blood-chocolate waters. Dugouts, fish
traps, fence posts, whole trees race maliciously to the sea under
murky and heavily burdened skies. Bloated animal bodies sometimes
bob to the surface in the raging current. And yet, the rains bring
new life; and for this the people wait.

Gray mildew and green mold cover clothing, books, sandals,
blankets, sheets. I scrawl an obscenity into the festering growth
upon the damp wall. Nothing is really dry, and the dank limpness
of everything pervades the soul, particularly of the Westerner; there
are fewer smiles and fewer words.

A sodden letter arrives in the week's mail: an ancient poem sent
by a fellow traveler who had gone her own way...still exploring the
paths of the East:

The autumn moon is half round
    above the Yo-Mei Mountain.
Its pale light falls in and flows
    with the water of the Ping-Chang River.
Tonight I leave Ching-Chi of the limpid stream
    for the three canyons,
And glide past Yu-Chow, thinking
    of you whom I cannot see.

             "The Yo-Mei Mountain Moon"
                      Li Po

Year of the Hare

For one unaccustomed, even after several years, to the monsoon's monotony, the drumming rains drill into the mind and allow the darkness of the skies to pass within. Ruminating thoughts turn deep cold gray with the clouds; and just when one concludes he has entered that realm of true insanity, there is silence.

Noises, which one thought he had come to ignore for their very persistence, reverberate only in memory and become conspicuous now in their absence. The constant drumming on the metal roof, on the broad-leaf plants, upon the land itself is gone...silent.

Then a gecko high on the inside wall barks his cadence of seven loud omens, impatient with the new quiet. A Cicada picks up the rhythm, trilling an impossible tempo in an unlikely volume. The tiny *Cuk-cuk* feels the beat, and echoes his name in the sliding scale of a hollow metal ball bouncing in ever decreasing arcs. The spell is broken.

The new sun sends down splintering rays, shattering watered mirrors lying over the land. The new brilliance is difficult to view, and we each squint and try to shield our eyes with a hand, but the brightness springs from too many changing angles.

> *...into a sky all brazen—all one brightening*
> *for gods immortal and for mortal men*
> *on plowlands kind with grain.*

175

Our small world becomes one of a million sparkling hues of living green: new fields of rice; young sprouts of bamboo shooting inches in a day; verdant mountain forests darkening in growth; succulent leaves of the lotus rising from murky ponds; new grass growing on hills and plains; cassava plants searching for the sky and potato leaves carpeting carved fields; newly mounded gardens springing forth with the greens of lettuce and onion and carrot tops and a hundred other varieties of emerald, jade, olive, verdigris, and viridian; and then the greens of the jungle.

The rejuvenation of the soil and its produce also marked a new cycle of growth for the swine project. We were ready to begin working in the villages. I was anxious to get the young crossbred breeding stock into the field. Not the least of our concerns was convincing the villagers that pigs kept for brood stock promised greater returns than those promised for the pot. In spite of the exigencies of a war-racked land we experienced little problem in this regard: a gamble these hardy refugees gladly accepted. In several cases, men, women, and sometimes children would walk from remote villages over steep mountain trails for several days and return carrying their prize pigs in baskets slung over their shoulders. They would care for the animals. I had no doubt.

By this time the program had gained a small notoriety. The local American Province Representative, on the lookout for good-deed projects—some said to take eyes off his military intelligence role—offered the helicopter which he had use of once or twice a week. I happily accepted, for we could speed the process of transport appreciatively. The pilot and crew were not quite as glad as I, nor as accustomed to the aromatic sweetness of swine scat.

The last day of chopper deliveries we swung southwest to Plei Rawak. The pilot lowered the craft into our self-made swirling dust bowl outside the village. Once the rotors had slowed, kids swooped in from all sides to help unload. Newly finished pens greeted the fresh arrivals. Food and water awaited them, as well as several hundred smiling faces. I'm not sure I ever felt quite so proud of what we had been trying to do. The proof was yet to come, but if enthusiasm had anything to do with portents of the future, my four-legged friends were well on their way to happy homes.

After another brief talk with the elders, we headed back to the silver Huey. I still had half a dozen pigs to drop off at Kon Mohar. Rotors began their slowly increasing whine; the helicopter lifted out of the blowing red dust and skimmed over the thick sylvan foliage towards the eastern hills. The pilot picked up the ox-bowed Dak Bla and followed its winding course into the rising lands. He brought the craft to a higher altitude, unsure of the friendliness of the jungle below.

The clearing we eventually approached sat on a high bluff of one of the great U-shaped bends in the river. We spun down quickly to the circle the villagers had marked off for our landing.

The chopper's crew was anxious to return. They still had a flight to Nha Trang and, unspoken, a slight apprehension of being so far north in this area. I wanted to spend more time here, and so decided to walk out later. The pilot was a little leery of leaving me, so after assuring him I knew the trails well and had many friends here who would take care of me, he finally offered to loan me his pistol for the walk out. I thanked him and explained that I felt much safer without it. He shrugged, flipped a few switches, and in moments had lifted off and disappeared to the south.

The arrival of the pigs brought a joyous mood to the village, and after checking on the state of the airlifted swine, I was ushered from one longhouse to another. Rice wine jars appeared and the day dwindled into a peaceful twilight.

Pleasant pastoral sounds took over the village evening. The rhythm of women and girls pounding rice in large teak mortars outside each longhouse set up a melody of answering drums; cocks felt it their duty to announce the closing darkness; children seemed intent on making the best use of the last minutes of light; their laughter was echoed by dogs running close behind and barking at their antics; and there it was—a magic flute sang mournfully from somewhere towards the river's edge.

> *Then we heard the Muses sing*
> *a threnody in nine immortal voices.*

Darkness swallowed the hills and the music of the village quieted as families returned to the evening meal. The village chief had invited me to eat and spend the night with his extended family; his was the largest house in the village. We sat around the jar, passing the reed straw from hand to hand. The meal was simple, but fresh and delicious. Nightfall passed amid laughter, stories, and the music of several traditional gongs and bamboo instruments. People began drifting off, either falling asleep next to the wine jar, or crawling onto nearby cane mats, covering themselves with hand-woven blankets.

I was loaned a blanket to keep off the chills of the highland night, and when I nodded off several times the host asked me to move to his prize possession, an army jungle hammock. I could not convince him that I actually preferred sleeping on a mat. Nothing would do but that I had to take over his swinging perch. I promised him I was telling the truth...he promised me he knew I was lying to be polite. I lost.

Dawn was cautiously making her way over the eastern hills; darkness and mists just as tentatively clung to the jungle surrounding the village. The drumming of the rice being separated from its hulls reverberated in my head, now a little more fragile from the previous night's wine. I eased from the hammock and stretched the aches from my back. A few giggles from children, and the chief's wife asked me to join the family close to the fire. The sun had yet to break the morning chill. I gathered the blanket about me and edged closer to the smoking blaze. A bowl of steaming rice was handed to me.

I felt better after the meal. Stepping from the longhouse, I handed back the comforting blanket, and stood a few minutes in the warmth of the new sun. Several children came up to speak, and we squatted in the rejuvenating radiance.

The sights and sounds and smells around me were thousands of years old. There was little here that was superfluous. True, there were maladies and pains, and inconveniences of such a primitive life; but, there was also a harmony with the elements and spirits that was palpable. But so fragile was that harmony. I was suddenly overcome with the responsibility that fell to one introducing change to a culture that had evolved so slowly over thousands of years. An ancient Chinese proverb says, "Step on a blade of grass, and change the course of the universe."

I paid my respects and farewells. Several youths had offered to escort me part way down the trail, but before I left a friend approached and silently placed a simple ring of brass about my wrist, forged from the jettison of war.

After a kilometer or two I assured the boys that I could find my way, and they turned about with farewells of *Bok Malung*, go well. I still had several hours of jungle path to myself before crossing the Dak Bla to the more populated area near the hospital.

Though I had been on this trail with others several times before, this was one of the few times I had been alone and so far from the security of home base. I admitted to myself a slight tingling of apprehension, perhaps fear, but I also relished the solitude and the beauty surrounding me. The mixed emotions produced a rare and mellow excitement that caused me to smile to no one but myself.

My bare feet felt the smooth warmth of the worn path, flecks of sunlight filtered through the jungle's roof, birds I still could not name whistled and called their claims to this territory. I was a stranger here.

Yet days of childhood came to mind, roaming the hammocks and woods so close to my home then; forests and joy now eradicated by the amoebic growth of malls and parking lots. The reverie ended with a softly spoken greeting. I looked up from the ground sliding beneath my feet.

A gray-haired woman in the traditional Bahnar skirt stood before me, her kind and wrinkled face smiling at my obvious daydreaming. Her gentle character was balanced by the carbine over her shoulder. She spoke slowly so I would understand. "You should not be out here alone."

> *...take care*
> *not to get hurt. Many are dangerous here.*

I smiled and thanked her for her concern. I told her I was heading back to the hospital now. I stepped from the trail to allow her by. She bid me a safe journey and continued hers. The rifle seemed nearly as tall as she. Until approaching the river crossing, I had the rest of the way to myself.

Two Bahnar boys, proud of their new Western clothing, were just stepping from a dugout. I noticed shoes with the high fat heels and square toes of current Saigon fashion. They greeted me in Vietnamese; and then I stood transfixed as one pulled from his shoulder bag a small cheap camera, and asked if he could take my picture. I laughed.

Weeks passed rapidly. The couple managing the barn and its brood were doing well, even charting breeding schedules and giving shots when necessary. I spent more time with the village projects, introducing new ones, checking on the ones already established. I traveled more with the New Zealand Red Cross Team, helping them set up similar village projects around Pleiku Province. I enjoyed their company. Mac and I would sit up late at night swilling philosophy and beer. We'd trade travelers' tales and promised ourselves a joint expedition into some wild outback when these days were gone.

My days as a resident of Kontum were numbered. I felt confident with the management of the herd, and Ya Vincent had promised to keep an eye on things. At this point the best thing I could do was to step carefully out of the picture. The director of CARE had asked me to do some photography of their varied programs around the country. It would be a chance to do some traveling, and I planned to visit Kontum every couple of weeks to check on things. It seemed a reasonable approach to phasing out my presence, and yet still monitor the progress of the program. I still had a couple more weeks to wrap things up.

I was stepping out the door of the house on my way down to the barn when I bumped into Nancy, one of the western staff from the Saigon office. I knew she had been working on plans for a Montagnard crafts project, but I didn't know she'd be visiting here so soon. She introduced me to her Montagnard assistant.

Mi-Lai nodded her head and smiled. She looked familiar, and then I remembered: the two attractive Montagnard nurses I had briefly encountered when they were interviewing for a position with CARE a month or so ago. They had just returned from four years of nurse training in Japan, funded by a Buddhist scholarship, but were having a difficult time finding decent nursing jobs back in their home country, which surprised me. Then, on hearing their stories I recognized the plague of prejudice that so often surfaced with Vietnamese/Montagnard relations. It was as if the four years of education counted for naught. And now, here was someone who had the capacity to alleviate pain...hustling baskets and weaving.

Hurrying, I paid my respects, started to turn away, then remembered that some close friends in the village of Kontum Ko'nom had invited John and me to their house that evening...I asked Nancy and Mi-Lai[3] if they'd care to join us. We made plans to meet later.

Light was dwindling in the Buddhist graveyard as we ambled the dirt road down to the small village on the outskirts of Kontum. The family who invited us were special people.

Before I had left Saigon for the Highlands, Bill had brought a young Bahnar girl to the big city for some corrective eye surgery. Actually she was being fitted for an artificial eye to take the place of the one that had been lost a couple of years previously in an accident of the war. Yanh was thirteen—and scared.

A young girl from a primitive village, to whom the "big city" was at the end of the mile or so walk to the market of Kontum, was put on a plane for the first time in her life and whisked off to the mega-center of the universe, Saigon. She spoke little Vietnamese. No friends, only strangers, with whom she could hardly communicate. The scarred empty socket in place of an eye kept her from looking

---

[3] A note on Rhadé names: Usually, several days following birth when it appears that a child will survive, a naming ceremony takes place. Female names begin with H'; male names with Y-. For example, Mi-Lai's given name is H'Cham; her son's, Y-Lai.

The given name is used until that person becomes a parent, at which time that person is most often called "Mother/Father of (named child)," Thus H'Cham became Mi-Lai, a contraction of Ami Y-Lai (Mother of Y-Lai). Ma-Lai is a contraction of Ama Y-Lai (father of Y-Lai). When a person becomes a grandparent the name changes again in a similar manner.

into any mirror, or anyone's face when she was spoken to...and then the strange foreign doctors. She was indeed frightened.

I was staying in a somewhat palatial house, *sans* furniture, which CARE still maintained on the tail end of a lease. I asked Bill if they would care to stay with me during their visit. My time was relatively free, and I knew Bill had a lot of errands to run for Minh Quy, so I offered to take care of Yanh when she was not at the hospital. I gave her a small stuffed toy at our first meeting; the pink dog was to accompany her everywhere. Her shyness gave way to curiosity of the many new sights of the big city, and it wasn't long before we became good friends. She enjoyed riding on the luggage rack of the bicycle, and we'd tour Cholon, or the city market. Her favorite destination, though, was the Saigon Zoo.

My love for animals led to mixed emotions over the zoo. Many of the animals were not in the best of condition, and sometimes I was appalled at the treatment afforded the poor beasts by Vietnamese youngsters, and even adults. Yanh and I watched as several city youths took turns spitting on various captive creatures. Yanh was as saddened as I; she seemed to have a different perspective than the other kids around us.

She stood for minutes on end talking to the Tibetan Bear and the Mandrill, but her favorite was the Hornbill. We purchased a bag of peanuts, and where most people would watch the delicate shelling process of the great-billed bird, Yanh took great pains to shell each nut for her beautifully colored friend. The Hornbill came to the edge of the cage and sat politely next to Yanh as she slowly and deliberately took each nut from its shell, and carefully handed it to the bird. He would not be enticed by any other offerings of passers-by.

Yanh shyly smiled as she tested her first ice-cream cone. I enjoyed our outings as much as she; and stood with shared pride as she first hesitantly glanced at her mirrored image, now with the new eye in place. Her self-esteem grew noticeably minute-by-minute. She no longer saw herself as an ugly deformed urchin, but as the pretty adolescent that stared back at her from the mirror; with open, beautiful eyes. I was a little sad at the airport departure of Bill and

Yanh, for I had no idea I would be seeing her newly ebullient face again.

Such memories of my first meeting with Yanh drifted through my head as we shuffled down the twilight road to Kontum Ko'nom. It hadn't been more than a week after my arrival at Minh Quy when Yanh showed up at the house with an invitation for me to meet her family the next day. The meeting turned into a ceremony; the best I could make out, something akin to my adoption into the family. From that time on I had ready-made Bahnar language teachers at my beck and call, and a local family, with all its responsibilities and joys. Other than Yanh, my favorite was Grandmother, who took no gruffness from anyone, and enjoyed a few practical jokes on the white man to boot.

We were headed to Grandmother's house, ensured that a rice wine jar and local meal would be waiting, as well as the warm hospitality I always found there.

The village was mostly quiet as we stepped down its main pathway, darkness having sent the last of the playing children inside the thatched houses raised up on pilings. The soft glow of cooking fires sparkled through the thatch; smoke filtered through the roofs.

The evening was joyful and laughter was the common tongue; but at one point in the night's frivolity, grandmother turned to me, actually pointing and wagging her finger, a rather rude gesture in this culture.

> *...until the gods*
> *make known what beauty you yourself shall marry.*

"You must take care and be nice to the young woman who comes with you," nodding at Mi-Lai, "for one day she will be your wife."

I didn't know what kind of joke she was making. I waited for her laughter. She only stared at me. Several minutes passed and no one knew what to say. Mi-Lai was as noticeably embarrassed as I. The Seeress and her African sister were the last to speak to me with such certitude of the future. It was a little scary, but then I attributed my scrambled thoughts to the effect of the rice wine, and finally the conversation took another, lighter turn.

We walked home in the waning moonlight, continuing in the joviality of the evening; but Grandmother's voice would not leave me in peace. In our reminiscence of the evening's fun, no one referred to those words.

***

As the time approached for the first CARE photo junket my head was a jumble of loose ends. Admittedly, I was only going to be away from Kontum for a couple of weeks, but I had the strong feeling that after that time I would only be returning as a visitor. I wasn't saying good-by; but I was.

The feeling grows that it's time to get on down the road. My temper is getting shorter with people; it's easy for me to find fault with a basically good operation and kindhearted group of folks...all of which is obvious as I prepare to leave. I'll miss Kontum and the friend I've made.

Ol' Blue, the spotted boar that, as a shoat, I first carried into the barn in my arms, and who never has acted according to the dictates of promulgated porcine behavior, greets me at the entrance to the barn. We never were able to keep him in a pen, and finally gave up. He had learned to open every latch we devised. As a youngster he'd run and jump up on anyone entering the barn, waiting for a friendly pat. The act used to be cute. Now, at over two hundred pounds, he still didn't see why he should stop his affable habits. He thought himself the head honcho, and would parade up and down the aisle between the stalls, ensuring the rest of his kind were in their proper places.

> *Fifty sows with farrows*
> *were penned in each, bedded upon the earth,*
> *while the boars lay outside—fewer by far...*

An intimate scratch behind the ear would send him into ecstasy, rolling onto his back, waiting for a good stomach rub. On special occasions he was known to swill his share of Biere Larue; any supplies of the liter beer bottles had to be kept off the floor of the feed room, for he quickly learned to open that door also. He rubbed his head on my leg and looked up into my face.

Little Yanh, the gatekeeper's son, had become my constant companion. He had grown, but still was unable to keep his pants up. No matter whether transport was a bicycle, motor scooter, pickup, or two feet, Little Yanh would be right there; he had an uncanny knack for always knowing when I'd be leaving the house. He had accompanied me, at one time or another, to almost every village site at which we had been working. He often helped interpret from Bahnar to Vietnamese. Little Yanh was with me now, trying to climb onto Blue's back. There were going to be some difficult farewells ahead, but at least I could postpone them for a while.

***

The photography went well, and the travel kept my mind mostly occupied. From Hué in the north to the Ca Mau Peninsula in the south, I was shooting daycare centers, orphanages, feeding programs, refugee camps, schools, and other special projects assisted by CARE.

I was always attracted by the children. At night their faces would grow from the darkness and keep me awake: faces that should have been ones of innocence, and were not; faces that should have been smiling, and were not; faces that should have been open, and were not. Each face stared at me, some questioning, some accusing...most simply gazing; few of them spoke, but their eyes, imploring, beseeching...*Bui Doi*, the Vietnamese called them, "the Dust of Life."

I lay awake on the soft bed of the CARE guesthouse back in Saigon, wondering on the future...if indeed in the great scheme of the universe, I too was simply a small grain of the Dust of Life?

The recent traveling had brought me back through Saigon on numerous occasions, and I had had the opportunity of seeing Mi-Lai several times. We enjoyed each other's company. I became friendly with her young son, whose father had been killed before he was born. The more I learned of their story, the more I realized how the trauma of war had affected everyone in this country. As we saw more of each other, a quiet attachment grew, as did the befuddlement of my mind. I wasn't prepared for the direction my thoughts were taking. I had made nebulous plans for soon leaving this country after finishing up my current work. Now I wasn't sure about anything. Thoughts of Mi-Lai continued to interrupt my mental ruminations.

Never mind, I was soon to be headed back to Kontum, where perhaps I could better sort out the confusion. I did know that the military and political situation was worsening, and sanity seemed to dictate at least making plans for getting out.

Returning to the Highlands proved a catharsis. In spite of the increased military activity in the area, a serenity of the land and its peoples, continuing to follow the cycles of thousands of years, worked into my soul and calmed my nerves. The Minh Quy Pig Farm was a reality, progressing nicely in my absence. The village projects were doing well. I was able to take my time, visiting the various sites and friends along the way. Christmas and New Year's were approaching, and I chose to spend those holidays among my companions.

Again, a strong feeling persisted that I was seeing Kontum for the last time, and I leisurely, but pointedly, made mental photographs of the simple, and yet so complex, surroundings: the miniature Buddhist temple at the end of the dirt lane where one could almost always find solitude; the quiet pedestrian traffic, where voices and laughter were often the loudest noises of locomotion; the crisp air and consistently majestic sunsets; the hushed ruins of bombed-out homes close to the airport, and the artistic patterns of explosive's scat on the remaining stuccoed walls, circumscribed with the graffiti of youth; the rusting hulk of the C-123 at the end of the runway; the bells of the Catholic church on Sunday mornings, penetrating the mist still sleepily lying in the valley; the smell of wood smoke rising from the small Montagnard communities; the emerald rice fields; the occasional *"Ong My, Ong My..."* of children running behind the bicycle. It was a unique world of concord surrounded by war.

And yet there was one question lying unanswered.

Will you change the will of the everlasting gods
in a night or a day's time?

No matter how I tried to occupy my mind, thoughts continually reverted to Mi-Lai. I could think of a thousand reasons why our relationship would not work, particularly if we were to leave this country. My head said one thing; my soul, another.

Sometimes I had a hard enough time taking care of myself...was I capable of handling a ready-made family? I will soon be working myself out of a job. What kind of prospects for the future could I offer? And, yet....

I was convinced that the demise of the present government was not far away. Whatever the new times brought for this ravished country, those ahead were not going to be easy. I was pretty sure I didn't want to be here during the changeover.

The fighting had moved closer to Kontum. All of the major outposts had fallen. Even long-time residents who had lived through the numerous offensives were shaking their heads. When the move came, that it would be launched here in Kontum Province seemed obvious. Even as far south as the Delta, the rumors were "Kontum is next."

Perhaps the communists' greatest weapon was their knowledge of the psychology of the masses. That they had been playing a waiting game for decades was admitted. Conditions were approaching, indeed had virtually arrived, for which they had been delaying. All of what had been happening over the last several months seemed in preparation for the final onslaught; and the people knew it. There would be those welcoming the change; most others lived in fear of the unknown.

***

A small group of friends waited with me on the tarmac as the aged C-47 dropped its tail to the ground and taxied towards us. The side door opened and the co-pilot ducked his head as he swung out the folding ladder. The several others who were taking advantage of the unscheduled Air America flight from Kontum to Saigon climbed aboard and disappeared into the hull's cramped dark cavern.

Quiet farewells. I turned towards the plane, when Little Yanh realized what was happening. He grabbed my leg and started bawling. Several minutes were required for others to pry him away, still screaming. My throat grew constricted, and I hurried into the inclined interior, settling morosely into a webbed jump seat. The ladder was pulled in, the door closed. We began rolling towards the end of the runway. Sister Michael, one of the Montagnard nuns, turned and commented, "the poor child," referring to Little Yanh; then she saw my tears, and remained quiet.

I will miss Kontum, but I try not to delude myself in thinking that I will be missed; I know better. I've seen too many come and go. But to face those tears of the present was to painfully rend flesh from my soul. I was taking something of Kontum with me, but I was also leaving a part of me behind, and the process was anguishing.

The flight was a leap into the new year. I had a couple of hours, withdrawn into my cocoon on the plane, to reflect on the changes taking place in my life. I was leaving behind a relationship with a land and its peoples that I had never known before. No place, or circumstance or people had affected me so.

Mi-Lai had visited over the holidays and we had decided to marry. In such uncertain times she would be giving up her whole world of family and culture for an unsure future. I was asking much of her and her son.

The motors hummed with an harmonic pulse that reached into me. I drew my jacket tighter as we climbed into the cool atmosphere over the blue mountains of the Central Plateau. The Chinese horoscope had said this year began a new cycle in my life.

I would finish my work with CARE, commence the irritating pile of paperwork required for our marriage and their exit visas, and get us out of the country as soon as possible. Perhaps I would explore the possibilities of continuing in third-world developmental work, somewhere with no war.

As the plane began its descent I realized that, in spite of the questions of the future, the relief and feeling of wellbeing that followed our decision was like a calming wave of tranquility. All of the trepidations that anticipated such a life-long commitment disappeared when that commitment was finally made. Obstacles would raise their heads, I knew, but I was confident now. Uncertainties existed, but doubts dissipated; I could now recognize the difference. A new cycle was indeed beginning, even if it was a small part of a much older one.

The tires screeched on the runway. I unbuckled the seat belt and lifted the tattered knapsack into my lap; and smiled to myself, remembering Monkey's playful adieu this morning. We, no doubt, would be meeting later.

***

I raced with time, as weeks sped across the calendar. I had not imagined the red tape involved in such an international marriage. At least some of the Vietnamese signatures could be bought; the American Embassy sometimes acted as though their official policy was to discourage any such union to the utmost of its ability. We seemed to invite whatever possibilities existed for complications; some documents had been destroyed in the Tet offensive of '68, others were nonexistent. Finally, in a car parked on Tu Do Street, we traded rings. Mountains of paperwork still remained unfinished.

I had moved into the classic flat at the end of a congested alleyway: two small rooms, with a hotplate and a shared bathroom in the hall. Besides a wife and son, a brother and sister going to school in Saigon shared the accommodations, along with several Montagnard friends, and Huynh, a Vietnamese friend of Mi-Lai who worked in the CARE office. I anticipated the bickering that

Westerners would expect of such crowded conditions, and was amazed at the harmonious synchrony of the extended family. Music lessons somewhere in the adjoining building—amplified scales continually wrought from an unseen piano and violin; the continual medleys of children's play; radios and tape players in constant melodious combat; and yet, it somehow all fit together, and the sounds combined into a coherent symphony of life. For a few piasters more the landlady, with a piquant grin, rented us the small adjacent bedroom. To my surprise, I learned the harmony possible from crowdedness. I was enthralled, and happy.

We journeyed to Ban Me Thuot, and the Buon, or Village, of Pan Lam to meet the rest of the family; the same that had hosted me to lunch almost a year ago. Mi-Lai had been in Japan at the time.

The great longhouse filled with friends, and, all of a sudden, I realized the makings of a Rhadé marriage were in preparation. I donned the intricately woven ceremonial shirt handed me, and Mi-Lai's mother presented us with a magnificent wedding blanket, also finely hand-woven. Sticky rice and unknown spices steamed in sectioned green bamboo over the hearth fire, along with pots of simmering meat and *djam trong,* the traditional Rhadé dish of hotly spiced eggplant.

> *When prayers were said and all the grain was scattered*
> *great-hearted Thrasmedeies in a flash*
> *swung the axe, at one blow cutting through the neck*
> *tendons. The heifer's spirit failed.*

Animals had been sacrificed to the spirits, and dishes of certain raw delicacies had been strategically placed for their approbation. Prodigious earthenware jars of fermented rice, some having been buried for several years, were uncovered from the nurturing earth and lined along the center of the longhouse. Old men entered, carrying ancient brass gongs; and giggling women, with more dishes of ceremonial nourishment.

I was awed by the multitudinous activity, and feeling somewhat lost when a brother led the two of us before a sage sitting on crossed legs, inspecting the augury of the earlier sacrifices. He frowned, then after a few moments, looked up and smiled. He motioned us closer together and to sit before him, then placed a large knife flat beneath our touching bare feet. With chanting words I had no way of following, he called upon the spirits of the land and sky to bless our union as he slowly dripped rice wine upon our joined feet. The family crowded around as we shared the first of the aged intoxicant.

Congratulations ensued, as extended family members queued to place brass bracelets on each of our wrists, followed by friends from the village and beyond. The weight of the amulets soon rose from our fingers to elbows, each bearer offering a blessing on placing the brightly shined ringlets about our arms.

The ancient melody of gongs began in earnest, as did imbibing from the jars of strong rice wine. More celebrants crowded into the longhouse, and the disharmonies of war were forgotten.

> *And now the suitors gave themselves to dancing,*
> *to harp and haunting song, as night drew on;*
> *black night indeed came on them at their pleasure.*

Lanterns dispelled the descending darkness, and youth of the village set up drums and guitars at the far end of the longhouse; I sat spellbound in the center of centuries' differences: gongs at one end echoing ageless tradition; a rock band at the other, trumpeting rebelliousness of the young. It was not unfitting for a marriage such as ours, borne across such gaps of culture and time.

The morning sun was winking through tree branches when the revelers began slowing, some making their unsteady way back to other longhouses and other villages. Sleeping bodies lay circled about the hearth and still-standing wine jars.

In an unexpected ceremony I discovered an unexpected acceptance; I wondered if a reciprocal acceptance would be forthcoming in my homeland of the still-deep South. Time enough for those concerns. We were tired and happy.

We stayed several days, walking paths of the villages, plantations and forests. Small girls played on flutes of bamboo, beneath red-berried coffee trees and towering teak. Boys played tag among the village houses. The constant sounds of war, to which I had become accustomed in Kontum, were absent. Mi-Lai picked up the beautiful shell of a cashew nut. She started to toss it away, but I slipped the memento into my pocket.

The return to Saigon came too soon, but it was all a joyous time. Life took on an air of pleasantry and familiarity unknown to me previously. Amid untangling the red tape and continued paperwork needed for the three of us to leave the country, I was still finishing up various reports for the office. Life had meaning, and danced through time as a fast waltz.

Mac Riding came by to wish us well. He was taking a two-week break, flying to Laos, and was going to see how far up the headwaters of the Mekong he could reach. We laughed at his friendly jibes at married life and my not accompanying him...he saw our happiness.

> *Here's a tight roof; we'll drink on, you and I,*
> *and ease our hearts of hardships we remember,*
> *sharing old times. On later days a man*
> *can find a charm in old adversity,*
> *exile and pain.*

We talked into the night, discussing subjects ranging from prejudice to communes. He presented the idea of basing a community only upon the desire of mutual friendship and the exchange of the mind, with no physical dependency implied...where an individual could come and go.

The neighborhood noise had long ago quieted; Mac looked at his watch, and rose to leave. We clasped each other about the shoulders. I wished him a good journey, and asked him to stop by on his return.

I lingered in the doorway, watching his self-assured amble through the shadows of the alley, then turned back to the candle light of the room. Words played back and forth in my head, and finally I turned to Gibran's *The Prophet*. I found and copied the words into my journal:

"Yet I cannot tarry longer.
The sea that calls all things unto her calls
me, and I must embark."

***

We needed one more piece of paper and signature from the local government in Ban Me Thuot, and then we'd be able to leave. I put Mi-Lai on the plane. She'd have a few days to visit with her family, pick up her son who was staying with his grandparents, and return with the needed form. They were due to return to Saigon on Sunday. I was getting anxious to be on the way. The military situation appeared to be worsening.

I received a message over the weekend that Mi-Lai was not yet able to get that last paper—the person responsible wouldn't be in the office until Monday, but she was assured it would be ready by then; a minor hitch compared to what we had previously encountered.

MONDAY, MARCH 10, 1975: About 0330 hours, Ban Me Thuot came under a very surprising and very heavy NVA attack.

They came
with dawn over that terrain like the leaves
and blades of spring. So doom appeared to us.
...our evil days.

Initial news reports play down the severity of the situation— ARVN says they'll have the area under control shortly. All civilian communications are cut. I've heard nothing from them.

I rushed to the office of a friend in the embassy. Paul, the local Province Representative for the consulate in Ban Me Thuot, was married to Mi-Lai's sister. It was possible they still had radio contact with him, and he might know the status of the family. Yes, the consulate had a plane over the area, which was still in communication with Paul. They'd try to find out. We waited.

The reports I could garner from the embassy were more pessimistic. The spotter plane reported that both airports appeared under NVA control. All the roads out of town were severed. North Vietnamese tanks were entering the town.

A report came in from Paul. He was holed up in the small American compound there. About twenty people, other Americans, Canadians, and a Filipino, contractors, missionaries, and families were with him. " 'All Americans are accounted for and are safe'...your family is all right...they're with him; if any evacuation is possible, they'll get out."

TUESDAY: I knew that all information was coming through the Consulate in Nha Trang. Any rescue operations would be conducted from there. I had to get there. The government plane leaving in an hour was booked up. Then I remembered that John was in town from the hospital, and was planning to return to Kontum today. Perhaps he was scheduled on that flight. I caught a ride to the Air America terminal. John's red hair was easy to pick out in the crowd. His ticket got me on board the crowded DC-3. Other passengers laughed and joked as we lifted off the ground. I ground my teeth and clenched my fists until blood rose to my palms.

The plane rolled to a stop. Passengers took their time debarking. I finally pushed my way through. I found the consular intelligence officer; he was a friend of Paul. He took me into their communications room. Tables had been pushed together in the center and covered with a mosaic of aerial photographs of the Ban Me Thuot area, covered with a large-scale plastic overlay map, marked with different colored wax pencils...notes updating the situation.

I mentioned the message I had gotten from the embassy. Ira picked up the microphone. The scratchy voice of the spotter-plane's pilot came back over the speaker. They'd check for me; they were maintaining radio contact with Paul. More waiting. I glanced at the photographs...I tried to orient myself. Static on the loud speaker. The pilot's voice again, "Your wife and son are not, repeat, are not with

Paul. The last he saw them was in the village Sunday night...we're having to gain altitude...starting to pick up AA fire...Over." I must have gasped. Ira looked at me. I moved over to the map and photos.

There's the military airstrip...across the road: Buon Pan Lam. I was amazed at the detail of the photos. An NVA tank sat skewed across the entrance of the village. Flames and smoke leapt up to me from the photos. The whole village seems either on fire or smoldering.

> *Dead companions,*
> *many, he saw there...*

One longhouse stood, apparently unscathed. It could be theirs. I remember Mi-Lai telling me about the bunker they had hidden in during the attack in '68. God...that they be safe...I wanted to cry. I remembered her telling me how frightened they had been in '68.

What were their options? Assuming they're still all right...they're either holed up in the bunker...or possibly could have taken off through the countryside to the east of the village. There would be big problems and obstacles with either choice. It's easy to say which direction you should go when you're staring at an updated situation map. It's another thing entirely to have the shit hitting the fan all around you and have to make a decision.

Buon Pan Lam was by far the most devastated area in the photos. I looked up at Ira; he explained.

The damage to the village was not from the NVA. Rumors had come in that FULRO was involved in the NVA attack; Vietnamese reported seeing Montagnards in the vanguard of the first troops entering the town. It was known that FULRO directives sometimes emanated from Buon Pan Lam. It was also known that FULRO was often the whipping boy of the prejudiced individuals in ARVN's command structure. I bit my lip, for I had slowly been piecing together what I knew of various relatives' and friends' involvement in the underground. The prejudice between the Vietnamese and Montagnard cultures was long standing and ran deep.

On the excuse of an NVA tank that had stopped close to the entrance of the village, ARVN called an air strike. The Vietnamese Air Force had simply rolled several 500 pound bombs out of the belly of a C-130 onto the buon. Certain Air Force officers were fairly open in their talk of reprisals against FULRO and the Montagnards. Early estimates suggested that over half of the villagers had been killed, more than 450. I couldn't keep the "ifs" from my mind, and tears dropped to the plastic overlay as I listened to the calm words. American planes, and American bombs, dropped by crews trained by Americans. I was leaving a world of sanity...if any such existed.

The Highlands are going. News had come in that Kontum and Pleiku have started taking rockets. The Western staff of the hospital is beginning to evacuate, according to word from the consulate.

Another report from Paul. Everyone in the compound is all right, but he doesn't know how much longer their food will hold out. They can hear fighting going on all around them. He's limiting his radio contact, trying to save the battery of the small portable set for as long as he can. Ira assures me they're doing everything they can to extract them when the time comes.

What can I do? I've never felt so useless in my life.

WEDNESDAY: Spotter reports that Buon Pan Lam is still smoldering. No life can be seen in the debris. They can see bodies.

Paul had reported that the fighting continues around their compound. He says they've hung out white flags and signs in Vietnamese stating, "We are foreign non-combatants—willing to surrender to anyone in authority." It's well known that the NVA considers any US government representatives as spies.

Ira suggests I get some rest; there's nothing I can do. He's arranged a room for me at the consulate complex. He'll let me know as soon as anything comes up.

I stare at four blank walls. I sit. I stand. I walk. I smoke. I can't stand being alone. I can't stand being with people. I can't keep from repeating to myself, "What if..."

People, and machines of people, killing people. Are we all blind? Jesus! What kind of hell are they going through? And I sit here.

God! I want to be with them.

There's a beach here to walk on. Kids are laughing. I see a son's face, laughing. I kick at a broken feather washed upon the sand. I crush seashells. I stare at the water. I listen to the sea. A child shyly approaches and wants to practice his English. I'm not very friendly. I pick up a smooth stone and turn it over and over in my hand. I return to the radio room.

No news. I sense that I'm becoming a bother. There's nothing they can tell me.

A rumor of Vietnamese refugees trickling out. Only a few. No Montagnards.

I talk with one of the pilots of the spotter plane. Fighting continues. "98% of Pan Lam is destroyed. All roads are cut."

THURSDAY: Radio communication with Paul was lost late yesterday. Nobody's been able to raise him. His radio's battery should have lasted longer than this.

Some refugees are beginning to come out to Khanh Duong District on Route 21. A truckload of refugees was reportedly ambushed by NVA. Nothing is certain. Rumors abound.

Ira and Spears, the Consul General, fly over the American compound in Ban Me Thuot. They make several quick low passes. "No damage...but no life."

"Basically, we're not trying anymore."

Reports that a commercial Air Viet Nam plane was shot down somewhere near Pleiku. The plane was coming from Laos. Jesus!... Mac was coming back at this time. Please be on another flight.

An embassy chopper comes in from Kontum. An American doctor and Philippine nurse from the hospital. Senia, the nurse, is crying.

More rumors: fifty-five Montagnard refugees are being brought into Nha Trang. No, they're already here and are being questioned by province officials. I desperately try to find out where they are. I ask at the Vietnamese provincial offices. No one knows anything about them. I've never known such frustration. Could they have possibly gotten out? Are my wife and son right in this town and I can't get to them? Finally I find out that no refugees have come in.

FRIDAY: I learn from McDonald, the Province Rep, that a Montagnard official named Y-Bling had escaped from a village near Ban Me Thuot and is now at the Ethnic Minorities Office. There could be a misspelling. Mi-Lai's father's name is Y-Blieng. He was one of the highest Montagnards in the provincial government. I run to Ethnic Minorities.

Wrong man. He knew the family, but had no news of Buon Pan Lam, other than that it lay in ruins. "There were many deaths," he said.

A Vietnamese Air Force Officer, Colonel Tuy, approached me and offered his sympathies. He had spent a number of years in Ban Me Thuot, had become fluent in Rhadé, and gotten to know Mi-Lai's family quite well. Her father had adopted him into the family, a rare occurrence for a Vietnamese. He was taking a chopper into Phuoc An…there were rumors that refugees were coming into that area. He'd let me know what he found out.

Back to the improvised situation room at the airport. A chopper's coming in from Pleiku. I stand outside on the pad, squinting from the sun's glare on the concrete. I hear the pulsing of the rotors before I see the craft. It comes in hurriedly, out of the westering sun, without the soft set-down of a normal flight. Leoni and two others of the New Zealand Red Cross Team climb out, even before the rotors have slowed. The two girls are just controlling themselves. Leoni sees me and runs into my arms, sobbing.

Mac had been on that flight from Laos. He's dead.

> *Salt tears*
> *rose from the well of longing in both…*
> *and cries burst from both as keen and fluttering*
> *as those of the great taloned hawk,*
> *whose nestlings farmers take before they fly.*

198

I didn't think I had any tears left.

We find a quiet corner in the terminal building. Leoni wipes her face. She's holding my hand, and trembling. They're waiting for a flight out to Saigon. Their embassy is pulling them out. In broken spurts she speaks of Mac. The last entry in the journal that he had surprisingly left behind." Death: one must accept it as one accepts life." I remembered his embrace, unusual for him, his shadow walking boldly into the alley's darkness; Gibran's words.

I watch quietly as they board the Saigon flight. My eyes burn in spite of the tears dropping from them.

> *But as things are, nothing but grief is left me*
> *for those companions.*

I return to sit in Ira's office while he's trying to arrange for transport of medical supplies to Phu Bon. Crackling on the radio, and I recognize the voice of the recently appointed Province Rep from Kontum. He was one of the more inept of the round-eyes running around. Granted, he had been in that particular post but a short time, but his lack of knowledge and understanding of what was going on was inexcusable. Now he was wanting a chopper to go to Dalat, his previous duty station, for an "animal husbandry seminar." Ira muttered, "Another $3,000 trip to go see his turkeys and girl friend...Jesus!" He looks at me, and shakes his head.

I meet John coming from Saigon on his way to Kontum. I know it will do no good, but advise him against going. Yesterday's chopper was the last guaranteed flight out. He still thinks he can help get Pat and the others out more quickly.

The feeling of uselessness comes over me again, and yet I don't dare leave here for fear I'll miss word of the family.

Mac...We'll miss you.

SATURDAY: I head for II Corps Headquarters, looking for Colonel Tuy. I meet a young captain, whose distress seems as real as my own. He tells me his pregnant wife and four children are in Ban Me Thuot.

I find Tuy fairly easily. He said he learned nothing the previous day. He's sincere in his concern. Mi-Lai's family is his own. He tells me again how her father adopted him. I know he had to be extremely busy. He looks at me pensively for several moments. A sad smile slowly evolves. He puts his hand on my shoulder. I felt strength from his compassion. Very quietly, very determinedly, he simply says, *"Di!"*

I almost have to trot to keep up with his pace leaving headquarters. Into his jeep. Within minutes we're on the tarmac of the airfield. A few quick words, and airmen are jumping. The motor slowly gains speed, as do the rotors. The whine continues its ever increasing pitch until it's lost to the wind. The gunship lifts off the ground, tilting forward to gain headway, across the active runway at a few meters clearance...we rise, and bank a little north of west, gaining speed and altitude. Tuy turns over his shoulder and shouts in my ear, for the doors are open and the wind and motor noise are loud, "We'll go to Kanh Duong first."

We settle down into the swirling dust. There's little activity, and Tuy wastes no time. No refugees. "They say they've sent 300 on to Nha Trang. Mostly Vietnamese." The rotors are still swinging and we're back in the chopper, quickly rising from the red dirt below. "Phuoc An is next."

.....tilting the red wind to the gods...

We circle once and drop quickly to a makeshift command post on a dirty red hill overlooking QL 21. The NVA have blocked the road several klicks further towards Ban Me Thuot. A few rockets are haphazardly coming into the area. There's a lot of confusion. About 700 refugees are stranded with the NVA on both sides of them. They can't get by. Several deuce-and-a-halves have loaded the refugees that have gotten through. But now they are likewise stranded. The road has now been cut to the east, also.

I walk by each truck, filled with exhausted humanity, looking, hoping. Only very tired faces, crowded into the backs of the trucks. More rockets coming in with a greater regularity. Tuy calls me, and motions towards the helicopter. He's anxious to get his crew out of the fire zone.

The Huey lifts her tail, swings in an arc, avoiding the road, and we quickly close on the other trucks stranded to the west...more rockets...small arms fire...whining shrieks heard over the engine roar, we lift suddenly, our nose turns again to the ground gaining speed, wheels sharply, and we head southwest, skimming close to the rough terrain.

In minutes we're back on the ground at Kanh Duong. More confusion, heavy shelling in support of an ARVN push up the road. We walk towards a group of young soldiers. They see Tuy's rank and the group opens a pathway into its center. A badly wounded NVA prisoner is kneeling on the ground. He looks up at me. Blood mats his hair and streaks his face. A kid. He's tired, hurt, and badly scared. The others are staring at him as if he were some weird animal at the zoo. I feel his hurt; I realize that his family knows nothing of him either. I don't have the words or courage to comfort him. I'm ashamed, and return to the chopper pad.

One of the pilots comes up and offers a cigarette. I take it and light his. He starts to say something, but chokes, and his eye rims grow red and moist. He looks at the ground, embarrassed, then blurts out in Vietnamese, "All...All my family...in Ban Me Thuot."

A small squad of men, almost all of them wounded, is gathered close to the chopper. Tuy decided to medivac two of the worst cases with us. I help slide a stretcher across the open cabin of the aircraft; I look down at the body writhing at my feet.

Dirt, blood, flesh and pain. He quiets, then subsides into a coma. I doubt if he'll make it.

Just as we're about to lift off, a soldier rushes under the spinning blades with a letter in his outstretched hand. He screams over the noise of the motor, "Please take to Nha Trang."

Tuy takes the note and we lift out of the searing dust. We're headed east, to a safer climate. Tuy opens the letter and reads it... folds the paper carefully and places it back in his pocket, clenching his teeth as he shakes his head, to no one in particular.

So we fared onward, and death fell behind,
and we took breath to grieve for our companions.

I fold into my own thoughts. Of all the refugees we've observed today, I've only seen two Montagnards, and they were Bru. All the rest were ethnic Vietnamese. Why?

The Vietnamese with whom I had spoken said they thought most of the Montagnards were staying in their villages. No one had any more news of Buon Pan Lam. I was praying to a god unknown.

On return to Nha Trang I check back at CONGEN's situation room. The embassy had decided to evacuate all their personnel from the Highlands. The Consul General: "We don't want another Ban Me Thuot." All the foreign staff from the hospital have come in on the last chopper with the exception of Christian, the quiet pediatrician, and Edric Baker, a New Zealand doctor. Scott's comment on their staying, "They've got no other place to go."

I'm glad that Pat, John and the rest are out. Ya Vincent, and all, *Oei ma long...*Stay well.

I'm tired and depressed. Maybe I haven't been trying hard enough. I take a walk on the beach in the late afternoon light. Every kind of thought passes, and even my thinking shames me. Scott is with me, but understandably quiet and a step behind. "To be on the beach with the two of you now, laughing..." and that thought breaks me.

Before the end my heart was broken down.
I slumped on the trampled sand and cried aloud,
caring no more for life or the light of day,
and rolled there weeping, til my tears were spent.

Only time in the present counts now, and I'm losing track of the days. Refugees are accumulating at Kilometer 62, and the government is trying to provide at least minimal supplies. Air America may be carrying in rice, so I wait for a ride in...it seems my only hope now is to try to at least find some who have come out from Pan Lam.

Others are beginning to notice the significantly few numbers of Montagnards among the refugees. One embassy underling suggests that the native highlanders are staying in the buons because of recent backing of FULRO by the NVA. Perhaps this could mean more safety for the Montagnards. But how can I communicate?

There is a possibility of getting back into Phuoc An by chopper, but those using the craft return too late from their "aerial survey," One told me that many refugees had gathered there, many on trucks; but three bridges are blown between them and Khanh Duong. Another day of waiting.

> But when day came he sat on the rocky shore
> and broke his own heart groaning, with eyes wet
> scanning the bare horizon of the sea.

As the sun reaches for the western mountains I wander listlessly back to a quiet spot on the coast, sit and try to let my mind flow with the ebbing tide. The eastern horizon darkens. A helicopter swings low over the water and back towards the air base. I see what looks like a small child's face pressed to the window as they pass over the beach. Maybe they are bringing some out. I remind myself not to let hopes get too high. Dark visions again.

Return to the room to wait. Can't. Walk back to the abandoned school where supposedly refugees will be brought. No life. Meet someone from Kontum. Says the rangers have pulled out. Only the Ruff Puffs, the local militia, are left. They've given up. Probably the best thing for the people there. Return to the room for the night. I stare at two photos. I have my fears. I'm ashamed of the darkness that lingers at times in my mind.

NEXT DAY: More frustrating attempts to get nowhere. Fewer and fewer people want to tell me anything, More rumors. A lot of military activity on QL 21. Are refugees getting hit? Phuoc An has fallen. I was just there. Refugees are moving by foot to Khanh Duong. Military chopper pilots are selling rides out. Six days ago the price in Pleiku was 50,000 piasters to get out. Three days ago, 335,000 P. An exodus is beginning from Kontum to Pleiku to Phu Bon. Some 50,000 to 75,000 refugees are on QL 21. The government can't get any rice in. The situation is getting bad.

ANOTHER DAY: Refugees coming in for real. I spend all day out at Ruri, a collection of old, very dilapidated wooden barracks through which the government is funneling the refugees. I walk through them all and talk to people. The only Montagnards are from the Bru tribe whose village was near Km.62, and there were very few of them. They had to come through the forest; there's too much fighting on the roads.

MIDDLE OF THE DAY: Busses of refugees from Kanh Duong begin arriving. Confusion. Everyone asking for families. A few more Bru. Kilometer 62 was on fire; they walked out at night. One man is wiping the dust off an ancient sewing machine he carried all the way.

There is no water, no rice, no check-in procedure. One boy is carrying a pair of pants with the legs tied as a pack. He spills his possessions on the ground: an empty water bottle and a few rags. Many torn feet. Two dogs make it; one, riding the last leg of the journey on top of a bus. I've never seen such fatigue and despair.

Like a forest fire the flames roared on...

Everyone is talking about fire. Fire...Fire...Fire throughout Ban Me Thuot! People listen to stories and cry. It seems that everyone arriving has lost family. Two little girls, around the ages of five and six, huddle together, very much alone. A TV crew and photographer arrive and stay for 10 minutes. They're obnoxious.

Some know of Americans, but don't know what happened to them. Two Frenchmen are trying to get information on their countrymen in the area. I recognize a few names.

> *Now the souls gathered, stirring out of Erebos,*
> *brides and young men, and men grown old in pain...*

Tears and more tears from tired faces. One talks of many planes bombing. Many leave dead children, dead wives, brothers, parents, behind. Twelve busloads have come in, having picked up the half-dead refugees at the last blown bridge. Water is finally brought in from Nha Trang. Drinking and bathing become sacraments. Someone tells of sixty to seventy people stuck in the cross fire at Phuoc An. Another asks why all the ARVN run away. "The NVA are everywhere." Some people actually leave the makeshift camp the first day with friends or family from Nha Trang.

One soldier asks me if I am married to a Montagnard in Ban Me Thuot. My insides clench.

"Yes...Do you know..."

"What village?"

"Buon Pan Lam."

"She cannot leave...cannot come out. Everybody dead... Everybody dead...Everybody dead."

Another soldier alongside laughs.

I have to turn away. I cannot see. I cannot swallow.

A young woman, aged beyond her years: "There were about 5,000 people, somewhat together, coming from Kilometer 62. Communists stopped them. Started shooting. Maybe five hundred got through. One woman with five children finally can no longer carry the youngest. Leaves the baby on a rock in the forest...and walks on. Five hundred people are coming down the mountain into Kanh Dung...and three soldiers start firing into the group with automatic weapons. Many die." She wiped her dirt- and tear-streaked face with the back of an equally grimy hand.

Another: "First day, as many province officials as could be found were rounded up, given a 'trial', and shot."

An old man comes out with one deer antler over his shoulder. People are falling into desperate sleep anywhere, even in the glaring sun. The narrow road is congested with slowly moving bodies. They're dropping to the ground, rubbing legs and feet.

I'm not comfortable being with the askers when they hear the fate of families or friends. Right now I don't think my family came out.

> *You shall hear prophecy from the rapt shade*
> *of blind Teiresias of Thebes, forever*
> *charged with reason even among the dead...*

I'm weary, and a little dizzy, and squat down in the shade against an outside wall of rotten wood. I must have drifted off. I'm looking up, through eyes not my own, lying on my back in front of *Ae*'s longhouse. A flash of pain to my left side. Individual faces come before me; most I don't recognize...it's as though I'm staring at a thin, side-lit negative. Some look familiar. It's all one family. One's eyes are closed. The eyes I look through are half-closed.

I fall asleep and dream: Books and bodies, loud music, and modern surroundings. I awake, tired; I don't move. I seem to know something...I don't want to listen, yet I feel serene for a while...until I talk myself out of such serenity and into unknown worry. Where is my mind? I see the right side of Mac's face; the rest is shadow. A letter. A tree.

My head nods hard. I open my eyes. They're sunburned, and hurt.

If they do not come out, and I hear nothing, what do I do? The kids: Y-Hem, H'Nina, Y-Sang. What about Paul's wife? She was in Bangkok when the attack began. Can I be a comfort to the kids in Saigon when I myself seek sympathy? I'm not strong. I'm afraid for them. I'm afraid for myself. I'm afraid *of* myself. Where do I turn? I only see the Void. And someone says, "It all works out for the best..."

I look up at the weary humanity around me. Crying...everywhere. Westmoreland's infamous statement that the Oriental does not prize life as highly as the Westerner: He was not here today.

(AP) Saigon...HE [VIETNAMESE OFFICIAL] SAID THAT BY PULLING INTO THE COASTAL ENCLAVES THE SOUTH

VIETNAMESE WOULD HAVE SHORTER SUPPLY LINES,
AND THE NORTH VIETNAMESE, LONGER ONES...

It's official: they're giving up the Highlands.

> *The rose Dawn might have found them weeping still*
> *had not grey-eyed Athena slowed the night*
> *when night was most profound, and held the Dawn*
> *under the Ocean of the East. That glossy team,*
> *Firebright and Daybright, the Dawn's horses*
> *that drew her heavenward for men—Athena*
> *stayed their harnessing.*

THE NEXT MORNING: I'm out at Ruri again. Some Rhadé from Buon Ha have come in. No news of Pan Lam. People are saying that those within the city, or near, could not get out. The refugees coming in are in worse and worse shape. Many swollen feet, bandaged with rags. The shelters are becoming crowded. Someone mentions that Air Viet Nam is now charging 40,000 Piasters for special flights from Nha Trang to Saigon. People here are afraid. Dalat is now evacuating. What to do, where to go? If only I knew something.

I break; I can't handle more today. I have to leave the swarm of death-speakers and sorrow. I catch a ride back into Nha Trang, and walk down to the waterfront. The ocean soothes. I find a shell to give to Mi-Lai. Children are playing behind me, "touch the American..." One small child approaches. Mi-Lai would give the shell to the boy... he takes it. I turn away. A little girl playing. She wants a little girl. God! I have to do something.

Go back to the CONGEN complex, enter the small American cafeteria. I'm not hungry, but know I should try to eat something. I find a corner table with my back to the room. A pilot comes over to the table...a nice face...asks if I'm having any luck; says people are starting to come into Dalat from Ban Me Thuot...Hopes rise...a safer route. Please let it be.

I lay uncomfortably on the soft bed in the sterile cubicle. I'm looking up again. A clearing in the forest, trees surround me.

There's a glow behind the trees, possibly from the moon...perhaps a conflagration.

MORNING: An acquaintance from the consulate says he spoke with someone from the village who came out. He didn't have a name. He thinks Mi-Lai is alright. He could say nothing more about the family. Said the NVA were taking all the young men from the village. How young? I hope he's at least partially right. He repeats other conflicting rumors. I have to find out more information.

I can tell my presence is wearing on people from the consulate. I know that some would just as soon have me gone, out of the way.

Rumors that the family may have gone to Buon Ko Tam. Was it her father's voice heard on the communist broadcast? The second or third VNAF bomb hit the middle of the house. What can I believe?

I get a line through to Bangkok from the consulate and speak with H'Lum, Paul's wife. She's coming into Saigon tomorrow.

Y-Klong finds me. He had helped me last year in Ban Me Thuot, and had introduced me to my future in-laws. I had gotten to know him fairly well, and liked him. He was close to the family. He says someone has come in from the village. Do I want to talk to him?

Our pace is hurried. We finally enter a small hovel in one of the poorer neighborhoods. Half-a-dozen Montagnards are milling around. They're speaking Rhadé. Y-Suin, the man from the village, is obvious; his clothes are torn and dirty. He was drawn. His father was the hamlet chief. They lived next door to Mi-Lai's parents. At last: someone who was there...someone I can believe.

I can't follow his words. He slows his speech. Y-Klong interprets. He asks if I'm sure I want to hear.

"I was in the village Monday and Tuesday. I left Wednesday. Monday there had been no activity to speak of in the village. The feeling seemed to be that the situation was similar to '68 and would soon be over. Virtually all the villagers elected to remain. Mi-Lai and your son were there and safe then.

"Tuesday, two NVA tanks approached the village. ARVN apparently called an air strike. The planes were very high. Your mother and father were in the bunker, most of the rest of the family were in the house. The first bomb hit the gas station out on the road. People became scared...the second bomb hit right next to the house, next to that area where people like to get together..."

I remember her mother sitting there holding a young child, gossiping and laughing. Mi-Lai has her laugh.

"I was standing behind the house, to the side. After the second bomb, those who could, ran out of the house...those in the bunker also ran out, very frightened. They all ran towards the coffee trees, the plantation...the people gathered. The third bomb hit in the middle of the people."

Y-Suin became agitated, enraged as he spoke.

"The concussion knocked people far into the air, far away. All the ground shook. The bombs were blinding...blinding...like many suns."

I asked if he had seen Mi-Lai.

"Yes, she was with her brother, Y-Ler."

When did he see her?

"That morning..."

But, right before the bomb...?

"Yes, she was with Y-Ler...Many, many people died. Many, many people died."

Did he know what happened to her and our son?!

"The bomb was blinding...Many, many people died."

Silence. Y-Suin is looking at the floor. The others are looking at me.

I'm finally hit by the meaning. I begin shaking...tears flow. Y-Klong's hand is on my shoulder.

Y-Suin goes on: "Two small children ran from the house...Y-Din, the youngest, and a girl about his size...after the second bomb. They ran back after the third explosion...looking for anyone. There were many bodies. They ran away, screaming...I think they ran towards Buon Ko Tam...where there is family. That afternoon Buon Ko Tam came under a very heavy ARVN artillery barrage. I do not know what happened to them..."

kerry Heubeck

Y-Suin goes on, explaining the NVA entry into Ban Me Thuot. I cannot listen. I start to leave. Y-Klong asks if I'm alright. I nod. I walk to the coast. I think how I wanted them to be here on the beach with me, laughing. I return to the room. I cry. I scream.

The next day, I fly out. H'Lum is coming. Saigon. I walk...and walk.

***

And now there came before my eyes Minos,
the son of Zeus, enthroned, holding a golden staff,
dealing out justice among ghostly pleaders
arrayed about the broad doorways of Death.

It has been more than a week now. I enter the pagoda across the busy street from our block.

It is relatively quiet. One can dwell within the mind for a few moments. I look up at the Buddha, then close my eyes...the phrase comes easily, "one must not mistake the pointing finger for the moon." I realize the mistake of seeking the void without...for it is within. I must keep my hand in touch with the earth. I make the error of feeling sorrow for myself, for ourselves; when it is for them we wish the serenity and peace. At whatever price.

I had approached the area of prayer during a service. I knelt quietly in a corner of the platform. The service was soon over and I was alone. I could not, in reality, disengage my mind from my body. I sat cross-legged, alone, reaching within. The lattice work of the windows remained behind my closed eyes. The image did not fade as I had expected, but soon began to rise higher and higher, until it was lost from the swirls of darkness by leaving that field of non-vision directly, rather than fusing into the darkness itself. The concept of time evaporated.

...but first came shades in thousands, rustling
in a pandemonium of whispers, blown together...

210

I felt I had been there only a short time. I realized I could see no more from this vantage point today, and that I should leave. Though it was cool, and a breeze was rippling at my shirt, droplets of perspiration made themselves felt, falling easily down my side. I wished for the relief of tears, yet realized this was inconsistent with the serenity symbolized before me. I retreated from the now-darkened sanctum, for the candles had been extinguished.

One quite aged woman had sat a little to my left, reciting. I wonder which she sees...the pointing finger or...

I turn around; a girl, perhaps in her twenties, stands between myself and the door. She holds an infant. We share glances, seeming of mutual sympathy, for an instant. She soon follows my steps out, and wanders about the upraised balcony of the pagoda.

I look from the door, adjusting my eyes to the too brilliant light of the sun...

An old woman, to my Western eyes featureless, excepting her aged face and somewhat withered body hidden within the likewise featureless *ao dai,* light brown, like so many old, and to me, featureless women wear. The unencumbered breeze blew at the looseness of her *ao dai.* It made her even lighter than she first seemed; almost ephemeral.

> *...or if some wind could take me by the hair*
> *up into running cloud...*

She held in her left hand a bamboo bird cage, itself darkened with age. I heard the chittering of finches...I couldn't see them within the finely crafted framework. She was lightly tapping the cage with her right hand...Then I realized the door to the cage must be open, for the birds were escaping and flying high, but with the wind, all in the same direction, as a kite would lift from a child's fingers, play erratically in the breeze for but a moment, then soar into the heavens.

Everything about her was brown; the brown of an aged and overused earth. And yet the air...the sky about her head was so brilliant. The birds were free; now left to their own makings of

211

fate. It was she who had set them free. She hardly glanced at their disappearance, but returned to the confines of the temple, and I saw her no more. I cannot know her thoughts, yet I think her a beautiful person.

The girl and infant continue to wander slowly about the courtyard of the pagoda, alone. I am hesitant to leave. I wish I could give solace, and instead, I seek it.

This is the same pagoda to which, a week ago in the darkness of a late Sunday night, Huynh had brought H'Nina and me. It had been locked, but she found the caretaker, and explained we had family in Ban Me Thuot. The monk opened the door and lit a few candles. I had been here before, but only as a sightseer. My vision had been altered, and this was now different. The monk departed, and the three of us entered.

> *Think, then, Akhilleus:*
> *you need not be so pained by death.*

I sat, knelt, and tears flowed easily; but so did a new feeling of strength and clarity. The confusion leaves me. It's all so simple. I will not leave. We will get the two kids out, whatever it takes; for now it seems that H'Lum and I are the only family they have. Yet, I still have hope.

The week goes by rapidly, trying to buck two bureaucracies for passports and visas for the kids. We also begin collecting funds to send in to Montagnard families who lost their homes and possessions at Buon Pan Lam, for we had made connections with Rhadé who had already opened underground communications with those behind the lines. It's going to be a long wait.

The Highlands fall...are given up. Lam Dong, gone; Hué, gone; the mass terror of Danang; the only communication from there now is from a ship standing off the harbor. Horror stories of refugees and planes...refugees everywhere, millions. We are witnessing a tragic addendum to history.

At this moment, I do not fear the military situation of Saigon so much as the political, for I want desperately to get the kids out. The president proclaims a new law: No male Vietnamese citizen over the age of sixteen can leave the country. Period. More red tape. I try to get help from the embassy. There seems little they can do at this point.

I talk to an American friend in the consulate. She says that many fear that Paul has been executed. The communists had issued a communiqué stating that honest foreigners would be treated fairly... it specifically excluded "American military advisors...who would be treated as the spies that they are..."

We have collected over 700,000 piasters to send into Pan Lam. We have no way of knowing if it will get there, other than trust.

Montagnard and Vietnamese friends consult mystics and soothsayers. Their reports are sad, but generally optimistic. One says we shall hear news within the week. Anything that is positive, from whatever source, I want to believe. The last four books that I have picked up have dealt with telepathy.

CARE has a new director. My god, what a time to change. Most of the old hands are gone. I am suddenly the one round-eye who has been here the longest. I begin assisting with the refugee relief operations. In a short time I'm in charge of half of them. The other Westerner involved is seldom around...gradually I take over more of the relief operations by default.

> So we moved out, sad in the vast offing,
> having our precious lives, but not our friends.

Americans are beginning to leave the country in noticeable quantity. Nha Trang looks as though it will be given up in a day or so. The refugee problem is becoming immense. The atmosphere here is the thickest I've ever felt. The Vietnamese of Saigon are frightened. It's official: "non-essential" Americans are going to be shipped out. I'm surprised and ashamed that leaving had ever entered my mind.

Huynh has become the true sister that I never had. She knows my despair, shares my grief, but always remains optimistic. Her help with the kids is fantastic; with cajoling, flattering, crying, pleading, she has gotten us into the Vietnamese government offices and secured paperwork the rest of us were unable to get. She's been relentless in pursuit of our goal of getting them out. At night she prays for our family. I've rarely met anyone so selfless. She has shared with me her losses, the memory of her fiancé lost in the war. She reads a poem she had translated into English for me:

April, nineteen seventy-two
In Binh-Ba's battlefield
You was killed
Our love never come true...

Why didn't you live?
For memories and our war country!

Remember the former time
You, eighteen years old school boy
Gentle and well educated.
I, a little schoolgirl
Was shy in the white dress.
Our families in the same village,
Same way home, we fell in love
A poor boy, you're fatherless
Mother's crazy, lives like died.
I loved you, words couldn't express...

Spring passed by, summer moved on.
In war time as the man you had gone
Tears came out when saying "good by"
Joined to Army, you left me behind
First love is difficult to forget...

Candidate school is still there
Where I used come to visit
With some plum and grapefruit
Needless precious things
A true love still could win

Out of training school you became a fighting man
From Binh Long, Duc Tanh to Phuoc-Hoa
God separated us far and far...

What a nice surprise for us to meet!
How long have we been away, my dearest?
How long have I begun to compose poem?
Send sad verse via cloud when lonesome...

On the light rainy evening
Hand in hand we're walking
You told me the soldier's hardship
Advised me, "That's life," not worrying
Explained me what's "Father Land"
Our love was beautiful, no concerning sex

By heart and by brain
Reason won intense desire
Your love to Viet-Nam
Stronger than to me

One day seemed dully
From the field fulling fire and blood
You died like a hero
Without telling me "Hello"
Without seeing me the last
With native land—you completed
With our love—nothing's finished!!!

Following you to the church-yard
You let me down with a broken heart
From now on, no more letters from the front line
You kissed me only one time
Then forever you stand me up
What a miserable girl in this life!!

Some gloomy evenings
Sat behind your grave
I sang softly for you sleep
A sleep all day all night
whether it rained or stormed outside...

Oh country, oh Vietnamese mother land
I lost my lover from this small hand
No one sharing with me the happiness
When this war to end...

Peace coming who will I get married?
Under deep ground
Peace coming what will you get?

Well, let smile and be on your feet

Still having water on ocean, still having sand on desert,
Still being a person, I love you, my dearest...

dedicated to the soul of
Capt. N. NGOC-HUYNH

She was wiping her eyes when I looked up from the paper.

"...Needless precious things..."

***

We were still having trouble getting the final papers for Y-Hem and H'Nina. I'm sleeping very little, and not well. A deep fit of depression sets in that even the kids and Huynh can't bring me out of. I take the afternoon off and return to the pagoda.

A service is going on. All of the people present are wearing mourning bands. My corner is empty, despite the gathering. I sit upon the cool marbled floor, let go a sigh. My eyes close easily. I release myself and flow with the soft chanting. Each sound of the gongs takes me deeper, and forms a continuity and rhythm to the escape of the mind.

I finally feel—see their two faces; Mi-Lai's soft smile...the child approaches and brushes by closely. Very, very slowly the vision fades as if I'm drifting backwards in space, slowly back. I rest in the darkness, and strength comes. Again, there is no element of time. I know I can see no more, and rise. My left leg is asleep, almost paralyzed.

I'm leaving. The woman of brown approaches, disappears. A white kite breaks free and floats to the ground. Its guiding string is picked up by two children...and it flies again.

I return to the office. Madam Bac tells me, "I'm sure Mi-Lai is alive. I see her in my dream."

John comes into the office. His was the last flight out of Nha Trang after CONGEN was evacuated by the Americans. His story is another of horror: men pulling guns on the plane, fistfights at the door, Vietnamese hanging onto the landing gear as the plane's taxiing. The Vietnamese Army was looting, destroying, killing.

More friends are carrying guns. Anti-American sentiment no doubt will begin soon.

> *You shall see, now*
> *souls of the buried dead in shadowy hosts...*

The nights grow worse. What sleep I do get is filled with horrible dreams. I awake in sweats, sometimes shaking. Flames and torn bodies, women screaming...more flames, and children coming apart in gory pieces. Pain rises with yet more conflagrations. I awaken exhausted. A friend had given me some Valium. It takes several to put my body to sleep, but my mind continues to wander as a lost soul. I reach out in darkness, but no one is there; there is no warmth.

Huynh finally gets portfolio numbers for the kids. They've been accepted for consideration as special cases to leave the country. There's still more signatures, papers, and pay-offs remaining; but it's looking a little better.

Thousands of refugees are coming down from the coast by sea. The government is directing them all to Phu Quoc Island in an effort to keep them from inundating Saigon.

I don't like leaving the kids, but I think we have the capacity to help a lot of refugees, and Huynh will be with them if anything happens. I virtually have a free rein now with CARE's relief operations. I see less and less of the other American that was recently hired. Last I heard, he was trying to get his boat out of Nha Trang.

The government plane drops towards Phu Quoc's airport. As we approach the seaside landing strip, memories of the quiet village of Navy days are replaced by the sight of swarms of humanity below. Every type of craft imaginable sits either off shore or beached on the tropic coastline, hundreds and hundreds of them. Several landing craft lie swamped near the runway extending into the calm emerald sea. SWIFTs, PBRs, junks, sampans, fishing boats lie abandoned on the shore. Another landing craft is approaching the beach, filled beyond capacity.

> *Here, toward the Sorrowing Water, run the streams*
> *of wailing, out of Styx, and quenchless Burning—*
> *torrents that join in thunder at the Rock.*

I wander the makeshift refugee camp in the old barracks area of the prison that once had housed "political detainees" with Colonel Thien and Major Mac; they're in charge of bringing organization to some 40,000 exhausted and starving people. I'm carrying a small camera in my pocket but can't bring myself to photograph the pain and misery before me. Some dignity must be left.

Little water, very little rice, no medical supplies.... The Colonel is doing the best he can with what he has. Children are crying from dry breasts, and mothers look up helplessly.

I think I hear my name, yelled from the crowd behind me...I don't recognize the voice, but I turn. A man, about my age, is waving and working his way toward the throng. As he comes nearer I recognize Quang, from the CARE sub-office in Nha Trang. He tells how he had to leave his family, fearing reprisals from the NVA for working with the Americans. We arranged for his return to Saigon with us.

Coordinating relief efforts to Phu Quoc as well as to other smaller groups was taking up increasingly more time. We had access to resources, transportation, personnel—it was just a matter of putting it all together. Hitches always arose; that was part of the game. I returned to the island several times. I felt good about what we were accomplishing. My respect grew for the Vietnamese staff working with me.

The work was tiring, and with the help of Valium, I was sleeping better. Mi-Lai and our son were constantly in the back of my mind. Huynh was doing her best, and making at least slow progress against horrendous barriers of paperwork for the kids.

> *Evil may be endured when our days pass*
> *in mourning, heavy-hearted, hard beset,*
> *if only sleep reign over nighttime, blanketing*
> *the world's good and evil from our eyes.*
> *But not for me: dreams too my demon sends me.*

I realized I had become dependent upon the Valium. I decided to go without for a night. I was tired, and fell into a slumber easily.

Startled into an eerie consciousness by the flashes...blinding, then the explosions...I fall to the ground, more eye-scorching flashes...I'm following a girl...I think I know her...I find a coat in excellent condition...I'll try it on...intestines drop from it and I slip on them...Someone is letting himself down from a high doorway...I try to help...the feet are stubs...bones and flesh follow...I grab hips... no, the chest, I'm looking through the face, literally...but it smiles, then I realize I can see through the cage of the chest...emptiness... nothing where a body should be, where a heart should be...I tell myself this person is dead...I knew him, or her, but not now...I lay the remains down gently, and yet the non-eyes look up at me, trying to smile; as I lay the corpse, so light, upon the ground, the right hand comes up and slaps my face, playfully...then it is no more. With greed I try to collect my belongings from the cabinet of this room...I'm trying to get the camera bag out...it won't come.

I awaken stiff, trembling, staring at the slowly revolving ceiling fan, feeling too hot, too cold, all at once. I don't want to awaken; I don't want to return to such sleep.

But death and darkness in that instant closed

All night I try to hold onto the shell of the cashew we had found together at the Buon. It keeps escaping, I keep losing it, losing myself...groping in the dark, supremely lonely moments of seeking in the obscurity—for a shell of what once was.

I have to return to the Valium tonight. I wonder what would happen with more… a *lot* more.

TUESDAY, 8 April, 8:30 AM: The sudden and frightening scream of a jet streaking immediately overhead. Thunderous jet wash shakes the building. Women scream; we hear explosions. Several of us run up the steps to the flat roof of the office; and from there we watch a VNAF A-37 fighter repeatedly circle and dive, bombing the presidential palace.

A coup? The kids are alone at the apartment, Huynh has left to visit her family in Vung Tau. Not knowing what to expect, I run back to the apartment. I had just returned from Phu Quoc the night before—I'm glad. Kids are OK, a little frightened. There will probably be a curfew; we need to stock up on supplies: candles, rice, canned goods. We race about the local shops. Everyone else has the same idea; scalper's prices...triple, quadruple. Can't find any kerosene for the stove.

10 AM: curfew announced; no news; the continual wail of sirens; *Tieng Goi Thanh Nien,* "Young People Stand up for Your Country," the Vietnamese National Anthem, is played continuously on the neighbor's radios. I never realized how desultory the song was. No announcements. Should have had the foresight to have a radio, and extra fuel for the stove. Army trucks rushing towards the palace. More screaming sirens. Streets are cleared of civilians—except two

vendors pushing their carts and ringing their bells as if all is well: the balloon man and ice-cream vendor...each crying out their wares over the shrieks of the sirens. God bless them!

Quang, the man from CARE's Nha Trang office who came back from Phu Quoc with me, is now living with us. I was dubious at first of his motives for leaving behind his family. He's helpful. There are many of us here. I wonder about the feelings of the Vietnamese having an American neighbor. A better feeling as to what is going on should come from the Vietnamese radio, yet I feel a sense of isolation, not listening to the American broadcast of Armed Forces Radio. The American office staff has gathered at the director's house, not too far from one of the USAID buildings. Still the monotonous playing of the national anthem.

We've gathered what we can, and now sit waiting, not knowing what will come, or how long—hours, days—we'll be here. Each has withdrawn into his or her own private activity; there's little talk. I pause over reflections in my journal.

Now the sonorous pulsing of helicopters overhead. How long will it take to know? I look about the crowded room. The flowers are dying, are dead. Will the world turn to plastic in order to survive?

Over and over again, the national anthem. I'm glad we're together. I'm going to have to turn over Phu Quoc trips to someone else until we get the kids out; I can't risk not being here if more trouble should come, or an opportunity should present itself. Should I get them to pack? Who will we see again; who won't be seen again?

Thieu's voice comes up on the radio at noon, saying that the coup was unsuccessful. That's all. Curfew still in effect. Children begin playing in the alley; toy guns and plastic airplanes.

3:00 PM: Curfew is lifted. Today was good practice. We learned a little more about self-sufficiency; the kids are more confident in themselves. I notify the new director that I'm not leaving Saigon until we get them out.

I have one more card to play. I'd met "Jake" Jacobson, a special assistant to the ambassador, when Paul's wife came into Saigon for those few short days. He seemed especially sympathetic to our quest to get her brother and sister out of the country. He had said he'd do whatever he could. I felt he meant it.

I got a call through to him. He remembered me. I explained that we seemed to be up against a brick wall. We were so close to getting the exit visas from the Saigon government...but there was always a Catch 22. I could hear the fatigue in his voice. He must be getting hundreds of such calls a day. He'd see what he could do. His tone didn't sound hopeful.

Several days passed. We continued plaguing the Vietnamese authorities. Huynh had returned, and she brought a new energy to the endeavor. Still we kept hitting that wall. More Americans were leaving. I had forgotten about the call to the ambassador's assistant.

The late afternoon sky was particularly brilliant, streaked with reds, oranges and yellows. A slight breeze had picked up. I had just returned from the office, and was sitting on the second floor landing, watching the teeming activity in the alley below.

A vintage Renault taxi, rusted blue and yellow and coughing thick oil-laden fumes, eased through the usual mob, occasionally beeping a weak horn at irreverent pedestrians; the small thoroughfare theirs by tradition. A larger car could not have made it, indeed any motorized vehicle was rare in the narrow passageway. Youths glanced into the windows of the snail-paced car. *"Ong My...Ong My...,"* the chant was picked up by the rest of the kids in the street. I watched the fun had by the children at this joyously unexpected event in the afternoon activities.

The taxi could go no further. The rear door opened. As at a circus, long stilted legs first emerged from the miniscule interior, followed by the remaining body of the lanky Westerner. He had unfolded from the cramped taxi, and stood with a small paper in his hand, squinting, and looking all around, obviously perplexed. He was apparently looking for a particular address in this hodgepodge of a neighborhood.

I could hear him trying to ask something in English. He towered over the gathering crowd. Responses, at him as much to him, giggled in polite Vietnamese; he was flustered. I was enjoying the show, but finally called down to him, and asked if I could help. His relief at hearing an American voice was noticeable. He hurried towards me as I stepped down from the landing.

"I'm looking for a...a...," he looked at the paper in his hand and stuttered. I recognized my name, and tensed.

"That's me," I replied weakly.

He muttered something about not knowing what all this was about and handed me the paper. It had been hastily typed...lines X'ed out. Handwritten notes were scribbled in the margins, as someone would make when getting leads towards finding something:

THOR NGOC HAU
201   Y-WER- HMOK

Contact Kerry Heubeck, CARE, 211 Cong Ly

Tel: USAID 4768

For Nina Struharik   age 18   *Home address*
For Y Hiem Struharik age 21 or 22
Dependents of H"Lum Struharik;--USAID Bangkok

Nina and Y Hiem are sole suvivors of Montagnard
family in Ban Me Thuot killed in recent fighting. Both
were in Saigon at time of attack.

H'Lum Struharik is wife of USAID province representative
in BMT who was captured by NVA during first week of
fighting. H'Lum is in safe haven (BKO) but U.S. Embassy
Saigon has said that she would be able to carry them as
dependents into the States order

Kerry Heubeck is husband of H'Lum's sister who was
killed in BMT attack. He has remained in Saigon trying
to get paperwork for kids done for kids so they can
return to States with him. He and
H'Lum plan to support them in the States,

Because of entire family's close connections with
Americans, these kids should be gotten out ASAP.

Destination is states: Get Struharik family address in
States from Heubeck.

Mike Rollis   Mr DAVIS (CAO)
who will   ED 2. As HBK

10-1100

384/48

My eyes flashed back to the third paragraph. The words glared at me: "sister who was killed in BMT attack." Was this a confirmation of Mi-Lai's death? No signature.

Tears welled in my eyes. I looked up at him. He's shaking his head.

He stammered again, "I don't know what's going on...all I know is that there's a colonel out at Tan Son Nhut with...," and he stretched out his arms full length, "balls *THIS* big, who says if you can get those kids to the DAO theater tomorrow morning, he'll get them on a plane out."

I started to ask him questions. He just shook his head and said he didn't know anything else. He didn't know who wrote the note... only that it was from someone very high up. I thanked him, and he returned to the waiting taxi. I turned back, still stunned, and reread the note.

DAO theater was on the military side of Tan Son Nhut airfield, its entrance separated from that of the civilian terminal. In the old days entrance would have been fairly easy dealing with American security. Now in Vietnamese hands, the airbase security had been increased tenfold since the recent coup attempt. I might manage to con myself past the guards, but how was I to get two Vietnamese citizens through?

I thought of another friend in the embassy. He had pinch-hit as province rep in Kontum for a while. Though we hadn't spoken of it, I knew he had connections with the spooks, the CIA. I trotted out to the main street and flagged down a passing Honda, giving directions to his apartment. Thank God, Cris was home. I explained my dilemma. He thought a few moments, and as he was turning to the phone said, "Get them here as soon as you can."

The kids threw what was handy into overnight bags. We're all nervous. Huynh joins us, and we catch a cab back to Cris' apartment. He opened the door and motioned us in, the phone crooked over his shoulder, its extension cord trailing behind him. He listened, said "OK," and trod back to the kitchen to hang up the receiver. He looked at me, smiled, and said, "We're on."

The night dragged out. We made imitations of eating...a couple of beers. Y-Hem fell asleep in the corner. H'Nina was tense. We tried playing cards. No one could concentrate.

At 7:30 AM a buzzer sounds. We grab the bags and head downstairs. A large black sedan is waiting: a driver, and someone literally riding shotgun. Blacked-out windows; diplomatic plates. The flag of the American Embassy hangs limp on the small post at the corner of the hood. Someone says, "Put the kids in the middle." Cris and I are next to the windows.

We ease through the gate and out onto Cach Mang. All of the car's occupants are silent. Within a few minutes we approach the entrance to the military base at Tan Son Nhut. The iron-barred gate is across the road. Five or six armed security guards stand outside the gatehouse. Several tanks are parked around the entrance.

A guard holds up his hand for us to stop. The driver lowers his window only enough to speak, and hands out a couple of I.D. cards. The Vietnamese guard is trying to look in the window. The driver blocks his line of vision to the back seat. The kids are on the floor. Cris and I stare straight ahead. The driver says something about, "diplomatic clearance...in a hurry...." The guard takes the papers into the guardhouse. Long minutes. He finally returns, hands the papers back, motions another to lift the gate, then to us to pass on. The relief is audible. I'm thinking we're home free...Three minutes past the gate a Vietnamese soldier steps into the road, his hand upraised demanding us to stop. Other soldiers, all armed, stand at the side of the road. "Damn!"

We're half way to DAO. The car eases up to the guard and stops. The other American jumps out and shuts the door quickly. I notice a holstered pistol under his jacket. He speaks with the soldier. There seems to be an argument. The American reaches under his coat. "Oh Christ!" No...he's just pulling out his wallet. A few bills change hands, and the American jumps back into the car. "Hurry up before he changes his mind."

We sped past the soldiers, finally pulling up at the side of the theater. Another American steps from the early morning shadows, opens the back door of the car and says, "through here," pointing at the emergency exit door of the theater.

A number of Americans sat about in the cushioned seats of the movie house. The huge silvered screen looked down blankly on the grouped conversations and piles of baggage. I presumed these were Embassy and USAID employees and families. An American with a plastic I.D. badge pinned to his shirt approached, asked if these were the Montagnard kids. I nodded. He told me to make sure they stayed right there, for them not to come back to the entrance of the theater under any circumstances. The lights dimmed to about half level. He waved me to follow him. I walked back up the aisle and turned into the lobby. Groups of Vietnamese officials were standing at the main door, checking the American passports of those entering.

I was taken into the theater office. Several men stood about, drinking coffee and smoking. One stood out in a gray-green flight suit. Silver oak leaves adorned his shoulders. "Colonel, this is the guy with the Montagnard kids." I introduced myself, and repeated the messenger's description of him yesterday. He laughed. I thanked him for what he was doing, and asked if he could tell me his destination so that I could let the kids' sister know where to meet them.

"Aren't you going...?"

I explained. He let it pass. "I'll let you know when we meet at the plane. Truth is I don't know yet. Just do whatever this fellow asks," nodding towards the man who introduced us. "Right now, we just wait."

I went back and sat with Cris and the kids. Cris nodded and walked up the aisle. He returned minutes later with sandwiches and cold drinks. The kids were worried: How would they meet their sister; where were they going? We waited. Names were called, and Americans started drifting out with their bags. The man with the badge reappeared. "Follow me."

Out another side door. A three-quarter ton truck with an aluminum box over the body, no windows, was backed up to the door.

"Tell the kids to get in, and no matter what happens, not to make a sound until the door opens again." He held open the portal. It was dark inside.

I grabbed Y-Hem by the shoulders. He put on a brave smile, nodded, and jumped into the truck. H'Nina was crying. We hugged tightly. "We got'ta go," said the man with the badge. H'Nina wiped her eyes with the back of her hand, forced herself to smile, and took my hand as she stepped up into the dark interior. The man closed the door, then put a lock over the hasp, and clamped it shut. It seemed so final. He looked at Cris and me, "Wait inside for a couple more minutes."

I watched the clock on the wall. Ten minutes. Fifteen. The side door opened. He waved us outside again. The truck was still there. Another black diplomatic car had pulled up alongside. "Change o' plans." He unlocked the door, and the kids climbed out, squinting at the sunlight.

"Into the car...no...Cris, front seat. You, left rear...No, she has to be on the right." More blacked-out windows. The driver got in. We left the theater and drove into an area of the base I didn't know. The man with the plastic badge kept looking at his watch. He told the driver to slow down. A couple of turns. He looked at his watch again.

"Now!"

The driver made a left turn and increased speed. We were heading towards the back end of the airfield. A closed security gate was ahead. As we approached a Vietnamese soldier walked up to the one on duty at the gate, said something, and pointed into the guardhouse. The one standing guard laughed and walked into the small security enclosure. The new guard raised the gate and waved us through. He wore a big smile. The bar dropped rapidly as we passed. "One down," said the man with the badge. He looks at his watch again. "We're doing alright." He almost smiled.

We turned onto the tarmac of a taxi runway. The gaping open tail of a camouflaged C-130 was several hundred yards away.

"Little slower," he said.

I saw the colonel. He and another officer in flight suit were walking with three Vietnamese officials, one with a clipboard in his hand, on the near side of the plane towards the tail. We had a hundred yards to go. The group passed by the tail of the plane. The colonel drew the attention of the lead official into the darkened belly of the plane. Fifty yards. He put his arm across the shoulders of the official, pulling a bottle out of his side pocket with his other hand. The giant loading ramp began rising slowly. As we were pulling up to the near side of the plane, the group of men were rounding the far side of the craft and disappeared from view. We braked. In seconds a side door of the enormous plane opened, and an aluminum ladder dropped down.

The badged man jumped out of the car, swung open the back door, grabbed H'Nina's hand and yanked her out—a loud whisper: "Move!" An airman had jumped out of the plane's door, shoved the kids up the ladder, and closed the door. We were driving away as the inspecting group came into view under the nose. I looked back and saw the head official admiring a large bottle of Johnny Walker. The others were laughing.

Minutes later we watched the C-130 climb and bank towards the coast, and Clark Field in the Philippines.

Dragon Fire Dying

Time becomes an amorphous entity; day and night lose their dividing lines, dates become irrelevant, schedules cease to exist, sleep is haphazard. There is only the now, fueled by adrenalin. The kids are out and with their sister in the Philippines; a great relief. I expect the senses to dull, yet they expand, often accepting more pain.

A wise man says, "They are alive...but it will be a long time."

A C5A has crashed—its cargo: 243 "orphans" of Operation Baby Lift. When I hear the news, I think of Van in Qui Nhon, who had been talked into sending her two children to an orphanage in Saigon, and hopefully on to the States for "a better life." The disaster of good intentions.

I listen to a sister sing Vietnamese anti-war songs. I have never heard that language intoned so tenderly.

Phnom Penh is evacuated by the Americans. Here an airlift has begun in earnest; C-141s and C-130s are now coming into Tan Son Nhut by the dozens. Our small flat is immediately below the approach to the airport.

> *Never were mortal men like these*
> *for bullying and brainless arrogance!*

Secretary of Defense Schlesinger publicly proclaims there is no crisis in South Viet Nam. Over 200,000 refugees are still trekking south from Kontum and Pleiku; 60,000 from Ban Me Thuot; over two million displaced persons in MR I; something over 50,000 refugees on Phu Quoc alone.

A French journalist is shot in the head by Thieu's police. The official report: shot while attempting to escape custody. Xuan Loc, near where we're trying to supply a refugee camp, takes over 2,000 rounds of artillery in one day. Front page headlines of *Stars and Stripes:* "2000 FACE DEATH..." Friends are leaving. Becoming more difficult to get supplies out to refugee sites where they are needed; our trucks get shot at, some drivers quit. I catch myself, about to go over a mental brink...

I must not eat before going. I must enter the side door, leave my sandals on the steps. I must sit on the right, to the far left of the inhabitant of the lotus blossom facing me. Do I see? I don't know. Wait.

An elderly person, close to the family has died; is wrapped in a dark blanket. Better I do not guess at the identity. The face of a mother is...all faces are drawn and sad. A son stares from an open window. I try to tell his mother to go to him and give comfort; she cannot hear me.

> *He led them down dank ways,*
> *over grey Ocean tides, the Snowy Rock,*
> *past shores of Dream and narrows of the sunset,*
> *in swift flight to where the Dead inhabit*
> *wastes of asphodel at the world's end.*
>
> *Here the newly dead*
> *drifted together, whispering.*

Mourners, shrouded in shadow, pass before a burial. With bowed darkened heads they transit my view, crossing the road through the village. I'm looking up, and they climb above me. A known child with a mother's left hand tenderly resting on his shoulder. Bowls are set in the same circular pattern as the petals of the flower before me...I become confused...I think it's a reflection of that flower, but the bowls are greater in number, yet the family is smaller...I feel her now. A revolution of the wheel, and the Yin is in a dominant status...

I can be there...sometimes I can call forth others, yet they cannot speak. Can they hear; do they know? I feel a perception...reception...I feel that I can offer a bit of serenity. I hear no wailing as before...I hear nothing. Time has become static.

If we choose those with whom we walk, where do we gather? It will simply happen, for there will be one mind. Some will not wish to go. Their road is different. Others will deviate...as myself. But if there be a gathering...?

A male face in large, plastic-rimmed dark glasses. I have not met him...but I will. I must try to avoid him. A younger female face...of the family; scarred on the left side. H'Dani...an accident. Freedom of the body. Freedom of the mind. And finally, freedom of the spirit. Strength is needed.

Arrogant days of sorrow...and the night lingers with such insistent memories. The morn of awakening from drug's stupor, a melancholy of aloneness. Before the sun rises, the dawn of Mind breaks and lies writhing, bound within the loss, so silently, so deafeningly, poured... tears release a pressure, yet the cup fills again.

Sporadically, the mind seeks the void. I can see myself. Again, I'm looking up. Always up. Becalmed waters at night. The gongs of the longhouse...no the gongs of Vien Nghiem, the pagoda. More are leaving. I must hold to this serenity.

Love hides love, and the wheel turns slowly; compassion, its spokes. The soft snow of time covers ever so slightly a remembered smile...the form remains and turns to two...I know now I gave naught...so much I could have shared. Now too late. Hiding myself within you. A net is closing in...inside. May the gods stand beside me.

I'm calm. I know not what to expect of the remaining future, but from the Tao, I have learned simply to be, and accept. My vision has changed, and I can look upon my frantic surroundings with detachment, resolutely and calmly doing what is needed. There never was a choice. I will be here when the land becomes one. My mind is prepared for any eventuality. I can look upon Chaos quietly. Can I continue to?

More friends leave. I send out journals and exposed film. The camp at Phu Quoc is shelled. Xuan Loc falls, reportedly under the onslaught of 40,000 NVA. Thieu resigns. Over 100,000 refugees have climbed onto the shores of Phu Quoc now. Loads of rice. Noodles. Water. Medicine.

Rumors race through the town that unmarried girls will be rounded up by the communists, to be wed to disabled and disfigured veterans from the north. Bar girls are going crazy.

A mighty explosion, and stories that the Americans have returned and dropped a nuclear bomb over the invaders. The truth is bad enough: A specially rigged C-130 rolls a CBU out of its pregnant belly, miles above Xuan Loc...hundreds of soldiers are immediately incinerated, or die of suffocation—not to mention the civilians—the last breath of a dying foreign dragon.

More death throes as politicians juggle hopes of forestalling the inevitable. Hopelessness descends upon any who possess even the slightest awareness of reality. The embassy has played on other hopes: those of the Vietnamese working for the government and American volunteer agencies. Not-so-secret lists are drawn up of possible evacuees and their families. Already large families swell in numbers. No one knows what possible recriminations will fall upon those having worked for the Americans. Yet there are many who relinquish the chance of evacuating with departing round-eyes, to continue working until the last minute...trusting the Americans still.

The half-dark night of the city has long descended. Those who have stayed on, helping to get relief supplies out as fast as possible, are exhausted. The last trucks have come back in safely, though several more have been shot at. We say tired good-nights. A few short blocks to the apartment. Some sounds of artillery and rockets in the near distance. And yet again, a rumor of quietude flows from the twilight. Curfewed streets are almost silent. An honest weariness beckons, and I allow it entry. Tired steps carry me to the second floor landing.

"Ma-Lai, there's a message for you. Here's the address...you're to go there as soon as you can. It's someone from Ban Me Thuot."

The adrenalin. I grab the Honda at the foot of the steps...out the alley...speeding down an empty Cong Ly...a cool wind, and perspiration...police ahead...into a side street...around parked cars...a turn taken too fast...that's the house...drop the cycle to the ground, run to the door and knock.

A dark face caught for a moment in the harsh glare of a street lamp as the door swings slowly...returned to shadows. Emaciated. Frightened. The image stays, as I stare into the obscurity. I identify myself, *"Kao Ma-Lai."*

A torrent of choking sobs. She is clutching me, and I feel her shaking fear. She tries to speak, but chokes again and again on her gut-twisting keening. She chokes on her own breath. She clenches more tightly and I feel nails biting through my shirt and into my skin. For minutes we stand thus, I and this girl/woman I have never seen before. I try to comfort her.

She calms, though still crying. She takes my offered handkerchief. Slowly, painstakingly, H'Doi's story unfolds.

A Montagnard, H'Doi had been visiting her family in Buon Pan Lam. Her American husband had remained in Saigon with their children. After the bombing of the village she took refuge with French friends. Finally she befriended a Chinese who was going to make an attempt at escape. Harrowing experiences of darkness, money changing hands, hunger, thirst, and fear, and long nights of walking, days of heat and hiding, guns and explosions, running in more darkness, a black sea, an overcrowded boat, far too overcrowded, bodies dying, parched, salt-caked heat, an angry surf, walking, walking, and more walking, and always the fear. Finally the lights of Saigon, and suddenly they're through the lines of battle, running with the last fringes of energy down the street...the house...empty!

At last a neighbor gives her the news: her older husband has deserted her. Evacuated. A free ride out with the kids...and a Vietnamese girlfriend. All of her belongings are gone. The car has been sold. Her American passport, and all legal papers: gone. Her children: gone. She, trembling, gasping for breath.

235

I have to ask, "and Mi-Lai?"

A cloud of Y-Suin's voice describing the bombing, and telling me what I do not want to hear, drifts into my consciousness. Within, I am pleading to the darkness.

"We were together...I was so afraid...the bombs fell, fire was everywhere...many dead bodies...shrapnel...her shoulder...her son, afraid...sick, both sick...but alive..."

What further words she spoke I know not. Filled with hundreds of screaming emotions, it was I who bowed my head and cried.

H'Doi's hysterics quieted, but I could feel the desperation just below the surface. She gathered her few things and returned to the flat with me. Other Rhadé were there, friends of Y-Hem and H'Nina who were staying with us. Huynh and her friend Gia. They all would help. We returned to a healing environment.

We had not been home long when the night flights began into Ton Son Nhut. The growing sounds of a C-141 approaching, dropping lower and lower, closer, louder...H'Doi's eyes grew wide, her skin blanched, she screamed, "THE BOMBS...THE BOMBS!" Her arms were flailing with the strength of a giant. We tried to hold her. She flung us off like Lilliputians. Chairs flew across the room. Finally diving beneath the table in the bedroom, curled into an adult fetus, shaking uncontrollably, all the time screaming until she had no more breath, dry wracking sobs, and still the fear that only memory knows.

The plane had passed with the minutes. Only the gasping for air between fits of tears, quieter...and then the second plane made its approach to the airfield; and the fear came anew. Each plane carried its own cargo of terror, known only to the deep recesses of a lonely mind.

Several days passed during which we attempted to evacuate H'Doi with the growing masses leaving through DAO, but even that proved hopeless, for she had not even the minimum identification needed to get through. Ultimately, in desperation, I visited "Jake" Jacobson, the man in the Embassy who must have been the one who had helped with the kids. That he had time to see me at all surprised me; his haggard appearance told me of the pressures weighing upon him.

I thanked him for his previous help, and began telling him of H'Doi's plight. He interrupted.

"That sonovabitch!"

I must have looked bewildered. He explained.

"Several days after the attack on Ban Me Thuot that bastard of a husband of hers came storming into the office, drunk out of his mind...the fumes were enough to knock me over. Ranting and raving, yelling that his government wasn't doing a goddamn thing to get his wife out of the battle area...it was the embassy's fault this all had happened...what was I going to do...? He wouldn't listen to what few words I did have...I took his belligerence for about ten minutes, then finally called the Marines and had him thrown out. So he left her, huh...? That sonovabitch!"

I finished the story. He shook his head. "Check back with my secretary tomorrow."

In the meantime we were still trying to get as many supplies out to refugee sites as we possibly could. I never saw the other American who was supposed to be working with us. The swelling refugee camp was cut off; we could get no more supplies into it. The NVA had control of the road. We were still funneling relief supplies out to the sites near Bien Hoa, but trucks were continually being fired upon. Supplies were still going into Phu Quoc.

Official word circulates through the American community: when the time comes for the final evacuation, Armed Forces Radio will announce the temperature at 105 degrees and rising, then play Bing Crosby's "White Christmas," It's supposed to be a secret among the round-eyes. All the Vietnamese of Saigon knew, and laughed, jitteringly. Pick-up points are established, changed, changed again. If such a last ditch evacuation proves necessary, it seems doomed from the start. The new director knows that I'm staying, and consequently I'm left out of what planning there is for such eventuality...which is alright by me, as hours are taken up daily in such discussions. This later proved a serious mistake on my part.

Rockets began coming into Saigon, causing more rumors than damage. ARVN deserters are falling back into Saigon, burning and looting near the Newport bridge. Thieu is out, on a "deep black flight" arranged by the embassy. Stories circulate of how he tried to take over $200 million in gold from the National Treasury with him, but was stopped at the last minute.

I was apprehensive about H'Doi. Her hysterics continued with every passing flight overhead. She had gotten hold of some whiskey, and no longer were planes necessary to stimulate her convulsions. She needed her family, children, and professional help.

Her passport was waiting for us. She has packed a small bag, and I drive her out to DAO. She's a legal American again, and I take her to the head of the line. Waiting officials already know of her case. She can go on the next flight. She's nervous. She's crying: she hasn't said proper farewells to her brother. She changes her mind; she'll leave the next day. I try to dissuade her, to no avail. We return to the flat, only a mile or so from the airport.

6 PM: The ear-piercing screams of low-flying jets shrieking just overhead. H'Doi is terrified. Continued screaming. I can hear the jets making passes over the airport. Bombs or rockets explode. I look up from the landing. Five A-37s sweep and dive repeatedly over Tan Son Nhut. Deafening racket. Minutes pass before the sporadic answering sound of AA fire. Finally the planes form up and head north. I see no other planes in pursuit. I wonder as to the fate of the "orderly" evacuation at DAO. Time has speeded its passage. Perimeters are closing in. We need to get her out before the big push.

My body wants sleep; my mind is a windmill, spinning in the hurricane winds of all that this last month-and-a-half have brought. More explosions nearby. I glance at the clock; it's 4 AM—Tan Son Nhut is taking rockets. Now the sounds of in-coming artillery. The intensity increases.

Rounds are coming in almost every minute, some quite close. A horrendous explosion. A giant fireball reaches into the dawning sky. A fuel depot must have been hit. I mentally kick myself for not forcing H'Doi onto the plane yesterday. Circles are closing quickly.

I take the scooter into the office; confusion in the streets. Though I'm early, most of the Vietnamese staff are already there. Some have overnight bags with them. A few families are sitting quietly in the back. The other Americans have not shown up. The staff is nervous. Artillery still plays overtures in the background; a symphony of rocket and staccato of small arms fire. I call the director's house. No answer. The Region III office. No answer. Other residences. Nothing. Drivers come in; they can't get to the warehouses. Someone calls me to the roof top. An Air American Huey is settling onto the flat roof of a nearby apartment building. The office radio is on, tuned in to the American station. The calm music comes into focus, the ancient voice of the old crooner himself.

Strange momentary flashes of forgotten memories...pristine snowflakes drifting through the halos of street lamps on the quiet night-time avenue of the wintery campus...a girl giggling as she falls in a snow bank and throws a crystalline ball in my direction... the radio reaching from the open window of the dorm, "of a white Christmas, just like the..."

"This is it," the secretary was staring up at me, expectantly.

The following days flow as a dream: disjointed, racing, slowing, emotional peaks and depressions; and I pass through the dream almost mechanically, minute by minute, reacting to the stimulus at hand as a dog in Pavlov's cage.

The phone: "He wants to speak to an American...He's screaming..." Another American is stranded near the airbase. There's small arms fighting all around him. He can't get out. I can hear intermittent shots over the line. Grab the keys to one of the cars. People are running in the street. More shooting. Faster. Swing left, away from the entrance to the airport...away from the tanks...men running in the street with guns, firing...I slide down lower in the seat...heavier pressure on the accelerator...I see the building, speed across the street, and screech into the parking lot, reaching over to swing open the passenger door...weapons on automatic, spitting out their rounds...he races from the doorway bent double and jumps into the still-moving car...foot slammed on the gas, across the curb and slam onto the pavement, swerving around some construction, heavy oily smoke from a fire...a crescendo of rattling weapons...windows shattering...ricochets...tires screeching...and then the relative quiet of lower Cong Ly. I realize I had been holding my breath. We're both frightened, but relieved. We ease into the office parking lot, behind the high white wall and stop, sitting still for a minute catching our breaths and calming nerves. H'Doi is on my mind...how am I going to get her out? This American might be able to help.

Y-Sang is waiting for me at the office. His calmness is energizing. Earlier, when the Americans had started evacuating Vietnamese citizens on a regular basis, I had offered to help get him out. He had declined, smiling, simply stating this was his country.

He asked what he could do to help. I asked him to take the Honda and bring H'Doi back to the office. In the meantime I'd keep trying to get hold of the director...maybe I could find out about evacuation plans for those of the office who wanted to leave. They are all looking at me as if I hold some magic key. I wonder when they would stop believing in the omnipotence of the Americans.

H'Doi arrives and she, the other American and I are back in the car, aiming for one of the apartment buildings used by USAID employees. As we draw near it becomes obvious this is one of the pick-up points; crowds have swollen into the main street a block away. Surprisingly, the throng opens up as it sees Western faces in the vehicle. We get relatively close to the gate, but the masses are more unruly, pushing towards the high cyclone fence. A dozen U.S. Marines are standing about on the other side, sometimes banging climbing hands protruding through the chain-link with butts of rifles. A guard sees us, and motions. For ten minutes we push and shove towards the gate. A Vietnamese mob tries to follow in our wake. Finally a huge black Marine pulls us through. Once inside, he grins a large toothy smile, "Congratulations."

More crowds inside but they're orderly. I recognize Walt Martindale, who had worked with the consulate in Quang Duc Province, just south of Ban Me Thuot. I knew he was sympathetic towards the Montagnards. He was directing chopper-loads onto the roof, one group at a time. There was a breeze on the flat-topped landing pad. He saw us. I spoke a few words.

"No sweat...give ya seats on the next one out..." The rotor wash of an incoming silver Huey was soon blowing in our faces. He smiled, "All aboard...," holding back the waiting group. H'Doi grasped my hand, then hugged me, rain from her eyes. The American clasped my shoulders, "Thanks," then reached into his pocket, handing me a wad of Vietnamese bills. "I won't be needing these any longer." I watched as the bird tilted and swung towards the coast. I relaxed and walked back down the stairwell. The same Marine stopped me at the gate.

"You what...?"

I explained again that I wanted to get outside.

"Man, you must be crazy...Good luck, Bro!"

The office staff was much more nervous. The director had called, left a number where I could reach him; had said nothing else to the secretary.

The number was an extension at the embassy. It rang; a gruff voice answered; I could hear yelling in the background. Much commotion. The director came on the line. The others were with him...had been all night. Asked if I wouldn't reconsider evacuating. I asked what plans he had for getting out the staff that had been promised a ticket out. Also it was the end of the month; the Vietnamese staff had not been paid. He'd get back to me.

I was angry that I had not been informed of the goings-on of the previous evening. We could have accomplished a lot during the night. If the staff was ever going to need their salaries, it would be in the unknown times ahead, assuming they weren't leaving.

Arguments existed for and against the evacuation of Vietnamese... yet with the attitude of the NVA towards indigenous who had been working with the Americans still unknown, the safest course seemed to be the allowance of a safe haven to those who wished to flee. Should the worse fears of a bloodbath prove wrong, they could always return to their homeland. Otherwise, there was no guarantee against any recriminations the NVA decided to levy. That there would be those who would take advantage of the situation seemed a small price to pay for the allegiance of the many others who had given so much for the Americans. The spectacle before us now was a shameful reminder of the vacancy behind the rhetoric of our leaders.

I later learned, far too late, that the last month's salaries, as well as money for retirement benefits, were right at my finger tips, locked in the office safe. A simple combination would have at least covered a minute portion of the white man's obligation.

I was amazed at the serenity exhibited by the Vietnamese around me, in contrast to the fright of many Americans. Exceptions, of course, existed on both sides, but the contrast was noticeable. I gained much strength from the examples of friends surrounding me.

The chaos on the street increased: more small arms fire; cars had been turned over, were burning; bands of ARVN soldiers, many having discarded their uniform shirts, were roaming in search of vacated American buildings that might be looted; what traffic there was traveled at frenzied speeds and in haphazard directions. A couple of loose soldiers wandered into the office compound; we got rid of them, took down the office sign, and locked the gate. We waited for evacuation instructions from those supposedly in the know at the embassy.

An old woman approached me. Since I could remember she had cleaned the office at night in exchange for a few piasters and a small room at the rear of the complex. We had become special friends in the last few weeks. I had been coming into the office early, before the others, in an attempt to give some semblance of organization to the upcoming day's hectic activities. It gave me a few minutes of quiet before the onslaught of the next twelve hours or so. Sleepless nights had aided in my early risings. The Ba had taken me under her matronly wing, chided me for not taking care of myself, and forced a simple breakfast and rich coffee upon me. I came to enjoy the few minutes with her in the cramped servant's quarters. At a street vendor's cart I would sometimes pick up a steaming portion of *soy*, a savory concoction of sweet rice, peanuts, beans, and spices wrapped in a banana leaf, to share with her. We would sit at her low table and she would bring me up to date on the office gossip. Her usual betel-juice stained smile was gone this morning, replaced by pain and tears.

Of the close to a hundred who had asked for personal help in leaving the country, none was so pitiful. But that was not the cause of her distress. A well-meaning son-in-law had successfully gotten her youngest daughter evacuated on one of the earlier flights. *The old Ba wants me to help get her daughter back! She's all she has left in this world. A cleaning woman, and she offers to pay me her life savings. All I can give her are hollow words.*

In two days she would kill herself.

I'm trying to decide if I should take the matter of the staff's evacuation into my own hands...possibly attempting an entry, carload by carload, into the pick-up point from which H'Doi left. Remembering the dangerous crowd surrounding the building, which could only have gotten worse by now, I realize our chances would probably be slim, and hazardous at best. There has to be a better way. *Why don't they call back from the embassy?*

As on cue, the phone rings. There's hope in the director's voice, and a hint of conspiracy. I'm instructed to get the staff, as unobtrusively as possible, to the CRS office, another well known volunteer agency. Its director, who had been here longer and in whom I had more confidence, was also at the embassy and had supposedly arranged a plan. I was to call back when the staff was regrouped there.

Timing could not have been much better. Armed soldiers are attempting to climb over the gate. We won't be able to hold them off much longer; the sounds of rifles firing, hopefully into the air, from the entrance. We're out the gate, drifting in groups of two or three, some in the office cars. Havoc behind us as more soldiers enter the compound, locks are shot off warehouse doors, others are smashed open with butts of rifles.

We regrouped fairly quickly at the other agency's office. The old timers had organized groups of about a dozen each, so that we could account for everyone at a moment's notice. I was surprised that the Vietnamese staff of the other agency was also present, not quite as well organized as our own. Gradually, the staffs of a few other similar but small organizations appear. There are no other Americans.

I make the call. Minutes pass as I wait for the director's voice. Anxious faces watch me. I can make out the noise of a nervous crowd over the receiver. Finally, he picks up the phone. He explains how there is a back gate to the embassy compound that can be reached from the one that we're in. I don't understand. We're blocks from the embassy. "How in the hell..." He's not familiar with this office, but he's sure he's correct. I ask to speak with this office's director... he can't find him...is there anyone else...can't find anyone... "There's chaos here," he says. I ask him to explain it to me again...the same words...that's all he can tell me..."Got'ta go...call back if a problem." I place the receiver down in its cradle. Am I so blind, so stupid?

I repeat the words I've just heard to the Vietnamese at my elbow. They don't understand either. We finally decide to send out a couple of men to scout the embassy. I can envision the crowds around it, but agree that this seems the only chance so far. They should check at the French Consulate and the police station that borders the American compound. The others decide that I should stay by the phone, to communicate with the Americans if the need arises.

The rest of us settle down to wait. Several babies are nursing. Small children play on the floor. I feel a heavy burden of responsibility to these people. I hope that I'm able to help them. The peacefulness within the building is in stark contrast to the pandemonium outside on the main thoroughfares. Not knowing what the future holds, several men decide to organize as best they can for the possibility of being together for several days. We check what vehicles are available, gas supplies, water. Someone remembers a small godown where food supplies are stored. It might not have been looted yet.

The scouts return. They've skirted the entire embassy grounds and can find no possible entry. The mobs at the front and sides are enormous and dangerous. A van has been overturned in front of the high walls, and is burning. More looters are on the street outside our own building. It seems only a matter of time when someone will realize a possible prize exists behind these walls too. The looters seem the most dangerous aspect of this day. Mostly armed, there is a forlorn despair about them, divorcing them from any moral inhibitions. Some are quite drunk. Most are ARVN soldiers who have fled their units.

I call the embassy back, a little surprised that the lines are still operable. A female Vietnamese voice answers in perfect English; a calm, rational voice. I ask if she might locate any of the CARE representatives. She'll try. Minutes later she returns. Can't find them; would I like to speak to one of the embassy officials? Her calm demeanor belies the chaos that I know must surround her. An American comes on the line. I explain our situation. With me are some two hundred people, workers and their families, who were promised evacuation by the Americans for whom they worked.

I'm informed that the last of the VOLAG Americans are on the chopper just now lifting off the roof. "Call back every hour, we'll try to arrange something." A desperation in his voice is inconsistent with the hope in his words. There was a clamor at our own front gate. I hung up the phone.

Several young soldiers were banging on the gate. Others were trying to climb over. A small crowd was milling outside. We had to do something before a riot ensued. A secretary suggests the director's house: it had a high wall, was off the main avenues, and had a phone. Families were quickly regrouped. Cars were loaded. Others stood outside the building to the side of the gates which one of the men opened when everyone was clear. A mob rushed in, heading quickly to the buildings behind us. The pedestrians and cars quickly passed onto the vacated street. I lingered, checking that indeed everyone had gotten out.

A wave of fatigue swept over me, accompanied by no small amount of despair. Of a sudden, the realization came that there was little chance of getting friends out. I sat down on the sidewalk, my feet in the gutter, my head in my hands. I was tired.

This way and that way raping the steep city,

I watched straggling scavengers run towards the building I had just left. Others picked about the debris in the street. Anything movable was carted out: chairs, desks, a wall clock. Intermittent rifle fire cracked.

I felt a hand on my shoulder, and with it the weight of those families who still maintained a faith in the round-eyes. It was a Montagnard nurse from one of the other organizations. She bore a tranquil smile. I got to my feet and we walked together to the director's house, immune to chaos.

Though not far from USAID II, one of the U.S. government buildings, the quiet street still maintained a semblance of normalcy. That there were no other foreign residences or offices in the vicinity must have kept the vandals unsuspecting. We were the last through the small gate, and a self-designated guard closed it behind us. Lengthening shadows stretched across the yard. A number of diverse vehicles filled the driveway and part of the manicured lawn. I could hear children peacefully singing a Vietnamese ditty inside the house. The leaders of the group were waiting for me.

Most of these people had gone without food since the previous night. Children, though politely composed, were hungry. Some of the younger ones were softly crying in their mothers' arms. Several women took over the kitchen, cleaning out the pantry for whatever had been left behind. Those who had gone to check one of the CARE godowns came back empty handed. Then we remembered a small storeroom behind the house where overflows were sometimes stored. Cases of dried noodles were still there.

Someone showed up with a bag of rice; another, with a large bag filled with freshly baked French bread. One other had a friend who ran a small store around the corner; I remembered the wad of bills the American had thrust at me this morning as he was climbing into a chopper...that would probably pay for a few cases of soft drinks. I was awed that in all the confusion there might be merchants still plying their trades.

A few minutes later several men came in lugging wooden boxes of bottled cola of all flavors. The last man entering had a huge smile on his face. He carried a case of large-bottled beer. Until now I hadn't noticed the thirst. I wasn't hungry; but I was suddenly very dry. One of the men popped a cap with his penknife and handed me a warm beer, and a smile. I needed both.

The rustling of leaves in the evening breeze could be heard even over the constant and distant sounds of Hueys and Sea Knights plying back and forth from roof tops to the distant coast and waiting offshore vessels. Darkness crept slowly but passionately into the ravished city. Flares could be seen drifting onto the horizon. Sporadic bursts of automatic weapons...green and red tracers arched into the sky and back to earth. An occasional rocket would whine into range, and then hit with a muffled explosion. Artillery sounds erupted from various directions.

I called the embassy to let them know where we were. The same soft-spoken Vietnamese answered. She recognized my voice and wished us all well. She called the same embassy official to the phone. His words still offered hope. I gave him our location. He asked the exact number we had. I told him. He asked my name again.

And then I made a grave mistake. I asked if he might do me the favor of getting word to my family when he got out, that I was alright.

"But you're coming...right?"

I answered negatively.

He mumbled something. Then I realized my error. There was much less concern in his voice now that he realized an American wasn't trying to get evacuated. Quickly said he'd see what he could do, and hung up. I cringed inside, hoping I hadn't ruined the chances for those around me. I kept my fears to myself, but I think a few close by saw the pessimism on my face. Someone brought me something to eat, but I had no appetite.

It was a curious night: quiet, and not altogether unpleasant. Floor space was completely taken up by bodies; small and large groups sat about talking quietly in the candle light. Others slept, or rested, almost serenely, as though all had been given up to fate. A placid resignation had calmed those few who earlier had been the most anxious. There were those who still held hope that the Americans would come swooping down out of the sky to rescue them from an unknown future, but most, by this time, had begun to realize that the embassy was having enough trouble getting its own out. The radio continued to repeat the ultimatum issued by the North Vietnamese the previous morning: Americans had twenty-four hours to leave the country. That presumably meant they would all be gone by the early hours of the coming day. We heard fewer and fewer choppers in the air.

What shame to be repeated of us, after us!

At sometime around 3 AM we decided to check back with the embassy. The phone rang longer this time. At last, the same Vietnamese voice, but not the same controlled soft tones. She was crying, catching her breath. "They left me...they left me! He's gone... gone...they're all gone..." She was close to hysteria, but still talking. "He asked me to stay on...the Ambassador...said he needed me...he promised that he'd make sure I and my family...before he went... Twenty-three years I worked for the American government...they got his *dog* out...what will happen to me...twenty-three years."

***

The previous day's sounds of choppers were gone, and in that respect, the dawning skies were silent. Small arms fire occasionally ricocheted through nearby streets; distant artillery from various directions still echoed about. At sunrise, two rockets exploded close to the house, one knocking out a high garden wall. Children became frightened. The radio is announcing, "The American Imperialists are gone...Our country will be unified!"

he cannot stir,
cannot fare homeward, for no ship is left him...

Some of the group leaders still have hopes of a rescue. The majority are more pessimistic. During the early hours of night they had placed a large American flag on the roof, as a signal to any helicopters. I suggested it was time to take it down. The removal of that symbol that had seen so many days in this country, for better, and now for worse, seemed to drown the last hopes of the few remaining optimists.

In spite of the gloom and loss of hope, the families decided to stay together for a while longer, until they could make out the direction of the tide. Steaming pots of noodle soup soon made their appearances from the kitchen.

I realize that soon the group will have to disband, yet to be surrounded by friends in such a traumatic time of change has been a comfort to me. However reassuring, I must face the fact that my association with any Vietnamese in the near future can prove only detrimental to their relations with the future regime.

Rifle fire in the fronting street...we can hear some yelling. Two men go out to the gate to check. Before they can reach the portal, shouting increases, shots are fired at close range. We can tell a mob is gathering. *"Nha My! Nha My!"* "American's house! American's house!" Several men in army pants and white tee shirts have climbed over the gates. They're drunk and armed.

Men from the house volunteer to try to hold off the onslaught of the lusted mob, while others attempt to funnel huddled families through a side gate opening onto another street. Shots are fired at point blank range into the lock of the front gate. It's slammed open. Men swarm through belligerently. I witness the mob mentality as I have never seen it before. More shots. Shouting. A woman screams.

> *Battlespoil they want from our...bodies*
> *to add to all they plundered here before.*

The mob has rushed into the house. I'm hoping everyone is out. The soldiers are fighting among themselves. Two pistols are waving in the air. The last of the families are filtering through the small side gate, mostly unnoticed by the invading looters.

Disregarding the chaos, friends stop to share a moment's farewell. Many eyes are tearful. Two of the younger secretaries...I don't remember leaving. I head back towards the house. The looters are so intent on their prizes they hardly notice me. I don't see anyone left in the house from the group.

I meet one of the drivers at the side of the house. He tells me the two girls got out by the front gate. Windows are being broken, more shots. He says, with quiet understatement, it's time to leave. We head for the side gate. One last look around at the madding chaos behind me. We're out the gate. He grasps my hand with both of his, "Good luck."

He's trotting down the vacant side-street. I can see the USAID building a block and a half away. Looters are carrying furniture out the front doors. I hear a motorcycle swing around the corner, heading towards me, and I turn around. It stops alongside. Y-Sang smiles, "Need a ride?"

A heavy weight has been lifted from my shoulders with the last of the Vietnamese families on their own, though I feel remorse at not getting them out.

My mind goes into another mode now. I must concentrate on survival and getting the family back. An English friend had suggested that I contact the International Red Cross Delegation. With the likely possibility that I would be picked up by the North Vietnamese soon after their entry into Saigon, it was important that someone know my whereabouts.

On the off chance that the lines would still be open, I had called the Red Cross during a lull in the previous night's confusion. The call went through; I spoke with the head of the delegation, and started to tell him of my situation...the friend had already told him. The deep Swiss voice suggested that I get to them as soon as I could. He could not keep me from being incarcerated by the NVA, but they could at least try to keep tabs on me when that happened.

At first I thought of returning to the apartment and picking up my few belongings; at least the passport I had absentmindedly left there in the bedlam of the previous morning. Then I realized that, at this point, any more association with the Vietnamese could only jeopardize them. For once, my best bet would be with other foreigners.

I climbed behind Y-Sang and directed him to the old apartment building and hotel that the Red Cross had taken over on Hong Thap Tu. We made arrangements to keep in touch and try to get word into Ban Me Thuot as soon as it was possible. We stopped at the gate. After a few moments Y-Sang raised his hand in good-by, and left me with his indefatigable smile. I remember letting out a great sigh.

There was nothing more I could do until communications were restored with the Highlands. I was tired. The sigh had released an enormous tension in my body. Three days without sleep were catching up. I could hardly keep my eyes open as I walked into the ICRC building. Pierre Guberon, the head of the delegation, led me into his office and asked the secretary for a couple cups of black coffee. The rich brew did little in the way of rejuvenation. I asked if there was a half-quiet corner, somewhere I might rest a few minutes. I remember someone showed me to a room on the far side of the building away from the street. I think there was a bed next to the wall. I simply knelt to the floor and spread out. I don't believe I ever achieved sleep so quickly.

Tortoise and the Dragon

I awoke to a growing sensation of vibrations in the floor of the building. Sunshine, and the approaching dissonance of rumbling and clanking came through the open windows. I lifted myself from the cool floor; aches of fatigue accompanied my slow movement out of the room and down the hall towards windows facing the street.

The harsh clamor was something I had never heard before. Army trucks were speeding southwest on Hong Thap Tu; soldiers with stripped uniforms filled the truck beds. Others were running in the street. But that was not the noise. It came from several blocks away, still approaching: NVA tanks.

I descended to street level and joined others looking through the iron grill of the gate. The first tank passed with a speed of which I would not have thought it capable. Its tread dug inches into the pavement. I felt the rumbling of its approach in my feet, and right up my spine.

Spread-eagled on the front of the lead tank, as if held there by the momentum of the invasion, was the corpse of an ARVN soldier. A dozen NVA infantrymen rode atop the speeding monster, laughing.

and more than men they seemed,
gigantic when they gathered on the sky line.

253

Other tanks followed at the same speed. Red flags with gold stars and others, red and blue, fought crazily with the wind. We could hear shooting to our right, several blocks away, and then the loosening of the tank's cannons. The remnants of the notorious Phoenix Group were making a last stand. It would be the last in the city. I watched, as a soldier climbed to the top of the facing building, tore down the banner of the South Vietnamese regime, and hauled up the PRG flag.

The mood of the populace was strange. Crowds lined the streets, once it was obvious that the war was over; cheering, some hesitantly, waving flags of the victors' colors that had appeared from nowhere. Long-time PRG sympathizers, as well as others taking advantage of the situation, donned armbands, helped direct traffic, and generally took over basic civic administration duties. Genuine joy was demonstrated by many, whether celebrating the victor's entrance or the end of a long war. Others were hesitant to show any emotions at all. Still there were those who rather blatantly decried the loss of freedom they felt would be following in the wake of the tanks.

The continued pouring into the city of the *bo doi,* the NVA troops, gave the impression that they were still catching up to their hasty success; that indeed, they hadn't quite been prepared for such quick victory. But within hours the shooting was over. New local authorities rapidly organized neighborhoods. Though most of any crowds were well controlled, I was surprised that the NVA allowed the looting of any deserted American establishments to continue, until the shells of the round-eyes' presence left nothing more to be taken.

I knew of several other Americans who had planned to stay behind the evacuation: a lab worker with one of the evangelical organizations; another running a home for street kids; the Mennonite group of three or four; one or two others, some from the press corps. Several new American faces drifted into the ICRC; a couple, extremely frightened.

Word circulated that the ICRC was responsible for handling political refugees. It wasn't long before crowds of Orientals, mostly ethnic Chinese, began gathering at the gates. Some were waving U.S. passports.

One of the Swiss delegates asked me if I'd care to join him on a short tour of the city. A Vietnamese driver pulled the car up to the door. The streets were orderly; most were open. Little damage could be seen from the car on the route that we took. The ugly statue of an ARVN soldier at the head of Nguyen Hue Street had been toppled. The day before a southern general had shot himself in the head at its base. A few military vehicles, trucks and jeeps, lay overturned and burned. The gates to the palace had been smashed open by tanks, a number of which were dispersed across the palace grounds.

We turned towards Cong Ly. The ICRC member suggested we attempt to retrieve at least my passport from our old apartment. We swung into the alley, creeping through the gathering crowds of kids. Small Red Cross flags flew from the hood of the car. A few friends spotted me and waved. Others simply followed to see what more excitement the day had to offer. I pointed out the building and the driver stopped.

The landlady was flustered. Earlier in the week I had explained to her that I was staying but would find another place to live so as not to place the burden of an American tenant on her hands. She had politely objected. She was kind, but also relieved that I was going to make other plans. Perhaps she now thought I was returning to stay.

We relieved her fears and asked if I might gather up my few belongings. Her face reddened. I noticed some of our household items on the shelves amongst her own. There was nothing left, she said: vandals. I looked pointedly at a couple of items I had recognized. She and her son fidgeted. When I mentioned that I really was just looking for my passport she seemed at first noticeably relieved...then reddened again. "The passport must have been carried off by the looters...or destroyed." I realized who had destroyed the passport, but I couldn't really blame her.

As we were leaving through the gate the son came trotting out to the car. He handed me a camera I had likewise left behind. "I think this might be yours..." An apology went without need of speech.

In the days that followed a certain tenuous normalcy returned to the city; a general feeling of relief that there were no immediate reprisals against the people of the South, no bloodbaths as prophesied by the propagandists of the Thieu and American regime. The first full day of Northern control, May Day, was marked by celebrations and parades and the first issue of a new newspaper carrying a front page picture of Uncle Ho, and renaming Saigon in his honor: *Thanh Pho Ho Chi Minh.*

Streets were walkable; more bicycles became evident, less smog and noise. Many of the old security barriers had been pulled down, less of the obnoxious concertina wire in evidence, and new areas were opened for pedestrians. On the green in front of the palace, soldiers from the North were meeting with families and friends, or just making new acquaintances. That edifice had been renamed, *Doc Lap,* Independence Palace. The lower house of the senate had been turned back into a concert hall. Banners and slogans streamed everywhere. "Viet-Nam is One!"

Watching the *bo doi,* I was immediately taken by their footwear: soldiers, with the pride of victory over the best equipped armies in history, wearing sandals made from discarded tires. It was an impressive sight.

Fully expecting to have been apprehended by the North Vietnamese upon their entry into the city, I counted each day of freedom as one of blessing. Y-Sang had assisted me in sending messages to Ban Me Thuot, and now all I had to do was wait. I had registered with the authorities, and they seemed to have no reservations about my presence.

Indeed, the number of Americans remaining in country had been larger than what I had expected. There were, of course, rather large groups of ethnic Vietnamese and Chinese with American passports, mostly spouses and some children who had been left behind. A few members of the American press corps had stayed. Several others like myself had remained on purpose of one reason or another. But the majority seemed to be those who never got the word, or were simply too late in their attempts at leaving—eighteen 'U.S.-born' Americans.

Two ex-G.I.s had come back into country only days before, looking for girlfriends. Several retired Americans living in the suburbs had failed to get their Vietnamese families to the evacuation points on time. One particularly jolly and drunken contractor had been locked up in a South Vietnamese prison before the attack, and was only released by the *bo doi*. Another contractor had spent the last day unsuccessfully trying to get his firm's employees evacuated, finally losing his own opportunity at escape. A self-proclaimed hippie, who seemed perpetually spaced out, had come into Saigon only the day before the evacuation to "see what was going on." He too missed his ride out.

As to the other foreigners in Ho Chi Minh City, the French seemed back in the majority, thoroughly enjoying their renovated role after being overshadowed by the Americans these some twenty years. Restaurants reopened; you could hear the French language again drifting from street-side cafes. Besides the normal European community of the town, advisors from some of the Eastern Bloc countries soon began arriving, mostly sticking to themselves.

The Saigonese were never without their humor, or at least not for very long. Jokes surfaced rather quickly about the invasion, and particularly, the rather countrified *bo doi*. Indeed, it was rather easy to poke fun at the newly arrived soldiers. Most had never seen buildings so high, and they craned their necks at such heights, often bumping into passers-by. Words circulated that they had received a bonus of several months pay in celebration of the victory, and city sharpsters were quick to prey upon the less sophisticated soldiers whose cravings mostly appeared quite similar.

What the South Vietnamese had lost in war they were regaining in street-side commerce. First a pair of dark glasses, preferably with mirrored lenses; next, a wrist watch with silvered expandable band that was too large for the Asian wrist, and whose works managed to operate for about a day; a life-size Caucasian doll; and finally, a bicycle from the south. With these items the sandaled soldiers' dreams were complete. Socialist ways had their limits.

The first story to make the rounds was of the *bo doi* newly ensconced in his Saigon quarters, complete with indoor plumbing, the first of his experience. After figuring out that the porcelain bowl on the floor in the small room must be for washing vegetables for his meal, he became distraught when, on pulling the lever to get more water, his greens disappeared down the drain. He went screaming to his leader that his quarters had been booby-trapped by the Americans before they left.

After registering with the Foreign Ministry it became evident that I was basically free to roam the city at will. I was still hesitant to visit Vietnamese friends. Some, more than others, still worried about possible recriminations in the future for their association with the Americans. It was a valid concern.

Many of those who worried less about the unknown days ahead visited at the Red Cross Headquarters. From them came more stories of the last hours. I learned then that the old cleaning woman at the office who had wanted me to retrieve her daughter from the evacuation had killed herself. The director's cook, an affable old man, had also died in some mysterious circumstances. The two young secretaries who had escaped the director's house at the last minute through the front gate had been attacked, their clothes ripped from them by the drunken vandals, and almost raped, had it not been for others who had not yet succumbed to the mob mentality.

For one of those girls I felt particular sorrow. Her brother had been in the Navy, and had offered to try to evacuate the whole family on one of its ships. Phuong had decided to work up to the last minute, relying on the promise of the American evacuation. The rest of the family had made it.

I also discovered why the other American who was supposed to be helping with the refugees was rarely around. He had only recently been hired locally by the director; his earlier job with the Consulate in Nha Trang had been phased out. The majority of his time during these hectic weeks was spent cutting deals with wealthy Vietnamese for their paid evacuation, using his connections with the embassy.

That revelation came as little surprise. What shocked me more were repeated, and later verified, allegations concerning another

American staff member of CARE, one of the more recent arrivals, who had also succumbed to Mammon's enticement. After their performance during the evacuation, and now these new revelations, I was becoming embarrassed to have been associated with such a well-known organization.

I had earlier queried officials at the Foreign Ministry concerning the possibility of American social welfare agencies returning to Viet Nam. Their reply was tentative, but optimistic. "Good" agencies would be welcomed in the reconstruction of the country. I later came to realize that the agency for which I had been enquiring had too many ties to the U.S. government to act independently in such a matter.

***

A week had passed, as had the anticipation of incarceration. My fortune, indeed that of most of the Americans remaining had surpassed my hopes. Now I simply had to wait.

Saturday night. The ICRC team was having a party in the penthouse at the top of the building. The boisterous music cascaded down the darkened stairwell. The nighttime curfew was still in effect. A knock on the door. "Someone to see you at the front gate... said his name was Y-Sang." Perhaps he had received some word. I slipped on my sandals and walked into the night-shrouded driveway, out to the massive gates. In the darkness I could barely make out Y-Sang straddling a bicycle. The shadow of an older child sat over the rear wheel. I started to say something...

"Ama..." Dad.

My mind went into a spin. I grabbed him to me. Y-Sang: "Mi-Lai is waiting for you. I can take you to her."

I held a son to my chest. Turned and raced to the stairs, clutching him. Up six flights running. I burst into the ICRCs party.

Within minutes, Pierre, the head of the delegation, had a car out front. Lights flashing, we careened down deserted streets. Y-Sang pointed out the house. Not waiting for the car to stop I jumped out and rushed through the door. A dozen Rhadé sat and stood about

259

the dimly lit room. A tired but beautiful smile greeted me from across the floor.

"Dearest companion, what has Zeus given me?"

Her story was harrowing and tragic. She still shook and cried while telling it. Miraculously, the immediate family had survived the bombing, but the village had paid a deadly price. They were there when the bombs fell. Y-Suin had been correct in his description of the scene, except in, to me, its most important aspect. Ae H'Muan, the old sage who had bestowed the blessings of the spirits upon our marriage, had been grotesquely killed, as had over 450 others, in that rain of death. A vision of the elderly man's body wrapped in darkness returned to me. Mi-Lai's dad and older brother had later been taken away from the charred village by the NVA.

Each of them had lost an enormous amount of weight, which neither of them could afford. Their weariness was not a transitory one, such as from a long trip, but rather stemmed from almost two months of fright and anxiety, surrounding death on a scale incomprehensible to most, and hunger and illness. Her eyes would sometimes stare blankly from deep and shadowed sockets as she recounted the horrors they had survived.

But we were together. They were safe, and we were together.

***

Weeks passed swiftly as we again attempted to gather all new papers necessary for us to apply to the new Ministry of Foreign Affairs and Emigration for an exit visa. The majority of foreign press had already departed, excepting the few obviously sympathetic to the new socialist regime. Some of the other Americans had already been allowed to leave on the few scheduled Air France flights. Lists were posted of others with permission to leave. Time weighed heavily on the majority of those waiting to get out. For us, any wait seemed a small price to pay.

More days. Foreigners were departing fairly quickly now, a few Americans on each flight. We'd occasionally pick up international news on the BBC or VOA. A petition was presented before the United Nations for seats to be allowed each of the Viet Nams, North and South; a political game of chess. The U.S. vetoed the measure in a session of the Security Council.

The next day, American names were removed from the departure list posted outside the Emigration offices. No officials would comment.

Twenty-sixth of June: Mi-Lai's birthday. Personal funds had dried up. We were living on the kind assistance of the ICRC. I had found a can of spam, wrapped it neatly in a page from the *Giai Phong*, the "Liberation News," and tied a bow of twine atop the insignificant birthday present.

Later that morning, I happen to mention to Pierre the date's special occasion. He grinned, "Wouldn't you like to borrow a few piasters?"

I now had the money to buy the material for a traditional Montagnard skirt. Mi-Lai had returned with virtually no clothes other than those she wore. We set off walking towards the center of town with a young married couple who had recently returned from Ban Me Thuot; she had come from the same village as Mi-Lai; he, an Italian, from one of the coffee plantations in that area. We laughed at inane nothings as we strolled beneath flamboyant trees shading the sides of the street. Francisco and I communicated in a broken Spanish that neither of us spoke very well, but enjoyed practicing. The girls giggled at our obvious mistakes.

A youthful soldier standing at an intersection stopped us. He asked for our identification. Francisco said in Spanish, "I'm not sure he can read...he's holding your paper upside down." We stifled laughs. The boy looked up from under his faded green helmet, smiled officially, and said in Vietnamese, "Come with me, please."

We were taken to the second floor of an office building recently taken over by the army. Another soldier asked us to sit at a large table taking up the better part of the room. Several older men came in wearing side-arms, obviously officers. They began asking questions to the wives, apparently assuming neither of us foreigners spoke Vietnamese. Sometimes their questions were curt. Why had they married foreigners? Were they planning to desert their own country? Our son became nervous. More men came in and sat at the table. More questions, some directed at the foreign males, still asked of the women. Where were they living? Why doesn't the American have his passport? Two men left the room. Another entered, but said nothing. Finally Francisco and H'Dam were told to go. They offered to take our son with them. The officers wouldn't say how much longer we were to be held. "Perhaps not too long."

After a few more questions, the officer who seemed in charge suggested that Mi-Lai should leave also. She refused politely. Questions became slightly more indignant. Now they were directed at me. I answered in the simple language of which I was capable. Finally, the officer made the statement that everyone knew Americans did not eat rice. My wife should go to the market and buy her American husband bread to eat; perhaps he would be here a little longer. She refused again. He reddened. He stood and turned to her. "You *will* go get your husband bread." I quietly mentioned to her in English that perhaps it would be better for her to return to the Red Cross and tell Pierre where I was and what the circumstances were. Then she could return with the bread.

All but the man who had entered late left the room as soon as Mi-Lai departed. Several minutes elapsed in silence. He stood. In Vietnamese: "Stand up Mr. American." His use of the polite title lacked the courtesy it implied. He called to two very young soldiers, each with an AK-47 slung over his shoulder.

"Take him downstairs, and wait out front."

The soldiers unslung their rifles. One motioned me forwards with a nod of the head and motion of his weapon. The expression on his face was serious, a little nervous.

Out in the street, we waited for several minutes. I was told exactly where to stand. The sun was bright. Sweat trickled down my sides, ice cold. The officer came out the door and addressed one of the young boys in arms. I could only catch bits and pieces of the words,...a building across town,...the Ben Ngie Canal. The soldiers were confused. The orders were harsher; directions apparently even more unclear. I didn't understand the last directive at all. The officer shouted at the soldiers, then stomped inside the building, slamming the door.

This was what I had hoped to have prepared myself for. I closed my eyes for a moment. I sought the serenity of an image of Buddha. I was relaxed. Several other soldiers gathered to look at the American. One of the guards asked something of the others. They shrugged their shoulders. I turned towards the guards behind me.

"Nhin dang truoc!" Face Forward!

They were nervous. The rifles were held above their waists, pointing at me.

"Di Di! Move it!

Something told me I shouldn't.

I replied that I didn't know which direction to go. One of them should come in front of me and lead the way. To myself, I just knew I would feel a whole lot safer with one of them ahead of me.

"Da khong!" They were adamant about staying behind me.

"Khong biet di dau." I don't know where to go, I repeated.

Then several things happened very fast. I am not familiar with the operation of an AK-47...but I heard a metallic sound...some spring mechanism being released on one of the weapons. I started to glance around, and in so doing caught sight of one of the young watching soldiers who was standing to the front and a little to the left of me....He had looked behind at the guards...his face blanched... his expression changed to one of abject fright; he took off sprinting across the narrow street in front of me...out of a possible line of fire from behind....The French journalist shot in the head "escaping" flicked through my mind...in that moment I realized how easy it would be for another prisoner to be shot with a similar excuse...I wondered if that was part of the instructions I had missed. And then, in that split second, the shadow of the boy racing in front of me caught my attention...at first I thought it was a small child keeping pace with the running shadow...it was gone from sight when I realized it was too small for a running child...and then I smiled. My good friend had come back to join me—Monkey, companion to the gods.

A moment stood still in the dimension of time, filled with all the tension of a long war. The moment stretched and stretched, grew tighter, as a strong rubber band, or balloon, about to burst.

Monkey. It would be alright, a sigh released. The tension was broken. One of the guards came up beside me, pointed ahead, and in a quieter tone, said *"Di."*

We walked back streets for some twenty minutes, heading towards the town center. A crowd began forming, following the American imperialist and his armed escort. We rounded the city market, already being rebuilt where rockets had caused large areas to burn. The crowd grew larger, but remained quiet. Turn onto Le Loi. Vehicles pulled to the side as we marched north up the middle of the southbound lane towards the National Assembly. We came to Tu Do. The boys were confused. They were talking. They told me to stop, still debating between themselves. I finally turned and mentioned that we should be heading in the opposite direction if they were taking me to the area the officer had mentioned. *"Cam on, Chu,"* he thanked me. We turned and headed back down the other side of the street, again forcing traffic to the side. The crowd continued following. We marched for some minutes. Pedestrians on the sidewalk stood and stared silently. The guns were still pointed at my back, but I knew now, more for a matter of face to those youth carrying the weapons. I was told to stop.

Then a token came to him from a woman...

I noticed a woman's kind face in the crowd before me. She stepped forward, almost as if she were about to offer me something. I smiled at her. The *bo doi* approached from behind. They asked her directions. She stared at them for almost a minute, silently. Though her face remained an image of strength, tears began falling from her unblinking eyes. Then she did a very brave thing.

She turned to me, pointedly ignoring the soldiers. Though her accent was strong, her words were perfect English. "The place that they wish to take you...you should turn left two blocks further on, go two short blocks...you will see the building on your right...God bless you." and then in Vietnamese, still addressing me, *"Di manh goi, da..."* Go well. She turned and looked at the soldiers, tears staining her cheeks, then turned her back and walked through the crowd.

The guards were at a loss, stunned by the performance. I repeated the directions to them in Vietnamese. One shook his head, then motioned me forward with his rifle.

An officer was waiting in front of the building. He dismissed the guards with an abrupt and grating order to return to their duty station. His appearance struck a familiar chord, but I couldn't just place it. The left side of his face was scarred, his eyes were covered with plastic-rimmed dark glasses...the dark glasses! The image returned from the visions within the pagoda. It was not an added element of fear that struck me, so much as one of caution.

Several younger soldiers approached. He ordered them away harshly. He rested his hand on the pistol at his side. "So you are a big man American, huh?" His Vietnamese was anything but polite. "Alright...we'll see...MOVE!" He was pointing up the steps leading to the second floor.

Trash and filth lay everywhere. The windows had all been smashed. He called to another soldier with a rifle to follow us. I was pushed into one of the rooms. Litter covered the floor. Several days' worth of human excrement drew flies to the far corner. An army cot, bared to its broken metal springs lay against the wall. I turned back to the doorway. The soldier stood, his carbine pointing nonchalantly in my direction. I started to ask...he told me to be quiet.

I sat upon the mattressless cot, resting my elbows on my knees. I needed to maintain the serenity. I let my eyes close. I was not actively seeking it...and the Void came quickly, effortlessly, peacefully.

My solitude was not long lived. Two chairs and a small simple table were brought into the room. A man whom I had not seen before entered and asked me to sit in one of the chairs. He sat across the table from me, placing a manila folder before him. His demeanor was polite. He seemed a kind person. He wore the same faded uniform as the others, with no mark of insignia, a side arm, and the same tire-treaded sandals. He glanced through the papers in the folder for a minute, then looked up at me.

In simple and slow Vietnamese he began asking general questions as to my experience in Viet Nam; less of an interrogation than a conversation. I avoided mention of my military involvement in earlier years. When my attempts at the language faltered he would help me out. At the end of perhaps thirty minutes he stood, apparently to leave the room. I asked if he might be able to tell me how long I could expect to be here...to be held. He replied that they had just wanted to ask me some questions...problems existed because of my lack of passport...probably not much longer. There were others, he said, who would like to speak with me. He would probably be back. In departing, he looked about the room, then turned to me and apologized for its condition. After he left the guard stepped back into the doorway.

I sat back down in the chair, kindling hope that I would be gone from here soon. Footsteps approached down the hall. I turned to see the man with the scarred face enter. His dark glasses were gone now.

"STAND UP WHEN I ENTER!"

He sat at the table. I remained standing. He began addressing me in a loud and bitter voice. His rapid speech gave no accommodation to my foreign ears, and I often had to guess his meanings. He would fire questions at me, then dress me down for taking a moment to decipher them or form my answers. Why had I said nothing in the previous interview about my military career? How many Vietnamese had I killed when I was in the Navy? Did I take pleasure in shooting women and children? He was growing angrier. My answers became more broken, my use of the language more inexact. What was the secret intelligence organization I belonged to when I was stationed in this country? Wasn't PSYOPS really associated with the Phoenix Group? I rarely completed any answers before he was shouting other questions.

It seemed the classic "Good Guy—Bad Guy" technique of interrogation that I had learned in Navy SERE training. My mind was operating on two different levels at the same time. I was trying to understand his rapid-fire Vietnamese and answer as best I could; and another part of me was playing back the lessons of interrogation I had had some six years previously. I was amazed at the accurate information this man had concerning my past, and how he intertwined it with gross exaggerations and extrapolations. He was pulling out even minute details I had forgotten.

What had I been doing in the remote Montagnard villages in the Highlands this last year? What was the name of the U.S. intelligence officer...spy...stationed in Kontum? Was it true I was married to one of the heathens from that area? Then he stood, shoving his wooden chair against the wall. He came around the table and stood close to me.

"Look at me!"

His finger traced the scars on the left side of his face. "Do not expect me to like Americans...they did this...They also killed my family."

His hand dropped from his face. A wrath boiled in his eyes. "Now is your turn. Do not expect to see your family for a very long time. You will be going away...to be educated...re-educated...far away. You will not see your family. Maybe they will not wait for you. He stared at me, then left the room.

I sat back down in the chair. Could I handle the uncertain future? How much of his bluster was to scare me? How much was true? Mi-Lai has no idea where I am. What will they do? I had known this could happen. I had tried to get my head right for such an occurrence. But now that it's really here...

The kind man entered; again asked me to sit. In spite of my trying to appear calm, I'm sure he could see my increased agitation. What did they want? I had nothing to hide. "Just a few more questions..."

The afternoon and evening continued with the alternating visits of the two interrogators. A third officer entered at one point; he seemed the neutral compliment to the triangle. He spoke a little English, and would sometimes mix Americanisms into his speech. Never was there evidence of any kind of mood in his words. He'd ask a question. I'd answer.

The sky had long since darkened outside the shattered windows. Mosquitoes, perhaps attracted by the bare glowing bulb in the ceiling fixture, swarmed about the room. The kind old man appeared to be growing weary. He shuffled the papers back into the folder and stood, stretching his back and shoulders as he did so. I asked him again how long he thought I would be held. He seemed sad. "I really do not know...I am not the one in charge here. It may be you will have to stay a while...or perhaps move to another place...I really do not know."

He left the room, then returned minutes later with a torn mosquito net. "Perhaps this can help you sleep...Good night."

I sat on the edge of the cot. I thought of Mi-Lai and our son. Could I maintain the integrity of my emotions? I tried to look at my situation as objectively as possible. I realized that I had had no food or water since the morning, but I had no hunger or thirst. My body was accommodating itself; could my mind continue to do the same? I still had control, but perhaps I was losing that control since I was wondering how long I could hold on to it.

I glanced towards the open door. A new guard stood there, rifle in hand. He would look my way every now and then—his expression did not invite conversation—and then he would look back at a small black and white television sitting on a chair placed at an angle across the hall. Classical Vietnamese dancing flickered across the screen. The volume was turned very low. I raised my legs up onto the cot and stretched out on my back. It was not so uncomfortable. I pulled the mosquito netting over me and closed my eyes.

Perhaps it was a trick of the optic nerves—a continued holdover pattern of the bare bulb in the ceiling. A light continued to shine behind my closed lids. It wavered and moved, centering itself to a position slightly above and between my eyes. Its form grew more amorphous, then jelled into a pulsing circle of glowing gold. It faded, returned, enlarged, and rose higher.

> *Alone*
> *he saw the field of time, past and to come.*

A sensation of lightness came to my body, as if it were rising with no discernable support. I could no longer feel the bed springs beneath me. I was at perfect rest, weightless. No sensations from my body at all...there was no body, only the golden light...as a sun rising above shadowed hills...a comfortable warm glow penetrated the mind, the warmth of a newly risen sun, slowly dispelling the night's gown of veiling mist. The sun was breaking through the fog, and forms in shadowed outline began to appear: the distant hills, their color growing from monotone gray to mottled greens. Limbs of trees in the foreground struck through the net of morning's earth cloud, baseless, divorced from the trunks I knew to be there.

In the greater distance, a form so large I had ignored it; now growing into sight as the sun dispelled, minute-by-minute, the soft mist. The great mountain: snow crowned its ancient volcanic peaks. I knew where I was. I had been here before. It was real. But it was different from the last time—everything was in its place but myself, of no form.

The matinal sounds of the African plain gathered hesitantly from the earth; and then I could make out the wildlife grazing in the near distance. A familiar chattering behind me. Monkey and his friends greeted me from branches above. Kilimanjaro loomed behind them. Kibo, its highest peak, rose from the dissipating cloud at its feet, bathing in the golden day and deep blue of a clear sky.

A lion, hidden from my eyes, roared a morning yawn. The zebras, gazelles and antelope paid it no attention and continued grazing, knowing the mood of the predator was not bent on prey.

The mood of the predator was not bent on prey. I knew now. The deep fear I had tried to ignore suddenly was gone. Two worlds were at peace. All that remained was harmony and serenity.

I opened my eyes. The light of a false dawn overpowered the dim illumination of the ceiling bulb. I was rested and calm. Whatever the day brought I could manage, I could simply be.

I heard voices outside the windows. I got up and went to the casements. I had not realized there was a large ledge, not quite a balcony, outside at floor level, a single story above the ground. Several young *bo doi* were standing there in the morning light. One leaned on the barrel of a rifle. They had been talking quietly. They saw me and came closer, simply staring. I had the feeling that I was the first American they had actually seen. They began talking among themselves again, this time about the *"Thang My"* under guard. I greeted them and smiled. They were taken aback for a moment, then one of them asked if I really could speak their language.

Their faces broke into open smiles, and then deluges of questions. Did I really not know how to eat rice? Where was I from? Was I married? Did I have children? What was my religion? Were there any other Americans still in Viet Nam? Could I use chopsticks? What did I eat? Why did I have hair on my arms? Do all Americans have beards? Do American women have great huge breasts? Where did I learn their language? How long had I been in their country? Was I in the army? What towns did I know in Viet Nam? Did I think Vietnamese girls were pretty...?

We talked across the broken glass of the window for perhaps an hour. Their curiosity was endless. At last, someone called to them. Before leaving they said polite farewells.

I sat down on the bedsprings and looked towards the door. Another guard stood duty, mute and unsmiling. I lay back down, my hands behind my head. I had not lain there long when Scarface appeared. His temperament had not improved. "Get up, you will be moving to another place."

I was marched outside to the opposite end of the building from which I had entered the previous day. Other soldiers were waiting. This time I had four armed guards. And they knew exactly where they were going. There was no talking. We walked briskly along mostly side streets. The guards discouraged any gawkers from following. We passed through a neighborhood I knew. We continued south, finally entering a large building, the old Ministry of Immigration, now dealing with foreign emigration. The crowd milling in front made way for the soldiers. Through the foyer and into an empty back room. I was motioned to sit at a bench. Three guards turned abruptly and left; one remained. We waited in silence. I tried to engage him in conversation. He nodded and looked straight ahead. I let my mind wander where it willed, not unpleasantly, and lost track of time. The soldier fidgeted at times and seemed impatient of the wait. Eventually a man in civilian clothes entered and sat at a single desk, asking me to take the chair alongside. He spoke pleasantly enough, asked a few general questions, then opened the portfolio in front of him. He said he wanted to ensure a few facts.

He then began reciting from the pages in his hands. It was a fairly accurate history of my presence in his country; more detailed than even the day before. He asked if there was anything that was incorrect; closed the folder, and lapsed into more general conversation for a few minutes, asking about my family, what I thought about the changes taking place in Viet Nam. He stood, shook my hand, and departed. I went back and sat on the wooden bench with the guard.

Finally, the guard could stand the silence no longer. "Does elder brother really have a Vietnamese family?" I figured this was no time to make distinctions between Vietnamese and Montagnard; I replied. He asked what town my wife was from, how many children I had. He began telling me of his family in the North; the ages of his children. He had a creased photo of his wife. She looked young. He missed his family. Did I know how to smoke? He would very much like a cigarette. I thought of the street vendors outside. I had some change in my pocket. I offered to buy us each a smoke if he wished to go get them. No, he couldn't leave me, but he sure would like a cigarette. A few minutes passed in silence.

Another guard entered; they spoke quietly and rapidly. He turned back to me and smiled. Could I buy his friend a cigarette also? I handed the coins to the other who headed for the front door. He returned promptly with three cigarettes, smiling. We lit ours with the glowing ember of his, already smoldering in his cupped hand. The guard told the other what he had learned of me, then he too had questions. The hand-rolled *Dong Nam* was strong black tobacco, slightly moldy, and a dizziness and light-headedness came over me as I inhaled. Quiet jokes were made about pompous bureaucrats and stuffy officers. The two finally dropped their butts onto the floor and squashed out the burning ashes. I looked for an ashtray, then followed suit.

The newcomer left us to our conversation. We sat for perhaps an hour more before two soldiers with rifles entered. The guard stood quickly to his feet. The smile was gone. They came behind me and motioned me out of the room and towards the front door of the building. *"Di."* One motioned me through the door with his rifle. The crowd outside parted. I wasn't sure which direction to go. The guards had stopped at the door. I looked back at them. Again, *"Di."* But they weren't following, though the rifles were still loosely pointed in my direction. I was in a quandary. I took a few steps forward; glanced back. Still not following, but watching. The crowd began filling in the space between us. The old guard smiled at me. I was free.

The experience had been a good lesson, the scare of which did not hit me until my return to our small apartment. As I sat on the couch there was a spinning of my mind, as if some mental reorganization was taking place; and then, in a moment, all was straight again, except in another more common mode. I found it difficult to describe what had taken place, and a phobia of venturing outside again crept upon me. The emotional strength I had known just that morning had dissipated, replaced by a weakness of the most common human frailty: fear.

For days I occupied myself behind the street-side walls of the ICRC headquarters, indeed, mostly in our minimal living quarters, making excuses to avoid the world beyond. Gradually my sense of reality resumed its proportions, and I became less worried upon stepping outside the protective gates. Yet it was rare that I went out alone. To be with my family was enough for the time being.

That remaining Americans were being detained from leaving, while other foreigners were granted permission, became obvious. Never was there a mention of a hostage situation, yet the displeasure of the regime over the American government's stance regarding Viet Nam's position in the U.N. and retributions for the wartime destruction was now clear. The hope of swift emigration palled and a waiting game began.

Money, not only ours, was becoming scarce. And yet, there were those who were spending as if the last day of the earth had been proclaimed. The black market grew to proportions far exceeding that of the days of the earlier government. The present regime seemed little concerned with its presence; in fact, its most usual customers wore faded green, pith helmets, and tire-soled sandals. One of the unanticipated benefits was the quantity of English language books piled high along several streets making up the black market scene. Along with looted volumes from the USIS Library, books in English were being voluntarily purged from private homes and sold for pittances.

Stereos and TVs lined the sidewalks, topped by framed portraits of Ho Chi Minh. American brands of toothpaste and watered down bottles of shampoo lay spread out on plastic army ponchos, along with other ponchos covered with vast arrays of plastic toy guns of all makes and caliber; revolvers, 45s, Uzis, M-16s, AK-47s, and a myriad of others, many of Chinese or Russian origin. Prescription medicines, unavailable in the local hospitals, their notices, "KEEP REFRIGERATED," fading in the tropic sun, lay piled in heaps in front of old and young vendors.

Banks either remained closed, or opened their doors for no purpose other than to notify customers that accounts were frozen. And yet many of the foreign community continued to thrive, some through previous hoarding, others with transactions with wealthier Vietnamese and Chinese who wished access to funds outside the country at a later date. Inflation rose, some goods became less available. The value of "green," U.S. bills of all denominations, increased, albeit exchanged behind closed doors or within darkened alleys.

The government was actively encouraging movement out of the cities, particularly Saigon, as Ho Ch Minh City was still called by less-than-enthusiastic residents. For the thousands of fairly recent refugees the opportunity of returning to their one-time homes was welcomed, and trucks and busses piled high with baskets of worldly possessions left the city daily. Other truckloads of saddened men could be seen, departing for "re-education" camps.

The government touted the "New Economic Zones" as the frontiers of the future, opportunities for a new beginning for anyone wishing to take advantage of new policies. Initially voluntary, movement to these hastily conceived and ill-prepared rural areas soon emerged as drop zones for the masses and mandatory termini for many of those who could not pay the bribes to remain in their city residences, whether stately homes on tree-lined avenues or tin shacks of the odiferous slums along mud- and sewage-filled canals.

Theft was on the rise, and it was common to witness a purse snatching or similar accosting in daylight hours. Two such incidents occurred below our apartment window in one morning. Though at times beggars would be swept from the streets in citywide clean-ups, the increase of those seeking alms for survival was apparent. In speaking with the mendicants who had been reduced to begging to feed undernourished children I came to understand the thin line beyond which one would step into the dangerously dark world of stealth and thievery, especially when confronted by those far wealthier, with seemingly unlimited resources. Raised in a world where the more obvious forms of dishonesty were absolute wrongs, I was beginning to understand the real lack of absolutes in our moral underpinnings. The concept at the time seemed less important than the shift in mentality that accompanied it; perhaps a time for re-evaluation of most values.

Since we were given no indication that we would be allowed to leave the country any time soon, the ICRC suggested the Americans under its aegis take up occupancy of an older apartment building the government had made available for foreigners, perhaps to better keep an eye on their activities. The move was actually a pleasant one, closer to the heart of town, on a quieter street, with more spacious accommodations.

Our new apartment let out onto a small rooftop patio overlooking the still tree-lined Gia Long Street, fronting the old French La Grall Hospital. Greenery of treetops spread below us, hiding street-side reminders of urban growth and decay below. Visions of the one-time beauty of the Paris of the East was not difficult to imagine.

Though finances continued to pose a problem, with some assistance from our friends, the ICRC, connections with the illicit black market, and frugal economizing, a few piasters remained at the end of each week for the purchase of a book of poetry or a beer or two at one of the street-side stalls on the sidewalk below our rooftop aerie. The whole foreign community, as well as many of the Vietnamese, seemed caught up in the waiting game; time lying heavily on most hands. Some made good use of that time, reading, writing, studying...others were less fortunate in discovering profitable utilization of the first "free" time they had had in their lives.

Vietnamese and foreigners alike were becoming more vocal in their comments and criticisms of the new rulers. The rhetoric of the conquerors, in spite of the new slogans constantly taking the place of roadside advertising, was dimming in meaning in light of their actions. All this was augmented by the rumors for which the city was so famous. One local friend, a photographer who had had the opportunity to leave the country with his family, and chose to remain, cautioned me with a phrase that was to become the current buzz phrase of the critical. In speaking of the communists, "Watch what they do, pay no attention to what they say."

Others, with leftist leanings or investment in the new order of things, remained loyal to their beliefs; but their ranks were thinning. Though too early to forget the travesties of the Thieu Dynasty, fewer were extolling the virtues of the new kings. The awaited blood bath had been a myth, and the earlier joy displayed at the end of the war was justified. The ever-present corruption of the old command was gone. Yet now, after several months of enthusiastic slogans, evidence of bribery within Uncle Ho's ranks was clearly surfacing, sometimes elaborated upon by the ever-existent rumor mill of Saigon. It was as if the corruption went with the scenery and not the puppets.

The economic situation certainly gave no cause for jubilation, but perhaps the most depressing aspect of the fledgling government was the policy regarding "re-education." Thousands of heads-of-families were being shipped off in the backs of trucks to re-education camps. Some had been gone now for a couple of months with no or little word reaching back to kin. Wives and children were anxious. Those who had not been called yet awaited their turns with a fear of the unknown. What little correspondence that did reach the families was less than optimistic.

> *...for Zeus who views the wide world takes away*
> *half the manhood of a man, that day*
> *he goes into captivity and slavery.*

Madame Thi, a previous secretary with CARE, spoke with choking sobs as she related the one letter she had received from her husband. He had written with a nervous hand, but in the circuitous and poetic style of an Oriental navigating the treacherous seas of censorship. He would be home, he said, to see the children at the time of year of the flowering of the tree they had planted in their yard. What went unspoken was that the type of tree they had planted was known not to bloom for a number of years from its planting as a seedling.

Waiting. Vietnamese waiting for fathers and husbands. Waiting for word from those who had evacuated, or who recently chose to escape. Businessmen waiting to learn if their small companies would be taken over by the government. Waiting in line for the monthly allotment of rice and soap. Waiting for new rumors. Waiting for a bottle of cooking gas, or if this was temporarily non-existent, waiting for the promised bag of charcoal. Waiting for news that Americans would be allowed to leave, waiting for hours in front of the immigration office, for emigration papers. Waiting for another signature.

We tended a small roof-top garden, toting dirt from the street below, up six flights of stairs. There always seemed another book to read; hours of negligible and philosophic conversations over inexpensive coffees at a diminutive table and stools alongside a seldom trafficked side street beneath the shade of ancient tamarinds; an occasional bowl of rich noodle broth from Ong Mi's soup cart, the leftovers always going to At Soy, Ong Mi's constant companion, the dog who always slept with him curled up at night upon the stoop of a drafty doorway.

Though I had managed to send out all of the exposed film I had taken over the years, a number of images would return to my mind, as clear as the sight through the viewfinder when they were made. Words wove their presence about the pictures; and soon I had a project to occupy my time, piecing together in my head fragments of poetry and scenes of children's eyes. Not only a project for the present, but something to look forward to physically constructing once out, and the opportunity was available.

The usual drudgery of boredom had set in heavily upon the shoulders of many, particularly the Lilliputian American community. Small-scale bickering, family feuds across the hall, gossip across the street. The foibles of each were adamantly discussed behind rotating backs. Our own rumor mill was being erected.

The second of September. Small explosions somewhere below. Shots fired. Rockets tracing red streamers in the air. Stories of a purported resistance came to mind, but the explosions and shots turned to firecrackers, and the rockets for display. It was the eve of a new Independence Day for the country; new for the South at any rate. Displays of incendiaries continued through the night, with the fervor of a steam valve releasing.

Our neighbor is marking days off the calendar, and the "X"s are protruding into October. A squad of *bo doi* are approaching below on the street in single file. The column of young soldiers is heavily armed—AK-47s, rocket launchers, 30 caliber machine guns—with the exception of the smallest warrior trailing the line of combatants. Over his shoulder he's gaily carrying a long cane fishing pole, a string dangling at its tip, and at the other end, swinging about in the cadence of the nonchalant, a wooden hand-made model airplane. My mind's eye envisions the figures scribed on the side of the makeshift practice target, "B-52."

Though I had to grin at the spectacle below, a headache caused me to draw the curtains and lay on the bed. A small hole in the curtain allowed a sliver of light to pass, and a quirk of optics created my own *camera obscura,* the soldiers marching upside down across the ceiling of the darkened room—the last still swinging his cane pole as some Eastern Huckleberry Finn sliding across on his head. I lay on my back watching a pageant of life pass above.

Christmas approached with a cold spell uncommon to Saigon. Only half jokingly the frigid air was blamed on the *bo doi* bringing it with them from Hanoi. It was the first Christmas we would celebrate as a family. Gifts were meager, token really, but the quiet eve gave space for reflection, and we were thankful to be together.

The Yuletide night was spent in company with a few friends, including a colonel of the NVA. His honesty, intelligence, and personable conversation impressed even Mi-Lai, who previously had had few good words for the communists. Simple generalities seldom sufficed.

With the coming new year, eight months had passed since the "Liberation" of Saigon. Our position seemed even less clear than in those early days after the American evacuation. We were not prisoners, we could roam the city at will though we were restricted to its boundaries; but we were unable to leave—simple pawns.

More discontent was rising in an increasing percentage of the populace. Even those who had been the poorest under the old regime were voicing dissatisfactions. The usual stories and rumors of Saigon were taking on more pallid colors. A small-time merchant told me, "I'm a Buddhist, but I read the Bible, and they [*the bo doi*] are just like the devil...We lost a cat and dog already. They eat cats and dogs, you know, just like the devils in the Bible."

The truth of the matter related more to the economic policies of the current administration than to dietary habits. Meat, as well as other items, was becoming scarce in the market, and prices for such items were climbing exorbitantly. The origins of chunks of "beef" drawing flies on the banana leaves of the open market was questionable, to say the least.

At a small birthday celebration I spoke with a North Vietnamese who was working at the state-run television station. He said his father has been Hanoi's ambassador to the Soviet Union for nine years. He had accompanied his father, and graduated in electrical engineering there. For four years after returning from Russia he was in charge of surface-to-air missile installations in the North. At the end of the war he had been sent south to manage the TV station. He gave the impression of having come from an educated and wealthy family. He was discouraged, and spoke openly of wanting to leave the country and even changing his nationality.

In the same room was a woman of the Koho tribe of Montagnards, whose French husband had been incarcerated in Dalat some six months previously for supposedly collaborating with FULRO. She had received no word from him in that time.

Rumors of counter-revolutionary activities by FULRO and other groups continued to spread. Two Swiss delegates of the ICRC talked of an ambush two days ago on the bridge outside of Saigon on the way to Nha Be. Ten people were killed, mostly *bo doi*. In the last several days and nights we've heard occasional gunfire and one distant but loud explosion.

In some cases the government is surprisingly admitting to continued resistance and sporadic fighting. Travel in some of the Highland regions is prohibited, even to Vietnamese, for "security" reasons. Stories come in from the delta of skirmishes between government troops and the Hoa Hao, the militant Buddhist sect, or the Cao Dai, followers of that unique religion with its Holy See in Tay Ninh. I found it interesting that these two groups, along with FULRO, had likewise been responsible for the most notable militant insubordination against previous governments of the South.

One of the few classes of items still readily available on the black market at very low prices continued to be the plethora of books in the English language, on every subject imaginable. I picked up a copy of James' *The Varieties of Religious Experience*, along with essays by M. N. Roy entitled *Communism in Asia; Problems of War and Strategy*, by Mao Tse Tung, *Autobiography of Mark Twain; Silas Marner; the Norton Anthology of Poetry*, and a copy of Frank Herbert's *Dune*.

For once it seemed I had all the time in the world to nourish my addiction to the printed word. When tired of one subject or style I would simply pick up another book, and in this way I ended up with half a dozen going at one time. Topics often complimented each other, and in books I escaped the stagnation of waiting.

***

The last week of January was filled with the loudest cacophony of fireworks since 1968 when they were outlawed. Tet, the Chinese New Year based on the lunar calendar, had traditionally been the largest holiday of the year. Now, more than a holiday, it served as a vent for built-up pressure. The sounds of all kinds of weapons fired into the air joined the noise of firecrackers throughout days and nights. Rumors persisted that counter-revolutionists would take advantage of the disorder to inflict some sign of their vitality; and indeed, on the first of February a series of distant explosions caught our attention. From the roof we watched a fireball rise into the sky somewhere between Newport and Bien Hoa.

The explosions continued, following one another in increasing intensity, for more than thirty minutes. Though several miles away, we could see more huge fireballs rising into an already burning sky, streamers streaking for several kilometers. The sounds and concussions of each blast could only be those of a touched-off ammo dump. Though rumors abounded, no official word ever offered any explanation.

We later learned that a child at the hospital across the street had been struck in the head by a stray bullet fired during the festivities. His death brought a sobering element into the local gaiety of Tet.

Traditions of Tet include frequent visits of friends and relatives, and many of our Vietnamese and Montagnard friends took the opportunity to pay us calls. It was during these visits that I learned of a Vietnamese who had paid one of the American staff of our "humanitarian" agency $2,000 to get evacuated. The Vietnamese who had done so was still here, the money gone.

Stories came to light of groups of Chinese and Montagnards who had walked from Ban Me Thuot, across Cambodia, to Thailand. An encrypted cable had recently arrived in Saigon notifying friends of their safe arrival. An exodus seems to be forming, though spoken of only behind closed doors. Rumor states that for the sum of one million piasters one can take a boat from Rach Gia to a small island near Phu Quoc, and from there a fishing boat to Thailand.

Hanoi radio announces that "search and destroy" missions are being conducted in the Highlands as well as the Delta, surprisingly admitting counter-revolutionary resistance. More rumors of another money change drive prices higher still. An Austrian friend, Helmut Kutin of SOS Kinderdorf, who was trying to keep a village of orphaned and abandoned kids open against desires of the regime, had just received his mandatory exit visa.

Frances Starner, the one American journalist remaining in town shows up at our door with another American I had not seen before. Bill Cooper had been imprisoned for the last nine months. His captors eventually told him that an American woman working with one of the religious groups that had stayed behind after the evacuation for a short spell had pointed him out to the new authorities as "a bad man working for the CIA." I had met the woman in question just before her "approved" departure. I easily could believe that she had said that. The *bo doi* had finally released the captive after finding no evidence to support the woman's claims. Bill stayed with us a while before making arrangements of his own.

I enjoyed our discussions, particularly those centering on how he had coped with his lengthy confinement. Upon placement in a solitary cell he had realized, "this could be it." He began meditation exercises that, he said, leaving any mystical or religious connotations aside, were responsible for maintaining what sanity he had left.

I thought back to my own short experience, and those of other friends who had survived, in fact had even seemed to have grown, during periods of extreme duress. Hiro, a Japanese Mennonite who had been held in a similar situation, spoke of "floating up to the clouds, *becoming* a cloud, flowing, dissociating...." Such practices, that at one time in the not too distant past had seemed only stories of fantasy to me, now had become as real as the sunshine outside. We all were growing.

On the seventh of February more explosions erupt from the Tu Duc area. *"Cach Mang Ngay 30,"* the johnny-come-lately converts to the revolution on the day of the Saigon victory, are rumored to be involved, and from this day on they are not allowed to carry firearms unless accompanied by the *bo doi*.

Without closing doors to churches or temples, the authorities have been able to significantly decrease religion's role in this society. Large meetings are suddenly suppressed on the grounds of security; the protestant groups are united under state officialdom. Job applications ask for religion, and if given, the applicant hears no more of the job opening.

The catechism of the revolution has taken over the market place, with Uncle Ho's Christ-like figure smiling down upon his children everywhere. Jingoes appear on every street corner, telephone pole, storefront. The regime easily forces its own religion into the minds of its people, especially those of the youth.

Another good friend visits. He had the opportunity to evacuate with his family along with the American exodus; he chose not to; he's now seriously seeking a way out. Three Montagnard women whose husbands are in re-education come by and talk of escaping, even leaving their husbands behind. "He told me if I had the chance to escape, to take it."

On the 14th of the month stories come in from Phu Tho of shooting in the area, a twenty-four hour curfew. A Frenchman's secretary calls in and says she can't get in to work because of fighting in the area. One informant says eight *bo doi* were killed, another says 80; a reporter returns from a press conference wherein the spokesman speaks of one killed and one wounded, and two counter-revolutionaries shot. The official version reported the rebels holing up in a Catholic church, where radios and a printing press were found. Authorities "were investigating the role of the Catholic Church in this latest occurrence of revolt against the revolution." There's no way to find out the actual numbers involved.

The following night, at 2:30 AM a loud banging on the door awakens us. The security chief of the *khom,* our local district, accompanied by a retinue of police and soldiers, enters for a security check. The chief is young; a Napoleon Complex had taken the place of politeness.

At daybreak I discover that we had been lucky to have had an internal lock on the door. Other Americans had been awakened at that hour in beds, with flashlights glaring in their faces. One says to me, "This *is* a police state, isn't it!" That day I begin reading *The Best and the Brightest*.

Several days later I am approached by a friend and asked if I would be interested in teaching English. If so, I was to meet with Madam Trinh Dinh Thao, the wife of a well-known revolutionary. The proposition sounded interesting; I was informed that I should say nothing about this endeavor to anyone.

I find the address on Hoang Van Thu Street in Vo Tanh. A spacious house, apparently vacated on the eve of Liberation, stands back off the street, a sign over the door, "Lien Hoa Tea Factory." A young girl ushers me into a side room. Madam Thao enters and introduces herself. She's a stately woman, comically trying to impress me with her broken English, as I am her with my unstately Vietnamese.

She tells me of how she took her family into the liberated zone with her husband some eight years ago. They were eventually taken to Hanoi, and from there ensconced on diplomatic missions to both Peking and Moscow. Finally, after giving me a tour of the factory, where girls stood stuffing tea leaves into small tins, she came to the point of our meeting. She had a "nephew" who would like to study English. Was I interested? She asked a few polite questions as to my background, made sure she could spell my name correctly, then said she would contact me in the near future.

A few days later I received a message to please come to the tea factory at a specified hour the next day. I took a pedicab to the area, deciding to walk the last couple of blocks. It was mid-day, and little traffic passed the narrow road on the way to the house. The sound of a mufflerless car caught my attention and I turned; automobiles had become uncommon in this new order because of gas shortage. The car turned towards me, the engine revving faster. I jumped into the ditch as it sped closely by, spewing gravel and dust. Several teenagers leaned from the windows, gesturing obscenely, shouting, "*Thang Nga!*" [f___g Russian!]

I laughed out loud. I had been mistaken for a Russian.

Another, more pleasant, surprise awaited at the tea factory. Madame Thao sat me down, laughed at my story of moments before, then launched into a very specific account of my history in her country. She smiled, asking if the information the foreign minister had supplied her was correct. I nodded, by this time surprised less by the information than the fact that she had it. "The President approves your appointment." I thought that perhaps I had misunderstood. What did the President have to do with this?

Still not quite comprehending exactly what was taking place, I was escorted to an upstairs room at the back of the building. A strikingly beautiful girl of perhaps eighteen stood and greeted me in excellent English. I turned and looked questioningly at Madame Thao. The woman smiled again and introduced me to her "nephew," who incidentally happened to be the daughter of Nguyen Huu Tho, head of the PRG and president of the new South Viet Nam.

English lessons proved more of a challenge than I had anticipated, for this was no beginning linguist. She spoke, besides her own Vietnamese, fluent Chinese, Russian, and French. Her English was superior to that of the majority of my countrymen. I should not be surprised to see her one day, a representative of her government at some high international gathering.

Towards the end of February we were invited to the home of the senior representative of the Indonesian community in Saigon. A group of some thirty people had gathered at a large house complete with swimming pool. Before we sat upon the mats spread over the floor to an exquisite meal of curries and other Eastern delicacies, a Muslim prayer was offered amid sweet-smelling incense hovering in a softly undulating cloud over our heads. I began speaking with an elder who seemed somewhat more despondent than the rest. He had been in this country for over sixty years, and now he was facing "going home" to a country he doesn't know.

Now, some ten months after the communist victory, early March was marked by a large demonstration in front of the municipal building by women demanding their husbands be returned from re-education. Frances Starner, the American correspondent working for the Pacific News Agency who had wisely convinced the authorities of her sympathies towards their cause, had her apartment invaded by the *bo doi* as she was watching the demonstration with binoculars from her window. Her film was confiscated. The next day the local press adroitly publicizes the demonstration as one for the recognition of the Paris Peace Agreements by the United States.

With the lack of news coming into the country, Saigon's reputation as the rumor capital of the world seemed well deserved. "Chinese troops were massing on the border with North Viet Nam...the U.S. was bombing Cambodia...there was going to be a crackdown on citizens associating with foreigners...Americans would soon be issued exit visas...fighting on Phu Quoc...negotiations being conducted at Tan Son Nhut with the counter-revolutionaries...the area south of the sixteenth parallel to remain neutral and the rich of Hue and Danang moving south...no, reunification would take place after elections were held..." Knowing what to believe was difficult.

One of the favorite gathering places of friends was at the soup cart of Ong Mi, habitually stationed on the side street below our apartment. Ong Mi and his constant companion, At Soy, a nondescript but loyal mongrel, became fixtures of constancy in times of change. Ong Mi cared little for the doctrines of the new regime, and didn't mind whom he told. He was happy for the business of the occasional foreigners, and payment for his bowl of noodles was entirely dependent upon financial conditions of the client at the time. At Soy never left his side unless Ong Mi chained him to the cart or had someone hold him when he departed for occasional affairs of state, usually to purchase a bottle of *basi de,* the locally distilled rice liquor. On one such occasion At Soy had been left behind, when two "cowboys" on a motorcycle roped him with a chain and drug him off yelping, presumably for the inflated meat market.

Ong Mi had often kidded that he valued that dog more than his wife. Days later he was still tearful. He aged before our eyes, rarely speaking. His soup lost its flavor.

At long last the constantly clear skies began clouding. The spring monsoons were approaching. The Ides of March found the sun hiding behind banks of darkly gray billows, mountains really, of cumulus. The atmospheric oppression presaged an eventual release, and late that afternoon torrents washed the sidewalks and streets. An early twilight burst through, the rains slowed, leaving diamonds where before lay dust. An unusual quiet pervaded the city. A refreshing coolness brushes past the curtains, more than coolness; there's a process of revitalization, rejuvenation entering the land with the monsoons. A restoration of the serenity of the spirit is brought on by the cleansing activity of nature.

Someone below our window this evening plays a silver-throated flute with both life and serenity. It is a sound of purity, solitude, gaiety, and sadness. Life forces the sprigs of green grass through the cracks in the pavement below.

***

Breaching the normally quiet street of Duy Tan, a circle forces traffic to slow around a somewhat modern statue supported at its base by a large turtle. I had never considered it very attractive, and consequently paid it little attention.

On the eve of April first an explosion ripped into the turtle, killing one soldier from the north who had been leaning upon its perimeter. Several civilians were wounded, as well as one killed who had apparently detonated the plastic charge attached to his bicycle. The act was impossible to understand until a Vietnamese explained it to me.

Back before the palace had been built, Diem had his favorite geomancer lay out the position of all the buildings. The palace itself symbolized the head of government, and as such represented the head of the great dragon that was Viet Nam. Some kilometers away the geomancer found the position of the end of the dragon's tail. It was at this point that he mandated that a turtle must be placed; for traditionally, as long as the turtle had hold of the dragon's tail there would be peace, for the dragon would be unable to swing his great weapon disrupting the harmony of society. The turtle had now been forced to release the tail. A man had willingly died to create a symbol of a symbol. After all this time in the East, I felt as though I was just beginning to learn, and that, only of the bare superficialities of a culture thousands of years old.

A friend whose husband was still in re-education told us of a visit she had had by a relative who was s colonel in the NVA. He told her to be careful should she happen to see any demonstration using the flag of the old government, "It will be to see who is loyal to the revolution." I thought, at the time she told me, of the rumor itself; what a great ploy to increase the fear of acting, no matter what happens. It was only a few days later that other friends told us of an anti-government demonstration in a small town some thirty kilometers from Saigon, wherein the old yellow and red banner had been used as a rallying tool, until the demonstrators were rounded up by soldiers.

Banners and signs throughout the city proclaim the upcoming elections on the twenty-fifth of April. Though voting will be mandatory for all citizens, there appears little choice on the ballots. In spite of crackdowns, episodes of rebellious actions increase. Recently an explosion occurred in a local movie theater being attended by a large number of soldiers. Reports have filtered down from the Highlands that bombs had been dropped on a rebelling Montagnard village north of Ban Me Thuot. Fighting was reported some fifty kilometers from that town.

A tale spread rapidly through town of the *Cai Luong*, the local traditional Chinese opera. The lead actor, in speaking to his errant son who had just asked for more money, said, "I don't listen to what you say, but I watch what you do," using the popular anti-government slogan. The house applauded wildly. After the performance the actor was carted away in a waiting jeep. A second occurrence of a similar nature closed the *Cai Luong* indefinitely.

The end of April marks the first anniversary of the victory of the revolution, and government-sponsored celebrations echoing slogans of peace, independence, and freedom—the same words we've been hearing for a year—seem more contrived and less spontaneous than a year ago.

Just as mysteriously as my teaching job appeared, it was discontinued, whether permanently or temporarily I know not. A friend had mentioned that the government had admonished many of its own for associating with foreigners, and perhaps this is the reason for the discontinuance of the studies on such short notice.

The end of a year in limbo had also forced certain reflections upon my mind. The education that this year has presented cannot be denied. In discussions of the situation I often find myself playing the devil's advocate or walking the middle road. Many others seem to think they have to offer a polarity in their opinions; perhaps black and white are easier to decipher, to program, than gray. Many of those who so heavily criticized the American involvement and its "puppet" regime appear to feel obliged to defend the present government at all costs. Ego becomes entangled in simplistic rationalizations.

I have no problem in disliking both contenders for power. As the old man said, "Power corrupts...." On the other hand, idealists are necessary for any society. It's putting one's ideals into effect that gets bogged down in the frailties of human nature.

As to our own plight in this game, there came a point at this time of simply being; perhaps fatalistically, allowing the course of nature its way. Though the anticipation of eventual release could not be denied, it seemed a less important aspect of our daily existence. Reading continued to occupy many hours of both day and night; however, I made fewer and fewer entries into my journal.

Three more months would pass, a total of fifteen after the revolution's victory, before we would find ourselves boarding a plane for Bangkok with the others who had been retained.

Clear sailing you shall have now, homeward now,
however painful all the past.

I remember the smile on the stewardess' face, the humidity within the cabin before the air conditioners took hold, the captain's "Welcome aboard," the revving of the engines, and finally the lift-off prompting a great and almost unanimous cheer...for I was quiet. I watched the landscape of the city, slums, and then rice fields slide further below our wings. The Mekong etched its muddy way out to sea. As we banked I could make out to the north the beginnings of the high plateau and mountains of the Highlands. Inexplicable emotions arose in my throat, and I turned back to the window so none would see my tears.

***

"'What is meant by that saying about the Northern Sea and Ts'ang-wu?' asked Monkey. 'A real cloud-soarer,' said the Patriarch, 'can start early in the morning from the Northern Sea, cross the Eastern Sea, the Western Sea and the Southern Sea, and land again at Ts'ang-wu. Ts'ang-wu means Ling-Ling, in the Northern Sea. To do the round of all four seas in one day is true cloud-soaring.' ' It sounds very difficult,' said Monkey. 'Nothing in the world is difficult,' said the Patriarch, 'it is only our own thoughts that make things seem so.' "

from *Monkey*

NOTE: lines of indented italics in the text have been taken from *The Odyssey*, by Homer, translated by Robert Fitzgerald (Garden City: Doubleday & Co., 1961), unless otherwise credited.

Epilogue

As mentioned below, although Mi-Lai had been able to return to visit her family as early as 1988, Americans, including H'Krih, our daughter, and myself, were restricted from traveling to the Highlands of Viet Nam until 1994. We took advantage of the lifting of those restrictions to visit family in Buon Pan Lam, near Banmethuot, as well as friends in Kontum, the site of Minh Quy Hospital. We then discovered that we were the first westerners involved with the hospital during the war who had returned to Kontum since that time. The below letter was sent out to those connected to Minh Quy with whom we still had contact in September of 1994.

....

My apologies for not addressing personal letters to each of you. As years race by more swiftly expediency sometimes wins out over nicety. We've recently returned from Viet Nam and I thought some of you might be interested in a few observations, as sketchy and haphazard as they might be.

The time seemed appropriate for introducing H'Krih to the other side of the family whom she had never met: grandparents were not getting any younger; H'Krih was headed off to college after this summer; we had received word that travel restrictions were generally being lifted and that Americans were finally being allowed up into the Highlands. We did experience some problems obtaining our visas and had to delay our departure a week, but once arriving in country travel went fairly well with few hitches.

As most of you are aware, 'Mi-'Lai (H'Cham) has returned on several occasions since 1988 to visit her family, so some of the changes that have taken place, particularly in the Highlands, did not come as complete surprises. The fact that close to two decades have passed since leaving might be sufficient reason to expect change, in addition to the political and social transitions.

Though we only spent a day there it was enough to see that Ho Chi Minh City will always be Saigon. The first mistake I made was the assumption that I would know my way around. Many streets have been renamed, some with old names of other streets; a number have been rerouted, others have been eliminated. So much for assumptions. Downtown still looks much the same, however new facades now grace a number of buildings (the famous open-air veranda of the Continental is now enclosed) and quite a bit of new construction is evident. Traffic is even worse than pre-end-of-war days.

I must say it was nice entering the country without a war going on. Coming in from the airport the streets were jammed at 11 PM with city dwellers out enjoying the relative coolness of evening; coffee shops, with "Video," were crowded onto the streets; soup wagons and sidewalk vendors all vied for noisy space. Uniquely conflicting smells elicited an instantly pleasant feeling of coming back to someplace I had once and only momentarily forgotten. We passed a moss-covered bunker and gun turret, other-worldly and out of place. My most recent and profound memories of that city stemmed from our fifteen month sojourn following the communist takeover. I somehow expected to see the myriad presence of military uniforms we had left then; gratefully, they were few.

While in Saigon we stayed at a small and pleasant hotel in Gia Dinh, off the main thoroughfare, and not to remain small much longer. Business has apparently been good.

Late night sounds quieted to the once familiar melody of the bamboo clapper of the soup cart pusher echoing his way along barely lit alleys...the things I thought I'd never forget.

Upon the gradual change of light before sunrise I parted the curtains of our up-stairs room and looked out over the salmon-rimmed horizon of cluttered upper stories of old Saigon: rusted metal roofing; potted monkey puzzle and palms; new wash being hung out on balconies; an old man in tee-shirt and shorts with old black plastic rimmed glasses perched on the end of his nose squatting and reading the morning paper; a gray-haired matron dipping water from a huge earthenware cistern and watering her roof-top garden. In the quiet alleyway below a feminine trio ranging from grandmother to child gracefully practices Tai-Chi. Others wordlessly appear from houses and gateways and join them until a long and silent chorus line stretches below, slowly moving in a semi-synchronous rhythm as a matinal breeze might sweep along the fronds of a palm, and a child on his bicycle winds his way among them. By 6 AM the horns and exhaust of cyclos, Hondas and trucks from busier streets dispel the early morning magic.

We traveled from Saigon, across the bridge at still-bustling "Newport," and out onto QL 1, through rubber plantations, old and new, rice paddies at every stage of growth and every shade of green, groves of posts supporting umbrellas of bright magenta dragon fruit, roadside vendors of pomelo and durian, guava, bananas, custard apples, papaya, rambutan and other fruit I still don't know. Until that drive H'Krih had thought Mexican drivers were crazy. Just south of the outskirts of Phan Thiet the unmistakably strong aroma of nuouc mam wafts through the open windows of the car.

The road winds along the coast passing small fleets of gently rolling fishing boats anchored off-shore, skirting Cam Ranh Bay and into the busy environs of Nha Trang before turning west towards the jade-colored mountains. This road is less well maintained and our journey is slowed by potholes and long jarring stretches of hand-crushed rock as the only surface. The close-to-three hundred mile trip will have taken some 14½ hours.

Passing through Ruri, Kanh Duong, Phuoc An, steadily climbing, the route is not without its flashbacks of pungent memories...the same road I had watched and paced as tens of thousands of refugees poured out of the Highlands following the Ban Me Thuot attack and bombing of Buon Pan Lam almost twenty years ago, hoping for some news or sight of my family, then caught in that maelstrom...the hill over there where I stood before a North Vietnamese prisoner crouched like a cornered wild animal, a kid, wounded and frightened beyond comprehension, surrounded by southerners unable to see themselves in his place... bodies, dead and alive, being thrown under my feet in the back of a revving Huey...abruptly arching over that roadway in the same VNAF chopper, witnessing several hundred people, having wearily trudged for three days through the jungle, carrying a few sacred possessions, the babies, the elderly, now caught beneath me in a heavy barrage of crossfire and terror from both sides and completely unable to move...walking this stretch of the road amongst the immeasurably dense masses of people, too exhausted to cry, people who seem to have lost even hope and yet continue on. They are overwhelming memories, filled with distinct smells, faces of agony, wounds, and stronger emotions, as if it were but yesterday. To transmit the power of these feelings from yesterday to the generations of tomorrow seems next to impossible, yet somehow the attempt seems important. Much of the jungle is gone now, clear-cut.

Higher elevations and we begin to see the familiar stilted homes of Montagnards. Lines of women walk the road barefooted, black skirts to their ankles, baskets on their backs, laughing. Another group further on, and a young woman, perhaps in her twenties, catches my eye, same skirt, same basket, but blond/brown hair, the same complexion and similar features as my daughter sitting beside me. The air is cooler; the mountains are closer.

The fringes of Ban Me Thuot have extended themselves over the years and even in the darkness of arrival I'm aware that the ruralscape that once surrounded Buon Pan Lam has been replaced by urban sprawl. Indeed the integrity of the village itself as I remembered has disappeared. In its place lies a gathering of traditional Montagnard longhouses interspersed and surrounded by Vietnamese homes and shops. It is here and now that I become aware of the second meaning behind the slogan, "Nuoc Viet-Nam la mot, Nguoi Viet-Nam la mot," the country of Viet Nam is one, the people of Viet Nam are one,[4] signifying not only the reunification of the country, but also an unwritten policy of cultural homogeneity. From the viewpoint of certain minority speakers such a tacit but seemingly obvious policy smirks of cultural genocide. From the proponents come the words of bringing the less-advantaged into a more modern society. In any case, we're quite possibly witnessing the potential demise of a culture thousands of years old. To be sure there are holdouts, as well as opponents even from the ethnic majority. Their success seems, at best, uncertain. I understand that outside Pleiku a "typical" Montagnard village has been built for the tourists to visit, with a $30 admission charged. Visits to actual villages in that area are reportedly prohibited. One wonders on the fate of such traumatized cultures.

Of course, one of the more obvious reasons for the "integration" of minority cultures lies in the relatively silent history of the Highlands over the last twenty years and even earlier. The influx of northerners since Giai Phong seems heaviest in the Highlands—the filling of a land-use vacuum that had its roots in early French colonial policy since the mid-1800's. However, the outside world has heard little of the

---

[4]   Southerners quickly transformed the expression to, "Nuoc Viet-Nam la mot, Nguoi Viet-Nam la hai," (hai = number two).

struggle continued after reunification by elements of FULRO, the Montagnard underground. Because of the closed nature of the society for many years following the war, virtually no news of armed conflict reached the international press. Sporadic, it nevertheless took place. The Cambodian jungles became the hiding place of those who refused to submit to the revolutionary regime, and until late 1992, security in the Highlands could not be assumed. In that year a worn group of some 400 Degas (the Montagnards' term for themselves) were evacuated from Indochinese jungles and flown to the U.S. For better or worse the fighting seems to have finally ceased. And for that I am thankful, for it has meant that finally our journey could take place.

The late-night family reunion was tearful, joyful and every other adjective you could imaginably relate to elders first embracing their seventeen-year-old granddaughter. Aunts and uncles, cousins, nieces, nephews and neighbors swarmed with laughter, tears and excited verbal commotion. H'Krih survived with grace. Ai (Grandfather) proudly pointed to the new bath house he had just built for her arrival.

Our stay in the village was an experience. A typical longhouse is not known for its accommodation to the western concept of privacy and it was only the outhouse that occasionally afforded that luxury so prized by us occidentals. Visitors appeared at most any hour, faces I hadn't seen for twenty years. Kids were now parents (with the appropriate but confusing name changes in that culture), parents now grandparents, and a whole new flock of toddlers and youth had appeared.

To take a walk more often than not meant an adventure with a gang of kids out to show you the sights. The tour would seldom proceed far without a polite but insistent invitation to visit a friend's home, always with some refreshment, often a meal, and certainly when available a jug of rice wine hauled from some dark corner. Consequently, our meanderings seldom got far.

Several days following our homecoming friends and relatives began arriving from more distant villages; a bullock and pig were sacrificed and quantities of waist-high earthenware wine jugs were hauled from cloistered shadows and staked along the center of the house. Time-tarnished brass gongs from the size of pie plates to great sonorous ones that needed to be hung from the roof beams were brought out. The animist priest began his chanting of prayers over the sacrificial offerings to the spirits and ancient music of gong and drum. Celebration and thanksgiving proceeded with prayers spoken over the new arrivals as we each sipped from the cane straw of every jug. Speeches, gifts of baskets, fruits and chickens and brass bracelets, each offered with words of blessing.

I watched these proceedings with awe, wondering just how old was the scene before me. Then a brother started carrying boxes into the other end of the house. Within minutes an elaborate electronic sound system and color video (complete with bikini-clad western beauties and Japanese subtitles) had been set up opposite the traditional ceremony at the other end of the longhouse, borrowed from god-knows-where. Betel-nut-chewing grandmothers, gaping adolescent boys and children barely old enough to stand were switching heads back and forth like center seat occupants at a two ring circus. Ai's speech had all the electronic echoes technology could provide. As to the question of the survival of the Montagnard culture I must admit to a "guarded optimism," not withstanding the necessary accommodations.

The following morning, after a ritual sip at the remaining wine jug, the three of us set out for Kontum. The road between Ban Me Thuot and Pleiku is probably one of the best in the country at this time. The sides of the road are almost completely lined with thatched and wooden homes of transmigrants brought in either from the north or Binh Dinh Province by the government over the last nineteen years, this being one of the major "New Economic Zones" of the Cao Nguyen provinces. So

much of the thousands of hectors of the dense forest and
jungle of the central plateau has completely disappeared
that wide vistas astonish eyes expecting to see only
triple canopy. There can be no doubt as to the drastic
altercation to the ecology of the area. True, much of the
now cleared land is in production: rice, coffee, rubber
and a variety of lesser crops. What this means to the
traditional cultures that so depended upon the jungle
and wildlife for thousands of years is obvious: major
change. I attempt not to place too many values on my
observations, but I must admit to a sadness upon seeing
the loss of such mighty forests and all they held.

Kontum. I was not prepared for the emotions
triggered by our arrival to this Highland town, a place
I and most of you had called home some two decades
ago. We crossed the concrete span over the Dak Bla
leading into town from the south, and nerves frayed as
familiar sights caught my attention and unfamiliar ones
disoriented my sense of location. The disorientation
not only played havoc with a sense of place, but more
unnerving, with a sense of time. Rushed back and forth
between a place I had loved those twenty years ago
and a provincial town attempting to come to terms
with modernity and growth today, I was simply caught
short. One circle through the town and I was lost. We
stopped for a bowl of soup and asked directions to the
old church close to Kontum K'nam.

The familiar old wooden structure calmed my
anxiety. A few kids were playing soccer in front of the
aged building, several more people sat beneath the
eaves conversing quietly. We asked to speak with the
priest or one of the nuns and one little girl trotted off
to find someone.

The priest seemed young and spoke with an accent
from the north. I explained that I had worked at Minh
Quy and was looking for any of the nuns or other
workers who remained from that era. Ya Gabrielle, who
had been imprisoned following reunification and was
now still providing needed help to neighboring villages,
was currently traveling to Hue and Hanoi. After a polite

conversation the priest called for a younger nun and suggested that she might help us locate some of the previous hospital workers and other friends. In spite of his friendliness I left the meeting with an uncertain attitude towards the priest who had explained that he had come here after the change of government. I realized later that he was probably holding some reservations of his own.

In the few short hours here we were all gaining a feeling of more intense repression than we had felt in the Ban Me Thuot area, although it was difficult to point at any particular example. Luh, the young nun who accompanied us from the church explained that the sisters were prohibited from wearing habits outside the church grounds and that past the cloistered fence were to be addressed only by their given names. Military presence in the area appeared significantly greater than any of the other places we had visited, and on inquiry we learned that the local command also consisted of a large military training component.

On entering Kontum K'nam we asked for directions to the house of one of the two men with whom I had most closely worked. In this Montagnard village, the dirt-floored home was more reminiscent of the poorest of Vietnamese houses. A woman sat on the ground of the darkened interior weaving on a hip loom. She turned in surprise at the commotion in her doorway, village kids surrounding the foreigner and retinue. Luh translated into Bahnar as I inquired for Hih. A quiet moment, then she explained that Hih had died several years ago; yes, she recognized me. She was his widow. Emotionally unprepared, I uttered condolences, then recognized the face behind the weathered features. I looked around at the children playing in the dirt beneath my feet; I choked on the lump rising in my throat.

Noisy excitement crescendoed outside and I turned to look out the door. The glare momentarily blinded me and then I witnessed the crowd part as an old man with a questioning look on his face approached. Geam, the other of the pig barn team, stood there and uttered my name unbelievingly. We embraced, tears rose and I could not speak. We stood thus for long minutes, I oblivious to those surrounding us. Holding hands, he guided me to his house. We climbed to the stark but clean interior. Possessions amounted to a reed mat which was quickly unrolled for us to sit on, a few rags of clothes and blankets neatly stacked in a corner, and several charred and battered pots. Geam, not more than a couple of years my senior, explained through a hacking cough how both his young wife and oldest son had died, leaving him with both children and grandchildren to care for.

I remembered most of the Bahnar villages that I had come to know as being generally poorer than those of the Rhadé to the south from which we had just traveled, but the difference now struck me hard. Indeed, these people had been uprooted more often and more severely than many others. Many villages had simply been resettlements of refugees, people fleeing the horrible chaos of war. In the Rhadé villages we had recently visited there had seemed at least some limited progress. The Bahnar villages, on the other hand, seemed even poorer than what I had remembered from the past. Even more apparent was simply a sense of helplessness seldom referred to but which nonetheless often hovered heavily during those silent breaks in conversation.

I should preface all remarks with the caveat that my impressions were gained from such a short period of time and few locales that they could well be quite off base. I accept that, and would welcome informed contradiction. In fact, I had heard from a friend who had spoken with a Bahnar acquaintance from the States who recently had returned to the Kontum area and reported people being better off generally, particularly since the Montagnards had begun growing irrigated rice in permanent paddies, as well as a local official (either district or province chief, I don't remember) quite sympathetic to the ethnic minorities of the area. I simply did not see such progress. It nevertheless may exist, I don't know.

In previously speaking with Luh I had inquired about Yanh, the little Bahnar girl I had come to know when Bill, the administrator for Minh Quy, had brought her to Saigon to be fitted with a glass eye due to a previous accident of the war. I had yet moved to Kontum, and as Bill was swamped with hospital business I offered to show Yanh the sights. She was fourteen at the time, and her ability with the Vietnamese language was not a whole lot better than my own. If you can imagine the mind state of a child whose entire world until then had consisted of the tiny primitive village from which she came, with neither electricity nor running water, and an occasional visit to the "big city" of Kontum, suddenly stepping into a giant silver airplane, lifting into the air, and dropping down a few hours later into a city of some four million people with whom she could hardly converse, surrounded by foreigners, with none of her own family or even people close at hand.... If you can imagine this for a moment then you might have an idea of the fright and confusion I witnessed in her one good eye upon meeting Yanh.

To add injury, in this case, to insult she seemed convinced of her ugliness with the gaping hole in her face and would most often stare at the ground even when she was speaking to you, often finding ways of covering that side of her face. I was there, twenty some years ago when, after being fitted with the prosthesis, Yanh looked into a mirror. I was a fortunate witness that day to a beautiful sight. Yanh hesitated to glance, she shied from the looking glass; then caught sight of the pretty girl within.... She smiled. Something I had never seen her do. She looked again. Smiled. And laughed.

A couple of days were left before Bill and Yanh could return to Kontum. In that time Yanh and I and a tiny pink stuffed dog toured the city, she and the dog clutching tightly to the back of me and a banged-up bicycle, sometimes silent, sometimes laughing, always, I like to think, with a new vision of the world and herself.

I remember the zoo. I had acquired mixed feelings about the place, some of its inhabitants were less than well cared for and often the Vietnamese attitude towards the animals appeared one of scorn, teasing them or offering inedibles in lieu of food (paper scraps to the elephant hanging his trunk over the iron railing, stones to the parrots). We bought some peanuts and stood before the Toucan's cage. Several Vietnamese boys were feeding it and watching in awe as the bird so adroitly shelled nuts with its beautifully colored large bill and fringed tongue. Yanh carefully shelled her own peanut and offered the bird the prized seed inside. The Toucan moved over next to Yanh and from that moment paid no attention to other offerings. Each nut from the bag passed in turn such transaction. But a few moments had passed, and yet that memory lingers still.

Upon moving to Kontum shortly afterwards I was greeted several days later by Yanh at the door to my room, with the gift of a Bahnar basket and an invitation to her home. That Sunday I climbed the notched log to the raised floor of the wattled house and entered a world of another culture, and one that day of such conviviality that the war only a few clicks away was completely forgotten. A ceremony took place which, to the best of my limited understanding, adopted me into the family. A cockerel had been sacrificed to the spirits, which quickly made off with the essence of homage leaving the more corporal aspects for our own enjoyment. Turns were taken at the rice wine jar and Yanh quietly placed a brass bracelet about my wrist. Grandmother (for those who know Where Feasts Come Rarely, hers is the full page profile a couple pages from the back), serious to the core, stated that now I was her son and would have to suckle at her withered breast. At that point I was brought bodily to her lap and I began to get seriously concerned and more than a little embarrassed. Only at the last minute was the cane straw of the wine jug substituted for the drawn dug and the charade was exposed for what it was, the first of many jokes the old crone was to pull on the round-eye.

It was almost a year later when I asked the Montagnard nurse who was working for the CARE crafts project, and who had just arrived on a visit to Kontum, to join me and friends at a party at this same family's home. In the midst of the joviality Grandmother assumed a serious air, pointed her finger at me somewhat rudely, and said, "you be nice to her." I knew she meant business. I asked why she had spoken to me like that. "Because she is going to be your wife." That set more than myself aback. A minute of startled silence must have passed before activities resumed. I had just met 'Mi-'Lai the day before.

All this is to say that obviously this family held a special place in my heart. I had inquired for the family in Kontum K'nam, only to be told that Grandmother, as well as Yanh's mother, had died. Ha, her father, was apparently at work. After arranging to meet Geam and others the next day we started to leave when a girl who appeared about the age of Yanh twenty years ago shyly approached. She was Yanh's sister, and said that Yanh was living in a distant village. She'd try to get a message to her.

We bounced slowly over the rutted road towards the hospital. A few moments passed before I recognized familiar sights. Memory somehow expects trees not to grow. A new pumping station stood beside the ochre-flowing river, intended for irrigation of the paddies to our left. Recent rains had flooded the lower parts of the road and we crept slowly forward, inching past Kon Monay Xalom, a vacant field, then the walls of the hospital, Minh Quy; vegetation grown up in areas, ill-kept, as so many older structures, but nevertheless in use. A military sign over the gate. We crossed the old wooden bridge, barely passable, towards Kon Monay Katu. The road worsened, seeming unused by other than foot, bike and cart travel. Luh partially alleviated my confused memories. Kon Monay Katu had been moved across the road to the west due to the water's erosion. We stopped before the second wooden bridge crossing a now peaceful stream entering the Dak Bla, its condition worse than the first. Luh, with me following, walked back through Katu, asking for anyone who had worked at Minh Quy. Silent faces peered from raised doorways, many too young to remember the hospital.

Leaving the village we crossed the broken boards of the second bridge by foot and stood on a high sandy bank overlooking an oxbow on the wide river. I tried to picture how the village had stood twenty years ago, then thought I saw the bank where John and I had quickly exited the waters after a rather foolish and chilling swim of some long hours down-river from Kon Mahar. It had been late afternoon and the women were bathing there, startled by our intrusion, laughing and covering themselves, making lewd jokes at the shivering whites who had emerged in their midst.

From that bluff the wide vista of what I had known of Kontum's beauty revealed itself in the warm late afternoon light, a simple panorama of green hills and mountains, the river and rice fields, and I was hesitant to leave. Nostalgia is a potent addictive.

Crossing back over the worn bridge I passed two young North Vietnamese soldiers who laughed unbelievingly when told I was American. Back past the hospital, Luh and I circled through Kon Monay Xalom, inquiring for Minh Quy workers. I was struck by the obvious poverty, worse than I had remembered. There was a commotion out on the road and we returned to the car to find Francois Huim and his wife and the same bicycle that was an antique two decades ago, and the same smile.

Huim and I had not been particularly close, and yet the reunion was still choking and tearful, as if my emotions were riding a very fine edge and any familiarity was sufficient to break down the barriers of restraints. A small crowd gathered around the car. Francois remarked that he would like to invite us back to his house, but he was apprehensive about possible repercussions from the "village committee." We agreed to meet at the church the following morning.

As evening approached we returned with Luh to the church. The priest was serving a mass to a bare few devoted in the candle-lit cavern of the old building. He had left a message inviting us to have dinner with him.

While waiting, Hy-Am and his wife appeared. He had studied radiography in Saigon and worked with Bob and Scott. He asked to be remembered to them as well as Pat, Bill, Marion, Phyllis, and John.

The priest joined us and I realized that my previous apprehension had arisen from his North Vietnamese accent; he chuckled and commented that his accent had been one of the largest barriers he had had to overcome in gaining the trust of the people after the takeover.

During dinner Hnet and Nea came in. You'll better remember them as Ya Francoises and Ya Christian. Still in habits, aged like us all, yet full of energy and joy I recalled from those earlier days. They were easily convinced to join us in toasting memories and wishes with the Beer 333 (care to guess its origins?) that the priest had thoughtfully acquired for the occasion. That evening succeeded in loosening any reservations I had wrongly held against Ong Cha. The priest likewise seemed to lose previous constraints and spoke quite frankly of the local situation.

He said his activities were rather severely restricted by the government, limiting the times and days he can hold mass, restricting his travel and service to outlying villages, curtailing activities of the nuns. Nevertheless, a few comments led me to believe that he had discovered ways and means of dealing with the authorities. We complimented him on the beautiful Bahnar Ceremonial house in the front of the church, and one of the nuns remarked how he had convinced the authorities to allow him to keep it after they had outlawed the unique structures in the villages.

He and the nuns are running the orphanage behind the church. He has permission to house some 75 children. Population runs around ninety-five. "They [the authorities] keep fining me for having over my

limit, but what can I do, turn them away? I think not."
Here's one more example of a Vietnamese who seems
to have come under the same spell as many of us did in
working with the Montagnards, perhaps more aware of
realities than many of us were. Whatever I have come
to think about organized religion, missionaries, and
the Tom Dooley Complex, I must applaud this one man's
conviction and dedication in the face of adversity.

Earlier in the afternoon the priest had directed us
to a small hotel. Centered in the crowded market area
there was no place to leave the car so we ventured on,
eventually approaching a new tourist hotel. Admittedly
devious, we asked the driver to inquire as to room rates:
equivalent to $5 and $7 depending on the room. When I
showed my face the rates increased to $25 and $35.

That night, on returning to the hotel, I was told
there was someone waiting for us outside. Returning
to the darkness I saw figures standing by the gate:
Yanh, a young mother with children, emerged from
the shadows, her father and husband quietly behind.
By now I had become less startled by my own tears
and emotions, but still I had difficulty speaking,
overwhelmed by unlabeled sentiments. I ultimately
managed words. They were hesitant to enter the hotel
so we talked in the night air and finally agreed to meet
at the church the next morning.

Stacks of piasters lay strewn across the bed. At a
rate of something close to 11,000 dong to a dollar, and
low denominations the norm, a lot often added up to
very little. Trying to decide what to leave with whom
proved a serious game of Solomon. I tried to figure what
cash we'd need for the rest of the trip, and generally
ended up feeling selfish just thinking that what we paid
for one night in the hotel could feed a family for a couple
of months. Gifts which we left behind, both here and
in Ban Me Thuot, continued to concern me throughout
the journey; I was never at ease either handing it out
or not handing it out. Something I've yet to come to
terms with.

No matter our status in western society, it is impossible not to be viewed as wealthy by the indigenous, and indeed this may be the greatest lesson in humility foreign travel or work in third world countries has to offer. Confronted by such abject poverty a realignment of values is forced upon us, whether we like it or not. Recognition is made that ultimately the gifts we leave are for ourselves, the salve of our conscience.

But there are places where a few dollars can make a difference: a bicycle to go to school on, school fees themselves (ever present, even in a communist society), specific medicines, and so forth. "Step on a blade of grass and change the direction of the universe." The Chinese expression suggests the ramifications of introducing change that invariably pass even the wildest imaginations. With the best of intentions, we quite often create havoc within a semi-balanced system (e.g. improve the potable water supply in a rural village without accompanying social programs and you've just introduced a major factor in population explosion and subsequent poverty). My apologies for such tangents, but they all seem connected. If there is one law that seems applicable in such situations, it might be that the ones who need the most are often the most silent... and vice versa.

On the way to the church we stopped for a <u>Banh Mi Thit</u> (perhaps the best tasting sandwich in the world) and I decided to walk the rest of the way to the church, a cobbled road through the more familiar and older part of Kontum; an elderly lady looks up from scrubbing a pan at the well and smiles in greeting, oxen and a wooden-wheeled cart approach at an easy pace, a few young children follow a short way commenting on my beard and laughing. One difference from the past: nobody's shouting, "<u>Ong My, Ong My</u>" [Mr. American] any more. And when they do ask where I'm from, they're generally surprised and think I'm kidding.

The car and family have already arrived in front of the church and I can see a crowd gathered. Huim comes by on his bicycle and walks the rest of the way with me.

On entering the grounds of the church I learn that the one foreign resident of Kontum, a British teacher of English, has been waiting the last two hours to see me. I excuse myself from the crowd, agreeing to meet them shortly and am escorted to an upstairs veranda.

Mark Richardson has taught at the Kontum Education Training Service for the last five months as part of the "Highlands Education Project." He plans to finish out a year there. With little or no training in Vietnamese, and certainly none in Bahnar, his stint as the lone foreigner in Kontum has had its difficulties. His impressions of local authorities are less than laudatory. Social contacts have been severely restricted, and I gather he has led a fairly lonely life these last several months. Just recently he was given permission to visit the homes of some of his students. However the first and only time he did so the student was "invited for an interview with said authorities." Such a different picture of accommodations to foreigners from what I had gleaned from Ban Me Thuot.

Mark commented on the stir our arrival had caused in the vicinity, apparently the first visitors associated with Minh Quy. He thought the visit was good—that it had brought a bit of "hope" to a somewhat despondent people. I wondered out loud if perhaps that was such a good thing, for I had no idea by what blessing such hope might be fulfilled. Had we, once again, inadvertently created false expectations?

I apologized for spending such a short time with him and walked back to the orphanage with H'Krih. We entered a large room with long table set. Yanh's family, Francois Huim and his wife, nuns and others surrounded us and once again I choked on indefinable sentiment. Yanh, in her inimitably quiet way, presented me a small basket and strikingly beautiful Bahnar blanket. A dozen conversations cross-currented at once. The sisters gave H'Krih and 'Mi-'Lai Bahnar blouses and skirts. In the midst of the conversational pandemonium a nun touched me lightly on the shoulder and I turned to see lined before me ten more people from the days of Minh Quy. There were quiet smiles and words of greeting from each weathered and aged face; as each took my hand the hardships of twenty years radiated from eyes and I simply cried.

These were people who had helped carry the sick and wounded from the hospital that day the rockets had screamed, blasting and ripping open the end of the main ward, killing several of their own. These were the people who had appeared daily to perform both the mundane and heroic deeds that always took place at Minh Quy; the men who, on hands and knees, had carefully cleared a hundred pounds or more of claymores, bouncing betties, smaller booby traps and other explosives from the overgrown land behind the hospital that had been mined by three different armies, so that they then could build a pig barn that might help feed the patients; the women who fed and cleaned and comforted and did a thousand other chores that kept Minh Quy alive and functioning.

Pea, Bia, Hrong, Moh, Lung, Dy, Drong, Rang, Oan, Chel, Deo. Men and women who had done so much even before I had come to know Minh Quy. What had we left them? What had they gone through in the last twenty years? I silently wished for more time to garner each of the stories behind their quiet eyes. The joy, in seeing once again these beautiful faces, was framed in pain.

There was one face missing from all this. The one who had taken me under her wing, as she did all children of Minh Quy, including the four-legged beasts. Ya Vincent had become a very special friend whose cheer I had come to count on. Not above teasing the ignorant Anglo; her laughter echoed from the smoky hospital kitchen lit by half a dozen wood fires under soot darkened caldrons of steaming soups, greens and rice. I remember her laughing so hard she had to hold her stomach, and tears were streaming down her face, as she pointed to the crazy American doctor, with stethoscope swinging wildly about his neck, chasing one of the geese around the kitchen building. When she calmed down enough to talk she asked if didn't he have a girl friend.

Over the last twenty years when I allowed myself to envision the possibility of returning to Kontum, it would be her sparkling eyes my mind would seek out. She throws her head back and laughs, holding a child with newly casted leg. The day before leaving the states I had talked to Pat who informed me of Ya Vincent's death.

As we were finishing the graciously offered meal, one nun excused herself and returned with photographs of the funeral. Ya Vincent's body, more slender than I had remembered, lay in the simple open casket, her last smile, serene.

The sisters invited us to spend the night at the orphanage; the priest, in a quiet aside, suggested it might not be wise to draw attention there since our overnight presence would have to be registered with authorities. We declined the invitation.

The rest of that day passed in a state similar to some sad dream one yet wishes to prolong for its melancholy sweetness. Reminiscences and laughter passed around with the cane straw (no longer amended with surgical tubing) of an ancient wine jar; inquiries of remembered friends (Bok Tuan, apparently still alive in a distant village; Yanh #2, my young Doppelganger and interpreter, the gatekeeper's son, gone away; others simply disappeared); En Luih and An, Marcelle's daughters came by to say hello—I remembered them helping in the kitchen as little girls—now pretty young ladies; a return to Kontum K'nam and visits with families and last minute gifts, photos, joy and more tears. Too soon we were headed south. I sat silent during the four hour trip. H'Krih asked if I were alright.

The remaining few days we passed with the family. Serene walks through effervescent groves of coffee, picking red and orange peppers, melons, durian, guava, rambutan. An outing to Buon Ea Katur and another multi-jug celebration with sacrificed beef and gifts of bracelets, fruits and kind words. More invitations than could possibly be accommodated. And yet my confused thoughts mostly lingered in Kontum.

One further surprise remained for me. Since our trip had been shortened because of visa problems, we decided that 'Mi-'Lai would remain with her family for two more weeks while I and H'Krih return as scheduled since she had to begin college in a few days. Arriving at a modern Tan Son Nhut terminal, we were faced with the usual completion of immigration forms, custom declarations, stamping of tickets, visas and passports. Waiting in line, looking through the glass-fronted departure lounge, I could see the many rusted hangars and dilapidated bunkers of yesterday, and an ungovernable imagination took me back to our harried exit from that country after fifteen months of uncertainty under the new regime, the strip searches, the anxiety, wondering if this time we really would be allowed to leave, and time again became amorphous. Even though my rational mind knew that all was well I grew nervous and even frightened, apprehensive every time I stood before those same uniforms that I had faced at an earlier time trying to answer the angry interrogations thrown at me. H'Krih recognized my nervousness and calmly led me through the lines.

A slight delay in departure. Finally we're on the shuttle to the Cathay Pacific flight (only Air Viet-Nam parks in front) waiting on a side apron, the same location of the C-130 parked here two decades ago into which we had covertly smuggled two frightened kids, Y-Hem and H-Nina, when we thought the rest of the family had been killed. Flooded with these memories, all of the anxiety and fear had surreptitiously returned with force. The stewardess calmly grinned, "Welcome aboard."

This letter has turned into something quite different than the couple of pages I had intended to write you of friends and places seen; it has evolved into something for me, forcing me to collect thoughts and perhaps gain some perspective on our journey, one which obviously necessitated heavier baggage than I anticipated.

I'd like to ask two favors.

Minh Quy, as an institution, no longer exists except in the memories of those of us fortunate enough to have shared some of its experiences. Even though I was only there for the span of one cycle of seasons, its role in my life was immense, and I suspect some of you harbor similar feelings. Pat Smith's creation developed into a legend in its own time, and I think the story of that legend should be recorded. I'm unaware of any current effort in that direction. I've a number of photographs from my time there; I'm sure there must be others from earlier days. I'd like to attempt a short history of Minh Quy with remembrances of those who passed its gates. If not commercially publishable, at least something for ourselves. To do so will require much help, so I am asking if you might be willing to share with me any material you might have, memories you'd be willing to put on paper or tape, knowledge of other sources of information or names and addresses of earlier staff that might be contacted. I promise to take good care of any original material you'd care to send though, where possible, I'd prefer copies. With your assistance, I think we can put together something worth both having and passing on to the future.

Second item. I realize now that much of the emotional confusion I experienced in Kontum recently had to do with the feeling of complete helplessness in the face of the poverty and destitution we witnessed among old friends. I know that a number of you have family still in Viet Nam to whom you've been providing help, and also that you're probably assaulted almost every day with further requests for one charity or another.

As I have mentioned, Ya Gabrielle, who in spite of her incarceration of several years because of her past association with us, continues to provide what healing assistance she can to villages in the area. I think we can help her, even from here. Other possible avenues exist into some of the local villages which I'd like to explore. I wonder if any of you might be interested in joining us in occasionally sending monies for Ya Gabrielle's projects and in seeing what other possibilities exist for returning some friendship to those who once made us feel so at home. I'm open to ideas, suggestions and criticism; I'd like your thoughts on the subject. Thank you,

Sincerely,

Kerry

Postscript:

In the fall of 1995 a reunion of Minh Quy alumni was held in Indianola, Washington. In addition to much time devoted to rich reminiscences, the group agreed to keep in touch through newsletters and attempt to provide some assistance to our friends in Kontum. Variously named "Friends of Minh Quy," "Friends of the Vietnam Highlands," and "Friends of Kontum," this group was able to occasionally get financial assistance to some of our Montagnard friends there.

As a direct consequence of "Friends of Kontum," Asia Connection Inc. (ACI) was formally established and was granted its official non-profit status as a 501(c)(3) in 2001. The initial aim was to support health and welfare programs in the Kontum area. While this continues to be a primary concern, ACI has broadened its focus over the years and now distributes grants to numerous projects in other needy parts of the world.

For more information visit: **www.AsiaConnectionInc.org**

Glossary

AFVN: **A**rmed **F**orces **V**iet Nam **N**etwork, American radio station in Viet Nam.

Aê: (Rhadé) grandfather, also honorary term.

Air America: Airline operated by CIA in Viet Nam.

AK 47: Chinese assault rifle used by communist forces in Viet Nam.

Arigato goziamas, Ojisama: (Japanese) Thank you very much, Uncle.

ASAP: **A**s **S**oon **A**s **P**ossible.

Altiplano: (Spanish) high plateau.

Ama: (Rhadé) father.

Amî: (Rhadé) mother.

Aó daì: (Vietnamese) traditional national dress.

ASROC: (military acronym) naval **A**nti-**S**ubmarine **ROC**ket (nuclear capable).

Autogetum: (military slang) automatic setting on M-16.

B-52: large American bomber, commonly used in Viet Nam.

Bà: (Vietnamese) honorary term for married woman.

Bahnar: tribe of Montagnards living in Central Highlands of Viet Nam, centered around Kontum.

Bakshish: (Arabic) gift; dole; alms.

Basi đế: (Vietnamese) distilled rice alcohol.

Ba mươi ba: (Vietnamese) the number "33," name of a popular beer.

Baobab: tropical African tree from *Bombacaceae* family with gourd-like fruit.

BBC: **B**ritish **B**roadcasting **C**orporation.

Bierre Larue: popular Vietnamese beer, produced in liter bottles.

Bộ đội: (Vietnamese) North Vietnamese soldiers.

Bok: (Bahnar) Mister.

Bơk: (Bahnar) to go.

Bơk ma lơng: (Bahnar) go well, farewell.

Bouncing Betty: (military slang) anti-personal mine designed to spring into air to chest height before exploding.

Bru: tribe of Montagnards living in Central Highlands of Viet Nam, centered around Cheo Reo and Khanh Dung.

BUFE: (slang acronym) **B**ig **U**gly **F**ucking **E**lephant; large ceramic elephant, popular in Viet Nam.

Bụi-đời: (Vietnamese) "Dust of Life," street urchins.

Bui-bui: (Swahili) black clothing (head-to-toe) of devout Islamic women in East Africa.

Buôn: (Rhadé) village.

Buzkashi: (Afghani) equestrian sport, forerunner to polo.

C5A, C47, C127, C130, C141: various military transport aircraft.

Cách Mạng Ngày 30: (Vietnamese) "Day 30 Revolutionary" - referring to Vietnamese who quickly changed loyalty on 30 April 1975.

Cài bí đao: (Vietnamese) melon the size of a small watermelon and texture of a cucumber.

Cài Lương: (Vietnamese) Chinese-style opera.

Cambodian Red: GI slang name of potent form of marijuana found in Southeast Asia.

Cám ơn: (Vietnamese) Thank you.

Cânsa: (Vietnamese) marijuana.

Cao Đà: indigenous religion of Viet Nam with Holy See in Tây Ninh.

CARE: American developmental and relief agency, (original title) **C**ooperative for **A**merican **R**elief **E**verywhere.

Caveat Lector Benevole: (Latin) Beware, Kind Reader.

CBU: Cluster Bomb Unit.

Cerveza: (Spanish) beer.

Chapandaz: (Afghani) the horsemen who play Buzkashi.

Charango: (Spanish) stringed musical instrument, smaller than a guitar.

Charlie: (military slang) Viet Cong.

Charlie-Charlie: (military) command and control helicopter.

Cherries: (military slang) new recruits.

Chi: (Vietnamese) elder sister, term of respect.

Chicha: (Spanish) local beer made with masticated corn.

Chi khana: (Afghani) teahouse.

Chillum: (Afghani) pipe used for smoking hashish.

Chin chin: Vietnamese drinking toast.

Chơlớn: (Vietnamese, literally "big market") Chinese section of Saigon.

Chopper: (military slang) helicopter.

Chú: (Vietnamese) Uncle.

CIA: Central Inteligence Agency.

CIC: see "COMBAT".

Claymore: anti-personal mine with thousands of little steel balls that blow outward, covering an arc of about 120 degrees.

CO: (military) Commanding Officer.

Cô: (Vietnamese) honorary term for unmarried woman; "Miss."

Cobra: American AH-1G helicopter gunship with maximum speed of 219 mph.

Coi di: (Vietnamese) Look!

Combat (also **CIC**): (military) short for **C**ombat **I**nformation **C**enter, compartment usually directly behind the bridge of a warship, often housing radar and sonar repeaters, communication equipment and duty personnel.

Combat unloading: method of unloading cargo while plane is still moving on runway.

Copal: (Mayan/Spanish) dried pine resin used as incense.

CONGEN: (American acronym) **CON**sul **GEN**eral, Regional Representative of American Ambassador in each of four military regions of Viet Nam during the war; the building housing his offices.

CRS: **C**atholic **R**elief **S**ervices, American relief organization.

Cumshaw: (from Chinese) to make a present of; to acquire in an illegal or unorthodox manner.

Cyclo (also *Xyclo)*: (Vietnamese) pedicab.

Daisy cutter: (military slang) particularly devastating antipersonnel bomb.

Đại U'y: (Vietnamese) military rank of army captain or navy lieutenant.

Đại Tá: (Vietnamese) military rank of army colonel or navy captain.

DAO: (military) **D**efense **A**ttache **O**ffice; complex of buildings at *Tân Son Nhút* Air Base.

DASH: (military acronym) naval **D**rone **A**nti-**S**ubmarine **H**elicopter.

DMZ: **De**Militarized **Z**one, area between North and South Viet Nam during the war.

DEROS: (military acronym) **D**ate of **E**stimated **R**eturn from **O**verseas.

Deuce-and-a-half: (military slang) 2 ½ ton truck.

Dhow: an Arab lateen-rigged boat of the Indian Ocean.

Đi: (Vietnamese) go; used after any verb it forms the imperative.

Độc lập: (Vietnamese) independence.

Đồng Nam: (Vietnamese) name of inexpensive and often moldy cigarettes available in Saigon after the communist takeover.

Farange: term used for foreigner in Greece and elsewhere.

Fantail: (naval) after part of deck on ship, usually overhanging the stern.

Finca: (Spanish) farm.

Fire zone: area receiving in-coming artillery rounds.

Flechettes: small barbs the size of fish hooks sprayed in large quantities from certain anti-personnel mines and "Beehive projectiles" containing 8000 such barbs capable of killing everything in its path fifty yards wide in a range of 150 yards.

Fo'c'sle: (naval) common contraction for "forecastle."

Forecastle: (naval) forward part of deck on ship.

Free fire zone: (military) area where anything moving (or not) can be shot at, no questions asked.

FNG: (military slang) "Fucking New Guy," new arrival.

FULRO: (French acronym) *Front Unité de la Liberacion de Resistance de la Oppressee*, organization of Montagnard underground in Viet Nam.

Furo: (Japanese) bath.

Futon: (Japanese) stuffed cotton mattress.

Giả Phóng: (Vietnamese) liberation; also term used for Vietnamese troops.

Gook: American derogatory term for Oriental, and Vietnamese in particular.

Hawaya: (Amharic) Ethiopian word for "foreigner."

Hoà *Hảo*: militant Buddhist sect of southern Viet Nam.

Hoà *lan*: (Vietnamese) orchid.

Huey: (military slang) helicopter used for gunship or small troop insertions.

I Ching: ancient Chinese book of divination.

ICRC: International Committee of the Red Cross, Swiss based.

In-coming: artillery round(s) coming into an area.

Indian Country: (military slang) enemy territory.

Injera wat: unleavened bread and sauce, common Ethiopian food.

j.g.: common term for naval lieutenant (junior grade).

Jolly Green Giant: (military slang) large transport helicopter.

Junk: oriental sailing craft; also term used for heroin.

Kafkan: lightweight man's gown commonly worn in Islamic desert countries.

Kâo: (Rhadé) I, me.

Khóm: (Vietnamese) government term referring to neighborhood district.

Không biêt: (Vietnamese) ... don't know.

KIA: (military) **K**illed **I**n **A**ction; term used in body counts.

Klick: (military slang) kilometer.

Lao hai: Laotian rice wine (usually home-made).

LAW: (military) M-79 rocket launcher.

Li: Chinese unit of measure equal to about one-third mile.

LOH: (military acronym) **L**ight **O**bservation **H**elicopter, pronounced "Loach."

LZ: (military) **L**anding **Z**one.

M-16: American military rifle used extensively in Viet Nam.

M-60: machine gun.

M-72: see "LAW."

M-79: grenade launcher.

Mazoongu: (Swahili) foreigner.

Medivac: (military) **medic**al **evac**uation.

MP: **M**ilitary **P**olice.

MR: **M**ilitary **R**egion; in Viet Nam, I through IV.

Muzzein: one who calls people to prayers in Islamic countries.

NLF: National Liberation Front, political front of Viet Cong.

Nước mắm: (Vietnamese) fish sauce.

NVA: North Vietnamese Army.

OAU: Organization of African Unity.

Obasan: (Japanese) "Aunt," polite term for older woman.

OD: (naval) Officer of the Deck.

Oei ma lơng: (Bahnar) Stay well; farewell.

Ông: (Vietnamese) Mister.

Ông Mì: (Vietnamese) "Mr. Noodles," play on words with "*Ông Mỹ*" (see below).

Ông Mỹ: (Vietnamese) "Mr. American."

Ops: (military slang) operations.

Out-going: artillery round(s) leaving an area.

Pathet Lao: Laotian Communist.

PBR: (militarty) Patrol Boat, River.

Phở: (Vietnamese) variety of noodle soup.

Phoenix Group: Clandestine organization of Vietnamese, established by the CIA to seek out Viet Cong, known for its brutality.

Pi-e: (Rhadé) rice wine, usually home-made.

Pisco: (Peruvian) rum.

PL 480: Public Law 480 which established "Food for Peace" Program; slang for commodities received under this law.

Popuh Vuh: Sacred Book of the Maya.

PRG: Provincial Revolutionary Government — government apparatus established by the Viet Cong.

PSYOPS: (military acronym) PSYchological OPerationS.

Puff the Magic Dragon: (military slang) C-47 cargo plane equipped with three electric powered Gatling machine guns capable of putting out 18,000 rounds per minute; named for popular song of the '60s.

QC: *Quân Cảnh*, Vietnamese military police.

QL: *Quốc Lộ*: Vietnamese national highway.

Ramadan: holy ninth month of Islamic year, one for fasting.

Rau muống: (Vietnamese) leafy water-grown vegetable similar to spinach.

Rhadé: tribe of Montagnards living in Central Highlands of Viet Nam, centered around Ban Me Thuot: also known as "Edé."

Round-eye: slang term for westerner, particularly American in Viet Nam.

Ruff-Puff: term derived from acronym **RFPF**, **R**egional **F**orces, **P**rovincial **F**orces, Vietnamese paramilitary units.

Rừng Sát **Special Zone**: from Vietnamese, "Killer Jungle," special area of Mekong and its tributaries assigned to naval operations and known for its harsh conditions.

Saigon Tea: "whiskey" (actually tea) purchased by GIs for bar girls.

Sea Bee: member of naval construction battalion (from initials CB of **C**onstruction **B**attalion).

Sea Knight: large naval transport helicopter.

SERE: (military acronym) "**S**urvival, **E**vasion, **R**esistance and **E**scape — controversial military course in which students are treated as prisoners of war.

Shifta: Ethiopian brigand.

Slick: (military slang) lightly armored transport helicopter.

Slope: American derogatory term for Vietnamese, referring to sloped forehead.

Spook: (American slang) CIA operative.

Spooky: (military slang) C-47, "Puff the Magic Dragon," equipped with extremely powerful searchlights and flares for night ops.

Swift: fast naval gunboat.

Tân Sơn Nhứt: (Vietnamese) name of Saigon air base.

Tết: Chinese and Vietnamese New Year celebration.

Thằng Mỹ: (Vietnamese) derogatory term for American.

Thằng Nga: (Vietnamese) derogatory term for Russian.

Thành Phố: (Vietnamese) city.

Thiệu Tá: (Vietnamese) military rank for major or naval lieutenant commander.

Tự Do: Saigon street famous for its bars and prostitutes during the war.

USAID: United States Agency for International Development.

USIS: United States Information Service.

Về đi: (Vietnamese) Go back!

Việt Cộng: South Vietnamese communist(s).

Việt Minh: (Vietnamese) Early Communist followers of Hồ Chí Minh.

VNAF: (military acronym) VietNamese Air Force.

VOA: Voice of America, radio broadcast.

Walia Ibex: rare Abyssian mountain goat.

WESTPAC: (military acronym) WESTern PACific.

Willy Peter: (military slang) white phosphorus (from phonetic pronunciation of "WP" markings on artillery rounds) — "the fire that won't go out."

XO: (military) eXecutive Officer, usually second in command.

Yankee Station: military designation of area in South China Sea off coast of Viet Nam.

Ya Ti: (Bahnar) "Big Mother."

YMCA: Young Men's Christian Association.

Zippo Raids: (military slang) attacks in Viet Nam in which villages are burned to the ground (refers to cigarette lighter commonly carried by GIs).

My Thanks

I am humbled by the pleasant task of thanking those who gave me succor, guidance and assistance throughout the days of journeying. I am indeed one of the most fortunate beings upon this planet to have such family and friends.

First, my most sincere appreciation to Jeff: "Ranger," guide and brother, who undoubtedly saved my sanity and my ass more times than any other.

To Hap, my thanks for the friendship and instruction in proper naval etiquette, both onboard and off ship—one of the best officers I've been privileged to know. To Stan C., who graciously suffered my ignorance and erratic ways aboard DD 867—I couldn't have asked for a better captain.

From the days of Pigs and Chickens, my hat is off to Jim N., top wrangler, who handled all the BS so that I could go out and play in the countryside of Viet Nam. Special appreciation to all the men of "Pigs and Chickens" who did an incredible job under less than ideal circumstances...Dolder, Moses, and all the rest: I cannot thank you enough; to Gary, Jim and the other Special Forces Veterinarians my thanks for your expertise, advice and friendship; to Lan and Mai, good friends who provided a hiding place when I needed it, you also preserved my sanity—thank you.

From the days of wandering, before and since, Punch and Penny have always been there with the correct prescription (it was they who had provided the 'found' whiskey on that less than festive New Year's Eve in Mexico); Kay and Thelma, sisters, introduced us to the Oglala, their hospitality will always be remembered; To Bay and David B., appreciation for the Montana guide service and Bay's putting up with all of us. Carol and Sandy: enough cannot be said about your kindness and concern, especially during our involuntary stint in Saigon—my most sincere appreciation (just remember to bring back the ice cream next time); to Jaime and Stella, who became my family in Colombia, taking in a lost child on many occasions and showering him with favor—*muchisimas gracias, con mi cariño;* to Alicia, Pablo and Daisy, who shared what they had and introduced me to "El Rancho," another place I've been able to return to in my mind when in need of serenity—my gratitude; and of course, *mil gracious* to Isabel who took two *gringos* under her wing and shared her love of land and culture with them—*encontremos en la misma esquina.*

Before embarking on the second circle Jack and Nancy of Nancy Palmer Photo Agency (alas, no more) encouraged a young photographer with words and publication, neither of which he probably deserved, and Sally gave advice on future travel and friendship to a confused being. Dave S. (gone but not forgotten) and Trinh gave shelter and kindness both in Saigon and Nairobi—had it not been for them I wouldn't have had my first meeting with Monkey; Louise and Mavis gave welcome to their home, stories of old Kenya, and an introduction to another world; the Sweet family extended their generous hospitality in Addis Ababa; it was also in Addis that John Peters shared his immense wisdom—to all these special friends my sincere gratitude.

Heading East by going east brought me to the doorstep of two Greek brothers who gave me a fun job and all the food I could eat (sorry about that platter of dishes...but it *was* worth an ouzo). To Sandy, Jean, Anita and Bruce, my thanks for your cherished friendships and kindnesses. And to Drew, I cannot thank enough—a true Taoist guide to whom I will forever be indebted.

Back in the Land of the Dragon, I owe a special thanks to the matron and occupants of "the compound" for giving me a home and a family of sisters from whom I was to learn much of life...*Cam on, va di manh gioi, da.* To Jim B., without whom I never would have had the opportunity to know Minh Quy, my deep appreciation. To Omega, in Vientienne, thanks for your kindness to a stranger and for remembering the words to "Annabel Lee."

To all those associated with Minh Quy Hospital I owe so much; Ya Gabrielle and all the nuns—how you put up with us ignorant round-eyes I'll never know. To Bok Tuan and the crew who risked life and limb gathering hidden and deadly explosives, all to build a pig barn, I applaud your courage and thank you for your friendship. To Geam, who quietly went about his job, and from whom I learned much, my thanks. My appreciation goes to Edric who took charge of the hospital during Pat Smith's absence; and, to George C. one of the finest people and pediatricians I've known. Gratitude to Bill for being the role model he is and for sharing his wisdom and his Dago Red (forgive the lack of political correctness); to Harry for supervising the construction of the barn and his amazing cumshaw expertise; and, to John, for all his help with everything. To Marion, Phyllis, Scott, Senia and Bob my sincere appreciation for their worldly advice and friendship; as well as to Dr. Pradahn for such interesting conversations, and to the rest of the crew who accomplished so much. To Yanh, her mother and grandmother of Kontum Ko'nom, and the rest of the family: thank you for taking me in. To Little Yanh, wherever you are, I'm glad you were my interpreter and sidekick.

My sincere gratitude to Ira, for his assistance in Nha Trang, as well as to Col. Tuy for his friendship and help. And of course a special thanks to the survivors of the New Zealand Red Cross Team of Pleiku, Leoni and Mary, for their companionship during somewhat trying times. Our walk into Kon Mohar that Sunday with Joe and Mac was one of the most idyllic days of my life.

Back in Saigon there was the entire CARE staff, Madame Bac, Madam Thi, Madame Chung, Co Phuong and all the rest who gave so much, and in the end, were let down by us. I am shamed by our (American) actions, but honored by your friendship. To Huynh in particular I owe so much for her support in troubled times—it would be impossible to find a better sister. To "Jake" J. and Cris C. a very special thanks for your part in getting folks out who needed out, as well as to the unnamed Air Force Colonel and his bottle of Johnny Walker. To Ong Co and family, I value your friendship; and to Y-Klong, thank you.

After the changeover of government there were many who helped in many ways. Thanks to Y-Sang for that last motorcycle ride as well as for getting the messages to where they were going. To Pierre G. and all the staff of the ICRC, we're glad you were there. To Helmut I will forever be indebted, not only for all your help, your continued friendship, and your introduction to SOS Kinderdorf; you also taught me that sometimes one needs to put down the camera—*danke schon!* To the Mennonite staff—Earl, Hiro, Jim and Max—keep up the good work, we enjoyed your companionship.

On our return to this world Butch and Ann could not have been more helpful, as were Carol P., Carol and Sandy, and others already named. Our most grateful thanks.

And, of course, there is family on both sides of the water. To Ami and all the clan my love and thanks for taking me into the family. A special note of appreciation to Brother Paul and Ami H'Rung for wise counsel and extended hospitality upon our return. To Y-Lai: a father's love and gratitude for the lessons you've taught me. To H'Krih, for the translations and for just being you—also, my appreciation and a father's special love. And to Ami Y-Lai: words are insufficient (but I'll try). *Khap!*

A particular thank you to a bunch of great impromptu editors: David N., Abby, Cynthia, Dorothy and especially Dexter, who gave freely of their time and read this manuscript in its poorest forms, and offered encouragement and advice that pulled it into better shape. The mistakes remain mine. To Jeff and Hugh: thanks for the saved letters. For final typing, Jan deserves special kudos, as does Rita for her expert, and often last minute, editing skills. To those who have gone unnamed: please forgive my faltering memory. Without you all, I should not be here now.

A number of folks are with us no longer, at least on this plane; nevertheless they are people to whom I owe a large debt of gratitude and I would like to acknowledge them here and honor their memories. First, of course, to my parents for their love and the opportunities they have given me; to Jack Heubeck, who unknowingly encouraged his godson into the naval tradition, and to his crew mates aboard the ill-fated Tang; to Ama who took a strange round-eye into his family with the utmost of grace. Very special praise goes to the memory of Dr. Pat Smith, who founded Minh Quy Hospital and became a legend in her own time. I had hoped she would share the story of Minh Quy as only she could tell it. Pat died in 2005. Bob Trott, Director of CARE Viet Nam, was the best boss I've ever had. David Schaer gave me crash courses in veterinary medicine and shelter when I was in need, more than once. Dat, Hih and Joe, you are missed. Ed Fortner and I.J. Hampton each shared their philosophies with me and taught me much. Ya Vincent, a very special lady, a friend to little children and four-legged beasts; I promised her I would return one day, but when I did it was too late. And Mac—there has been no friendship so short that has been so meaningful.

Peace,

Kerry

About The Author

Following his military service in Viet Nam, kerry traveled and eventually returned to that country in 1973. His work there with humanitarian programs eventually led to meeting his wife and their remaining there for 15 months following the end of the war.

After leaving Viet Nam, kerry worked in both Indonesia and Latin America for international nonprofits. He also established a commercial and editorial photography business in the States.

He and Mi-Lai, his wife, currently reside in northern New Mexico. His interests range from sustainable living design and photography to his involvement with two philanthropic foundations: Asia Connection, Inc. and Quail Roost Foundation.

The author's royalties from the sale of this book will be donated to **www.AsiaConnectionInc.org**.